Sentries Along the Shore

Elinor De Wire

Elinor De Wire

Sentinel *Publications*

P.O. Box 654
Gales Ferry
CT 06335

For Richard DeAngelis
Retired editor of *Mariners Weather Log* at the National Oceanic & Atmospheric Administration.

Direct inquiries to:

Sentinel Publications
P.O. Box 654
Gales Ferry, CT 06335

Printed by:

Franklin Impressions
Norwich, Connecticut

De Wire, Elinor, 1953-

Sentries Along the Shore / Elinor De Wire. - 1st ed.

Indexed.
ISBN 0-9657313-1-6

1. Lighthouses - History - United States - International.
2. Lighthouse Keepers.
3. Navigational Aids

Other Books By Elinor De Wire

The Guide to Florida Lighthouses, Pineapple Press, 1987
Journey Through the Universe, Mystic Seaport Planetarium, 1989
Activities for Young Astronomers, Mystic Seaport Planetarium, 1990
Reach for the Sky, Mystic Seaport Planetarium, 1993
Guardians of the Lights, Pineapple Press, 1995
The Lighthouse Activity Book, Sentinel Publications, 1995
Lighthouse Victuals & Verse, Sentinel Publications, 1996

Front cover watercolor of Nauset Lighthouse, Cape Cod, "Light and Shadow," by Jim Mahanes, 1995
Back cover photo of Elinor De Wire at Ponce de Leon Inlet Lighthouse by Jonathan De Wire, 1983

Contents

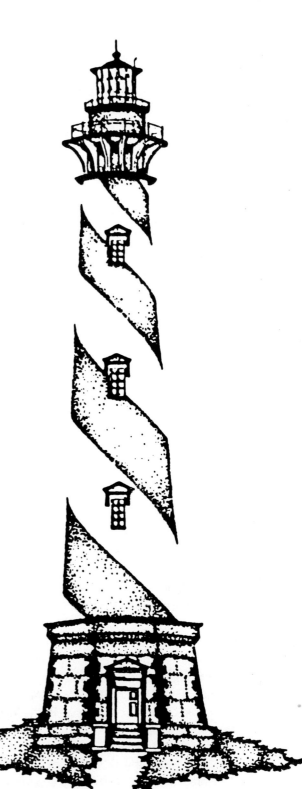

Author's Note

Not long ago, I decided to compile a notebook of "tear sheets" for use with my submissions of article ideas to magazines. In editorial lingo, "tear sheets" are copies of an author's best published work, intended to showcase both talent and dependability. They say, "I have great ideas, and I can deliver when I'm given an assignment." The name "tear sheets" comes from old publishing days, before photocopiers, when writers actually tore the original articles from magazines and sent them to editors.

After nearly twenty years as a successful (that means "minimally frustrated") freelance writer, you can imagine the amount of material I've collected. I own boxes full of magazines containing my byline - heavy, disorganized, yellowing heaps of print that may someday reach kindling temperature in my attic and set fire to the entire house.

Perhaps technology will allow me to put it all on laser disk soon. In the meantime, I need to have it handy, because not a week passes that someone doesn't write or call asking for a copy of a particular article. Off I go, deep into the dusty realm of cardboard, wondering in which box a particular magazine is located. That idea of a notebook full of alphabetized "tear sheets in the form of photocopies" was a time-saver. And it was enlightening.

In the process of categorizing the 200+ articles I've published since 1983, I discovered that nearly half were related to lighthouses. In addition, I wrote (and continue to write) a column on historic lighthouses for *Mariners Weather Log*, the in-house magazine of the National Oceanic & Atmospheric Administration. I felt this was a valuable collection. The subtopics were varied enough to lend themselves to a book, and there was definitely an audience.

In the spring of 1995 I produced a small test run on a high-speed copier of a simple, comb-bound collection called *The Lighthouse Keeper's Scrapbook*. All 50 copies sold at the New England Lighthouse Foundation's Annual Meeting on Cape Cod, and several people went away disappointed that I had no more. My husband said: "Looks like a winner!" So, I printed another 75 copies, and they were gone by summer's end. It was time to think seriously about making this a better quality book.

You hold in your hand the result. *Sentries Along the Shore* contains about fifty of the best lighthouse-related articles I've written. Much time was devoted to updating information in the articles, and I've added some interesting author notes and highlights. Now that it's complete, I can reflect on the many hours spent producing it - brainstorming for ideas, finding places to send them, querying editors, researching, digging and interviewing, writing and revising copy, waiting for publication, waiting to get paid. It's a long process from germination of idea to deposition of a check.

Writing has taken me on many journeys and opened lots of doors that otherwise would have remained closed. Wherever I go, my writer's antennae are up and tuned to a good topic or story line. I've written science, history, human interest, short fiction, how-to articles, foodways, travelogues, poetry, nostalgia, promotional materials, inspirational pieces, and a great deal of curriculum. For a time, I was even a humor columnist!

My best and most animated work, however, has been about lighthouses. Their granite and mortar and metal are the foundation of my writing career and will inspire me for years to come. Twenty years ago, few people were as passionate about lighthouses as I was. Today, there are dozens of societies and groups who love them and bookstores and gift shops full of titles and trinkets about my favorite subject. I only hope my work has, in some small way, contributed to this "Lighthouse Renaissance."

Many people have helped me along the way: my family - Jon, Jessica, and Scott - who always support my projects; artists Lee Radzak, Paul Bradley, Jr., Leo Kuschel, and Jim Mahanes (whose splendid rendering of Nauset Light appears on the cover); Ken Black of Shore Village Museum; Tim Harrison and Kathy Finnegan of New England Lighthouse Foundation; Wayne Wheeler of the U.S. Lighthouse Society; the folks at the Outer Banks Lighthouse Preservation Society and at the Great Lakes Lighthouse Keepers Association; and the many helpful people of the U.S. Coast Guard. The biggest *thank-you* goes to Richard DeAngelis, my editor at *Mariners Weather Log* from 1987 to 1995. Without his enthusiasm and appreciation for "all things maritime," and his desire to present a diverse publication, many of the articles in this book would not exist. Thank you R.D. I hope you're enjoying retirement!

Elinor De Wire, April 1997

Sentinels on Watch

A Brief History of Lighthouses

On August 7, 1989, the United States celebrated the 200th Anniversary of the Lighthouse Service. Officially, this benevolent organization has existed since 1789, when it was established under Alexander Hamilton in the Treasury Department. But lighthouses have been a part of the American way of life for much longer. In fact, there is considerable argument over just how to define a lighthouse, for we know beacons of all sorts have been used to guide vessels safely for thousands of years. And though not all of them embody the tall, conical form we traditionally imagine a lighthouse to be, such structures fulfill the same purpose — the concern for and safekeeping of human life.

Lighthouses exist in every geographic region of the globe to mark the oceans and inland lakes and the arteries feeding them. Their origin can be traced to antiquity, when crude fire beacons guided the first intrepid mariners. For centuries, a blazing brazier or hillside bonfire was the seafarers' only sentinel. Then about 450 BC, plans for the world's first formal lighthouse were finalized, and construction of a gigantic tower was begun on an island in the Nile Estuary at Alexandria. Its marble and limestone, quarried and dressed in the hills north of Giza, and purple granite taken from Assouan, were hauled miles overland and lightered to the island on huge rafts. No records indicate how long this monumental task took, but historians estimate the tower was probably under construction more than a decade,

When completed, the Pharos, as Ptolemy I named the magnificent sentinel, rose nearly 500-feet tall (the Washington Monument in 555-feet tall) and held a large brazier in its crown. Doubling as a temple, it was tended by priests whose slaves continually hauled wood up its massive courses to fuel the hungry beacon.

The mighty Pharos presided over Alexandria Harbor until about 800 AD, when its costly beacon was deemed unnecessary. The structure stood another 500 years before being toppled by an earthquake, after which its island eroded and

disappeared into the estuarine murk. Thanks to ancient historians like Pliny the Elder, we have excellent descriptions of the Pharos, but even more recently, a diving team uncovered pieces of the original collapsed structure, buried in the silt of the Nile Delta. Mapping of the debris-fall and examination of some of its stones confirms Pharos' size and appearance and justifies its claim as one of the Seven Wonders of the Ancient World. This great tower remains a part of history even today, having given its name to the modern-day study of lighthouse construction and illumination — pharology.

The Egyptians were not the only ancient people to build sentinels. Greece had several, including the Colossus, a 50-foot copper statue of Apollo straddling the entrance to the port of Rhodes and holding aloft a flaming brazier. The Greek Hellespont and Sigeum in the Troad were also marked by lighthouses of sorts. The Romans built a lighthouse at Ostia around 50 BC and lit thirty others before their empire collapsed. All of these, save the Greek Colossus, were of stone or wood, had a predictable squareness to their shape, and were illuminated with fire baskets.

At the height of Roman rule, great beacons were built at Coronna, Spain and the harbor of Boulogne, France. Other lesser lights were raised but crumbled by the time of the Dark Ages, when, as their name implies, few lighthouses were built.

In 1160 AD, however, Italy re-illuminated the world with the great lighthouse at Genoa. Among its early keepers was one Antonio Columbo. His young nephew, Cristoforo, spent much time exploring the slender, stone lighthouse and grew to love the sea during his years here. Perhaps, by its sheer height, which elevated one's perspective of the horizon, Genoa Lighthouse influenced the course of history, for Cristoforo later sailed west from Genoa to prove a revolutionary claim that the world was a globe and the Indies lay just beyond the Ocean Sea.

During the Middle Ages, various nations throughout Europe built lighthouses of one type or another, though most were crude stone structures with feeble beacons. Many were established and maintained by monks. France's Cordouan Lighthouse is significant, however, due to its elaborate, durable design and its unusual location on an erosive peninsula at the mouth of the Gironde River. Designed in 1584 by architect Louis de Foix, it required 27 years to build and rose nearly 200-feet over the water. Foix's plan included an apartment in the center of the tower for the king and a chapel just above the royal chamber. The huge lantern burned oak, and its lowly keepers, who were forbidden to enter the royal rooms, carried their faggots of wood aloft by way of a narrow passageway inside the walls surrounding the lighthouse. The royal apartment was never occupied, however, and erosion has since sequestered the lighthouse far offshore from its original position.

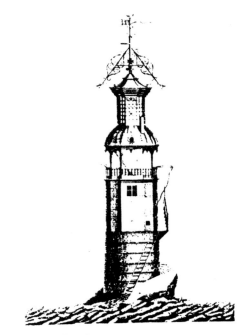

The first Eddystone Light, 1698

Up until the 18th century, lighthouses had been built on solid foundations, either onshore or on islands very near the shore, but much of the need for marking navigational perils lay offshore in the clutches of rocks, ledges, sandbars, and shoals. In 1698, England revolutionized lighthouse construction by building the first seaswept lighthouse on a treacherous site in the English Channel known as Eddystone Rock.

Henry Winstanley was the brave architect of the first sentinel on the site. Hewn and hammered from virgin timber, lightered to the rock piece by piece, assembled and anchored with iron rods driven deep into the rock, Eddystone Lighthouse was a bold experiment under the scrutiny of all Europe. It towered 60 feet over the sea, but heavy waves in the channel easily sent spray over the lantern and snuffed the tower's five dozen tallow candles; hence, Winstanley was forced to increase its height to 100 feet soon after its illumination.

Thought tall enough to escape the spray, the tower still shook miserably in gales, but Winstanley

2

boldly maintained that his masterpiece could withstand the worst of the sea's pummeling. In 1703, after a storm mildly damaged the lighthouse, he confidently journeyed to the tower to make repairs. While work was still in progress, a more severe storm blew in on the heels of the first and destroyed the lighthouse, killing Winstanley and his entire repair crew. Meteorologists today say it was the worst storm in British history.

Three years later, British architect John Rudyerd began work on a new tower at Eddystone Rock. This one, built primarily of wood, was taller and stronger, due to its stone foundation and iron-sheathed interior. It was also considerably simpler in form than its elaborate predecessor, with a sleek design to provide minimal resistance to wind and waves. It suffered through several trying gales, then tragically met its end one night when the wooden lantern caught fire. The keepers fled down the wooden stairs and to the outer rim of the rock. As the lantern burned, its lead parts melted, and huge blobs of hot metal fell downward, splashing into the sea with a sizzle. One unfortunate keeper looked up at the blazing inferno, mouth agape, and swallowed a gob of molten lead. He died a few days later at a mainland hospital from burns and lead poisoning.

John Smeaton and his 1759 Eddystone Light

Undaunted, the British called on civil engineer John Smeaton to build the fourth Eddystone Lighthouse. Against the advice of his colleagues, Smeaton chose masonry for his structure and adopted a conical shape that flared gently at the base and just

beneath the lantern. This shape had the effect of minimizing contact pressure with waves and throwing them back upon themselves. His sentinel was lit in 1759 and stood for a century before being replaced by a taller structure. It was the first successful sea-swept lighthouse in the world and a harbinger of the great towers engineered in Europe and America over the next century.

While England was experimenting with seaswept lighthouses, Scottish engineers were contemplating sentinels for their growing international trade. Scotland's jagged, rock-riddled coastline required strong masonry structures, many located on offshore islets or on submarine foundations. The Stevenson family, well-known marine engineers who had built numerous bridges, viaducts, breakwaters, and seawalls, were pressed into service for the Scottish Lighthouse Board.

Five generations of Stevensons — excluding Robert Louis Stevenson, who gained fame as a literary figure — designed, built, and administered the great sentinels of Scotland. Among their most admirable achievements are the gargantuan towers at Bell Rock in the North Sea, Skerryvore in the Hebrides, and Dubh Artach off the Ross of Mull. Each of these sentinels is a marvel of marine engineering, even today.

Unique obstacles challenged the Stevensons at all three sites. Wave force at Skerryvore can equal three tons per square inch, and Dubh Artach, though situated some 300 feet above the sea, has had boulders thrown against its base by storm waves. Bell Rock, perhaps the supreme achievement in 18th century architecture, once had one of its doors ripped off and imploded into the tower 60 feet above the waterline by the backdraught of a wave. In fact, Bell Rock Lighthouse has become such a legend among educators and historians, it is studied world-wide and utilized as a training post for novice lighthouse keepers, marine scientists, engineers, and architects.

While England and Scotland were grappling with offshore construction, and France was perfecting better illumination, the American Colonies were growing in both population and trade. When the first colonists arrived in the 1600s, there was no welcoming light to guide them ashore, but by 1716, Boston had raised the first Colonial sentinel on Little Brewster Island at the entrance to the harbor. It served until the Revolution when the British spitefully blew it up on their retreat from Boston. It was rebuilt and still stands today — active and the nation's last attended lighthouse.

Numerous other Colonial lighthouses appeared before the Revolution. Most were located in New England, primarily in Massachusetts Bay Colony, but one was built at Tybee, Georgia. Of the Colonial lights remaining today, only those at Tybee and Sandy Hook, New Jersey, are original structures. Sandy Hook's lighthouse, built in 1764, is in good condition and still serves as a navigational aid. It is an octagonal, brick tower with a base diameter of 29 feet tapering to a 15 foot diameter at the top. The lantern is iron with a copper roof, and the entire structure rises 103 feet. It was built by Isaac Conro, and at a ripe old age of over two centuries, it is a testament to his fine workmanship.

Because of advances yet to be made in illumination, lighthouse architects and engineers in the 18th and 19th centuries grappled with problems of identifying beacons. Along one stretch of New England coast, for example, nine white lights were in view at once, and mariners complained of difficulty differentiating them. This confusion was blamed for numerous wrecks and plotting errors and demanded a quick solution. Since optics had not yet been developed which could emit a characteristic signal, or flash, the problem was solved by clever design of multiple light stations.

Matinicus Twin Lights

These consisted of double towers, often called twin lights. Such sites as Thachers Island, Massachusetts, Navesink, New Jersey, and Matinicus Rock and Cape Elizabeth, Maine were given this type of system. Scituate, Massachusetts had, for a time, a creative foray into piggyback lights in one tower, and Nauset Beach, Cape Cod even had triple lighthouses. These elaborate systems proved cost-inhibitive and

never gained general usage. In fact, not long after the first twin lights were established in the United States, France introduced a revolutionary optic capable producing a flash characteristic. This eliminated the need for multiple light towers, yet they continued in use until the 1920s, probably more for sentimental reasons than practicality.

Thimble Shoals Light, Chesapeake Bay

Up until the mid-1800s, lighthouse construction confined itself to onshore sites or solid submarine and wave-washed foundations, but the need for sentinels on unstable foundations, such as murky river estuaries, erosive beaches, and coral reefs, had grown paramount. Places like the Florida Keys, the Chesapeake and Delaware bays, and the alluvial Gulf Coast desperately needed to be marked, yet heavy masonry towers could not be adequately anchored on such unstable surfaces.

Again, Britain would find a solution to the problem. Experimenting with wharf pilings, a blind engineer named Alexander Mitchell came up with a type of anchorage called the screwpile and successfully used it in the mucky estuary at Maplin Sands, England. Mitchell's Maplin Sands Lighthouse looked like a giant spider standing knee-deep in the water. It consisted of a small house and lantern atop eight iron piles which were literally screwed through the silt and anchored in solid bedrock. Mitchell's lighthouse was a phenomenal success, spurring engineers throughout Europe and the United States to design similar systems.

In the southeastern U.S. and Gulf of Mexico, the screwpile and its variations were ideally adapted to the Florida Reef and the continually shifting beaches between North Carolina and Texas.

Mid-Atlantic bays and sounds also benefited. Five huge towers of screwpile design were built on the Florida Reef between 1840 and 1880, requiring specialized stabilizing disks where their piles entered the coral. Each tower was of open framework design to allow hurricane wind and waves to pass through unimpeded. Sturdy keepers' quarters were incorporated into the towers at suitable heights above the water, and state-of-the-art optics were installed in their elevated lanterns.

In less tempestuous bays estuaries, and sounds, the screwpile design featured a small house low to the water and sitting on deeply anchored pile legs. Two problems quickly became apparent with this new design — the threat of collision by ships off-course and, in northern areas, by floating chunks of ice. This was solved in the 1880s when major David Heap of the Army Corps of Engineers designed and built the first caisson lighthouse at Fourteen Foot Bank in the Delaware Bay.

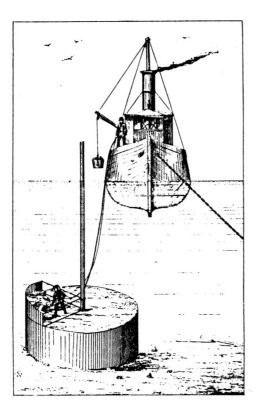

This diagram from the Coast Guard Archives in Washington, D.C. shows a cross-sectional view of the preparation of a submarine caisson.

Heap's caisson was a 73 foot vertical iron cylinder of 35 feet in diameter, fabricated onshore, towed to the site, and sunk in the bay bed. Seawater was suctioned out to allow workmen to prepare the foundation, then it was filled with concrete and riprap, and the iron sheathing was removed. Riprap was also placed around the base to fortify the caisson. The superstructure included a two-story cast iron dwelling with a lantern projecting from its roof and a Daboll fog trumpet in its basement. Later, hollow caissons were fabricated onshore, then towed to their sites to be sunk and filled. This design proved so successful, it replaced most screwpile lighthouses north of Florida.

Atop such caissons were built a variety of house styles. Among the most familiar was a design of several tiers, each decreasing in diameter as the structure gained height. Humorous nicknames were given to such sentinels by local residents and boaters. Orient Point Light in Long Island Sound has always been called The Coffeepot Light. Mile Rocks Light in San Francisco Bay was called The Wedding Cake before it was demolished some years back. Deer Island Light in Boston Harbor was called The Sparkplug. Its successor, a slender, white, cylindrical tower atop the caisson is called The Cigarette. Ironically, it lights up every night!

One of the most difficult caisson lighthouses to build was Race Rock Light in Long Island Sound, situated at the eastern edge of the perilous current caused by tides roaring through the opening between Fishers Island and Great Gull Island. The sentinel was constructed by F. Hopkinson Smith, who also built the massive foundation for the Statue of Liberty — herself originally a lighthouse.

First, Smith created a plinth with a mass of concrete 60 feet across that was poured in four concentric layers using large iron hoops. A second pier, smaller in diameter, was poured over this to a height 30 feet above the foundation. The entire base was then reinforced by the addition of 10,000 tons of riprap, and the superstructure, consisting of a granite dwelling with a tower rising from it, was completed in time for the beacon to be exhibited on New Year's Day, 1879.

Almost simultaneously, lighthouse architects and engineers ingeniously solved another problem related to instability. In areas where beaches were hard packed enough to support massive concrete foundations, but erosion was rapid and unpredictable, the collapsible lighthouse was put to the test. This design provides for fast and inexpensive dismantling, moving, and reassembling of lighthouses, somewhat akin to our modern modular and prefab buildings.

The central feature of this design was a series of cast iron plates, which were bolted together on a concrete foundation and stabilized with a lining of bricks. In addition, the stairway and lantern also could be assembled or dismantled in pieces. Such forms proved ideal in the Southeast, where beach topography is constantly in flux.

Hunting Island Lighthouse near Frogmore, South Carolina is typical of this design. Its original masonry tower toppled and was replaced by a collapsible structure in 1875. After erosion changed the shape of the beach in 1889, this tower was dismantled and relocated to a more effective site. Cape Canaveral Lighthouse in Florida is similar in design to Hunting Island Light and also has been moved since its original construction in the 1870s.

Several other natural hazards have necessitated special lighthouse designs. In Northern California, where the San Andreas Fault runs close to shore, reinforced concrete towers are in use to thwart possible collapse from earthquakes. Point Arena, California had a masonry lighthouse at the turn of the century that was destroyed in the Great San Francisco Earthquake of 1906. For construction of the second tower, the government hired a firm specializing in industrial chimney construction. A new lighthouse was built of reinforced concrete strengthened by massive cement buttresses at its base. Special cushioning in the foundation allows the tower to sway a meter from vertical in high winds or severe earthquake shocks. So far, the structure has not been tested by more than small tremors, but engineers feel it could withstand another catastrophe of the 1906 magnitude.

Lightning rods are a must on all lighthouses, though for a time early colonists refused to use them, citing their interference with divine strokes of power. After Boston Lighthouse was struck and damaged by lightning several times in the 1700s, it was agreed such an edified structure tempted the powers of heaven too much, and a lightning rod was installed.

Certain familiar features of lighthouses, regardless of their beauty, function as aids to navigation and are intentional elements of design. Daymarks are as important to lighthouses as their beacons and constitute all aspects of a tower's visual appearance. Descriptions of lighthouses in Coast Guard's *Light List* include shape. (cylindrical, conical, truncated, telescoping, pyramidal, square, etc.)

The height of a lighthouse is dependent upon its required visible range and the elevation of its base.

In the case of landfall lighthouses, those built on high headlands and promontories require little additional height to elevate the beacon's focal plane. They are likely to be short and squat to create stability and prevent wind damage. Landfall lighthouses built on low, flat beaches or at the waterline require height and slenderness to elevate the light's focal plane and reduce excessive weight.

Color is equally dependent on function and physical surroundings. White or beige beaches usually require dark-colored lighthouses. Heavily forested or snowy areas need bright markings, usually red. Stripes, diamonds, checkers, and comely other designs are used when neighboring lighthouses need differentiation. For example, along Tidewater Virginia and North Carolina's Outer Banks this progression of colorful daymarks is found — red and white horizontal stripes at Assateague, white pile legs at Cape Charles, black and white checkers at Cape Henry, red brick at Currituck Beach, black and white stripes at Bodie Island, black and white spirals at Cape Hatteras, white at Ocracoke, and black and white diamonds at Cape Lookout.

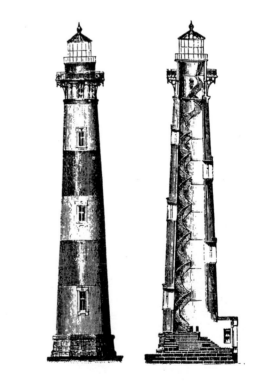

Bodie Light, North Carolina, showing its handsome daymark and an interior view of the spiral staircase. *Harpers Magazine*, 1874.

Additionally, sentinels in channels and harbors must conform to the color schemes of navigation, such as "red on right returning."

Diminutive Jeffries Hook Lighthouse, where the George Washington Bridge spans the Hudson River, marks the Manhattan shore with a bright red daymark. This small lighthouse gained fame in the 1940s when Hildegard Hoyt Swift immortalized it in a children's book called *The Little Red Lighthouse and the Great Gray Bridge*.

Entryways to lighthouses vary greatly with location, climate, and overall design. In the heyday of lighthouse keeping, the New England lighthouse often had a covered passageway connecting the keeper's dwelling to the tower. A footbridge might also have connected the tower with shore if it stood below the high tide mark. Where towers were incorporated into the plan of the keeper's dwelling, a small rotunda, foyer, or storage room usually stood at the base of the stairwell. Most lighthouses, however, were separated from keepers' dwellings and had their own entry on the leeward side.

Doors and windows are among the possibilities for exterior ornament on a lighthouse and, indeed, architects often embellished them with elegant hoods and lentils. Porthole-style windows and eyelets are often seen, and many of the house-type sentinels sport gabled windows. Lantern windows vary greatly in design, but must attend to the function of emitting a clean, unobscured beam. Latticework in the astragals (metal framework) facilitates drainage and snow removal, however, the majority of lighthouses have horizontal astragals with handholds built into the metal frames to aid cleaning the windows at perilous heights.

Brackets supporting the lantern may be very handsome additions. Florida's Reef Lights, often criticized for their cold, stark ironwork, still exhibit Antebellum beauty in their delicate, scrolled brackets. Similarly, a number of New England lighthouses have decorative railing finials in the shape of miniature lighthouses. Lovely Cape Neddick Nubble Lighthouse at York, Maine is an example, as is Nobska Light at Woods Hole, Cape Cod.

Numerous stairway styles can be found in lighthouses. Most towers have wrought iron staircases bolted or bracketed to the interior walls. These may have continuous steps or be interspersed with landings at which windows, and sometimes alcoves, are placed. Currituck Light, on North Carolina's Outer Banks, has a beautiful stairway, decorated with intricate scrollwork and railing knobs.

Given the dominance of the conical shape in lighthouse architecture, most staircases are spiral, but many forms exist. Pile design lighthouses usually have a central stair cylinder that is exceedingly narrow, cramped and dark — a claustrophobic's nightmare that can become oven hot on summer days. Wooden stairs are common in many house-top sentinels, and a few rare stone staircases still exist, including fine hand-hewn examples at Stonington, Connecticut and Amelia Island, Florida.

The pile-design tower at Sanibel, Florida, showing its central stair cylinder. *Harpers Magazine*, 1874.

Arrangement of the upper portion of light towers depended on the size and type of illuminating apparatus used to operate the beacon. In the years prior to electricity, huge weights were suspended in a lighthouse to power the revolving mechanism of the light, and a large pedestal for the lens was incorporated into the watchroom, just below the lantern. When electric motors took over the task of turning the beacon, the clockworks mechanism and weights became obsolete, and generators were installed in the watchroom. Today, one can also find devices such as timers, solar batteries, photosensitive cells, and lightbulb changers to perform the functions of lightkeeping automatically.

The last traditional lighthouse was built in 1928 at Point Vicente, California — a concrete cylinder with a hint of Spanish mission architecture, in keeping with its neighbors at nearby Palos Verde Estates. More modern pyramidal structures were built in Hawaii in the 1930s, with sleek lines and self-sufficient beacons, but they lacked the conventional appearance that was, by then, familiar to lighthouse fanciers.

The most recent lighthouses, and no doubt the last of their kind, are the ultra-modern Sullivans Island Lighthouse at Charleston, South Carolina and

Oak Island Lighthouse near Wilmington, North Carolina. Sullivans Island Light, built in 1962 is a triangular tower of steel coated in porcelain. It sits on a hexagonal base, has an elevator, and wields a 28 million candlepower beam. Except for minor flooding, it withstood the ravages of one of the worst storms of the century — Hurricane Hugo.

The 1958 Oak Island Lighthouse is a concrete cylinder with its buff, gray, and black daymark poured directly into the concrete; thus it never needs repainting. It sits on a cushioned foundation to allow sway in high winds and has a dual-intensity beacon. The beam's high-intensity function is capable of searing skin and requires special insulation in its components and throughout the lantern room. Green-tinted glasses are worn by maintenance crews when working in the lantern.

It is unlikely that lighthouses, in the traditional sense, will ever be built again — a sad admission to progress — but as the lights have been discontinued or automated, the Historic Preservation Act of 1966 ensures they fall into the care of new keepers. These preservationists view lighthouses as wholly unique structures ubiquitous to all parts of the world. They seek to preserve the important role lighthouses have played in history by safeguarding their material remains and the documents related to them.

Numerous groups now exist solely to perpetuate the history and lore of lighthouses. Among them are the nationally recognized U.S. Lighthouse Society, based in San Francisco, and Lighthouse Preservation Society of Rockport, Massachusetts, regional groups such as the Great Lakes Lighthouse Keepers Association in Michigan, the Florida Lighthouse Association, and the New England Lighthouse Foundation of Maine, as well as dozens of small groups devoted to the preservation of a particular lighthouse. The work of these groups in educating the public and making lighthouses accessible is beneficent and praiseworthy.

Few structures transcend time, place, and culture, or so perfectly capture the charitable ideals of humanity the way lighthouses do. Few have suffered more trauma and triumph in their evolution. Surely, none ever will again conjure the same romance and excitement or embody such perfect solicitude.

This article originally appeared in *Mariners Weather Log* as a two-part series in the Summer and Fall 1989 issues.

One of the Seven Wonders

The Pharos Lighthouse of Alexandria

The word *pharos* has become synonymous in many languages with the word lighthouse, and its etymological offspring, *pharology*, with the study of the history and technology of such structures. It's popularly believed that this word first came into use as the name of the immense lighthouse that stood at the mouth of the Nile River in the great Egyptian city of Alexandria. But Pharos was really the name of the island where the lighthouse was located. Roughly translated, *pharos* means light, in the sense of the wisdom and guidance of a great leader, and derives from *pharoh*, the name the ancients gave to their kings. These monarchs supposedly obtained their power from the sun and were the great political lighthouses of their realms.

Long after ancient Egypt's glory and splendor diminished, the young Macedonian conqueror, Alexander the Great, began a search for a grand capital for his sprawling empire. According to legend, Alexander had a dream in which he saw an island in a beautiful harbor and heard a voice quoting from Homer's *Odyssey*:

An island is there in the dashing sea,
Before the shores of Egypt — Pharos named.

Alexander traveled to the Nile Delta to see the island of his dream and decided it was perfect for his vast metropolis. It would be a center of the arts and sciences, religion and learning, and its magnificence would outshine all existing cities of the time. Construction of this enormous cultural seaport began around 322 BC, and naturally, Alexander's architects included a lighthouse in the plans. The entire project was so colossal, however, it required decades to complete. Alexander died before the Pharos Lighthouse was even begun.

Work continued after his death, overseen by Ptolemy Soter, one of Alexander's favorite generals and commander of Egypt at the time. The Pharos Lighthouse rose to completion on the eastern shore of the island about 279 BC. Ptolemy Philadephus, son of Ptolemy Soter, dedicated it to his parents and to the mythic and immortal brothers, Castor and Pollux, celestial beacons themselves and the brightest stars in the Gemini Twins, the favorite constellation of mariners.

Sostratus of Cnidus was the architect for the job, which took more than two decades to finish and involved thousands of slaves, huge barges for bringing stone blocks up the Nile, and hundreds of artisans to dress the stone and sculpt and paint the tower's ornamentation. As with other vast projects of the ancient era, no one knows how the gigantic blocks were lifted and placed. In this, the Pharos remains as much a mystery as the pyramids.

Legend holds that Sostratus was told to carve the name of Ptolemy Philadelphus into one of the cornerstones at the base of the tower so that the king would receive credit and honor for the building of the great lighthouse. Cleverly, Sostratus had his own name carved in the cornerstone, then covered it over with a thin layer of cement-like material. Years after the Ptolemys' were forgotten, wind and water wore away the veneer to reveal the true mastermind behind the Pharos Lighthouse:

Sostratus of Cnidus, son of Dexiphanes, dedicated this to the Savior Gods protecting those who sail upon the sea.

There is considerable disagreement over the size and appearance of the Pharos Lighthouse. It has been described by noted historians, including Pliny the Elder and Strabo, and for many years was said to have been the second tallest structure in the western world, next to the Great Pyramid of Cheops, and one of the Seven Wonders of the Ancient World.

The marble and limestone tower had four stories and telescoped to a dizzying height between 400 and 500 feet. (Historians greatly disagree on its elevation.) An estimated 50 million cubic feet of stone blocks, each weighing 40-75 tons and strapped together by metal ties, were used in the construction. The bottom tier was a broad, 300-room barracks to house the tower's keepers, mainly priests, and their servants and slaves. Above that was an octagonal tower containing a staircase and possibly a hoisting apparatus for the beacon's wood fuel. A third level was similar to the second, only smaller. The lantern rested amid four ornate columns and was topped by a statue of Poseidon, the Roman god of the ocean.

The nature of the Pharos' beacon also has been hotly debated. That it consumed forests of wood, we have no doubt, and surely slaves labored nonstop chopping wood, hauling it to the pinnacle, cleaning the creosote from the marble, then carrying down the ashes. Possibly, the wood was treated with oils to make it burn longer. The beacon's exhausted attendants would have suffered miserably to keep the hungry brazier burning 24 hours a day.

By day, a plume of smoke rose from the tower and was seen many miles at sea. At night, the fire beacon shone. Some historians believe the light was visible 30 miles at sea, so bright sailors often mistook it for a star near the horizon. In order for this to be true, some sort of reflecting or magnifying device had to be in use. Pliny the Elder was told that a great convex mirror stood behind the brazier and was used not only to intensify the light, but also to capture the sun's rays and focus them upon an approaching enemy ship to set it afire.

The Pharos was a tower befitting both Alexander's conquered empire and the grandeur of Egypt. It represented the opulence and high culture of Alexandria as well, a city illuminated by the arts and revered as a repository for the work of the ancient world's greatest thinkers. In addition, Pharos Lighthouse had the longest operative career of any lighthouse on record. The beacon shone for nearly a thousand years before a Byzantine emperor, in search of Alexander's rumored treasure trove, sent his soldiers to ransack the island. They dismantled the tower's lighting apparatus, then brought the great mirror down from the lantern and hid it. A short time later, the colonnaded lantern itself was removed.

Pharos Lighthouse remained standing another four centuries, unlit but an imposing monument visible miles at sea. An earthquake around the year 1000 destroyed its third story. The rest of the structure collapsed in more severe quakes in the 1300s. An Arab traveler visited the site in 1349 and noted that so much rubble lay about the place he could not find the entrance to the tower.

In the years that followed, erosion claimed part of the eastern end of the island and toppled what remained of the lighthouse. The shattered pieces of Alexandria's great sentinel sank into the muck of the estuary and soon were forgotten. A century later, an Ottoman fort was built where the tower once stood, obliterating any trace of it.

Almost 700 years passed, with Pharos merely a subject for historians and romantics. Alexandria's residents claimed they saw dark outlines in the estuary, which they believed to be the larger pieces of the fallen tower. Then, in the 1970s, an Egyptian diver discovered the remains of the great Pharos strewn over the seabed. By this time, the island had reconnected to the mainland to form a peninsula.

An underwater photographer filmed the ruins in 1979. His pictures revealed a long fall pattern that suggests the tower may have been 600 feet tall. Also photographed were dozens of statues, both Roman and Egyptian, indicating the tower's adornments may have changed fashion several times. A few of the smaller statues were brought ashore, but the giant blocks of the lighthouse were too large to be recovered.

More recently, a commercial venture has begun that may culminate in the construction of a replica of the Pharos Lighthouse on the tip of Pharos Peninsula, where the original lighthouse long ago stood watch. Plans for the second Pharos show it serving as a navigational beacon, but also as a posh hotel and tourist attraction. One major innovation since antiquity would be the addition of an elevator to take visitors to the lantern where they could view the harbor that so captivated Alexander the Great some 23 centuries ago.

This is an unpublished article in the author's collection.

10

Turn on the Light!

The Development of the Fresnel Lens

The heart of a lighthouse — indeed, its very soul — is the great beacon beaming from its lantern. Like the Cyclops of Greek mythology, it surveys the sea with a single, gargantuan eye, sometimes winking sleepily, sometimes gazing with catatonic boredom, but always pre-empting the night with a brilliant, guiding ray.

Such sentinels evoke an aura of romance and imagination, of solicitude and simplicity; yet, their origins are exceedingly complex. The lighthouse's thin pencil of blinding light, so captivating for photographers, painters, and poets, is no ordinary beam, rather a technological achievement rooted in pure science and showcasing the grandest talents of craftsmen and engineers.

The variety of lighted aids guiding today's navigator would certainly have confused the ancient mariner, who felt fortunate to have even the crudest aids by which to steer. The earliest lighthouses had wood braziers for beacons. The famous Pharos of Alexandria, the lighthouse that guarded the Nile River Estuary and one of the Seven Wonders of the World, had a huge brazier that was maintained by priests, whose slaves carried wood up the 500-foot tower and ashes down.

Candelabras were used in some early lighthouses. These could be titanic in size, with dozens of tapers that required hours of work to maintain. The renowned Eddystone Light in the English Channel began its career in 1698 with tallow candles suspended from the ceiling of its lantern. The first Boston Light is believed to have been lit by a chandelier of 46 candles. In the 1500s, coal braziers came into use, but as with wood and candles, soot was a problem. In addition, these early beacons cast a feeble light upon the sea and were fire hazards.

In fact, both the Eddystone Light and the Boston Light burned when their tallow-soaked, wooden floors caught fire.

Oil lamps followed in the 1700s, with numerous improvements in their designs to magnify the light and produce a cleaner and steadier beacon. The zenith of lamps came in the 1780s with Ami Argand's tubular-wick lamps, which produced a bright, smokeless flame equivalent to seven candles and was further intensified with reflector pans placed behind the lamps. This design was improved by Winslow Lewis of Cape Cod, who added a parabolic, silvered reflector. Even so, only one-sixth of the light of each lamp was reflected out to sea.

Candelabra in Smeaton's 1759 Eddystone Light
The Strand, 1909

And the problem remained of identifying beacons at night. Prior to the 1820s, all seacoast lights were white and fixed (did not flash). Colored lights were unsuitable for landfall navigation, as they drastically reduced the range, or distance a beacon could be seen, and engineers had found no effective means to make a beacon flash a signal. The American and European coasts were lit by a necklace of steady, white lights that sometimes confused the unwary mariner. Maine was typical, where one stretch of shore showed nine white, fixed lights, all visible from a single vantage point.

Efforts were made to produce flashing light characteristics as early as 1800. Highland Lighthouse on Cape Cod had a peculiar eclipser installed shortly after it went into service to distinguish it from the

Boston Light. The apparatus consisted of a semicircular screen that revolved around the 15-lamp beacon once every eight minutes. Eight minutes was too long a signal period, and complaints were made about the beacon's range, which extended only about 10 miles from shore and less during bad weather. Ships nearly ran onto the shoals of the cape's backside trying to find Highland Light, so the eclipser was discontinued.

In 1822 a French physicist named Augustin-Jean Fresnel (pronounced Fray-nel) introduced a revolutionary optic that drastically improved lighthouse illumination and became the basis for all modern optics. Fresnel's design, though devised through complex physics and mathematics, was a creation of unparalleled beauty. A fragile aggregation of prisms and brass, shimmering like an ornate ballroom chandelier, it transformed the light of an ordinary oil lamp into a blinding beam.

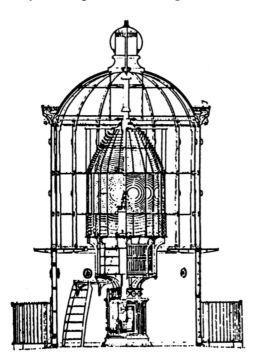

Fresnel was born in Broglie, Normandy in May 1788 and was a sickly child whom his teachers considered dull-witted, for by the age of eight he could neither read nor write, and he never mastered English or Latin, the scientific languages of his time. Yet, young Fresnel exhibited such superior talent in mathematics, he was accepted into the famed Ecole Polytechnique at age sixteen and continued his formal training at the famous Ponts de Chaussees (School of Bridges & Roads), graduating as a civil engineer.

By 1814 Fresnel had prepared his first paper on the science of illumination — a discussion of the aberration of light. Somewhat of a maverick, Fresnel boldly disputed the 150-year-old theories of Isaac Newton and outraged the scientific community. Newton had vaguely defined light as a swarm of particles moving through space longitudinally, each with a different mass, according to its color, and each with identifying characteristics which allowed it to be refracted, reflected, or moved randomly. Fresnel, on the other hand, believed light traveled in waves in a transverse manner.

His discovery that beams of light polarized in different planes do not exhibit interference led him to produce the first circularly polarized light. He went on to apply his formulas of interference, double refraction, and polarization to the design of his magnificent dioptric (beehive-shaped) lighthouse lens. Although he is best remembered as the founder of modern wave theory in physics, it should be noted that his discoveries were made while attempting to devise a better lighthouse beacon.

Fresnel's system did away with multi-lamps and reflectors and replaced them with a single larger lamp placed at the center, or focal plane, of the lens. His beehive-shaped lens was composed of a central panel of magnifying glasses surrounded above and below by concentric rings of prisms and mirrors properly angled to gather light and direct it toward the focal plane where it was intensified and projected seaward. The Fresnel lens was first tested at the celebrated Cordouan Lighthouse where the Gironde River flows into the Bay of Biscay. The beacon's excellence was quickly recognized by the maritime world, and demand for Fresnel lenses burgeoned.

Several types of Fresnel lenses were available by the mid-1820s. Fresnel's fixed lens exhibited a steady beam of light by means of a smooth, central barrel of convex glass. The flashing lens had flash panels, called bullseyes, arranged around the focal plane of the lens to funnel light into separate beams. (When viewed from above, the flashing lens resembles a great wheel with spokes of light spewing from it!) The number of flash panels determined the number of flashes over a select time period as the lens revolved. As few as two panels could be used, in the case of bivalve and clamshell lenses, or as many as twenty-four panels could be used.

A fixed-flashing combination lens was developed later that used both bullseyes and a smooth central band to give a versatile signal. Colored panels were also employed to warn of specific danger areas, such as underwater rocks or sandbars. Thus, Fresnel not only introduced an improved optic, but also a means of distinguishing one lighthouse from another at night.

The drawbacks of the Fresnel system were its weight and cost. A first-order lens could easily weigh five tons, and on today's market it might fetch more than $1 million. The heavy lenses were lifted up to lighthouse lanterns in pieces, then assembled on large, ornate pedestals. Flashing lenses were rotated by clockworks with huge weights suspended in the towers to power the cogs. Some were mounted on chariot wheels or ball bearings; others floated in troughs of high-density, low-friction mercury. Lightkeepers had to wind up the clockworks several times a night and were kept busy polishing the brass and prisms. But the expense and ponderous nature of the apparatus seemed small compared to the savings in life and cargo it effected.

Europe, namely France and Britain, embraced the design immediately and launched industries to manufacture Fresnel lenses. Chance Brothers of England and Henry-Lapaute and Barbier & Fenestre of France were among the well-known lens craftsmen. Americans were less enthusiastic. The parsimonious chief of the Lighthouse Service, Stephen Pleasanton, refused to dish out funds for the new system, citing the expense as inhibitive. He continued using the archaic lamp and reflector system patented by Winslow Lewis, who was his personal friend.

Fresnel died of tuberculosis in 1827, but by 1835 nearly every major European lighthouse had been converted to his lenticular system. Meanwhile, sailors complained of the poor quality of American lighthouses and extolled Europe's brilliant sentinels. As criticism increased, particularly from shipping interests with government influence, Congress decided to investigate. Two Fresnel lenses were purchased from France and installed for testing in the south tower at New Jersey's Navesink Twin Lights in 1841. They were quickly dubbed the best lights in the nation.

Immediate conversion to Fresnel lenses began, and the administrative workings of the old Lighthouse Service were overhauled to ensure that personal friendships did not interfere with progress and that, in the future, the U.S. would rank near or at the top in navigational aids. By 1860, practically every U.S. lighthouse exhibited a Fresnel lens. Conversion to gas illumination and, eventually, to electricity around the turn of the century only enhanced the power and beauty of the system. Though many of the old lenses were damaged during the Civil War and have since suffered from age and exposure, a number remain in use at lighthouses across the nation. The firms that manufactured them went out of business long ago, but their products shimmer timelessly along many coasts.

This article originally appeared in *Lighthouse Digest*, May 1996.

Turn on the Light

Dark! Dark! Comes the night;
Time to turn on the light.
Tread! Tread! Up the stairs
Goes the keeper with his wares.
Snip! Snip! He trims the wick,
Stirs the oil, clear and thick.
Strike! Strike! Goes the match;
Fire on the wick does catch.
Glimmer! Glimmer! Spark takes hold
Of the wick so pale and cold.
Flame! Flame! Burns the oil,
All night long it will not spoil.
Flash! Flash! The beacon warns
Beware of rocks! Beware of storms!

Elinor De Wire

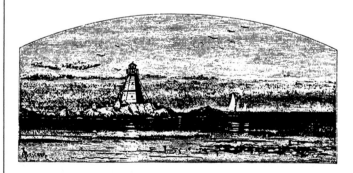

Fenwick, who was on duty one night, lent me a pair of black glass spectacles, without which no man can look at the light unblinded, and busied himself in the last touches to the lenses before twilight fell....One star came out over the cliffs, the water turned lead-colour, and St. Cecilia's Light shot out across the sea in eight long pencils that wheeled slowly from right to left, melted into one beam of solid light laid down directly in front of the tower, dissolved again into eight, and passed away.

Rudyard Kipling
from The Disturber of Traffic

Let there be light...

...on a dark, stormy night.

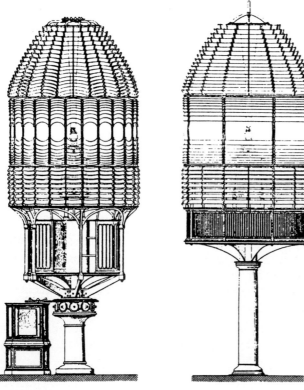

Upper Left: Augustin Fresnel
Smithsonian Institution

Upper Right: Winding up the Clockworks
The Strand, 1909

Lower Left: First-Order Flashing Lens
First-Order Fixed Lens
National Archives

14

Daymarks

Perhaps it's our love-affair with lighthouses that makes us view them as something more than the utilitarian structures they really are. Their sheer height, jewel-like optics, spiral stairs, and candy cane stripes seem as natural to the coastal landscape as sand and seagulls. They lure the photographer, painter, and poet, enchant the vacationer, bedazzle the beachcomber. Even the navigator is awestruck by their beauty.

In the bright light of day, with their beacons asleep, we easily forget that picturesque lighthouses are still on duty. Their size, shape, and color broadcast a daytime message as important as the brilliant rays of light they send seaward after dark. Bold stripes, skeleton legs, octagonal walls, buttressed bases, tiered chambers — all combine to identify a particular lighthouse.

"Nothing that has to do with the appearance of a light tower is by happenstance, but by carefully planned design and all for purposes of easy identification," wrote maritime historian H.C. Adamson in his book, *Keepers of the Lights*.

The barber-pole beauty of Cape Hatteras Lighthouse has made it America's best-loved sentinel, but its trappings are not merely cosmetic. Invariably, whenever contractors are hired to sandblast and repaint the 208 foot brick tower, someone suggests that its world-famous black and white spiral paint scheme be changed to red, white, and blue. But Cape Hatteras Light has worn its distinctive daymark for over a century, and barring any unforeseen circumstances, the Coast Guard has no plans to alter it.

Every sailor knows how valuable daymarks, or daybeacons, are for navigation. At night, the lights show the way with their unique colors and flash sequences, but during the day the navigator must judge position by known landmarks. Brightly painted lighthouses in a multitude of shapes — conical, cylindrical, octagonal, square, housetop, telescoping — are reliable guideposts guaranteed to be dressed according to their descriptions in the *Light List*.

Along with Bowditch, a Coast Guard Light List is the navigator's bible, cataloguing all the lighthouses, buoys, daybeacons, channel markers, and fog signals along our coasts. These nautical reference books provide detailed descriptions of the location and appearance (day or night) of every navigational aid. They are updated frequently and relied upon heavily by shipping of all types, from the smallest sailboat to the titanic tanker.

Ancient navigators sailed by the seat of their pants, without sophisticated instruments or manmade structures to guide them, but they did use daymarks. Old Viking sailing directions mention odd-shaped rocks and curious headland profiles. In Medieval Britain, certain stretches of coast were distinguishable by their great stands of trees, and so pressing was the need for these natural daymarks, the monarchy deemed the cutting of them a crime punishable by death.

Natural daymarks were also well-known in early America. Among these were the brilliant clay cliffs of Gay Head on Martha's Vineyard and the sparkling Diamond Shoals along the Outer Banks of North Carolina. Mountain peaks and unusual rock formations were also used. When the Gold Rush sent an armada of ships to the West Coast, via Cape Horn, California's bold headlands and the arches and stacks of Oregon and Washington pointed the way.

As recently as 1937 the government reaffirmed the navigational value of natural landmarks by utilizing one at Isle Royale, Lake Superior. In that year, the lighthouse tender *Amaranth* painted "a jutting rock for use as a daymark." The rock's black face was painted white to clearly differentiate it from its dark surroundings and facilitate safe passage into Rock Harbor.

In our nation's infancy, daymarks were simple. In channels and small harbors, various kinds of barrels, spindles, cages, and tripods marked the safe routes. All twelve Colonial lighthouses, from Portland, Maine to Tybee, Georgia, were built with conical or octagonal walls, white-washed to help them show up well against backgrounds of tawny beach, gray rocks, and green forests.

Their keepers were kept busy maintaining the bright daymarks. Gallons of white-wash and paint were used up and brushes were worn down to stubble. Keepers rigged scaffolds and sling-chairs to do the painting and scaled the exterior and interior tower walls like human spiders. It was dangerous work that sometimes resulted in injury or death.

At lofty St. Augustine Lighthouse in Florida, keeper Joseph Andreau may have become too complacent about the dangers. He fell more than 150-feet to his death when his improvised scaffold broke during a tedious 1850 repainting of the tower's daymark. Other keepers found themselves dangling from catch-lines when the scaffolding broke. Lighthouses were not places for acrophobics!

Shortly after the Revolution, the fledgling Lighthouse Service, under the guidance of Alexander Hamilton, increased the number of lighthouses in the nation and began to mark them more distinctly. In the Northeast, gray winter scenery, fog, and snow made daytime identification difficult. Following the Canadian practice of painting lighthouses red, or partially red, to make them stand out against a background of snow or fog, New England and the Great Lakes differentiated some of their beacons with attractive and colorful daymarks.

"Big Red" at Holland Harbor, Michigan can't be missed in a blizzard. West Quoddy Head Lighthouse, near Lubec, Maine, still cuts a comely profile with bright red and white horizontal stripes

that show up even in a pea soup fog. Nearby Head Harbor Lighthouse on Campobello Island has a huge red cross

St. Augustine Light
Courtesy of the Junior Service League of St. Augustine

on two of its sides. Nova Scotia's Sambro Island Light wears brilliant red and white stripes.

Canadian lighthouses also have brightly painted lanterns to contrast with their surroundings. Peggy's Cove Light, near Halifax, is well-known for its red lantern, and the range beacons on the Canadian side of the Niagara River entrance sport bright red caps. Dalhousie's range lights on Lake Ontario have green lanterns.

Southeast sentinels also employed red and green. Virginia's Assateague Lighthouse wears a red and white striped cloak, a pattern that shows up well against the pine barrens surrounding the lighthouse. Florida's Jupiter Light is bright red to differentiate it from neighboring lights at Hillsboro Inlet and Key Biscayne. St. Augustine wears a red lantern to avoid confusion with Cape Hatteras Light, since both towers have black and white spiral bands. Many copper-roofed beacons, such as Virginia's old Cape Henry Light, have turned green with age.

Along the Outer Banks of North Carolina, aptly dubbed "The Graveyard of the Atlantic," accurate marking of the low, beige capes and beaches is crucial. Five lighthouses stand watch within a stretch of 150 miles, and to easily identify them by day the government devised distinctive daymarks that good sailors have committed to memory. A chorus line of handsome towers identifies each section of the Outer Banks:

Currituck Light stands on the northern reaches with a natural red brick daymark. Bodie Island Lighthouse at Oregon Inlet is encircled by black and white horizontal bands. Cape Hatteras Light, at the elbow, boasts the familiar and much-loved spiral bands of black and white, and Ocracoke Lighthouse on Pony Island is entirely white. Guarding the lower extremity at Cape Lookout is a tall, whimsical lighthouse in a black and white diamond drape.

Black lighthouses show up well along the flat, buff-colored beaches of the Gulf of Mexico. Mississippi's Biloxi Lighthouse was given a black daymark shortly after the Civil War, causing a rumor that it wore a shroud of mourning for President Lincoln. But the Lighthouse Service was merely responding to claims that a white tower was difficult to see against the background at Biloxi. After the switch to black failed to resolve the complaints, the lighthouse's white daymark was restored and remains today.

The light towers at Bolivar and Matagorda, Texas are also black. A popular explanation is that the black daymark celebrates Texas oil, but both lighthouses stand on low, tawny beaches and are more easily seen in black garb. This was not true for Alabama's Sand Island Lighthouse, but it too was painted black so sailors would not confuse it with its neighbors.

New Yorkers' enthusiasm for the little red lighthouse beneath the George Washington Bridge was dampened a bit when they learned its red color was not in honor of a celebrated children's book, but by its position. Daymarks — even the prettiest ones — are purely functional. Jeffries Hook Light, as the tiny sentinel is correctly called, is a Hudson River daymark and, being situated on the starboard side of the channel, must be painted red.

White daymarks have always stood out well against the rugged headlands and capes of the West Coast, Alaska, and Hawaii. Lofty Makapu'u Light, northeast of Honolulu, looks like a tiny white spike high on the windward cliffs. Yaquina Head Lighthouse rises high over the Oregon shores in a pillar of white surmounted by a black lantern cap, and the white tower of Southeast Five Finger Island in Alaska shows up well against its rugged, timberland background.

Banded daymarks are also used at some spots on the West Coast. Pyramid Rock Light at Kaneohe,

Hawaii is a nontraditional, box-shaped affair with diagonal black and white stripes. The original lighthouse at New Dungeness, Washington had a black lower half and white upper half. Bright rings of horizontal black and white stripes encircle Cape Disappointment Lighthouse on the Columbia River entrance and on the Race Rocks Lighthouse in British Columbia. Prospect Point Light, another Canadian sentinel on the West Coast, has a prominent red band slashed across its front face.

Daymarks can be changed when the need arises, and many lighthouses have switched fashions over the years. Twin lighthouses were built at Cape Elizabeth, Maine, but seamen frequently confused them with Cape Ann's twin lights and those of Matinicus Rock, Maine. So the government changed Cape Elizabeth's white daymark, first to two brown towers, then a mismatched pair with a series of uneven red stripes, and finally back to white.

Cape Cod's Nobska Light wore a ruddy daymark in years past, as did the Nubble Light off York, Maine. Texas' Bolivar Light and Sabine Light both had stripes early in their careers before being painted solid colors, and Georgia's Sapelo Island Light long ago wore stripes. Photos of these former colors and designs are quite valuable today.

Shape can distinguish a lighthouse as well. Most are conical, a contour that offers less resistance to wind and water and is stable on most types of foundations. Some sentinels have unusual shapes well-known to navigators. Seven Foot Knoll Light in Baltimore looks much like a big kettle drum, Long Island's Orient Point resembles a coffeepot, and San Francisco's Mile Rocks Light was the "Wedding Cake Light" before automation decapitated it.

Duxbury Pier Light, Plymouth, Massachusetts

Occasionally, lighthouses create their own daymarks. Hardly a sailor today doesn't recognize Sharps Island Lighthouse in the Chesapeake Bay. Some years ago, the caisson foundation of the cast iron lighthouse gave way, and it slowly leaned to one side. Though threatened with destruction, it's a perfect example of what daymarks are all about —

By rendering a structure absolutely unique in appearance, a daymark helps make it as welcome a sight to mariners by day as by night. It's not just another pretty face, but an indispensable visual clue for determining inshore position.

This is an updated version of an article that appeared in *Offshore Magazine,* February 1987 under the title "Not Just Another Pretty Face."

Dungeness Light, Washington, in its taller years.

Nov. 15, 1983

Dear Mrs. De Wire,

I am really interested in light-houses and the prism. You're a great friend and you're the Best.

your friend
Albert

Nov. 15, 1983

Dear Mrs. De Wire;
Thank-you for showing the slides on towers. I noticed you have been in many towers. I have never been in a tower or have seen one. I bet they are neat. Here is a tower I drew.

Sincerely,
Anita

18

Twin Lights

Sentinels from the Past

They were the pride of America's early lighthouse engineers, tall and graceful columns lifting twin lanterns aloft and casting double beams over the Atlantic from Matinicus Rock to Navesink. In the late 19th century, an uninformed sailor might have thought he was suffering from double vision when the twin lights of Plymouth, Massachusetts rose over the horizon and twinkled their greeting in the night. As his ship drew nearer the Gurnet, and the seaman realized not one, but two beacons guarded his port, he may have felt twice as secure.

The idea of building two lighthouse towers at one station came about in the latter half of the 1700s, and was not rooted so much in security as in mistaken identity. Ironically, the task of marking the Colonial coast with lights had led to some confusion. So many lights had been erected around important harbors, mariners began to complain that one could not be distinguished from another.

Unfortunately, it was not until 1842 that the need for distinguishing light characteristics was stressed. Inspector I.W.P. Lewis of the old Lighthouse Service made a government-ordered inspection of lighthouses that year and reported:

"In two different places on the coast there are nine lights to be seen at one time, which must confuse the navigator. All the lights require distinction. They should be colored or made to revolve, or something to recognize them on a dark night."

But no such investigation had been made prior to Lewis's travels. Eighteenth century pharologists — lighthouse designers and builders — realized the need for identifying characteristics, but they were ignorant of the methods Lewis later proposed in his 1842 report. Colonial beacons had no distinctions save architectural differences and daymarks designs. At night, each possessed a steady white beam and, though some seasoned mariners could discern one light from another by the intensity of its lamps, many were bewildered by the string of white rays spewing their warnings over the treacherous coast.

"Eclipsers" were installed in the lantern of Highland Lighthouse on Cape Cod in 1797, making it the first beacon to exhibit an intermittent characteristic, but revolving, occulting, and flashing mechanisms came later. The Lighthouse Service sought a solution to the problem of identifying lights from sea, and the idea arose of building two beacons, or twin lights, at selected sites along the coast. It was reasoned that two lights within a few hundred feet of each other could be classified as one station and their double-beacon characteristic easily identified.

The theory seemed sound at the time, but such factors as the merging of light beams from certain perspectives or the effect of the earth's curvature as lights disappeared over the horizon made the system less than perfect. Nonetheless, the project was undertaken with great optimism and seven double-beacon stations were eventually built.

Their navigational merit is best measured by individual opinion, since they undoubtedly aided some mariners while confusing others. But the beauty and technical achievement associated with the twin light stations, as well as the special circumstances confronting their keepers, cannot be denied. The unusual design of twin towers, all constructed between 1768 and 1877, made them unique among the world's lighthouses, and their histories comprise a colorful part of maritime lore.

Gurnet Twin Lights, from an old postcard.

The first twin-light station established in America was at Plymouth, Massachusetts. The site selected was called the Gurnet and was situated at the tip of a small peninsula extending out from Plymouth Harbor. The Pilgrims referred to it as "the Gurnet's nose," from the name of a fish that was plentiful in their homeland along the Devonshire Coast of England.

Land at the tip of the Gurnet was owned in 1768 by John & Hannah Thomas. The Province of Massachusetts made arrangements with the family to build a lighthouse on the point that year. John Thomas was appointed keeper and was paid a paltry five shillings a year. Cost for the lighthouse was 660 pounds.

It was an odd wooden structure, 20 feet tall, 15 feet wide, and 30 feet long, with a lantern at each end of the building. Each lantern had two lamps and, because the structure was situated on a high bluff, they could be seen some distance out to sea. It was the first twin light station in America and the ninth lighthouse to be established.

During the Revolution the lighthouse at Plymouth was hit by cannon fire. A few years later the brigantine *General Arnold* wrecked off the Gurnet, killing 72 of those aboard. Many of its crew and passengers survived the wreck only to perish in the frigid December water.

The lighthouse had to be repaired in 1783 and when it was ceded to the Federal Government in 1790, widowed Hannah Thomas was still tending the lantern. Her son then took the job and was on duty the night of July 2, 1801 when the lighthouse caught fire and burned to the ground. By 1803 a new lighthouse had been built, again constructed of wood, and the government purchased the land from the Thomas family to establish a permanent station.

An 1838 inspection of lighthouses indicated the Gurnet's lanterns were often confused with nearby Barnstable Lighthouse, since on certain bearings the twin beams seemed to merge. Captain Edward W. Carpenter, who conducted the inspection, suggested a single tall tower be constructed with two lanterns — one at 65 feet elevation and the other at 110 feet. It was decided this piggyback system would also cause problems, merging into one beacon at a distance or, because of the earth's curvature, one light might appear above the horizon before the other. The piggyback plan was abandoned, though such a design was later tried at Massachusetts' Scituate Lighthouse.

The twin tower tradition continued at Plymouth with two white octagonal towers replacing the old ones in 1843. More powerful lanterns were installed in the 1870s, but Plymouth's importance as a seaport eventually diminished and there was no great need for the twin beacons. The opening of the Cape Cod Canal returned the point to prominence, however. In 1924, the government re-evaluated the light station on the Gurnet and decided to reduce it to a single beacon. The remaining twin still stands guard over Cape Cod Bay.

The second twin light station to be built in America was at Cape Ann, Massachusetts. Situated off Rockport and often called Thachers Island, it was the scene of a terrible shipwreck during the New England Hurricane of 1635. The only survivors of the tragedy were a Mr. Anthony Thacher and his wife. Since the Thachers lost all their children and personal possessions in the wreck, they were given the island as small compensation.

The Province of Massachusetts Bay Council bought the boulder-strewn island from the Thacher heirs in 1771 and built two light towers on it, 300 yards apart. A Captain Kirkwood was appointed keeper of Cape Ann's towers, each with eleven lamps, and remained in his position until the Revolution when his political leaning prompted removal. The lights remained dark until 1776.

The 1800s witnessed several important changes at Cape Ann. Winslow Lewis, an engineer who built most of the illuminating mechanisms used in our nation's early lighthouses, experimented with the hollow-wicked Argand Lamp at Cape Ann in 1807. Invented in Europe by Ami Argand, the lamp alleviated the problem of smoke haze on the interior of the lantern, thus intensifying the light and saving work for the keeper. Lewis's test of the Argand Lamp proved successful and it was installed at many lighthouses over the next few decades.

Cape Ann's north twin (*Harper's Magazine*, 1874)
Thacher's Island Association logo.

Cape Ann's towers were rebuilt in 1860. Truly twin lights, they were both conical, stone towers 124 feet tall on the northern and southeastern ends of the island. Each tower held a sparkling new Fresnel lens and both beams flashed from a height more than 160 feet above sea.

The north tower served until 1932 when the Bureau of Lighthouses deemed it surplus. A motorized flash-controller was fitted to the southeast tower and it was electrified by submarine cable.

Baker's Island, five miles off Salem, Massachusetts, was the site of the third twin light station in America. Citizens of Salem had erected a daymark there in 1791 and pressured Congress for a lighthouse after shipwrecks continued.

A large granite keeper's dwelling was built with two tall towers at either end. The twin lights were first lit in January of 1798. But government officials decided two lights were unnecessary at Baker's Island and extinguished one of the towers only a few years into the 19th century.

The wreck of the cargo ship *Union* in 1817 and another ship soon after brought a flurry of complaints concerning the dark twin at Baker's Island. Residents claimed the ships were unable to discern Baker's Light from Boston Light and urged Congress to reinstate the dark twin. As a result, Baker's Island was returned to a twin light station in 1820.

Its double beacons continued to shine almost a hundred years more. In June 1916, the shorter tower was permanently extinguished and the taller tower's beacon was strengthened.

Chatham, at the elbow of Cape Cod, received the nation's fourth set of twin lights in 1808. The first set of twins here were made of wood, each 70 feet all, with the keeper's dwelling separating them. By the 1830s the government had replaced the rotting wood towers with more durable masonry structures. These were whitewashed, conical in shape, and flanked either end of the keeper's house.

Their lifespan was short, however; the southern tower had to be rebuilt in 1863. Only fifteen years later the sea began a serious assault on the light station, eroding the towers' foundations until they were in danger of toppling. A new site was selected several hundred feet inland and two cast iron towers were built 100 feet apart. A handsome house separated the white beacons, but they were not attached to it.

Meanwhile, a hurricane swept up the coast in 1879 and, though no damage was done to the new towers, the foundation of the old station completely washed out, revealing several pits. Local children found old coins in the pits, and it was decided that Chatham's beach had once been a stowage area for a pirate's booty.

In 1923 Chatham's north tower was dismantled and moved to Nauset Beach some 15 miles up the cape. It was reassembled on a high bluff where three miniature lighthouses had once stood. Aptly named the Three Sisters of Nauset, they were the nation's only set of triple lights. The trio had been discontinued, and Chatham's relocated twin became Nauset Beach Light. Its upper half was painted red and the lower half remained white. As a tribute to the three little beacons it replaced, it was given a three flash characteristic

Matinicus Lights, from *Harper's Magazine* 1874

Matinicus Rock, 22 miles off the Maine Coast at Rockland, received its twin towers in 1826 — two wooden beacons connected by a keeper's house. John Shaw was appointed the first keeper at a salary of $450 a year. His wife accompanied him to the station and, at times, tended the lights herself. Keeper Shaw died while in service at Matinicus Rock, and his successor, Phineas Spear, also died there. It was a harsh and isolated assignment.

In 1846 two new granite towers were built, attached to either end of a new keeper's residence. What remained of the old beacons was leveled, but the old keeper's house was used for storage. Samuel Abbott kept the twin lights from 1839-1853, during their transition period from old to new.

Matinicus' most celebrated resident arrived at the desolate ledge with her father in 1853. Abbie Burgess was fourteen then, but she soon took on the mature responsibility of running the lights. Her father was away frequently, tending his lobster traps or on the mainland, and Abbie was left not only to care for the towers, but her invalid mother and small sisters as well.

In 1861, with the election of Lincoln, Keeper Burgess was removed from his assignment at Matinicus, due to the political favoritism that influenced lighthouse appointments. Abbie, then twenty-two, remained at the station to acquaint its new keeper, Capt. John Grant, with the duties. She intended to stay only a few weeks, but Grant's son, Isaac, became so enamored of Abbie, she decided to remain longer.

The arrangement culminated in marriage, and the following year Abbie and Isaac Grant were officially appointed assistants to Capt. John Grant. The couple had four children while at Matinicus and later transferred to nearby Whitehead Lighthouse where they served for many years. At Abbie's death in 1892, a request was made for a gravestone in the shape of a lighthouse. Many years later, a small lighthouse ornament was placed on her grave in Spruce Head Cemetery, Maine, by lighthouse historian Edward Rowe Snow. Today, only one of Abbie's beloved towers at Matinicus is lit. The extinguished twin has lost its lantern cap and only its masonry walls remain. The Audobon Society's "Puffin Project" team occupies the old keeper's dwelling.

Both Navesink, New Jersey and Cape Elizabeth, Maine received twin lights in 1828. Navesink, on a 240-foot high headland overlooking the Atlantic, was given rubblestone towers placed 300-feet apart, one fixed and one revolving. Not far to the north on a narrow peninsula sat Sandy Hook Lighthouse, the gateway beacon to New York Harbor.

Navesink Twin Lights, *Harper's Magazine*, 1874

A great step forward in American pharology occurred in 1841 when the Lighthouse Service

decided to use the Navesink twin towers to test the revolutionary Fresnel lens, invented by a French physicist in 1822 and considered the apex of illumination at the time. A first-order fixed lens was installed in the south tower and first-order flashing lens in the north tower. A Congressional investigation ten years later concluded that Navesink's beacons were the best on the Atlantic Coast, but its towers were badly in need of rebuilding.

Though American lighthouse construction had previously been characterized by simplistic, functional design and frugality, the government opted for unique blueprints at Navesink. Two brownstone towers were built in 1869, one square and one octagonal, connected by huge walls. The completed station more closely resembled a Bastille castle than a light station and drew visitors worldwide. Why such an extravagant and handsome design was sought is unclear, but residents of the Highlands had no complaints, for the towers have always been exceedingly attractive to visitors.

The original Fresnel lenses were re-installed in the new towers, but soon the government began further experiments in illumination. In 1898 an electric arc lamp was placed in the south tower and the north tower was discontinued. The new lamp's 60-million candlepower quickly overshadowed the old oil lamps and ushered in a new era in lighting. The intensity of the beam was welcome to mariners, but local residents soon tired of the bright beacon's invasion of their sleep.

As a result, the west sides of the lantern panels were blackened and later, the brilliance was reduced to 9-million candlepower by way of an incandescent electric light. Still later, the light was reduced to a mere 5-thousand candlepower and made automatic. The station was inactivated in 1954 and given to the Borough of Highlands. Today it is an historical landmark complete with a museum and gift shop.

Maine's Cape Elizabeth twin lights have witnessed many interesting events in their career, including the wreck of the steamship *Bohemian*. On board was John F. Fitzgerald, Irish immigrant and grandfather of future president John F. Kennedy.

The first Cape Elizabeth Lighthouses were established in 1828 on twelve acres of land near Crescent Beach. The towers were rubblestone and raised at a cost of $4250.

In 1865, an unusual color-scheme was devised for the lighthouses to be used as a daymark.

The west tower was given a broad, vertical, red stripe; the east tower was painted with four horizontal red bands. About the same time, the Cape Elizabeth lighthouses were intensified with Fresnel lenses.

Two tall cast-iron towers were erected in 1873 to replace the old stone lighthouses, and a new keeper's house also was built. One beacon revolved; the other was fixed. A fog siren replaced the old locomotive whistle that had previously served as a fog signal.

In the 1920s the west tower was darkened and its lantern dismantled. The shell was offered for sale. Many people objected, for the twin lights had become a tradition in Southern Maine and the area had come to be called "Two Lights." Regardless, the government deemed the twin light system useless and expensive. Only the east tower was retained, but as luck would have it, the importance of the old station was not lost. Artist Edward Hopper captured the beauty of the remaining sentinel in 1929 with his famous painting "Lighthouse at Two Lights."

When Cape Ann's north tower was extinguished in 1932, the last of America's twin light stations passed into history. Except for Navesink, all were situated on New England shores and established over a period of 71 years. Double towers still stand at Matinicus, Navesink, and Cape Ann. They are remnants of an era when pharologists built double and triple lights as a solution to beacon ambiguity.

This article originally appeared in Mobil's *The Compass*, No.1, 1983.

Author's Note

In the fifteen years since this article was submitted to the editors at Mobil's in-house marine/maritime magazine, my research has uncovered several other sites in the U.S. that may have had twin lights. Some sources have confused twin lights with range lights — beacons that, when lined up, provide guidance into a harbor or through a channel. There are numerous authenticated sets of range lights, such as those at Lovells Island in Boston Harbor and on the Kennebec River, Maine. Among the possible twin light sites not profiled in the foregoing article is Block Island's Sandy Point. According to various historical records, a house with short towers on either side was built on the point in 1829. The reason for these twin lights was to differentiate Block Island's southern extremity from Montauk Point on the eastern tip of Long Island. It had a single, fixed white beacon at the time. Mariners might easily have mistaken a single beacon on Block Island for the Montauk Light. The double towers at Sandy Point were inefficient and shabby. They served only a decade before being replaced by a second set of lights. These also were abandoned in the 1850s after the newly-formed Lighthouse Board deemed them obsolete, due to the advent of flashing lights. A single beacon on a granite house became the permanent sentinel at Sandy Point. It was eventually discontinued and remains on site today as a museum.

Americans were not the only builders of multiple light towers. A number of these stations existed in Europe, particularly France and Britain. As we've seen in America, one of the towers was sometimes not used. This is certainly the case at an unusual station in England.

"The Cow and the Calf" was the nickname for the set of double towers at St. Catherine's Point on the Isle of Wight in the English Channel. A coal-fired beacon was first established here in 1314 after a ship carrying wine to the monastery in Picardy was lost. A better light was established here by Trinity House in 1840, but it proved too tall for its beacon to be seen in the heavy fogs that envelop this coast. The tower was shortened in 1875.

Because of the thick mists, a fog signal was placed at the edge of the cliff below the tower. Over the years, erosion crumbled away the cliff, and in 1932 the fog signal house had to be rebuilt. Architects decided to place it next to the lighthouse, and in a fit of whim, built a smaller replica of the St. Catherine's light tower on the foghouse. No beacon was ever placed in it, but as a daymark the station was distinct. Sailors began calling the towers -- one large and one small -- "The Cow and Calf."

Triple light towers were seen in Europe too. The Casquets, a sandstone rock which lies in the English Channel about halfway between England and France near Alderney, was so dangerous an obstacle in the shipping lanes its owner, Thomas le Cocq, was petitioned by merchants to mark it with a beacon. Because so many lights shone in this area of the channel, le Cocq opted for three towers on the Casquets, each showing a coal-fire. The towers, first lit in 1724, affectionately became known as St. Peter, St. Thomas, and Dungeon. They were problematic, like all multiple lights, but Trinity House rebuilt them in 1854. They continued in use until 1877 when two of them were discontinued. All three still stand today, although only one shows a light.

FOG SONGS

A History of Fog Signals

Fog. The very mention of it conjures images of a vague and treacherous course. Light as a bride's veil or opaque as *pea soup,* it has bewildered even the keenest navigators since time immemorial. Yet this cloak of saturated uncertainty — a commingling of minuscule water droplets that may number 25,000 to the cubic inch — has not failed to inspire humankind. Whenever fog shrouds the seaway, a symphony unfolds. Lilting chimes, monotone clanks and bongs, shrieking sirens, mournful horns warn an unsure mariner when lights fail to penetrate the murk. The musicians in this briny orchestra have often been ridiculed for their harsh and repetitious tones, but they perform a critical service to mariners, guiding their course by the characteristic and number of sounds produced.

They are the humble, unapplauded fog signals — nostalgic troubadours of the sea whose songs have echoed through the centuries.

Early seafarers employed crude noisemakers to steer in the fog. Fishermen's wives banged pans or whistled through the thick air when it was time for their husbands to return home. Warships listened for the sound of a gun in foggy weather. A pounding drum led the Vikings to safety, and an imperial gong aided ancient China's eggboats in the freak mists of rivers.

An old trick in fog that is still used by Maine lobstermen is to listen for echoes from nearby headlands and cliffs. A toot of the horn or a hearty shout will bounce back to the sender. Some skippers believe a barking dog aboard ship gives the best echo. It might also set shore dogs barking in response, in which case the seaman knows the ship is too close to land.

Other seasoned old-timers claim to be able to identify a fog-obscured coast by its smell and go about with their nostrils dilated in expectation of a familiar scent.

Echoes and salty aromas aside, the best guidepost in fog, other than today's high technology radio and satellite communications, is the dependable and noisy fog signal. Even the captain of a huge oil tanker, with every state-of-the-art navigational gadget at hand, will tell you a groaning foghorn imparts a sense of security unequaled by modern bleeps and pings. But sound signals do have drawbacks.

Fog, particularly thick fog, plays tricks with sound. It may refract sound waves, causing them to travel unexpected paths that lead the listener to mistake their point of origin. Fog may also reflect sound waves away entirely, in which case the listener is unable to hear them. Since the density of fog can vary greatly, it is not impossible for the mariner to pick up a sound signal miles away, lose it upon drawing nearer, and then suddenly be overwhelmed by its loud return only a short distance from its point of origin.

In 1719, the third keeper of Boston Lighthouse petitioned the town for "a great Gun to answer Ships in Fogg." His suggestion was approved, and a cannon was positioned near the lighthouse and was fired every half hour in periods of low visibility. At the behest of this former sea captain, who was undoubtedly familiar with the tricks of fog, America had its first, official fog signal.

Boston Light, National Archives

West Quoddy Head, Maine and Point Bonita, California were among the other coasts in the nation to employ fog cannons. Point Bonita's rumbling gun came from Benicia Arsenal and went into operation in 1855. A retired army sergeant was placed in charge of it, but the fortitude he had demonstrated as a soldier did not sustain him through San Francisco's fogs. Only two months after being hired, he submitted his resignation, and three months after that the big gun also met its successor — a mechanical fogbell. At $2,000 per year for gunpowder, the cannon had proven an expensive headache for its keeper and Congress.

The Fog-Bell, *Harper's Magazine*, 1874

Fogbells came into use in the United States about 1820 and remained popular for many years. America's first one replaced the cannon at West Quoddy Head, Maine. The bell weighed 500 pounds and was struck by hand by the lighthouse keeper, who received an extra $60 a year for his labors. If conditions permitted, the bell's warning was heard up to 5 miles, but sea air often played ominous games with it, speeding up or slowing down its doleful sound or obliterating it.

By 1860 fogbells of titanic size were being cast, and mechanical strikers were developed for them. The huge bell at Ediz Hook, Washington weighed 3,150 pounds and caused the metal parts of the entire station to hum each time it struck. The 4,000 pound bell at Trinidad Head, California was anchored into a cliff 126 feet above the sea with its striker powered by heavy weights suspended beneath it. The keeper wound up the weights every few hours but, during a persistent fog in 1900, the cable holding them snapped, and they plunged into the sea never to be retrieved.

About 1850, a Canadian music teacher named Robert Foulis came up with the world's first steam powered fog signal. Coming home one night, Foulis heard his daughter playing the piano and was amazed to discover one particular low note stood out above the others. Foulis identified the note and reproduced it using a steam whistle mounted on a steam boiler. The Canadian government allowed him to install the steam signal at the harbor of Saint John, New Brunswick. When the first heavy fog rolled in, the deep voice of Foulis' extraordinary apparatus droned well beyond the harbor, ushering in a new era in fog warning.

Celadon Daboll of New London, Connecticut took up where Foulis left off with experiments involving compressed air signals. Daboll constructed trumpets of varying sizes to amplify the sound created by compressed air vibrating a reed. His largest experimental trumpet was installed at Boston Lighthouse in the 1890's.

Daboll was also innovative in the power sources he created for his noisy signals. In 1852, the strangest of his inventions went into service at Rhode Island's Beavertail Lighthouse. Its power source was a concoction of hay, grain, and water, for that is what kept its steadfast, old draft horse plodding slowly around the windlass hour after hour. Though the system appears to have worked well, the horse lost his job to a steam whistle with a cantankerous boiler that had to be fired up whenever fog crept in.

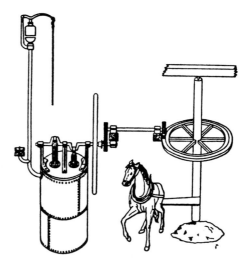

Lighthouse Service Bulletin diagram

A clever fog signal powered by the rise and fall of the tide was installed at Maine's Whitehead Lighthouse in the 1830's, but a more glamorous sea powered signal went into service at California's Farallon Islands in 1859. The source of energy for this sea-actuated apparatus was a big blowhole over which engineers built a brick chimney with a locomotive whistle in its top. A writer with *Harper's Magazine* in 1874 romantically described it as a "huge trumpet, blown by the rush of air through a cave or passage connecting with the ocean," but the signal was not problem free.

The sea is normally calm in periods of fog, and wave motion within the cave was not sufficient to force air through the whistle. On the other hand, when days dawned clear and windy, and the sea roared through the cave, the whistle screamed continuously as if it were a train gone berserk. During one storm, water forced through the blowhole exploded into the chimney with such power that it blew the structure completely off its foundation. Convinced the idea was worthwhile, engineers rebuilt the signal, and it remained in operation until 1871 when a second severe storm destroyed it.

A siren fog signal was developed in the United States in 1868 using compressed air forced through a disk. The Canadian Lighthouse Service introduced a two-tone diaphone horn a few years later by forcing compressed air through a slotted, reciprocating piston. Along with the diaphragm horn, developed in the 1880's and able to produce sounds of varying tone, these three types of signals became the mainstay of twentieth century fog warning.

Until the conversion to electricity in the 1920's, compressed air signals were powered by huge, fuel-hungry engines. The diaphone horn at lofty Point Reyes, California consumed 140 pounds of coal an hour and required a long serpentine chute to bring down the fuel on a cable car. With Point Reyes logging over 2,500 hours of fog a year, the signal needed to perform flawlessly, but it did not.

Point Reyes Lighthouse, *Harper's Magazine*, 1874

In 1875, the coal cable snapped, sending its little car careening down the chute and into the lighthouse. Additionally, vibrations from the station's blasting horn were causing rockslides and undermining the cleft on which the lighthouse was perched. As if these mishaps were not enough, the son of one Point Reyes lightkeeper was seriously injured while using the coal chute for a sliding board.

The groaning horn at Destruction Island, Washington performed satisfactorily, but caused raucous behavior on the part of one of the island's residents. The keeper's prize bull, alone amid a harem of cows, mistook the bellowing horn for a rival male and set out to establish his supremacy. Several weeks and a number of fences later, the beleaguered beast mellowed a bit, but he was always alert for any intrusion upon his domain when the horn roared into action.

Despite the blare of foghorns and the screech of sirens, bells had not disappeared from service. The government was continually improving bells and their striking mechanisms. By the 1920's, bells were electrically operated, and a device had been developed to automatically actuate their strikers. The hygroscope contained a moisture-sensitive cell that triggered the electrical power to the bell striker when humidity approached 100 percent.

At Baltimore Lighthouse Depot in 1921, an unusual hygroscope composed of human hair was tested. Experiments had shown hair responds to dryness by stretching and to dampness by contracting. A long, Chinese pigtail was attached to the electrical switch of the striker on a 2,000 pound fogbell, and its designers anxiously awaited a foggy day. Their invention came to life unexpectedly a few days later during the dedication ceremony for the Francis Scott Key Memorial. The day was sunny and clear, but fireboats were rocketing water over the harbor in celebration. Moisture drifted across the harbor to the fogbell, and the Chinese pigtail began to contract. In the middle of a moving speech by President Warren Harding, the insubordinate bell suddenly came alive, sending its urgent clangs over a fogless bay.

Bells also proved ideal as warnings on buoys. Bell buoys have been in use since 1885 and depend upon the motion of the sea to actuate their clappers, or make sound by means of a timed hammer powered by batteries or compressed gas.

Gong buoys produce a distinctive, resonant sound and are easily differentiated from bell buoys. Their melodious tune, usually four-toned, is produced by separate clappers mechanically struck, or haphazardly gonged as the buoy rocks on the waves.

Whistle buoys were developed in 1876 for use in open areas where the sea's motion is sufficient to produce compressed air and force it through a whistle head. By 1930, a trumpet mechanism powered by electric batteries induced their shrill warnings. Today, combination buoys employ several methods to issue warnings, but most still rely on the archaic but dependable bell as a backup system when ultramodern technology fails.

A certain romance of sorts surrounds the song of the buoy. People who've grown up hearing the clang, bong, or whistle of a buoy nostalgically recall it long afterwards. But the dangers of buoy work are well-known to the Coast Guard buoy tenders who must position these heavy, metal objects, then haul them out of the water for periodic cleaning and maintenance. Such perils were recognized early on by Rudyard Kipling, who immortalized them in his poem "The Bell Buoy":

I dip and I surge and I swing
in the rip of the racing tide,
By the gates of doom I sing,
On the horns of death I ride...

The music of foggy bays and harbors has not always been appreciated, particularly in large cites

where the noise extends over a populous area. When New York City's Great Captain Island received a sparkling, new fog siren in 1905, nearby residents protested. A local newspaper reporter used such comparisons as "an army of panthers...roar of a thousand bulls...wail of a lost soul...moan of a bottomless pit...and groan of a disabled elevator" to describe the unpopular siren.

The government did what it could to mollify annoyed neighbors of the fog signals by installing deflector panels and extolling the virtues of sound signals in aiding those at the mercy of the sea. But even the keepers of the signals sometimes objected to their endless din.

It was the crusty, old bulimic fog signal at remote Point Reyes, ravenously consuming coal and uttering its warnings with a belligerent belch, that drove one keeper mad and, in the words of a San Francisco reporter, made "its jaded attendants look as if they had been on a protracted spree."

The grateful mariner aside, there are few individuals who feel a genuine affection for the lowly fog signal. Both Rudyard Kipling and Robert Southey extolled the perilous watch in their writings, and a composer from California once wrote a symphony based on the sounds coming from San Francisco Bay during fog. School children in Canada still sing "The Foghorn Song," an energetic rendition of the sounds a music teacher heard in Vancouver Harbor.

One individual, according to Pacific historian James Gibbs, was unable to fathom the purpose of a fog signal or the need for it. He was an Indian and a descendant of the Continent's earliest seamen. After watching a foghorn being installed on the West Coast in the 1800's, the sage old man observed both the sea and the blaring signal for many days. He then concluded that the horn was useless, for despite its terrifying noise and hideous appearance, it failed to frighten away the fog, which came in with the same regularity it had for untold millennia.

This article originally appeared in *The Compass*, No.3, 1984. A variation appeared in *Sea Frontiers*, May 1987. Reprints appeared in *Mariners Weather Log*, Fall 1987, *Western Boatman*, August 1988, and *Weatherwise*, October 1991.

At left: The Coast Guard strictly forbids interference with the benevolent work of a buoy, including tying up to one or climbing on it, as is pictured on this old postcard from the turn-of-the-century. Author's Collection

Screwpile Lighthouses

Sentinels Secured to the Seabed

When most of us think of a lighthouse, we picture a lofty stone tower perched on a rocky headland or rising high above a long stretch of lonely beach. But lighthouse engineering did not confine itself to solid ground alone. Many of the world's lighthouses stand watch in bays and harbors and on sea-swept offshore reefs. Here, they warn the mariner of peril by risking their own safety.

Screwpile lighthouses stand on huge iron legs screwed directly into a seaswept rock or reef, or into the sea floor itself. They were first developed by an Irish marine engineer, Alexander Mitchell, whose experiments in the 1830s with methods for mooring ships led him to design a pile that could be anchored firmly in the soft, alluvial beds of bays and harbors. When Mitchell's pile design proved successful, he developed a similar design for a lighthouse at the mouth of the Wyre River in Lancashire, thus opening the door on a new era in marine engineering.

Mitchell's work was made more incredible by the fact that he developed his revolutionary designs after going blind. He had been born with poor eyesight, and by age 21 was completely blind. Despite his infirmity, Mitchell had managed to educate himself in mathematics, mechanics, engineering, and science. He worked as a brickmaker in Belfast, but spent his leisure hours tinkering. His wife and son served as his eyes and helped him assemble and test his inventions.

They assisted him in 1832 when he tested a sail he had designed for high winds. Prior to this, Mitchell had lain awake nights listening to storm winds rage outside his bedroom, and he wondered what he could do to help sailors survive in such dangerous weather conditions. He knew ships lost their ability to maneuver if their sails were ruined, so he began experimenting with designs for sails that could withstand high winds.

His experiments were not successful, but they led to a more important invention. Mitchell and his wife and son were testing a sail with a flanged screw on its lower end when a gust of wind grabbed the sail and screwed it into the muck of Belfast Lough. So firmly was the screw set, Mitchell could not remove it. He returned the next day to find it still anchored, and it remained so even after a storm the following week. Mitchell had developed the screwpile.

He patented his invention in 1833, and five years later it was used in the construction of the Maplin Sands Lighthouse. The tower consisted of nine iron disk-footed piles — eight forming an outer octagon and the ninth as a center support — screwed 22-feet into the unstable river muck and supporting a house for the keepers with a beacon on top. Mitchell, with the assistance of his son, had designed the entire structure and oversaw its construction.

Maplin Sands Light
Trinity House

The marine engineering world marveled at this technical advancement and its designer. Mitchell was extolled not only for his invention, but also his devotion to the numerous screwpile towers that were constructed in the decades following his discovery. He visited many of the sites to inspect work and cheer the crews who toiled on dangerous, wave-swept sites. Men were amazed to see Mitchell crawling on hands and knees, using his sensitive fingers, to assess workmanship, or leading the chanteys the crews sang as they marched around the great windlasses that drove in the monstrous screws.

In the United States, the first screw-pile tower was built in 1843 at Black Rock Harbor in Connecticut. Capt. William H. Swift of the Army Corps of Topographical Engineers was the architect. He had traveled to England to study the Maplin Sands

Lighthouse and talk with Alexander Mitchell. After the success of his 36-foot Black Rock screw-pile tower, Smith felt confident and eagerly accepted the job of building a lighthouse on treacherous Minots Ledge off Cohasset, Massachusetts.

Construction of the Minots Ledge Lighthouse was difficult and costly, and only a year after it was lit, the tower was completely destroyed by the sea and its two keepers drowned. The 1851 storm that claimed it earned the memorable name "The Minots Light Storm." Investigation showed the tower's iron piles had not been properly braced and had snapped like match sticks under the intense pressure of wind and waves.

Fowey Rocks Light, Florida, by Paul Bradley

Other screwpile lighthouses fared better. About the same time Minots Light was under construction, a massive screwpile sentinel was also underway in the Delaware Bay. Marine engineers, Maj. Hartman Bache and Lt. George G. Meade, were both young and energetic when they were appointed by Congress to design and build the Brandywine Shoal Lighthouse, eight miles offshore. Alexander Mitchell sailed to Delaware to serve as a consultant on the project. The 46-foot lighthouse had 32 screw piles supporting a keeper's house and was fortified by tons of riprap dumped around its base to prevent ice floes from shearing off its legs. The pricetag was $53,317. and the beacon was lit in October 1850.

No sooner had Meade finished work in the Delaware Bay than he was sent to the Florida Keys to build a screwpile lighthouse on Carysfort Reef. More than sixty known vessels had met their doom on this shallow coral reef, including the frigate HMS *Carysford*, for which the reef is named. A lightship had been assigned to the reef in 1824, because no lighthouse could be built there, but duty was perilous, owing to the lightship's position in "Hurricane Alley." It was repeatedly blown off station and damaged.

The screwpile lighthouse for Carysfort Reef had been designed by I.W. P. Lewis, a civil engineer, and its metal parts had been fabricated in a Philadelphia foundry, then shipped to the Florida Reef. Meade had to make modifications to the design when it was discovered the coral reef was not solid but was a hard shell over sand. Meade knew the screws would not hold in sand, so he designed disks to rest on the coral crust of the reef and distribute the weight of the huge 112-foot tower.

Meade went on to build screwpile lighthouses at Florida's Sand Key, where a masonry tower had been destroyed in the Great Hurricane of 1846, and on Sombrero Key near Marathon. He left the Florida Keys in 1860 and went on to play an important role in the Civil War as commander of the Army of Potomac, which defeated Robert E. Lee's army at Gettysburg. Other engineers took up Meade's work of erecting a string of sentinels along the Florida Reef, from Fowey Rocks off Miami to Rebecca Shoal's confluence of the Atlantic and Gulf waters.

Major screwpile lighthouses were built also in the Chesapeake Bay and along the shores of the Gulf of Mexico. Mitchell's archaic pile-driving raft, with its windlass and chantey-singing crew, was eventually replaced by a steam-powered 2000-lb. hammer. Not only were lighthouses built in far-flung and tempestuous places, but wharves and docks benefited from the screwpile technology.

Thimble Shoal Light, Chesapeake Bay, *Harpers Magazine*, 1894

29

Today, a number of screwpile lighthouses still stand in mucky bays and harbors, and on the reefs and sandbars of Florida and the Gulf of Mexico. A few in ice-prone areas have been replaced by caisson lighthouses, whose monstrous concrete platforms easily withstand the pressure of moving ice. Diminutive Hooper Strait screwpile lighthouse is among those that have been retired. It now stands a peaceful watch at the Chesapeake Bay Maritime Museum in St. Michaels, Maryland.

Visitors may go inside the sentinel and explore its strange, octagonal living quarters and the small beacon that juts up from the roof. The lighthouse's legs are sunk in the ground and afford a closer look at Alexander Mitchell's amazing technology. Near the base of the tower is the most fascinating relic of all — a screw from the end of a pile that was once sunk into the floor of the bay.

This article originally appeared in *Mariner's Weather Log*, Fall 1995.

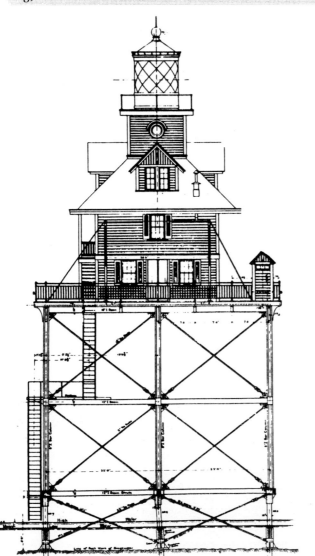

Recommended Reading

Dean, Love. *The Reef Lights*. Key West, Florida: Historic Key West Preservation Board, 1982.

This excellent book on the screwpile lighthouses of Florida was recently reprinted and is available from the U.S. Lighthouse Society and Lighthouse Depot.

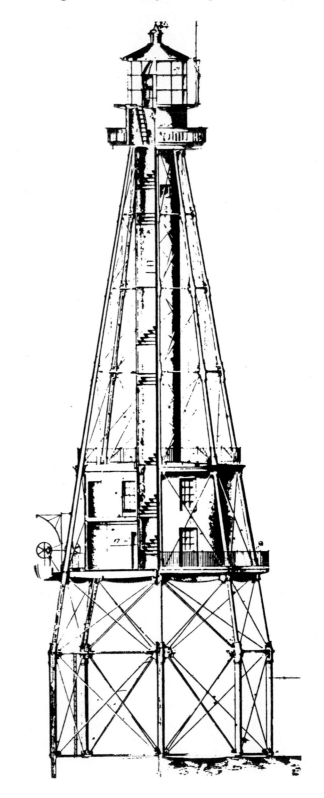

Light Breezes

In the traditional sense, the job of "lighthouse keeper" is obsolete today. Automatic machinery and high-tech navigational aids now perform the same work human hands once did, and for a fraction of the cost. But a mere fifty years ago more than 5000 intrepid "guardians of the lights" were on duty along the world's seacoasts and larger inland lakes and waterways. A wealth of lore surrounds these men and women, much of it quixotically colored by the drama of natural calamities.

Storms were center stage, of course, with fog offering a stunning secondary performance. Waterspouts, earthquakes, and tsunami made occasional showings too. But on a smaller, less noticeable scale, wind had the dominant role, for it was part of nearly all the scenes. The lighthouse breeze relentlessly wore down everything, from the paint on the tower to its sand foundation, from the station flag to the nerves of the keeper. Storms came and went; fog settled and lifted; quakes and tidal waves made infrequent cameo appearances. But the wind was almost always there.

Sometimes it came as a welcome air — clement and healthful, moisture-laden, and carrying the pleasant perfumes of the sea. More often it stole in unnoticed to gnaw, abrade, purloin, pilfer, tatter, and chisel everything within its reach. Over time, the surreptitiously subtle ocean breeze was the most destructive force at a light station.

The late Frank Jo Raymond, who served in the 1920s at Connecticut's Latimer Reef Lighthouse in Fishers Island Sound, found few things disagreeable about his solitary life on a waterbound lighthouse. But there was one aggravation:

"That wind! Almost never stopped. It got on my nerves some days. Storms were different. I could handle a storm because it kept me busy, and I knew it was going to end at some point. But the wind, just blowing and blowing and rattling and whistling all the time; that got to me. The worst thing was when it grabbed hold of something and just kept banging and banging it."

The stiff breeze snatched anything hung out to dry and hastily shredded ensigns and pennants; it absconded with the garden topsoil and plucked the petals from the flowerbeds; it scoured painted surfaces and sandblasted the windows frosty dull. It filled the foghorn trumpets with sand until they barely uttered choked, congested honks.

Fish stories paled in comparison to tales of the scurrilous wind: A lighthouse keeper from Nova Scotia swore he'd sat down to a meager dinner of boiled potatoes one blustery evening only to have a fat duck blown through the kitchen window and plopped neatly on his plate. Another from Cape Cod made the dubious claim that he'd put a splice in his cat's tail so that he could slip it over a hook and prevent the feline from being blown off its windy lighthouse home!

Few could spin a yarn as well as a lighthouse keeper, but for every tall and windy tale there was an equally true one:

During the lightkeeping years at Battery Point Lighthouse off Crescent City, California, it was risky to open the front door. Facing the full force of the Pacific, the portal often took its pedestrian for a wild ride, while violently testing its hinges. Evidence of the station's ceaseless wind was everywhere. Cypress trees, hunched and bent, stood with their backs to the sea and their limbs festooned with seaweed and foam. The rocks were grotesquely sculpted by invisible hands; the TV antenna on the lighthouse roof was a tangle of wire and metal.

31

Wind-blown Monterey cypress at Point Pinos. Author's Collection.

Some 300 miles down the California Coast was lofty Point Reyes Lighthouse with its persistent, buffeting wind. Perched nearly 300 feet above the sea, the squat iron-plated tower was literally bolted to the cliff to prevent it from succumbing to the unremitting bluster. A ramp and a steep exterior stairway were built into the rockface to connect the tower to the keeper's quarters. Another longer and more treacherous stairway snaked down from the lighthouse to the fog signal station, still about 100 feet above the sea.

Keepers often tethered themselves to the stair railings to prevent being swept off the cliff as they descended the 217 foot ramp and 307 steps to the lighthouse, or the 638 giddy steps to the fog signals. Gusts of 100 mph were not unusual on a typical sunny day; a steady 25 mph wind was routine. On numerous occasions the lightkeepers remained in the tower for as long as 36 hours rather than risk the windy trip up the stairway to the house.

The Weather Bureau was intrigued by the winds at Point Reyes Lighthouse, but also by the periodic fogs. It was, and remains, a place of weather extremes: First the wind howls fiercely, then silent fog blankets the point in stillness and gloom, only to have the wind spirit it away again. From 1870, when the sentinel was built, its keepers were required to maintain detailed daily weather records. Few entries neglected to mention the maddening cycles of murk and squall, so the Weather Bureau decided to examine first-hand the peculiar conditions at Point Reyes.

An official weather station was established at the lighthouse in 1900, with its resident meteorologist sharing quarters with the lightkeepers and their families. Data was collected for 27 years and revealed what the lighthouse keepers always knew. "Better to dwell in the midst of alarms than reign in this horrible place," penned one weary attendant. Clocking wind speeds and duration of fog were the major concerns of the Point Reyes meteorologists. In 1915 fog hung over the station more than 2300 hours, and an average wind speed of 23.5 mph was recorded. Point Reyes was dubbed the windiest, foggiest place between Canada and Mexico.

That same year an assistant keeper barely escaped death when the wind tossed a timber through his bedroom window. Fortunately, the man had awakened early that morning and gone to the kitchen for coffee. The timber shot into the bedroom like a missile, grazed the bed on which the keeper's nightclothes still lay warm, and penetrated the wall opposite the window. The keeper rushed to his room to find his pajamas riddled with splinters and hanging on the timber.

Across the vast Pacific on the eastern shores of New Zealand's South Island, lightkeeper Tom Clark was toughing out duty in the 1950s on wind-blown Akaroa Lighthouse. In his memoirs Clark noted that the station's power cable was frequently ripped from its connection to the powerhouse by the "southerlies," resulting in the failure of the beacon. His family relied on rainwater runoff from the roof of their house to fill the cistern, but the wind devilishly polluted it with sand and salt. His wife's efforts to keep a garden were continually thwarted by the ever-present breeze on which was sometimes borne a deadly salt mist: "Great dollops of spindrift would float in the air like toy balloons....only the burned tops of the crops remained."

The activities of the blue penguins at Akaroa Lighthouse were analyzed carefully by Clark's wife, a native Polynesian, who claimed she could tell what kind of weather was coming by listening to the penguins' calls. The birds lived in the 12 inch crawl space beneath the house and would cry miserably when the pointwinds of a southerly blow arrived. They were especially unsettled on a night in July 1956 when the high-pitched squeals of wind through the floor planking signaled the coming of a gale. The following night, as Mrs. Clark was cooking the evening meal, the wind tore off the baffle on the top of the kitchen chimney and sent a burst of air down through the stove, coating the roast in ash and smoke. Never one to admit defeat, Meri Clark scrubbed the tainted meat and chopped it up in a vegetable soup.

The full fury of the open sea accosted Atlantic lighthouses too. Cape Cod's Highland Lighthouse looks out over the North Atlantic, with nothing to obstruct the wind for 3000 miles. When Henry David Thoreau visited the lighthouse in the 1850s, he marveled at its beauty but also its exposed perch:

"Over this bare Highland the wind has full sweep. Even in July it blows the wings over the heads of young turkeys, which do not know enough to head against it; and in gales the doors and windows are blown in, and you must hold on to the light-house to prevent being blown into the Atlantic."

Highland Light had handholds built into its lantern windows, and numerous replacements of glass panes were made during its long career due to blowing sand that frosted the windows. Dunes moved surreptitiously about the station, alternately exposing and concealing anything in their path, while the relentless, sea-driven wind pilfered sand from the steep Clay Pounds. The lighthouse has stood watch for nearly two centuries and until very recently sat precariously near the edge of the cliff. Fortunately, funds were raised to relocate it several hundred feet inland. International Chimney Corporation moved the massive lighthouse in the summer of 1996.

Highland Light as it appeared in Thoreau's day.
Harper's Magazine, 1874

Winds blowing across miles of uninterrupted lakewater were also a test of will for lighthouse keepers. Winter wind was particularly brutal on the sentinels of the Great Lakes and Lake Champlain. Tiny, windborne droplets of water were dashed against the lake lights day after day until they more closely resembled ice castles than lighthouses. Their keepers were kept busy chipping and scraping and hosing with hot water to prevent becoming entombed before the close of the shipping season in December.

But troubles often began sooner, in September or October. Harriet Colfax was working at Michigan City Lighthouse, Indiana in October 1886 when she discovered how dangerous Lake Michigan's winds could be. Michigan City Lighthouse was just what its title implied, a house with a lantern on its roof. Harriet lived in the comfortable rooms below the beacon and had a relatively uneventful career in her early years as lightkeeper. But in 1871 her work was made doubly difficult by the addition of a second beacon on Michigan City's east pier, which extended some 1500 feet out into the blustery lake. Each night after lighting up the beacon on the roof of her house, Harriet trekked out the narrow, windswept walkway to the ramshackle pierhead tower, carrying cans of lard oil.

A few years after establishing the pierhead beacon, the government decided to move it across the channel to the west pier where it would better serve mariners. This meant Harriet had to cross in a boat, then walk some distance along a sloping ramp to reach the beacon. Once there she climbed a ladder to the lantern, filled the lamp, and lit up for the night. The trip to the west pier beacon was difficult at best, but outright treacherous in bad weather, especially for someone in skirts and high-button shoes. Harriet was injured on several occasions, but in October 1886 she nearly lost her life.

A gray pall of clouds hung over the lake all that day, with temperatures hovering around freezing. By afternoon a wet heavy snow began, its huge flakes swirling like confetti. Visibility was severely reduced, so Harriet decided to light the beacons. As the lard oil for the west pier heated on Harriet's woodstove, she bundled herself warmly for the arduous trip. The row across the channel took longer than expected due to a steady head wind. Harriet was discouraged to find the west pier awash but managed to scramble up the walkway during a lull in the waves and set the lamp in place. The lard oil had congealed in the cold air; still, she was able to coax a flame on the lamp wick, and soon the tiny lantern was bathed in light.

The snow had turned to sleet and was pelting the lantern roof and windows. Harriet felt the tower shudder in the wind and thought it best to quickly tend to her duties and leave. She stepped out on the narrow platform surrounding the lantern and scraped away the snow and sleet, then climbed down the ladder, skirts flapping in the wind. She had gone only a few steps on the walkway when a terrific gust of wind surged over the pier. She heard wood splintering and metal twisting, and turned just in time to see the lighthouse tip over and slide into Lake Michigan. Had she dallied a minute longer, she would have perished with it. Her close brush with death was downplayed, however, by a cursory entry in her logbook. Harriet Colfax, like most lightkeepers of her day, came to expect such calamities. Of course, she also might have been much relieved, even happy, to have the wind push that pesky pierhead beacon into the murky lake.

From *The Strand* magazine, 1909.

Life on the wind-swept coastal lighthouses was dangerous, but the rock lights on the open sea were far worse. One mile off Tillamook, Oregon, "Terrible Tilly" lived up to its nickname with tormenting winds that sometimes left its crew marooned for months -- unable to get ashore in their small dories and out of reach of the supply ship. Tillamook Rock Lighthouse also had a reputation for its eerie sounds, caused by wind coursing through the station. The veteran keepers were accustomed to these daily peregrinations of wind and water, but new keepers found them very unsettling.

Maritime author and former Tillamook lightkeeper James Gibbs recalled that the "sigh" of damp air current moving up the column of the tower on windy days could not only be heard, but also left a fine dew on the skin and a feeling of indescribable discomfort. Everything outside was kept tied down, every day of the year; at times the men went from place to place outside on their hands and knees. Wind and sea tossed rocks upwards more than 100 feet and deposited them on the deck.

But there was a lighter side to life on this desolate station: Gibbs comically noted that using the lighthouse latrine was a definite challenge when the wind had kicked up, because the bowl was open to the sea. Visits to the privy on these occasions were chilling experiences that, according to Gibbs, "could greatly hamper nature's calling."

The lightkeepers of Britain's infamous rock lighthouses also deftly recorded their struggles with wind. New men assigned to Wolf Rock Lighthouse off the Cornwall coast were always given grave warnings about the wind and hastily acquainted with the macabre legend of "The Wolf." Cornish wreckers supposedly despised the rock because it warned mariners away with a loud, lupine howl whenever the wind was forced through a blowhole in the crags. To silence its warning cry and thus increase their salvage profits, the wreckers hauled stone out to the rock and filled in the wolf's maw.

Wolf Rock Light
Trinity House

34

When a lighthouse was built on Wolf Rock in 1870, it was as unpopular as the howling hole had been. Crews were difficult to get and harder still to keep, for it was a dreadful place. Work at the top of the tower was particularly dangerous, often necessitating the wearing of safety harnesses. Due to its exposed location at the extreme southwest tip of England where the North Atlantic surges into the English Channel, stout gales incessantly pummeled the tower. Landings were difficult, with the keepers rarely getting on and off the lighthouse on schedule.

In 1973 the Wolf Rock lightkeepers were given a reprieve from the impositions of wind and sea when a heliopad was constructed on the top of the lighthouse. Wind could still dictate the men's arrivals and departures, but less so with a helicopter. As a safety measure, heavy netting was draped around the deck under the heliopad to catch anything the wind might try to carry away during landings and takeoffs. As every man knew, once the wind took something it was gone forever.

Equally turbulent were the rock lighthouses in the English Channel. Journalist Tony Parker spent several harrowing weeks in the 1970s on several of these wave-swept sentinels to record the daily life of their keepers. His effort culminated in a book that candidly revealed an existence regulated almost entirely by the weather. For the keepers of these lights, the wind was a mischievous friend. One man summed it up this way:

"As relief day gets nearer you get up each morning and wonder what the chances are going to be; you listen to the wind in the night, wondering if it's starting to change direction and whether it's for better or worse. I've always found a kind of excitement in it -- the wind's deliberately letting you know it's deciding if it'll let you go or not. It never seems malicious. I think of it being a kind of schoolboy practical joker playing pranks."

Said another keeper of the incessant wind: "I'm always conscious of it; I think I always shall be. It's played such a big part in my life. I don't think I could ever live somewhere now where I couldn't hear it and everything was always quiet and still."

On these exposed lighthouses the wind often blows a steady Force 8 or 9 for a week, nonstop, and brews up a swelling sea that pounds the towers mercilessly. During the years when resident keepers were aboard, the windows and doors were kept tightly sealed, and the air inside the stations became stale. Men described the roar and boom outside as sounding much like distant artillery fire. Weeks of it forced them to look for a variety of diversions.

One innovative watchman assigned to a North Sea lighthouse decided to amuse himself with a few creative entries in his weather journal. He laid aside his Beaufort Scale and instead used a chamber pot to measure wind speed. Each wind state was listed according to the way the contents of the chamber pot behaved when tossed out an upper window. For example, a trickle straight down meant a calm sea state. If the contents blew away quickly, a moderate gale was up. If pot and all disappeared out the window, it was a full-blown hurricane. Needless to mention, his superiors were not impressed.

In tropical climes, warm winds could be just as challenging. The keepers of Florida's "Iron Giants" -- a bright brigade of cast iron, sea-swept towers with legs screwed into the coral beds of the shallow Florida Reef -- grew accustomed to the ceaseless whir of wind through the pilings and braces of their peculiar offshore homes. They were thankful for any breeze on a balmy summer day when the metal decks of the towers became too hot to stand on and the lanterns felt like ovens. When cooler evening breezes swept in, these towers groaned and screeched as their metal joints contracted. The sounds gave rise to numerous ghost tales.

Double-Headed Shot Lighthouse in the Bahamas has its ghost stories too, thanks to the wind and a keeper who refused to stay in his grave. When the man died suddenly in the scorching summer heat in the 1920s, his bereaved family promptly went in search of a place to bury him. Their station boat was not seaworthy enough to reach the nearest island, so they chose a final resting place on their idyllic cay. The keeper's body was carefully lowered inside a coral cavern and covered with crushed shells.

It seemed a suitable grave, but a few days later the wind picked up and roused heavy seas. The widow and her children heard muffled booms as the ocean surged into the sealed cavern where the keeper had been interred. Swells increased until the inevitable happened: Compressed air exploded through the cavern, sending the keeper flying out of his pelagic purgatory like a novice angel. He landed on the sandy lawn in front of the lighthouse. The horrified family gathered up the poor man and hastily proceeded with a second burial, this time at sea with the body heavily weighted.

Wind was certainly a curse at most lighthouses, no matter where they stood; but it was sometimes a blessing too. At no time was that more true than at Southeast Lighthouse in the 1940s when the children of keeper Howard Beebe were passionately into baseball. Their home was a handsome Gothic tower with attached house overlooking the Monhegan Cliffs of Block Island south of Newport, Rhode Island. Mrs. Beebe was the island's foremost amateur weather watcher, with a reputation that shamed the local meteorologists. For this reason, she was consulted about baseball. Her daughter, Barbara, who officiated at the friendly ball games on the lighthouse lawn, nostalgically remembers:

"We waited for just the right conditions before challenging the neighborhood kids. Mom would study the wind, then signal us what to do. With a little help from a stiff northerly breeze, you could hit one into the sea. That was a homer because there was no chasing a ball down a 200-foot cliff into King Neptune's court!"

This article originally appeared in *Weatherwise*, August 1994.

Interesting Trivia

Sailors of old believed that a cat could stir up wind by playing with its tail or chasing string. They also believed a cat carried a gale in its tail. This idea came from the fact that petting a cat during dry weather produces a spark of static electricity. Sailors, of course, thought it to be a small version of lightning. For these reasons, tailless cats were preferred on ships. Since many lightkeepers were once sailors themselves, it's not surprising that they believed these same superstitions. The lighthouse cat had to watch his step indeed!

Author's Note

Here's a windy lighthouse story my family loves to tell, and in mixed company too! In August 1983 we vacationed on the Outer Banks for a week with my brother Tom and his family, who live in Maryland. My family traveled north from Florida, where we lived at the time. After terrific side trips to Hunting Island Light and Cape Lookout Light, we took the ferry from Harkers Island to Ocracoke, then crossed to Hatteras on the Federal ferry. Our cottage was in Avon, just north of the lighthouse.

The weather was beautiful as the ferry pulled away from the pier at Harkers Island. Gulls were chasing it, feasting on the chum the big screws churned up and hoping for handouts from passengers. My kids fed them a bag of corn chips. The only drawback that day was my pretty sundress with its billowing skirt. As I stepped out from behind the cars at the stern, the wind caught the skirt and lifted it over my head. I fought the material for what seemed like minutes before recovering. A lot of folks were grinning at me, and my embarrassed family was nowhere to be seen!

Split Rock Light, Lake Superior
Pen & Ink by Lee Radzak

Winged Visitors

Birds at Lighthouses

Certain lighthouses, because of their location along the great migratory routes, attract birds. These include the tall, bright sentinels at Fire Island, Cape May, and Assateague. All three lie along the great Atlantic Flyway — the Eastern Seaboard's busy, feathered freeway. A number of Great Lakes lighthouses witness great waves of birds migrating between the tropics and Canada, and most of Britain's lighthouses stand along the busy migration routes to and from Africa.

In the spring and autumn, these lighthouses witness thousands of birds passing overhead during the daylight hours, but at dusk the weary flocks may fly in and roost on aerial wires, rooftops, clotheslines, and the towers themselves. In the process, the bewildered, avian travelers are sometimes injured or killed:

"I remember being on Bardsey Island off the coast of North Wales on what experts called a 'bird night,' wrote birdwatcher Wynford Vaughn-Thomas in 1985. "The swarms of small birds poured onto the island, some of them exhausted after long flights from distant Africa. They could not resist the attraction of the night light and, when dawn came, the evidence of that fatal attraction lay sadly at the foot of the tower."

So great is the bird problem at some lighthouses, a screen has been installed around the lantern to protect the windows and lens, and a bird spike is mounted on the top of the cupola to discourage birds from perching and fouling the ventilation opening to the lantern. Keepers of yesterday spent much of their time cleaning the outside glazing and scrubbing the gallery decks and railings. At stations where rainwater was caught on the roof and drained into a cistern, birds were sometimes even a menace to health.

Long Island's Shinnecock Lighthouse had chicken wire wrapped about the lantern to protect the glazing, but huge flocks still pelted the tower during migrations, often snagging in the wire screen. So many were killed that the keepers dug a trench around the lighthouse to make disposal of the dead bodies easier. The problem appeared to be solved until hunters invaded the station, lured by the prospect of easy targets. The government was forced to declare the area a wildlife refuge to protect the lightkeepers!

Exactly what lures birds to lighthouses is still unknown. Tall towers, with brilliant, flashing beams seem to hold the greatest attraction, but any lighthouse is a target, whether by accident or deliberate aim. Logbooks make frequent mention of encounters with birds and are prolific sources of information for ornithologists.

The most recent theories of bird navigation suggest long flights are accomplished using a combination of celestial cues (the position of the sun, moon, and stars), known landmarks, and a keen sensitivity to the earth's magnetic field. Birds appear to have amazing built-in compasses and sextants, not to mention excellent memories for the lay of the land, that allow them to monitor their flight patterns, comparing them against magnetic north and true north.

Lighthouses may disrupt this navigational ability and disorient birds. Perhaps the birds mistake the bright beacon for the moon or the sun, or on starless nights it becomes an immense, blinding star. A flashing or revolving beacon adds to the confusion and may contribute to the inexplicable bird-suicides and bird-attacks that have occurred at some lighthouses.

Whether by choice or by necessity, many lightkeepers became avid birdwatchers. The keepers at Boston's Graves Lighthouse were beguiled by the cheerful little rock plovers who visited the rocky islet. The Shanahans of Sanibel Island Lighthouse in South Florida tamed a pelican in the 1880s, one of many wild animals that kept the thirteen children of the keeper amused. Matinicus Rock's keepers worked amid a breeding ground of comical, clown-faced puffins, members of the auk family who return to breed in the burrows from which they hatch and fledge.

Heligoland Lighthouse, in the North Sea thirty miles off the German coast, is so often the scene of massive and noisy flybys that an ornithological observatory has been set up there. According to German bird authority H. Gatke, October is the most active month when "under the intense glare of the light swarms of larks, starlings, and thrushes career around in ever-varying density, like showers of brilliant sparks or huge snowflakes driven onwards by a gale." Sometimes he observed predatory owls swooping through the beams in pursuit of a midnight meal. On October 28, 1882, so many tiny, golden-crested wrens swarmed about the lighthouse, the keepers could only describe them as a "blizzard of birds."

New Zealand's Arakoa Lighthouse had several families of blue penguins living under the porch of the lightkeeper's house each winter during the 1940s, when T.A. Clark and his Maori wife, Meri, kept the light. A perceptive amateur naturalist, Meri Clark noted that the little warm-blooded creatures were seeking the warmth of the brick chimney foundation. The cries of the penguins, which the family likened to those of unhappy children, forecast the arrival of storms with incredible accuracy.

Barnegat Light
Harpers Magazine, 1874

Great rookeries of seabirds live on a number of lighthouse sites. Navassa Light, between Jamaica and Hispaniola, sits on a 250-foot high coral atoll and guides shipping to the Panama Canal. Commissioner of lighthouses, George R. Putnam, described the island as having "the appearance of a great petrified sponge." Pock-marked volcanic limestone, extreme drought, and unbearable remoteness from civilization made the desolate island a difficult assignment for yesterday's lightkeepers. Other than the lighthouse, the only human activity there has been the collection of guano for use in making fertilizer. Tons of it are still harvested annually, due to the large numbers of seabirds that make their home on the island.

Southeast Farallon Light off San Francisco also has a rookery of seabirds. Nineteenth century lightkeepers, though miserable from the noise and smell of the birds, were thankful for their presence. Bird eggs were an important part of their diet and also a second source of income, for the eggs were a coveted exotic food in San Francisco, particularly in Chinatown. "Egg wars" erupted when collectors argued over who should harvest the eggs. Gathering them was no easy task. The island's rough terrain and the aggressiveness of the nesting birds called for enormous personal fortitude.

Harper's Magazine, April 1874

Ornithologists have long known that lighthouses provide excellent opportunity for the study of birds. In 1860, Texas lightkeepers were asked by the Smithsonian Institution to collect wild bird eggs, and great effort was made to educate the keepers, not only about the proper methods for collection, but also the importance of bird study. More than one lightkeeper became an avid birdwatcher, and by contrast, a few birdwatchers applied for lighthouse positions so that they could enjoy their hobby.

This was certainly true of Norman McCanch, a British lightkeeper who served in the mid-1970s. He had been interested in birds since his childhood on the Welsh coast and later the shores of Pembrokeshire. Trained as a taxidermist and passionately interested in birds, he joined the ranks of Trinity House and spent three years at various light stations. His experiences as lightkeeper, birdwatcher, and artist resulted in the 1985 publication of *A Lighthouse Notebook,* a handsomely illustrated personal journal dedicated to the winged traffic at the massive towers of Coquet, Cromer, St. Mary's, South Bishop, and Longships.

McCanch's deft pen and paintbrush perceptively captured the avian world of the lighthouse keeper: "Then, without warning, a small, brilliantly-lit shape dances momentarily in the beams of the light and is gone. Gradually another appears, and a couple more, until perhaps twenty or thirty small warblers and chats are flickering in the dazzling light. Unable to pinpoint any other landmark in the drizzle and mist, they fly towards the light, circling in its beams until exhaustion or daybreak frees them."

McCanch was licensed to ring birds, thus his detailed journals on their populations, physical conditions, and movements provided valuable data for British researchers and wildlife managers. He often caught birds in special nets as they flew near the brilliant lantern at night. Birds that collided with the tower and survived were nursed back to health and set free.

A one-legged, sickly herring gull was befriended after it awoke from a slam into South Bishop Rock Light. McCanch and his comrades hand fed the scruffy outcast and grew quite fond of it. Though the gull was eventually returned to the wild, it often came back to visit the keepers. Most birds that collided with the towers did not fare as well. Those that were merely stunned recovered quickly and flew off, but injuries were usually fatal. McCanch used dead birds for dissection or taxidermy.

The late and noted bird expert Roger Tory Peterson has never been a lighthouse keeper, but in an article for *Smithsonian Magazine* he admitted:

"For years I had wanted to spend a night in a lighthouse when the birds were flying; to see the small travelers pouring out of the darkness into the dazzling beams." Peterson got his wish in April 1952 when he and fellow birders, Guy Mountfort and Keith Shackleton, received permission from Trinity House to visit St. Catherine's Lighthouse in the English Channel.

St. Catherine's is a lonely sentinel on a prominent headland of the Isle of Wight. At the time of Peterson's visit, the beacon was about 6,000,000 candlepower and a great enticement for weary migrating birds. In its earlier years, when the beams were nearly three times as brilliant, the keepers recorded enormous loss of birds, as if they were lured to their deaths against the light by some invisible force.

The night of Peterson's visit, conditions were nearly perfect for birdwatching — no moon and a gentle change from fair to rainy weather was due. With no celestial beacons to guide them, the radiant beams of St. Catherine's Lighthouse became artificial stars in the heavens for the birds traveling over the English Channel. Near midnight, a fine, misty rain began to fall, and the local foghorn commenced moaning its warning to sailors.

"Then we caught sight of our first real night migrant," Tory remembers. "Flickering and ghostly, it darted toward our high catwalk and swept over the top of the tower into the darkness. Soon another came in and another, like moths to a street lamp. During the next two hours there must have been hundreds."

Tory believed the birds were navigating across the 75-mile channel by a kind of avian dead reckoning — knowing direction and speed. The lighthouse may have temporarily suspended their direction-finding ability and caused them to veer off course and behave erratically, or it could have been a known landmark on their route north. Either way, it's likely the birds would fly near the tower and perhaps even land for the night.

On the American Eastern Seaboard, there have been numerous documented instances of huge gatherings of birds during the spring and autumn migrations. Some coastal points — Cape Hatteras, Cape Charles, Cape May — regularly see this phenomena, which Tory believes results from cold winds from the northwest pushing migrating birds toward the eastern shores where they experience a kind of avian traffic jam. Alfred Hitchcock's fictional "The Birds" thrilled movie-goers with this theme in the 1960s, but at one lighthouse it was more fact than fiction.

Hog Island Light along the barrier islands of Virginia was attacked by birds in 1900. The two keepers were not surprised when a flock of birds collided with the lantern around 8:00 PM that February night, for this was a rather common event at the lighthouse, which was situated in the busy Atlantic Flyway. It seemed a few weeks early for such accidents though. When the birds did not immediately depart, one of the men climbed to the lantern and fired a shot into the darkness to frighten them away. It seemed only to increase the frenzy, so more shots were fired.

Soon both keepers were firing into the night, then taking aim at individual birds. The feathered raiders persisted, breaking glass and spattering blood. One even pierced the lantern glazing and lodged itself in the delicate prisms of the lens. The onslaught continued for several hours. When the keepers used up their ammunition, they took up clubs, then finally retreated to the base of the tower. Morning revealed the carnage — 68 dead ducks, geese, and brandts.

The men rigged a makeshift screen around the lantern and managed to repair the lens. But two nights later the berserk birds returned and once again battered the tower. Considerable damage was done to the lens this time, and at dawn the keepers counted more than 150 dead birds on the lantern and the ground. No explanation was found for the attack and it remains the worst on record at an American lighthouse.

Sand Key Light, Florida Reef,
National Archives

A lighter side to birdwatching at lighthouses can be found in the logbooks of Florida lightkeepers stationed aboard the wave-swept sentinels along the Florida Reef. Atop the keeper's quarters at many of the Reef Lights were lofts for carrier pigeons, which were used to communicate with shore before the advent of radio transmission. The gentle, cooing doves were much-loved and reliable messengers. If a ship in distress was sighted or the lighthouse crew needed help, pigeons were the quickest emergency couriers.

Far north, at Maine's Boon Island Lighthouse, a different sort of assistance was rendered by birds. One Thanksgiving almost a century ago the keepers faced a holiday without family or the traditional fare of turkey and its trimmings, for the weather had not allowed them to row nine miles to shore for supplies and no visit from the lighthouse tender was impending. The keepers sorrowfully concluded that holiday dinner would be potatoes and bread.

But to their surprise, a flock of geese crashed into the 137-foot lighthouse on Thanksgiving Eve. The next day, the aroma of roast goose, slathered with rich gamy gravy, wafted through the lighthouse and proved the perfect complement to potatoes and bread.

This article originally appeared in *Lighthouse Digest*, December 1995.

Interesting Trivia

Joshua Strout, a turn-of-the-century keeper at Portland Head Lighthouse, had a pet parrot named Billy who cussed and predicated the weather. "It's foggy! Turn on the horn!" was one of Billy's lines. On one important day, Billy's frenetic squawking saved the assistant keeper's son from drowning after the boy had fallen into the sea trying to reach a toy boat. Billy was also known to discipline (and sometimes curse) the keeper's hyperactive dog, Bos'un: "Down, Bos'un! Down boy!" Billy retired with Keeper Strout and enjoyed listening to the radio in his old age. He outlived the keeper and died in 1942 at the age of 90.

* * *

Matinicus Rock Lighthouse is the site of the Audobon Society's venerable "Puffin Project." Ornithologist, Stephen Kress, has successfully lured the Atlantic Puffin back to the island with decoys and research knowledge about the birds' mating habits. Puffins are among several bird species that return to their hatching island to mate. These buffoon-faced seabirds were welcome cohabitants for 19th century lightkeepers at Matinicus. Environmental changes in the Gulf of Maine caused them to disappear from the islet. Thanks to the "Puffin Project," they have returned.

* * *

Block Island's Old North Light sits in the midst of a seagull rookery. Barbara Beebe Gaspar, daughter of the lightkeeper in the 1930s, tried to catch the seabirds and tame them. "You had to be very sneaky and fast. I caught quite a few. I always let them go, though. I just wanted to cuddle them for awhile." Early 20th century lightkeepers on Block Island donated the bodies of dead birds to a colorful, local character named Mrs. Dickens, who was a bird lover and taxidermist. Her large collection of specimens is now in the care of the local historical society. Many of the little feathered "stiffs" assumed their odd poses after a night of aerial misjudgment around the Southeast Light or the Old North Light.

* * *

The foghorn at Maine's Seguin Lighthouse has such a powerful concussion it can knock flying seagulls out of the air if they pass too near it.

Lured from far,
The bewildered seagull beats
Dully against the lantern...

Robert Louis Stevenson
The Light-Keeper II

41

The Sea Comes Ashore

Great Waves Pummel Britain's Lighthouses

The seacoast of Britain is surely among the most dangerous in all the world; it is fringed by sinister rocks with equally sinister names -- the terrible Lizard, Cape Wrath, precipitous Dubh Artach whose name means "the black one of death," Inchcape with its legendary warning bell, and Wolf Rock where the sea rushes through a blowhole with a demonic howl.

English fogs, converging currents, whirlpools, strong tides, boreal winds, and heavy seas are among the mariners' nightmares here. These have challenged marine engineers too, particularly those who built Britain's magnificent rock lighthouses. Some of the world's tallest and most exposed towers stand watch here. Rising from the rocks like cathedrals, they light the 350-mile English Channel and perilous spots on the North Sea, Irish Sea, St. George's Channel, and the Hebrides.

Engineers learned to build lighthouses on these exposed sites by trial and error, often with many lives lost in the process. Some thought they had achieved success only to witness the sea tear down in one night what had taken years to build. Most startling was the incredible size and force of certain waves described here by author Tony Parker:

"A distant thud as though someone had swung a gigantic sledgehammer against the base of the tower. The electric lightbulb twitches, the plates on the dresser rattle; coffee slops out of a full cup onto the table. Outside the window a suddenly obliterating surge of creamy white, like a bucket of whitewash thrown against it — the crest of a wave breaking 85-feet above sea level."

Parker wrote of his experiences while visiting one of England's rock lighthouses in the 1960s. He spent several weeks living with the keepers, recording life on a dismal stump of masonry miles at sea, and returned to shore red-eyed and frazzled from the incessant din of the waves crashing against the tower. It caused him to marvel at the mettle of the men who tended such lights, but also of the men who built them.

The most renowned engineers of wave-swept lighthouses were the Stevensons of Scotland. They built massive stone towers that still stand at Bell Rock, Skerryvore, Dunnet Head, Dubh Arttach, and other perilous sites. Their most celebrated son, Robert Louis Stevenson, declined a career building lighthouses and took to pen and paper instead, but his view of the world seems to have always passed through the prisms of a lighthouse and was greatly influenced by his family's struggle to mark Scotland's treacherous coast.

Robert Stevenson (Robert Louis Stevenson's grandfather) was the patriarch of the family and one of the world's most knowledgeable marine engineers. With his son, Thomas, he designed a wave dynamometer to measure the force of waves striking a solid surface. It consisted of a 6-inch diameter plate mounted on a stiff horizontal spring. A rod behind the spring moved each time a wave struck the plate.

During a winter gale at Skerryvore off the Hebrides, where the Stevensons built their most magnificent lighthouse, wave force was measured at 6,083 pounds per square inch. A century later, a force more than double that was recorded by waves that tore up the stone breakwater at Cherbourg, France. Blocks weighing 7,000 pounds were hurled as far as 60-feet, ominously proving what the Stevensons already knew: The Atlantic could heave 3,000 miles of unbridled anger against the coastlines of Europe.

Skerryvore Light
Trinity House

Logbooks from Britain's rock lighthouses contain incredible accounts of waves, recorded by the keepers who experienced them. Some did not live to tell their stories. This was true of the keepers of the Eddystone Lighthouse in the English Channel off Plymouth. It was the world's first sea-swept sentinel. Waves easily passed through the lantern of the tower, 40-feet above low water. Still, it was an amazing structure for the year 1698, and its architect, Henry Winstanley, taught engineers much about building lighthouses on exposed rocks. In 1699 he strengthened the original tower and swore that nothing would please him more than to be in his lighthouse during the greatest storm.

Unfortunately, he got his wish in November 1703. (See "England's Great Storm.") The powerful gale on the 26th of the month was likened to a ceaseless tornado. "Trees fell like grass before a great scythe, leaden roofs of churches and cathedrals were rolled up like gray carpets," wrote a contemporary historian. The Eddystone Light stood gallantly for most of the night, then disappeared into the turbid channel, gone forever.

Subsequent towers on the Eddystone Rocks revealed important things engineers had learned. Ornamentation was gone — no fancy finials or embellished windows for waves to grasp — and a flared base proved best, to cause waves to be thrown back upon themselves. Tower bases were constructed of solid masonry several courses high, and blocks were dovetailed to anchor them more firmly. The idea was to make a rock lighthouse an extension of the rock itself. Titanic waves still came, but the towers stood strong, and the keepers lived to recount their experiences.

The sea had an alarming habit of opening doors to some lighthouses, almost as if waves had fingers that could pick locks and turn knobs. Most times they didn't bother to knock. A keeper at Unst Light in the Shetland Islands in the 1850s saw his door rip off its hinges and disappear into the darkness, never to be recovered. Similarly, in 1840 on a relatively calm night at the Eddystone Light, an unusual wave crawled 50-feet up the tower and blew out a door. The keeper was surprised to find that the door had survived in initial crush of the wave but had given way to the backdraught due to pneumatic pressure — the heavy and abrupt release of force as the wave withdrew from the door.

During the building of Dunnet Head Lighthouse in 1831 opposite the Orkney Islands, workmen were shocked to find that waves could scale the 300-foot cliff face below the lighthouse. Not only that, but stones of considerable size were tossed upwards like gray beach balls and landed on the tower, damaging it. If 300-feet of cliff face were no deterrent, what of a 100-foot lighthouse?

During the construction of Dubh Artach Light in 1842 between Skerryvore Light and the island of Colonsay, 14 blocks weighing 10-tons each were torn out by waves 37-feet up on the tower. Robert Louis Stevenson wrote that the waves over this rock in the Hebrides "growled about the outer reef forever, and ever and again; in the calmest weather, roared and spouted on the rock itself."

David Stevenson, builder of Dubh Artach Lighthouse, believed the sea here to be the most violent he had ever witnessed. Investigation showed that the rock lay at the head of an 80-mile long submarine valley which funneled and concentrated the waves hitting Dubh Artach. Stevenson estimated there was a wave force of 3-tons per square foot during winter gales; hence, he opted to make the tower's base solid block to a height of 64-feet.

Concerns about the power of the waves at Dubh Artach were confirmed only a week after the lighthouse went into operation. November seas wrenched a copper lightning conductor off the tower at a height of 92-feet on the lee side. The conductor had been snugly nestled in a channel running down the side of the tower and secured tightly with screws. The waves bent the conductor upwards and tore its screws from their sockets.

Tale upon tale could be told about the destructiveness of waves and the woes of the rock lightkeepers, but in fairness to the sea, which can give as easily as it takes, a happier ending is in order. It involves the first lighthouse to be built on the Smalls, along the tempestuous coastline of Wales. It was a strange structure for its time, a house and lantern perched on wooden stilts anchored to the sprawling reef 21-miles west of St. Ann's Head.

The year was 1777, and four men were stationed on the Smalls Light: the two keepers, plus two workmen who had come to repair the rickety legs of the tower. The weather deteriorated, and before the men could leave, a typical stretch of foul Welsh weather set in. There was no risking a trip to the mainland, especially after the waves stole the lighthouse boat. With four people eating rations meant for two, supplies soon ran low and spirits fell.

Desperate for help, the men wrote a message to the local agent, sealed it in a bottle, and cast it into the sea. The waves carried the little parcel toward shore, where it was picked up after the storm by a fisherman only a short distance from the home of the man too whom it was addressed. A boat was sent immediately to the Smalls Lighthouse. The rescued men were amazed that the plan had worked; the merciless waves had proven to be their salvation.

This article originally appeared in *Mariners Weather Log*, Fall 1993.

Author's Note

For many years I kept a correspondence with British lightkeeper John Mobbs, who served at Inner Dowsing Lighthouse, among others. As its name implies, Inner Dowsing takes a pummeling from the sea. Lightships served at this shoal 14-miles northeast of Skegness until a drilling platform, built to plumb the submarine coal field here, was transferred to Trinity House in 1971 to be used as a sentinel. Three keepers were assigned to the waterbound station. John Mobbs was assigned there when I first received a letter from him in the early 1980s via the editors at *Sea Frontiers* magazine. He had read one of my lighthouse articles and wondered if I would correspond with him.

John's letters were long and newsy, particularly about the weather, the routines of the lighthouse, and his passion for collecting postcards of lighthouses. I never seemed to assuage his appetite for "more cards," though his letters showed enormous gratitude for the few I did send, and he sent me dozens of photographs and postcards in return, along with copious amounts of handprinted stationery. As time passed, John's letters became fewer and shorter, no doubt because mine were scarce and postage rates were rising. Eventually, he gave up on me. I can't blame him. My busy shoreside life had plenty of distractions, and writing time was channeled mostly into articles and books, not personal letters. I still regret that I was neither as verbose nor as regular a corresponder as John. He had many interesting tales to share, especially regarding the sea and its fickle character.

Inner Dowsing Light stretches its metal legs down into the brine more than 50-feet to the sea floor. When the North Sea gets angry, it throws its wrath onto and sometimes over the lighthouse. The platform is strongly anchored; still it shudders under the immense pressure of storm waves, as it must, to resist destruction. John never complained about such things, only reported them as he would have reported a soft breeze. It must have been a mentally challenging place to live in the days before it was automated — the sea like a mirror one day and bubbling like hot soup the next. John expressed much regret about automation in his last letters to me early in the 1990s. He seemed to feel a human presence was important, even on a dismal, sea-swept place like Inner Dowsing. I'm told he's retired now, and I'm sure he's enjoying his cards and books and letters. At least now there's ground under his feet, rather than waves.

Haunted Lighthouses

Spectral Oases, Without a Doubt!

Has there ever been a lighthouse that wasn't haunted? Of course not. We all know ghosts have a hard and fast order of preference as to their residences: Cemeteries are great locations, along with old, dilapidated houses, particularly in and around Amityville. Old church towers aren't bad lodging either. But no self-respecting ghost can pass up a lighthouse. We're talking prime, supernatural real estate here!

Over a period of some twenty years, I've had the opportunity to visit several hundred lighthouses around the nation to research and photograph their contributions to maritime history. In the process, I've heard enough lighthouse ghost stories to fill Ripley's from cover to cover. Though I've yet to meet a real "lighthouse ghost," I never discount the possibility. Some very strange things have occurred during my travels to America's sentinels, and at the very least, I'm convinced lighthouses have an eerier ambiance than most of the classic haunts.

Lighthouses are natural settings for the unexplainable. Wind steals through the cracks in lighthouse walls with a high-pitched squeal, fog inches its misty fingers into every crevice and cubby, and rocks and sand move about covertly, uncovering skeletons from the past and burying others. Doors and windows at lighthouses have a nasty habit of opening and closing on their own. And the echo of a spiral stairway is enough to send any veteran ghostbuster scurrying.

"It was an experience to stand on the spiral staircase and listen to its shrill cry...then to feel the moist breeze that passed over, as if being brushed by a wet blanket," recalled lightkeeper-turned-author James Gibbs of Oregon's Tillamook Lighthouse.

Not surprisingly, Tillamook Light took up an even stranger career after it retired as a navigational aid. It became a columbarium where the eccentric among us may have our ashes interred after death.

The chances of this lighthouse being haunted have increased mightily!

A lighthouse beacon — that hypnotic beam wheeling and flashing in the black of night — has also triggered busy imaginations. Sweeping the sea like a huge Cyclopean eye, it creates myriad ghostly images and evokes a sense of power. Writers haven't overlooked this fertile possibility, nor have Hollywood movie producers. Yaquina Head Lighthouse on the Oregon coast has been cast in several films, one featuring the lighthouse as a sort of omen of death pointing its fatal beam on the next unlucky victim. Another film had its beacon possessed by an evil spirit and in need of an exorcism.

Celebrated sci-fi writer, Ray Bradbury, couldn't resist the strange appeal of lighthouses. Among his short stories is one in which a lighthouse beam reveals a dark, monstrous silhouette rising from the sea to frighten two lonely lightkeepers. Edgar Allan Poe also used a lighthouse as the setting for a horror tale, and Daphne DeMaurier's classic, *Jamaica Inn*, had a treacherous Cornwall Coast sentinel as a stronghold of ruthless mooncussers.

In New England, haunted lighthouses abound, and people who live in or near them take their ghost stories very seriously. The Coast Guard crews who kept Connecticut's Ledge Light were convinced a prankster wraith inhabited the lighthouse. Nicknamed Ernie, he was blamed for missing tools, strange sounds, and unexplainable events, such as a boat set adrift or a piece of furniture mysteriously moved. Even the media was bewitched by the stories. Rarely did a Halloween pass that the local newspaper and TV station did not run tabloid-type interviews with the lightkeepers or send a psychic in search of Ernie.

U.S. Coast Guard Academy Library

Maine's Sequin Lighthouse off the mouth of the Kennebec River was automated a few years ago, but a number of folks who live on shore near the lighthouse claim one of the keepers stayed on to watch the beacon — albeit a ghost keeper. She came to the station over a century ago with her husband, the lightkeeper, but found her island home a dismal and terribly lonely place, particularly in winter when she was confined to the house for weeks at a time. The keeper saw his wife's anguish and rowed to the mainland to find a cure. He returned a short time later with a piano, which he hoped would amuse her and soften her despair.

But the woman could play only one song, and this she played over and over again, hour upon hour, to ease the misery of her isolated existence. As time passed, it became evident to the keeper that his wife was teetering on the edge of sanity, but no matter how he tried, he could not coax her away from the piano. The song played endlessly, tormentingly, and seeped into every corner of the house and tower. The keeper was finally driven to madness himself. In an uncontrollable rage, he took an ax to both the piano and his wife. Her ghost haunts the station — a pathetic poltergeist whose melancholy endures in the form of a faint tinkle of piano keys that is sometimes heard across the water at nearby Fort Popham.

The *Boston Herald*, September 18, 1938, carried this eerie rendering of Joseph Antoine's ghost at Minots Light.

The wave-swept Minots Ledge Lighthouse off Cohasset, Massachusetts, had a reputation for being one of the worst assignments in the Lighthouse Service. A mile from shore, the dark, forbidding tower is perched on a jagged ledge exposed only at low tide. It is occupied only by spiders and seabirds these days, but during its manned years lightkeepers came ashore with odd complaints. One man claimed the round tower drove him crazy with its lack of corners, and another keeper slit his throat before a cause for his difficulty could be found. Other men remained on duty but spoke of the lens and lamp being mysteriously cleaned and filled, strange rapping noises in the tower, and a near-drowned spectral figure clinging to the ladder at the base of the tower.

These supernatural occurrences were attributed to the original tower's two assistant keepers, who died when the iron-pile lighthouse washed into the sea in an April storm. The men had often signaled to each other by rapping on the iron parts of the lighthouse. Even after a new lighthouse was built, the rapping was heard and strange events took place. Passing ships reported seeing the ghost of one of the keepers at the base of the tower warning ships to "Beware of Minots Ledge!" On one occasion, when the beacon accidentally went out, the keepers were alerted by an unlatched door on the lantern that the wind banged loudly. Unable to explain how the door became unlatched, they decided the ghosts of the light's dead keepers were still on watch.

Lighthouse ghosts have been known to polish up the brass or clank about on catwalks, but at St. Simons Lighthouse in Georgia, it was the keeper's dog who received the wrath of the tower's resident ghost. The devoted canine was named Jinx, and he came to the lighthouse around 1900 with the Svendsen family. But soon after settling into his comfortable home, an invisible pair of feet began stomping about the tower.

The phantom footsteps were heard on the lighthouse stairway, and occasionally an unseen hand would open a door or move something. The Svendsens grew accustomed to their noisy houseguest, but Jinx was tormented by the ghost throughout his time at St. Simons Light. His owners believed he could actually see the specter, for his eyes seemed to follow the sounds wherever they went. He always bared his teeth and bristled if the footsteps came too near, and more than once he tucked his tail between his legs and fled.

The nation's most haunted lighthouses — those with a host of ghosts reportedly dwelling within their ancient walls — are California's Battery Point Light at Crescent City, with no less than five ghosts cohabiting with the tower's caretakers, and Point Lookout Lighthouse at the confluence of the Potomac River and Chesapeake Bay. Point Lookout's housetop tower has been haunted by dozens of eerie spirits, many of them the subjects of paranormal investigations. Caretakers of the old sentinel, now inactive and part of a state park, have heard footsteps, sighs, singing, and voices and have seen visual anomalies in the lighthouse. Ghosts are often reported to wear Civil War era clothing.

The Maryland Committee for Psychic Research examined the old lighthouse in 1980 and discovered some startling evidence that the structure truly is inhabited by ghosts. Photos taken in front of the lighthouse show concentrations of light where ghosts have been reported to lurk, and tape recorders set up at random spots around the station captured unidentified voices. During one investigation, parapsychologists experienced feelings of sorrow and grief in one room of the lighthouse, where records indicate a child died. At night, this same room takes on a foul odor.

Minots Light
Harpers Magazine, 1874

Battery Point Light is a Cape Cod-style sentinel, though it stands watch some 3000 miles from New England. When settlers came west, they brought their architectural preferences with them; hence, Battery Point is a quaint little house with a lantern rising from its roof. For years, the caretakers of the lighthouse were Jerry and Nadine Tugel, who looked after the collection of relics in the tower that belonged to the Del Norte Historical Society.

The Tugels cheerfully received visitors who dared to roll up their pantlegs and cross the tidal spit connecting the point to land. The islet on which the lighthouse sits is strewn with cobbles and driftwood, and stands of Monterey cypress resemble gnarled old skeletons with their backs to the sea. The tower is almost a century and half old and looks every bit the ancient part it plays.

No less than five ghosts are thought to inhabit the old sentinel. The Tugels say many residents of the lighthouse have reported strange activities. A rocking chair rocks by itself and gives off a pleasant odor of pipesmoke, and a presence can be felt on the stairway leading to the second floor. Footsteps are heard in the lighthouse during storms and fog. Once, organ music was heard in the night.

Nadine Tugel recalls that she was suspect of the reports when she first came to the lighthouse, but strange things soon occurred. She was awakened one night by the voices of a man and woman talking. A complete search of the house and grounds was made, but no one turned up. On another occasion, Nadine was giving a tour of the lighthouse when several people reported that they felt invisible hands touching them near the stairway to the second floor.

Stranger still was the night the Tugels returned to the islet from the mainland and found warm spots on their bed. The couple also experienced lost items that turned up in odd places and objects that mysteriously broke. Nadine explains:

"There was the day I was working in the radio room and heard a crash in the living room. My first thought was to kill the cats, but both of them were standing beside me, looking as surprised as I was. Imagine my surprise as I walked into the living room and found the cranberry glass chimney from an antique candleholder lying shattered on the floor. There was nothing else out of order in the room."

The Tugel's cat, Frisbie, was particularly sensitive to the spirits in the lighthouse. She cried incessantly in the Museum Room of the house, as if something in there disturbed her, and she avoided the bedrooms whenever possible. Nadine notes that when Frisbie did come in the bedrooms, she only walked on the furniture, not the floor. Once while Nadine was putting away laundry in her bedroom, Frisbie came in and immediately jumped onto a chair. Moments later her hair stood on end, she hissed and growled, then bolted from the room. Nadine found her sitting in the hallway peering through the bedroom door but unwilling to come inside.

Two other cats the Tugels owned while at the lighthouse also reacted to the "Misty Friends," as Nadine calls the ghosts. Jeffrey and Samuel came to the station as kittens after Frisbie died. On several occasions something unseen terrified them. Nadine reports that there was a corner in the radio room that frightened the cats. They often stared at it intensely, as if they could see something there.

Nadine Tugel's 1985 sketch of Battery Point Light

Oregon's Heceta Head Lighthouse, perched on a magnificent headland in Suislaw National Forest, is haunted by a ghost that often appears in the form of an old woman. She has been seen in the attic and sometimes peers out the attic window. Her resemblance to a cloud of gray smoke has earned her the name "Gray Lady."

Investigators think she is searching for her child. A small stone near the lighthouse supposedly marks the grave of an infant girl who died at the station many years ago. Her mother grieved endlessly for the child and is thought to have returned to find the baby. The "Gray Lady" moves objects and keeps the attic tidied up. Her tiny, high-button shoes make a clatter on the attic floor that can be faintly heard on the lower floors of the house.

She once swept broken glass into a neat pile and replaced rat poison, which she surely felt would harm her child, for a silk stocking. She appeared before a worker in 1975 while he was repairing some woodwork in the attic. He described her as an elderly woman with gray hair, a very wrinkled face, and an expression of sadness. She wore an 1890s style dress and dainty black shoes. The worker refused to return to the attic after his encounter with the "Gray Lady," but later saw her again as he worked on the outside of the house. She peered out a window with the same imploring expression.

Two lighthouse ghosts have been positively identified, but supernaturalists will be disappointed to know they are attributed to natural phenomena. One of these specters persistently patrols her territory at Point Vicente Lighthouse at Palos Verdes, California. The earliest keepers of the lighthouse, which was built in 1928, believed the lovely apparition had been the wife of a fishermen in life. Her husband had drowned off Point Vicente, and she had thrown herself into the sea with grief. Lightkeepers believed her restless spirit was still searching for her lost husband.

Her regular nocturnal walks about the station lacked the heart-wrenching shrieks and eerie moans associated with some ghosts. She was a serene and beautiful spirit, waltzing about the lighthouse like a toy ballerina in a music box. Keepers weren't too modest to admit they felt a measure of affection for her. Consequently, no one attempted to frighten her away or look for a logical cause for her nightly visits.

But one young lightkeeper, just a few months into his tour at the lighthouse, could not accept the old-fashioned and naive idea that a ghost haunted the station. He determined to find the cause of the nightly occurrence. Her strolls around the lighthouse lawn seemed far too consistent in time and place to be of unearthly origin, and she could be seen only from certain vantage points at the station.

After watching her for many nights, he realized she was a product of the tower's huge prism lens — an illusion created from light reflected off the lens's curved surface. As light passed over each stanchion of the lens, a reflection in the shape of an hourglass was cast into the trees and swept along slowly as the lens revolved. It looked strikingly like a woman — an angel in a white gown — dancing around the tower.

The restless spirit of Florida's Carysfort Reef Lighthouse was blamed on a grouchy old keeper named Captain Johnson, who died at the lighthouse soon after it went into service in the 1840s. Johnson was said to have been a great sinner who cussed and drank and abused his companions. Only a few weeks after his death, an unseasonable hot spell settled in, and the ghost made its presence known.

About sundown the keepers of the light were greeted by shrieks and groans and moans unlike anything they had ever heard. The noise continued until well after midnight, then subsided. But the next evening it started again and raged on until nearly dawn. The men on the lighthouse, a spidery-legged iron tower standing in the warm waters of the Florida Reef, were convinced Captain Johnson had returned to torment them.

No one attempted to find a reasonable explanation for the nightly clamor until 1927 when a fisherman named Charles Brookfield was invited to spend the night in the lighthouse after his boat broke down. When darkness came and the distressing sounds began, Brookfield bolted from his bed to find the cause. He was told the lighthouse was haunted, but he refused to accept this simple explanation.

The next day he examined the lighthouse, particularly the connections between the huge iron plates, and decided the noises had something to do with the structure of the tower. That night, his theory was confirmed when the screeches and groans began shortly after sunset. Brookfield told the lightkeepers that a rapid contraction of the metal tower occurred when evening brought a sudden drop in temperature. This created stress at the joints, which caused the noises. Shortly after midnight, when temperatures moderated, the tower returned to normal. So much for Captain Johnson's ghost.

Lighthouse ghosts are finding it more difficult to keep up appearances these days, with only the machinery of automation to bother. While the Coast Guard is unsympathetic with a ghost's need to frighten people, local residents and tourists are only too willing to indulge the unsettled spirits. Every Halloween, dozens of seaside communities around the nation report unusual activities around their lighthouses.

Folks in Humboldt County, California swear the stretch of beach where their old lighthouse once stood still glows at night, and never a Halloween passes at Ocracoke Lighthouse on North Carolina's Outer Banks that someone doesn't report an iridescent light from Blackbeard's lantern swinging to and fro at Teach's Cove. Probably the worst places to be on a windy, full-moon night are ominous Yaquina Head Lighthouse and the bleak tower on Minots Ledge. Such places are the perfect destinations for kids looking for a dare.

The fact is, if you look and listen close enough, something out of the ordinary is bound to happen at a lighthouse. After dark, the wind picks up and changes from a soothing whisper to a macabre moan. Weak, shapeless shadows take on menacing forms; stairways become portals to other worlds. By day, a tall graceful tower can be inviting, even romantic, but at night it becomes a frightening monolith.

Lighthouse ghosts? Some people definitely believe in them. I've visited numerous lighthouses and have yet to encounter the ubiquitous "lighthouse ghost." But who knows? There's always a first time.

This article originally appeared in *Offshore,* October 1987.

Author's Note

Who doesn't enjoy a good scare once in awhile? If you're looking for the surreal in lighthouse stories, *Lighthouse Horrors* is for you. Produced by Down East Books and edited by Charles Waugh, it contains some of the finest frightening lighthouse fiction ever written. Ray Bradbury's haunting tale "The Foghorn" is there, along with Kipling's "The Disturber of Traffic." My personal favorite is "Messengers at the Window," by Henry Van Dyke - a tale of a lightkeeper haunted by his own misdeed.

The genre we might call lighthouse horror has long fascinated me, and I admit I've tried, rather unsuccessfully, to write it. Unfortunately, the best morbid tale I've written in this genre was lost years ago to an editor who had slated it for publication, but disappeared when the magazine suddenly folded. She cleaned out her desk and vanished with the only copy of my manuscript, "The Light on Petrel Rock."

That was back in the days when my writing was done on an ancient Royal typewriter with a smudged lower case letter h, which made every "the" look like "tbe" and kept me busy with whiteout. If I had change to spare, I hiked to the local library in Deltona, Florida and made photocopies of finished manuscripts. Sadly, I didn't make a copy of that one, and all efforts to recreate it have failed.

Perhaps, someday, I'll try again, for it *was* a very good tale. The old man who tended Petrel Light had begged the Coast Guard to take him off the station, not to put another lightkeeper there ever again. It was the sea, you see........something very dark and terrible and tormenting about the sea.

Keepers in Skirts

Women of the Lighthouse Service

During the last several decades, America's uniformed services have made admirable progress toward nondiscriminatory employment of women, who now seek and receive many assignments once given exclusively to men. One branch of the uniformed services, however — the old Lighthouse Service — employed women since before the American Revolution. Women's contributions to this organization, a precursor to today's U.S. Coast Guard, comprise a large part of our current knowledge of a lifestyle now obsolete.

Lighthouses no longer require keepers to live on station and tend them on a daily basis. Modern advancements in navigation, coupled with automatic devices that operate the beacons and fog signals, have rendered resident caretakers unnecessary. Little by little, since the 1920s, lighthouses have been converted to self-sufficient operation.

Abbie Burgess in *Harpers Young People*, 1882

But there was a time when lighthouse keeping was a critical service. About 1500 lighthouses were operating in the U.S. at the turn-of-the-century, each requiring at least one keeper and some having as many as five keepers. Because of the perils associated with it, the occupation of lightkeeper carried a generous measure of prestige. Dangerous storms, unnatural social deprivation, and occasional physical injury were all part of the job.

Women, nevertheless, eagerly competed for appointments and assured the government they were capable of handling the sometimes demanding work.

"I know how to row, and run and engine, and steer a boat," wrote one applicant, "...[and I] shall wear trousers instead of skirts."

The lighthouse service actually began in 1716, with the building of the first official colonial beacon at Boston Harbor, but a uniform and set of regulations were not issued to lightkeepers until the mid-1800s. Early lightkeepers learned their trade on duty, and, since the old candelabras and oil lamps were simple to tend, the majority of the lightkeeper's duties involved housekeeping. Women of the time were natural candidates for the job.

The first lady lightkeeper in the colonies was Hannah Thomas of Plymouth, Massachusetts. That settlement's first beacon was built on the Thomas family's property in 1769, at the end of a long finger of land the Pilgrims had named the Gurnet, in honor of a plentiful fish in the waters of their homeland.

Plymouth's 20-foot wooden towers were twin lights connected by a 30-foot long building, a unique style of lighthouse construction that involved two towers, two lanterns, and twice the usual work for the lightkeeper. The idea was for the sailor to see two beacons side-by-side and be able to differentiate them from other lights in the area.

Hannah Thomas assisted her husband with keeping the lights and raised her family. When her husband left home to join the Continental Army in 1776, Hannah was left alone to tend the lights. Her neighbors built earth berms around the twin lighthouses to serve as protection in the event the British attacked. The effort did not entirely shield the towers, for in 1778 cannonfire from the British frigate *Niger* hit the station. But Hannah managed to keep the lights burning. Not long afterwards she watched, helpless, as the brig *General Arnold* grounded in a winter blizzard and 72 of the crew died.

Plymouth's twin towers were originally illuminated with candles, but when Hannah took over, flat-wick, whale-oil lamps were in use. They were dirty and required Hannah to clean the lantern windows often. She worked every day of the year unless she was able to find someone to relieve her, for the colony provided no assistant.

Apparently, Hannah's husband was killed in the Revolution and she was given an official appointment as keeper until the new Federal Government took over in 1790. Records are unclear, but it appears Hannah's son, possibly himself a veteran of the Revolution, took over as keeper and served until 1801 when the lighthouse burned. Little else is known of Hannah Thomas, but she occupies a unique place in history as our nation's first woman to keep a lighthouse.

Like Hannah, most women who served at lighthouses inherited their jobs from their husbands. The government, it seemed, had few reservations about appointing women with several years apprentice-type experience. Those without such experience almost never received jobs. By 1851 thirty widows had succeeded their husbands as lightkeepers. Records indicate that as a group women served longer careers and moved less frequently. They also fared better during inspections, perhaps because of their flair for housekeeping.

Among the nation's widows who succeeded their husbands was Maria Younghans, whose husband Perry Younghans had been given an appointment to Biloxi Lighthouse in Mississippi as compensation for loss of his brickyard business during the Civil War. He died less than a year after taking up his duties. Maria was his replacement, having earned the respect of the local lighthouse inspector in her short time at the lighthouse. She remained on duty until 1919, then passed the work to her daughter, Miranda, who served until 1929.

Catherine Murdock had recently given birth to her third child when her husband, the keeper of Roundout Lighthouse on the Hudson River, drowned. Possibly in sympathy, but more likely because of her excellent recommendations, she was given the job. The lighthouse sat on a granite pier out in the river. It was a lovely structure referred to as "the castle" by reporters of the day. Catherine remained on duty until 1880 when her son took over as lightkeeper.

California's "Grand Dame" of lighthouses was Emily Fish, the respected widow of a San Francisco physician. Emily obtained her position, no doubt, by virtue of her son-in-law's work as an inspector for the Lighthouse District in San Francisco, along with her late husband's notable status. The government might also have been eager to appoint a woman because Point Pinos Light had a history of excellent care by feminine hands. Charlotte Layton had served before Emily's arrival and had the unique distinction of having a male assistant.

Despite her privileged appointment, Emily Fish did a respectable job. Her Chinese servant, Que, kept her gardens and domestic stock, but Emily tended the beacon herself. Not only did she operate her brilliant charge efficiently and economically, she was a prominent social leader as well. Her assignment was a pleasant one, interrupted only by an occasional Pacific storm and the 1906 San Francisco Earthquake.

Considerable damage was caused to the station during the earthquake, which came near dawn, but Emily and Que were not injured. Emily's step-daughter, Juliet Nichols, was serving at Angel Island Lighthouse in San Francisco Bay and witnessed the destruction of that great city by the quake and the fires that followed it. Juliet is best remembered for her devotion to the Angel Island fogbell, which she once struck by hand for twenty hours when its striking mechanism broke down.

Life in a Lighthouse, *Outlook*, January 1908

Another keeper who had political connections was Harriet Colfax of Michigan City Light on the south shore of Lake Michigan. Her cousin, Congressman Schuyler Colfax, no doubt influenced her appointment. She began her duties in 1861 at the age of 37. Rumor had it Harriet was fleeing from an unhappy love affair when she received her appointment as keeper. She never married and was devoted to the lighthouse for 43 years.

During Harriet's tenure as keeper, a beacon was placed on a pier extending out into the lake. She was responsible not only for the shoreside lighthouse but also the pier beacon, which was reached by an elevated wooden walkway. On stormy nights, lighting the pier beacon was death-defying.

Ice, wind, water, and the constant threat of vessels hitting the pier were among the perils she faced. On one occasion, she had just finished lighting the pier beacon and was returning to shore when she heard a loud crash. The pier beacon had collapsed into the lake.

There were pleasant moments too. Harriet colorfully recorded in her log of seeing rainbows, a mirage on the lake, eclipses, and the beautiful aurora. She was asked to collect data on the species of birds and insects around the lighthouse, probably for a scientist. And throughout her career she kept up a faithful friendship with a girlhood friend, Ann Hartwell.

Daughters sometimes followed in the footsteps of their lightkeeping fathers. Catherine Moore succeeded her father as keeper of Connecticut's Black Rock Lighthouse on Fayerweather Island. Her father was appointed in 1817 after a shipboard accident had left him badly injured. Catherine learned to keep the light at age twelve, and because her father's health was so poor, she tended the beacon and looked after him until his death in 1871. The government then officially appointed her keeper and she remained until 1878, retiring at age 84.

Besides tending the light, she kept chickens, cows, and sheep, and worked seeding the oyster beds in the sound. In her leisure time, which was seldom, she carved decoys. Catherine was credited with saving 21 lives while at the lighthouse and was probably aided by the Newfoundland dogs she kept as pets. She taught herself to read and amassed a large library at the lighthouse. At her death in 1900 she was 105 years old!

America's most famous lighthouse daughters are, undoubtedly, Abbie Burgess and Ida Lewis. Abbie lived at Maine's remote Matinicus Twin Lights from 1853 to 1872. Her father taught her to tend the twin towers when she was only 14, and twice she kept the beacons lit during fierce storms when her father was detained ashore. Sailors told stories about her youthful courage, and a legend of sorts grew up around her.

When her father lost his position in 1860 due to political favoritism, Abbie remained at the station to acquaint its new keeper with the duties. Her stay became permanent when she fell in love with the keeper's son, who was also the assistant keeper. The two were married, and Abbie was appointed assistant to her husband when he took over for his father. She earned $440 a year.

The couple had four children and went on to care for nearby Whitehead Lighthouse. Shortly after retiring from lighthouse work in the 1890s, Abbie became ill. On her deathbed, she reportedly requested a gravestone in the shape of a lighthouse. Her wish was granted many years after her death when historian Edward Rowe Snow placed a small replica of a lighthouse beside her gravestone in Spruce Head Cemetery, Maine. In the early 1990s the New England Lighthouse Foundation raised funds to have the aging gravestone cleaned.

Ida Lewis rescuing soldiers. *Harpers Magazine*, 1869.

Ida Lewis sought an appointment at Lime Rock Lighthouse at Newport, Rhode Island after the death of her father, who had kept the light from 1857 to 1872. She is credited with the greatest number of recorded rescues of any lighthouse keeper in America. Her picture appeared on the cover of *Harper's Weekly* in 1869, with an account noting that her rescue of a drowning man "was a most daring feat, and required courage and perseverance such as few of the male sex are even possessed of."

Suffrage leader Susan B. Anthony gave Ida a passage in her journal *Revolution,* and letters poured into Ida's mailbox from all over the world. Some contained marriage proposals, and while Ida did have a brief marriage to a fishermen, a husband and children were not among her needs. When an intrusive reporter asked her why she had shunned marriage and a family, she replied: "The light is my child."

In 1879 Congress finally approved Ida's official appointment as keeper of Lime Rock Light. Her popularity soared. Among her fans was president Ulysses S. Grant, who swore he'd roll up his pantlegs and wade through the water to visit her. She worked until her death from a stroke in 1911. Her grave in Newport Cemetery reflects her courage and the love of Newport for the "Grace Darling of America."

Sketch by Barb Kachel, "Lighthouse Lady"

With the introduction of sophisticated revolving machinery and steam operated fog signals lighthouse work shifted from mostly housekeeping chores to complicated mechanical work. It meant fewer women sought lighthouse appointments and fewer still received them. By the 20th century, women in the lighthouse service were rare.

Fanny Salter of the Chesapeake's Turkey Point Light was the last civilian woman to serve at a lighthouse. When her husband died at the lighthouse in 1925 she asked for the job but was refused because of her age. She appealed to her senator who convinced President Coolidge to grant approval.

Fanny had no electricity at her station until 1943; hence, she tended oil lamps in the lantern. Life was pleasant at the pastoral station, but also difficult at times. In winter, snow often blocked the access road, leaving Fanny marooned on the point. The Coast Guard assumed control of lighthouses in 1939, and Fanny worked until 1947, retiring with the simple excuse that her feet were tired.

Only two women worked as lightkeepers in the Coast Guard. Karen McLean tended three beacons on the Kennebec River, Maine, and Jeni Burr kept Dungeness Light along the Strait of San Juan de Fuca, Washington. Both women admitted their lives were far more comfortable and their duties much easier than their female counterparts of the "old days."

With automation completed in the 1980s, lighthouses no longer needed lightkeepers. Only Boston Light remains attended, as a memorial to lightkeeping. Three Coast Guard personnel reside at the station. At this writing (April 1997), no women have served at Boston Light.

This is an amalgamation of articles that appeared in *Sea Frontiers*, January 1983 and *American History Illustrated*, February 1987. A children's version appeared in *I Touched the Sun*, D.C. Heath, 1989.

Recommended Reading

Anyone interested in women's history, and specifically women who served at American lighthouses, would enjoy *Women Who Kept the Lights*, by J. Candace Clifford and Mary Louise Clifford. It's by far the best assemblage of material on lighthouse women and their contributions to maritime safety. As noted in the foregoing article, numerous woman served in official capacities during the years lighthouses were attended. Unfortunately, their efforts have received little recognition until very recently. The Cliffords, a mother and daughter team, profile about 25 of the more notable ladies of the lights in their book. Their research is meticulous, and the archival photos are especially wonderful.

Women's history, and gender bias in particular, has been a special interest of mine since the mid-1980s, when I was welcomed aboard the staff of the planetarium at Mystic Seaport with a well-meant but highly biased comment about my being the "lone Venus in a cosmos of male celestial bodies." As you can imagine, I set out to identify and eradicate as many gender biases as possible.

During this self-imposed campaign, I discovered an enormous amount of material on women's roles in maritime history. "Women of the Lights" grew out of that search. It was plagued by inaccuracies and gaps of information when I approached *American History Illustrated* with it, since there was little material available. But the editors felt it was an extant topic that would foster more research. It did. The subject became so popular that I created a slide talk called "Women on Watch," which I always dedicate to the Cliffords. I owe the them many thanks.

Grace Darling's Daring Deed

Who has not heard of Grace Darling and her plucky rescue of survivors from the wrecked steamship *Forfarshire*? Thanks to flowery Victorian journalism, and the British bent for fanfare, Grace's single and simple deed earned immortality. As her biographer, Jessica Mitford, puts it, "Grace Darling can be precisely and anachronistically described as the first media heroine."

At dawn on September 7, 1838, Grace and her father, William Darling, the keeper of Longstone Lighthouse off England's Northumberland Coast, awoke to the howl of wind and crash of sea about their home. Spume filled the air as they looked out on the North Sea morning, yet Grace's keen eyes spotted a ship aground on Big Harcar Rock, almost a mile away. A look through the telescope revealed survivors clinging to the wreck. Grace, 22-years-old and anxious for excitement, beseeched her father to attempt a rescue.

The lighthouse coble, a short, flatbottomed boat, was lowered. Grace and her father were able rowers, but the violent tide pushed the stout little boat off course several times, making their journey to the Forfarshire twice as long. They reached the wreck and took off five of the nine survivors, which were taken back to the lighthouse. Grace stayed with those rescued while her father and two of the rescued seamen made a second trip to the wreck to fetch the remaining survivors. (A report later confirmed that forty people had drowned before the Darlings arrived!) When the rescued were safely aboard the lighthouse, Grace and her mother tended to injuries and cooked meals. It was three days before the survivors could be taken ashore.

On September 11 newspapers and broadsides of the day printed the story of the loss of the *Forfarshire*. There was no mention of the Darlings' bravery, as arguments over the cause of the wreck and the possibility that the *Forfarshire's* owners had willfully sent a disabled ship to sea eclipsed the news of the rescue. When the scandal died down, a "penny-a-liner" reporter grabbed the Grace Darling story for his gossip broadside and gave it his melodramatic best. The deed leaped from paper to paper, with each account more thrilling and courageous:

"Surely, imagination in its loftiest creations never invested the female character with such a degree of fortitude as had been evinced by Miss Grace Horsley Darling on this occasion. Is there in the whole field of history, or of fiction even, one instance of female heroism to compare for one moment with this?"

Painters rushed to Longstone to capture Grace's dainty face and slight figure, then drop it in exaggerated scenes of angry seas and suffering humanity. Poets and minstrels wrote tributes to the "Grace of womanhood and Darling of mankind," and peddlers hawked locks of her hair and swatches of fabric from the dress she had worn on the rescue. A public conscription for the Darlings raised a gift of several hundred pounds, to which the Royal Humane Society added gold lifesaving medals and a silver tea set. Grace Darling had captured the public imagination.

Longstone Light, Courtesy U.S. Coast Guard Museum

Not unlike today's superstars, Grace spent the next few years dealing with the media, such as it was in the 1830s, and pursuing privacy and a quiet life. She continued to live on Longstone Light with her parents, but was besieged with mail, visitors, and requests for appearances. She went ashore to Bamburgh in April 1842 to visit her sister and attend to financial affairs, but was soon stricken with the influenza that had struck northern England. Grace never recovered.

In October 1842, four years after her brave accomplishment, Grace died, probably of pneumonia — a tragic finale that caused much public grief and elevated her image to saintly eminence. She was buried in Bamburgh churchyard before a huge crowd of mourners, who also contributed money for a memorial to be built over her grave. Even Queen Victoria sent £20. St. Aidans Church had a stained glass window made showing Grace rescuing the shipwrecked.

Over the years, Grace's legend grew. She became the model for Victorian girls, her story of feminine courage repeated so often in magazines of the day that her name was absorbed into everyday English as a term meaning "brave woman." Naturally, the town of Bamburgh has a museum dedicated to her, and Longstone Lighthouse doubles as a navigational aid and tourist attraction. Not to be outdone, Americans produced Ida Lewis of Rhode Island's Lime Rock Lighthouse, who rescued time and again; yet Ida was often called "America's Grace Darling."

Even today, the name Grace Darling brings awe to our hearts. Her image endures, according to Jessica Mitford, because she has been successfully "transmogrified," an unwieldy term that describes the cult hyperbole that might apply equally to Amelia Erhart or the Grand Duchess Anastasia. She has been re-invented so many times, we wonder who she really was.

This article originally appeared in *Mariner's Weather Log,* Summer 1994.

Grace Darling Museum, Bamburgh

Dogs of the Lighthouses

Companions to the Keepers

The history of American lighthouses is replete with tales of heroic rescues, deeds of courage, and steadfast duty to the lanterns. Stories have been told in briny taprooms for generations about the strength and dedication of lighthouse keepers and their battles with wind, waves, and sands.

The keeper's life was, for the most part, monotonous and lonely. Occasional jaunts to town or the mainland, in the case of offshore lighthouses, highlighted his schedule. Otherwise, except for the occasional shipwreck or visitor, or the crash of stormy seas over his luminous charge, the keeper's days were consumed by repetitious log entries of trips up and down the stairs and daily housekeeping chores in the tower.

For obvious reasons, companionship became a desperate need of many lightkeepers. Even those whose wives and children joined them in service at lighthouses often kept pets. Abbie Burgess, for example, the famed daughter of keeper Samuel Burgess of Matinicus Rock, Maine, raised hens on the lonely rockbound island and is said to have risked her life to save them in an 1856 storm. Tom Small, who tended Deer Island Light in Boston Bay with his brother, had an aquatic cat who climbed down the lighthouse ladder, leaped into the sea to fish, and returned on the ladder with the catch in her mouth.

More interesting, and certainly more heartfelt, are the stories of famous dogs and their masters who lived at lighthouses. The careers of these faithful dogs, though often as colorful as the keepers', were rarely documented in logbooks or lighthouse records. Without them, more lives might have been lost, and the keepers and their families would surely have led a drearier life.

Probably the best known dog of lighthouse lore was a huge, friendly Newfoundland-St. Bernard mix named Milo. His fame came more from a painting than his feats of lifesaving. Entitled "Saved," its artist skillfully captured the security and protection Milo was known for at Egg Rock Lighthouse, one mile offshore northeast of Nahant, Massachusetts.

Milo came to the rock in September 1855 with the first keeper of Egg Rock Lighthouse, George B. Taylor, and his family. Workers were still finishing the tower when the Taylors arrived, and they liked Milo so well they left a small hole in the stone entryway to the lighthouse to give the dog his own private entrance.

Milo's strength and determination were first exhibited shortly after arriving at Egg Rock. Keeper Taylor had tried to shoot a huge loon for the family meal, but had succeeded only in wounding it. Milo jumped into the ocean on the east side of the island and began swimming after the bird. The loon took off when Milo came near it and flew a quarter-mile before landing on the water again. Milo continued to pursue it.

As he reached the loon a second time, it again took flight. The chase continued this way until both Milo and the loon disappeared from the keeper's sight. Milo was gone all that night. The family was certain he had drowned, since he had paddled east, away from the mainland.

Late the next day, however, Milo was seen swimming toward Egg Rock, this time from the west. He had apparently attempted to return to the rock

56

after dark the evening before and had missed the island entirely. He swam all the way to the mainland where he rested for the night. The next day, he swam home to Egg Rock.

Milo's fame as rescuer came later and prompted a local artist named Edward Landseer to paint "Saved." Details regarding Milo's many rescues are sketchy, but he is said to have saved several children from drowning at Egg Rock. Keeper Taylor's son, Fred, is pictured in "Saved" resting safely between the giant dog's paws. Sadly, Fred Taylor later drowned on a boat trip through Shirley Gut. Had Milo been with him at the time, he too, might have been saved.

Owls Head Light
By Paul Bradley

At Owls Head Light, Maine, at the entrance to the picturesque seaport of Rockland, a Springer Spaniel named Spot gained fame after saving the local mailboat. Spot belonged to Pauline Hamor, daughter of lightkeeper Augustus Hamor who began service at Owls Head in June 1930.

Spot's entire world seemed to center on the lighthouse, and rightfully so, Owls Head is not only one of Maine's most beautiful lighthouses, it's also responsible for guiding the busy shipping traffic in and out of Penobscot Bay.

Spot's favorite pastime was ringing the station fogbell. He loved to watch for boats nearing the point of Owls Head, and as they passed, he ran to the fogbell and gave a hearty yank on the rope with his teeth, pealing the bell loudly. Often, the passing vessel answered with three short toots, which sent Spot racing for the water's edge and barking excitedly.

A mailboat serviced the remote islands of the Gulf of Maine in those years. It was piloted by Capt. Stuart Ames, a good friend of the Hamor family. Mrs. Ames, who lived in Rockland, often phoned the lighthouse in the evening to ask if the mailboat had passed. In this way, she was able to know when to have dinner ready for the captain.

The Hamors never had trouble knowing when the mailboat passed. Capt. Ames was Spot's favorite pilot, and the dog never missed a chance to ring the fogbell when the mailboat passed Owls Head. Every so often, though, the weather became foul and the mailboat was late.

One evening a storm blew up quickly, as they often do in the Northeast. By nightfall the mailboat had not returned. Mrs. Ames became worried and called the lighthouse to ask if Spot had seen the boat. The dog was summoned from his warm bed by the kitchen stove and led out into the storm. Laboriously, he trudged through the blizzard to the fogbell. Snow had piled high against the bell, and Spot could not reach it. He barked his frustration, then disappeared over the edge of the cliff.

Keeper Hamor followed, working his way over the cliff and down to the point nearest the channel. Spot was standing on the promontory, muzzle to the wind, barking loudly, The keeper could faintly hear the whistle of the mailboat heading toward Owls Head. Spot barked continuously until he heard the mailboat give its signal of recognition — three short blasts.

The dog's insistent barking enabled Capt. Ames to find his bearings in the storm, and Spot did not stop barking until the mailboat was well past Owls Head and headed safely into Rockland Harbor. Keeper Hamor finally dragged him, half frozen and exhausted, back into the house. Two hours later, the Ames family called the lighthouse to thank the Hamors for Spot's heroic performance. Years later when Spot died, as a memorial to the dog, the family buried him beneath his beloved fogbell.

At St. Simons Island, Georgia, a different lighthouse canine story unfolded about the turn of the century. It is undeniably less heroic than the previous accounts of Milo and Spot, but fascinating nonetheless — especially for those who believe in the supernatural.

The lovely white brick lighthouse at St. Simons Island and its Antebellum keeper's house were completed in 1872 at the expense of several lives. As with many of the southern beacons, malaria plagued the work crews in this mosquito-infested area. One in particular — the contractor in charge — died while on he job at St. Simons in 1870. No one is certain, but it is believed that it was his spirit that returned to haunt the completed lighthouse.

In 1907, Carl Svendsen and his wife moved to St. Simons to keep the beautiful lighthouse. The Svendsens had a fine-tempered dog whose name, oddly enough, was Jinx, though he had never brought them a day of bad luck. The Svendsens settled comfortably into the two-story keeper's house and took up their routine duties tending the light tower.

From the beginning of their stay, Mrs. Svendsen made a habit of spreading the supper table each evening when she heard her husband's boots descending the lighthouse stairs after he had lit up for the night. Jinx, who never cared to accompany the keepers on his daily trips up and down the lighthouse, remained in the kitchen with Mrs. Svendsen.

One evening as Mrs. Svendsen prepared supper, she heard footsteps on the stairs and spread the table as usual. But when the footfall reached the bottom of the staircase, her husband did not appear. Jinx rose from his napping place and growled low in his throat. The hair on his back bristled. Slowly, he backed into a corner and began to whimper.

Mrs. Svendsen went to the base of the stairway and looked up through its lacy spirals. There was no sign of her husband. She climbed slowly and cautiously to the top where she found him still working in the lantern. She told him about the footsteps she had heard and Jinx' incensed reaction. He dismissed her idea about a lighthouse ghost, since no more noises were heard in the tower that night. But a few days later, Keeper Svendsen also heard the phantom footsteps, and he agreed something unearthly did indeed inhabit St. Simons Lighthouse.

Though alarming at first, the sounds caused the Svendsens no trouble, and they soon grew accustomed to their noisy, anonymous guest. In fact, the footsteps eventually grew almost pleasant to the couple, who remained at the lighthouse about 40 years. Jinx, on the other hand, disliked and even feared the eerie presence. He hid whenever the poltergeist roamed the tower and was tormented for the remainder of his years at the lighthouse.

For every heroic deed of a lighthouse keeper, or strange occurrence at his light, perhaps one goes untold of his canine friend. Dogs have followed their masters into more human realms than these, but ask a weary keeper who has trimmed the wicks for the night and washed the salty taste from his beard, and he'll admit: When the light is safely lit and the storm rages outside the tower walls, it's good to have a soft ear to scratch and a cold nose in one's hand.

This is part of an article that originally appeared in *Dog Fancy,* December 1988.

Author's Note

Since the submission of "Dogs of the Lighthouses" to *Dog Fancy* back in the mid-1980s, I've met numerous lighthouse dogs. Almost every lightkeeper I interviewed over the years had a dog or two; some had pictures of their family mutts. The late Harold Jennings sent me a charming photo of his Scotty dog greeting the tender crew in the 1920s when coal was delivered to Lovells Island Range Lights. It reminded me of a story I knew about Katie Walker, who kept Robbins Reef Light in New York Harbor after the death of her husband. She once rescued a Scotty dog from the harbor and nursed him back to health. He was great companionship for her, and she admitted feeling quite miserable after he was returned to his owner.

Most Coast Guard crews at lighthouses had dogs, even in recent years. Striker greeted me with loud, threatening barks from behind the fence at Highland Light in 1989. I was assured he would cease his menacing charade the moment I entered the gate, and he did. Striker was a watchdog — important work at a lighthouse visited by thousands of curious tourists each year. Had it not been for Striker, many visitors would have invaded the lightkeeper's privacy or ventured too near the fragile cliff behind the tower.

My friend, Barb Kachel, who has the honor of living at North Head Lighthouse, Washington, sent me an amusing photo in 1992 of her two dogs posing by their "Lighthouse Doghouse." Such demonstrations of love for the lighthouse hounds show how truly appreciated and needed they were and are.

Canine Crewman Aboard!

Before the days of automated lighthouses, isolated lightkeepers were thankful for lighthouse tenders. These ships and their lonely, stalwart crewmen brought all manner of supplies and assistance to the men and women who watched over our nation's sentinels. Both lightkeepers and tender crews anticipated these visits, for with them came not only material necessities — food, medicine, books, mail, oil — but provisions for the starved spirit as well.

One such benevolent tender was the *Hyacinth*, whose watery territory was the Great Lakes. The tender was captained by H.W. Maynard, a gentle and sensitive man who understood the special needs of those sequestered away in the service of the lighthouses. In 1914, when the *Hyacinth's* crew pulled a near-dead, mongrel pup from the Milwaukee River and tenderly revived it, Maynard knew there was only one thing to do — adopt the little dog as the ship's mascot.

The lanky, emaciated pup was named Sport. During his twelve years aboard the *Hyacinth,* he gained immeasurable popularity and proved himself a worthy crewman. Whenever the *Hyacinth* neared a lighthouse, Sport would grab the heaving line in his teeth, dive into the water, and swim to the waiting lightkeeper, who took the line and pulled the tender into position.

Sport also played baseball with the crew, ate in the galley with his messmates, and took regular shore leave. On one such occasion, Sport accompanied Captain Maynard ashore at Chicago and became separated from him. The captain searched the city wharf, but was unable to find the dog. Sadly, he returned to the *Hyacinth* alone and told the crew Sport had been lost. But a few hours later, the skipper of the passenger vessel *Indiana* knocked on Maynard's cabin door. In his arms was Sport, who had magically turned up on the piers just after the *Hyacinth* lifted anchor. Needless to say, the crew and Captain Maynard were ecstatic to have their shipmate returned.

On July 19, 1926, Sport died peacefully of old age aboard the *Hyacinth*. He was placed in a canvas bag, and the crew solemnly mustered on deck for his burial. As Captain Maynard spoke of Sport's useful career as a tender dog, and the joy and help he had brought to lightkeepers and the crew, there were tears in all eyes.

The men agreed that since Sport had been pulled from the water as a pup, he should be returned to it in death. A final farewell salute was given by the bosun's whistle, and Captain Maynard announced that a trusted and loved comrade was departing. Sport's body was lowered into Lake Michigan and disappeared into its depths.

This article originally appeared in *The Beacon*, Fall 1985, publication of the Great Lakes Lighthouse Keeper's Association..

Lighthouse Cats

Feline Friends to the Keepers

They were strong, hearty creatures, at home where land touched water and the sweep of a powerful beam pierced the night. They knew the sea in all its fickle moods, ruffling their fur with stormy winds, coating their whiskers with salt and foam, or quietly lapping a rocky tidepool where they played.

They were the lightkeepers' cats -- nemesis of lighthouse mice and insects, and the recipients of an excess catch. They warmed the keeper's hearth on stormy nights and brought good luck to his ocean home. He cherished their companionship and welcomed their offspring. Their luminous eyes and rumbling purr were reminders of his sentinel home, with its huge lens turning softly on an iron pedestal, a guidepost bringing ships safely into port.

Since the first glimmer of candle flame appeared in our nation's original lighthouse at Boston Harbor, cats have stood watch with lightkeepers. Many were colorfully remembered by their owners in lighthouse logs and diaries. Others were captured by writers, photographers, and storytellers. All possessed that unique feline poise and adaptability that made them ideal lighthouse pets.

Some lighthouse cats survived generations of families, because keepers' positions frequently changed. It was not unusual for one or two cats to produce an entire colony of cat kin at a light station.

Born in the dampness of a tower storeroom, or behind a warm wood stove in the family kitchen, these cats knew no world other than the sea.

Other cats were brought to lighthouses to earn their keep as mousers and ratters. With so many structures at light stations made of wood, including the light towers, rodents found ample refuge and could do enormous damage. These pesky rodents often swam ashore from shipwrecks and multiplied to uncontrollable numbers.

Rats were not the only survivors of shipwrecks. Old lighthouse records and local legends tell of cats rescued from sinking ships and floating debris, for cats were popular pets aboard ships in the days of sail. In his book, *The Outermost House*, Henry Beston speaks of items from wrecks salvaged by shore residents and lightkeepers of Cape Cod: "...the cat purring at your feet may himself be a rescued mariner."

Such an event took place during a cold February years ago when the *Castagna* wrecked off Cape Cod. Coast Guardsmen found two survivors on the storm-ravaged ship -- a screeching canary and a purring, gray cat nestled peacefully in the captain's cabin. The bird perished in the freezing air while being taken ashore, but the cat survived and took up residence at a Cape lighthouse. It left its keeper a dynasty of descendants.

Lighthouse cats, like their owners, experienced a lifestyle unlike that of their landlubbing peers. Despite their distaste for wind and water, many were avid swimmers and could traverse blustery ledges with agility. An old New England folktale relates how a lightkeeper prevented his feline friend from blowing off an island in a gale: He drove a spike into a rock and cut an eye-splice into the cat's tail. When the wind blew up, the clever kitty simply dropped its tail over the spike and was safely anchored in place.

The antics of lightkeeper Tom Small's cat in Boston Bay are less legend and more fact. In the 1930s, the lighthouse Small tended at Deer Island was a metal telescoping structure on a concrete caisson, reached from water by a ladder. To the amazement of the Smalls and their friends, their gray and white cat would climb down the ladder, leap into the bay, and return with a fish in her mouth. Author Edward Rowe Snow, who often visited the Smalls at the lighthouse, snapped a photo of the unusual "fishing cat."

Tom Small's two brothers, Arthur and Judson, were also lightkeepers in Boston Bay who loved cats. At Narrows Light, Arthur Small had a rough and tumble tomcat aptly named Stripes. Small frequently made trips in his dory to a nearby island to visit a friend who owned Stripes' brother, an identical striped tom.

On one particular trip, Stripes stowed away in the dory and was not discovered until Small neared Fort Warren where his friend lived. Once ashore, Stripes and his brother mingled. Neither owner could tell them apart, and in typical feline fashion, neither cat answered to his name. The men tossed a coin. Small won and took his pick of the cats. He was never quite sure if Stripes was the cat that returned home with him that day.

Some cats traveled on their own. At lonely Sable Island, a desolate crescent of sand off Nova Scotia, a log entry at the weather station in the 1960s comically mentioned the resident cat, Stinky. Like most male cats, Stinky had restless feet. The closest neighbor was a lightkeeper who owned a female cat. The logbook explains: "Stinky was away for three days, but the prodigal cat returned this evening, only to eat a can of salmon and take off again. Stinky must be in love or something."

The most famous of America's lighthouse cats was Cape Neddick Nubble Lighthouse's rotund Sambo Tonkus. In the 1930s, he amused visitors to this picturesque Maine lighthouse by swimming the narrow channel between the Nubble and the mainland. There, he would carouse with the local cats, catch a fat mouse, then amble back to the channel, dive in and swim to the Nubble Light with the prize firmly clenched in his giant jaws.

Nubble Lighthouse, by Paul Bradley

Born on the Nubble in the 1920s Sambo was the pampered pet of Keeper and Mrs. James Burke.

With the death of Keeper Burke, his widow left the island. She felt Sambo belonged to the light station, so she gave him to the new lightkeeper, Eugene Coleman. The cat had grown to a hefty 19 pounds by this time and was eagerly adopted by Coleman. Between 1930 and 1934, Sambo Tonkus entertained more than 4,000 visitors and was profiled in the local newspaper on several occasions.

As late as 1989, when one of the last Coast Guard families was stationed on the Nubble, feline companionship was still an important part of lighthouse life. John Terry and his wife, Karyn, kept alive the tradition of the Nubble cats with their two pets, Tuffy and Tiny. Though these kitties were somewhat slimmer and less fond of the water than Sambo Tonkus, their role as companions and mousers continued.

Tiger-striped Tuffy enjoyed chasing the many seagulls on the island. His owners admitted they were seldom bored because Tuffy was quite the showcat, with acrobatic antics on the fence and the rocks in pursuit of the gulls. He was also quick to catch bugs inside the lantern, where there was never a shortage of them. Cape Neddick's powerful beam, like all lighthouse beacons, attracts thousands of insects nightly, and Tuffy considered them a treat.

Glossy black Tiny was the shy cat at the Nubble in the 1980s. He preferred the security of the comfortable keeper's house to the wild winds and openness of the outer island. The dark, enclosed stairwell of the light tower was among his favorite places. He was known to race up and down the stairs in the evenings, as if chasing some invisible foe. (Such night time crazies are well-known to all cat owners, but they must be especially fun at lighthouses!)

On Sanibel Island along Florida's Gulf Coast, lightkeeper Henry Shanahan's thirteen children amused themselves with a menagerie of pets, including cats. Sanibel was a pristine wilderness a century ago when the Shanahans kept its spider-legged lighthouse. The beach was strewn with shells, seabirds circled overhead, and there were many wild creatures to tame. Among the family pets were deer, raccoons, and a seagull. But the most unusual pet was the family's talented cat.

He was not the typical reticent, reserved feline. Keeper Shanahan had noted the cat's exceptional intelligence and eagerness to play from the start. The flamboyant tom could out-perform a circus monkey with tricks the keeper's children had

Sanibel Island Light, by Paul Bradley

patiently taught him. He amused everyone by walking on his hind legs, rolling over, playing dead, and doing flips.

A cat at lonely Destruction Island Light, off the coast of Washington, was less enthusiastic about pleasing humans. Yet he was thoroughly perceptive, as his owners discovered one chilly night more than a century ago. The lightkeeper had tended the beacon for the night and retired to the kitchen to read. His wife was at a table nearby with her sewing. The cat had taken up his usual spot on the rug by the warm woodstove. Everything was quiet, save the creak of the keeper's rocker and the soft whir of wind outside. But a noise in the attic interrupted the peaceful evening.

Footsteps were heard on the floor above, then down the wooden stairs, slow and measured. The stairway door swung open gently, as if pushed by an invisible hand, and something tapped softly over the floorboards. The cat raised from his nap, arched his back, and hissed angrily, backing into a corner. The phantom footfall passed by both the keeper and his wife, then paused at the door. The latch lifted and the door swung wide, teetering in the wind a moment

before slamming shut. The ghost had disappeared into the howling night and was never heard from again. Thereafter, any small noise in the attic sent the cat into the nearest corner.

As navigational technology has progressed, lighthouses have been automated or, in some cases, rendered obsolete. Some now stand grim, dark, and in disrepair. Others are being transformed into handsome museums showcasing the historic life of yesterday's "wickies," as lightkeepers were once called. At a number of these museums, cats still reside, keeping down the populations of rodents and insects and reminding visitors of an era when the lighthouse cat was nearly as appreciated as the beacon itself.

Ponce de Leon Inlet Lighthouse Museum, south of Daytona Beach, Florida, proudly exhibits its history in a lofty, brick sentinel -- the second tallest on the eastern seaboard -- and its three quaint keepers' houses. A number of cats live at the station today, representing their feline ancestors, who were companions to the keepers in the years when the lighthouse was isolated and lonely.

The cats at the museum are mostly foundlings, dropped off at the end of the dirt road where the lighthouse stands. Museum staff began feeding them in the 1970s, and over the years, the lighthouse has become a refuge for unwanted cats and kittens. These orphans, which often number more than a dozen, now have a happy home. A donation jar in the museum gift shop helps buy their food and pay the vet bills. Whenever possible, the cats are placed in loving homes.

The days of the lighthouse keeper treading up spiral stairs to tend an old lantern have ended, but the romance and history of lighthouses remains a beguiling subject. As newer navigational aids upstage the old towers and beacons, only memories of their human and animal attendants remain. Logbooks tell of storms and shipwrecks, of the travail of wars and the pleasures of visitors who stopped to "see the light." Here and there, interspersed among the yellowed pages, are less crucial records of life along the sea -- the passing of migrating birds, the colorful sunsets and moonrises, spring's first flowers, the birth of a child.

Here also can be found kind words for the small, whiskered friends who curled peacefully on lighthouse hearths and brought immeasurable happiness to the families who tended the lamp posts along the sea.

This is an updated version of an article that originally appeared in *Cat Fancy*, June 1985. A translation into German appeared in, *Ein Herz Für Tiere*. Similar articles appeared in *Purrrr!* and *Lighthouse Digest*.

Author's Note

My closest friends know I am ridiculously fond of cats. I've had the companionship of many over the years and, at this moment, am hampered in my work by the presence of two of my three felines, who feel they must always be in my company. That cats should be a part of my lighthouse research is no surprise. Their stories rank low in historic importance, but are heartwarming. Such tales reveal something of the character of the people who tended lighthouses and the nature of their work.

Hootie, now eleven and beginning to feel the infirmities of age, is a true lap-lighthouse-cat. Seldom is he more than a few inches from me, and always he keeps vigil over my work. He has presided over many an article or book and feels obligated to lay on my papers or sprawl by the computer. Occasionally, he steps on the keyboard and adds his own thoughts, however scrambled.

Buster, our manx cat and the curmudgeon of the house, inspired a character named Stumpy in my first novel for children, *Libby at the Lighthouse*. (With lots of work and luck, it will appear in print soon.) Zsa Zsa, the capricious feline lady of our home, enjoys chasing the cursor on the computer screen and attacking the laserjet printer as it ejects sheets of copy.

Other cats have traveled with me through lighthouse history and lore. In August 1985, my family moved from Pearl Harbor, Hawaii to Groton, Connecticut - a military transfer. Accompanying us was our family cat - Warhead. (The silly name was bestowed by my husband, who works with Navy ordnance, torpedoes in particular.) Warhead visited a number of lighthouses with us on that trip.

My fondest memory of his antics took place at Admiralty Head Light near Seattle. The children had tried to train him to walk on a leash. *Tried* is the watch-word here, for he never really walked on that leash; rather, he lurched, leaped, tugged, and flipped, as if some demon had taken over his body.

After a long morning in the car, he was emancipated in the parking area at Admiralty Head Light. It was a warm August day, and there were many visitors. People watched in disbelief as Warhead sprang from the car and began a wild escapade around the lighthouse grounds, kids in tow. A woman took his picture, amazed to see a cat leading kids on a leash.

As a Christmas gift a few years back, I received a signed Cheryl Spencer Coilin figurine of Rock of Ages Lighthouse. Cheryl is known for the detail and animation she infuses into her pieces. I have many of her fine works in my collection. I was particularly delighted with Rock of Ages, as it has a racy black cat zooming around the lower deck of the tower. Any why not? Surely the keepers of that waterbound light needed a furry friend and crewmate to help them carry out their benevolent mission.

Lighthouse Tenders

Workhorses of the Sea

Their dainty floral names - *Marigold, Dandelion, Geranium, Lily, Arbutus, Wisteria, Violet* - belied the hard work and toughness of the lighthouse tenders. In all kinds of weather and often under stress, these modest, round-hulled vessels traveled the waterways to build and maintain the nation's navigational aids. On their sturdy decks buoys were chained, awaiting repair or ready to be positioned on some perilous, watery station. In their holds were myriad stores - coal, lamp oil, fresh water and food, tools, building materials, machine parts, even furniture and livestock.

Servants of the seaways, lighthouse tenders were the backbone of the old U.S. Lighthouse Service and the forerunners of today's rugged, state-of-the-art Coast Guard buoy tenders. From their official designation of duty in the 1840s until their transfer to the Coast Guard in 1939, lighthouse tenders were indispensable. Tender crews did the dirty work, often in harms way and with little thanks

beyond personal satisfaction. The job was not glamorous, but it was critical: "Never in the entire history of the sea have smaller ships and fewer men been entrusted with bigger jobs or performed them with greater credit," wrote Hans Christian Adamson of the "tender boys."

Though lighthouses, fog signals, and buoys have served American seamen since Colonial days, a fleet of ships to maintain them was not inaugurated until the expansion and improvement of the nation's lighthouses in the middle of the 19th century. Prior to this, navigational aids were built and maintained through contracts with private vessels, usually small schooners that could squeeze into the tight spots required of buoy and lighthouse tending.

In large busy ports such as New York, Philadelphia, and Norfolk, local harbor pilots were paid to set and maintain buoys. Charter vessels and government ships, including those of the Navy and the Revenue Marine, handled most of the needs of lighthouse keepers. As late as 1838, with some 230 lighthouses and lightships on duty, only one tender was employed full time by the Lighthouse Service to maintain them.

An investigation that year revealed serious problems with the nation's navigational aids, particularly lighthouses which had fallen into a deplorable state of disrepair and were inferior in quality to those of Europe. In addition, lightkeepers were found to be inadequately trained and poorly supervised. A more rigorous budget was set aside to

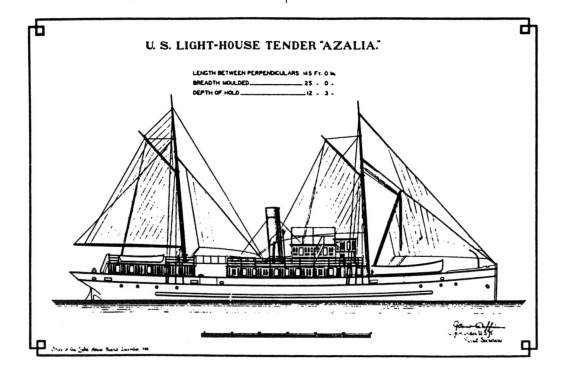

U. S. LIGHT-HOUSE TENDER "AZALIA."

LENGTH BETWEEN PERPENDICULARS 145 FT. 0 IN.
BREADTH MOULDED _____ 25 - 0 .
DEPTH OF HOLD _____ 12 - 3 .

upgrade and sustain all U.S. navigational aids, and this meant an armada of workships was needed -- to build more lighthouses, repair those that already existed, provision the lightkeepers and conduct inspections of their stations, and make the searoads safer with more lightships, buoys, and fog signals.

The first of the tenders belonging to the Lighthouse Service was the *Rush,* a former Revenue Marine cutter purchased in 1840 and refitted for its demanding new job. It served mainly along the shores of New England and the mid-Atlantic, working side-by-side with chartered vessels. Within a few years the *Rush* was joined by other government-owned tenders, including the *Lamplighter* and *Watchful,* two schooners purchased and overhauled in 1856 for service on the Great Lakes.

The California Gold Rush sent the West Coast into a flurry of maritime activity and spurred Congress in 1852 to authorize the construction of 16 lighthouses between San Diego and Cape Disappointment, as well as numerous buoys to mark the perils of San Francisco Bay. Private contractors submitted bids to build the lighthouses, while the Coast Survey was charged with sinking the crude wooden spars that served as the West Coast's first buoys. Congress was also quick to recognize the tasks that lay ahead - more lighthouses to be built and buoys to be set, not to mention the problem of fog.

In 1857, $60,000 was authorized for the construction of the first Pacific Coast tender, a sidewheel steamer built at the Philadelphia Navy Yard exclusively for the Lighthouse Service. The 140 foot *Shubrick,* named for Navy Commodore W. B. Shubrick, president of the Lighthouse Board, went down the ways on November 25, 1857. Its red paddle wheels stood out brightly against the black painted oak hull as it steamed out of Philadelphia a month later, bound for San Francisco. The single-expansion steam engine produced about 285 horsepower, enough to turn *Shubrick's* paddle wheels twenty times a minute for a speed of eight knots. Under sail, the tender was rigged as a brigantine. In the event of attack by Indians, *Shubrick* was armed with a cannon and guns to defend itself.

In the Straits of Magellan *Shubrick* struggled in headwinds that nearly used up its coal supply. The master ordered the ship's handsome wood paneling ripped out and its furniture dismantled to feed the boilers and keep the sidewheel paddles turning. At Valdiva Bay, Chile the crew went ashore and cut wood to keep *Shubrick* going until it reached the coal bins at Valparaiso. After an exhausting voyage of 155 days, *Shubrick* steamed into San Francisco and immediately went to work.

For the next thirty years *Shubrick* tended navigational aids from California to Alaska. Among its notable accomplishments was the marking of the Columbia River in 1859 from its mouth to Astoria, a voyage that took *Shubrick* almost to the river's headwaters. During the Civil War *Shubrick* was transferred to the Revenue Marine Service and assigned to police Puget Sound. At the end of the war it spent a brief period in the Navy on a mission to lay a submarine telegraph cable across the Bering Strait. Though the task was later abandoned, *Shubrick's* master, Captain C.M. Scammon, had collected considerable research on Pacific gray whales which he included in his 1874 book, *Marine Mammals of the North Western Coast.*

Shubrick returned to the Lighthouse Service in 1866 and was soon put to work hauling construction materials for the precipitous Cape Mendocino Lighthouse, some 200 miles north of San Francisco. Heavily loaded, *Shubrick* encountered fog a short distance south of the site and ran aground. The chief engineer managed to refloat the tender by removing all stores and machinery, then moving the empty ship on skids to a suitable launching site. In the process it was discovered that a large rock had imbedded itself in *Shubrick's* port bow. It was removed with gunpowder and left a gaping hole. Nevertheless, *Shubrick* was able to return to Mare Island Shipyard in San Francisco where it was repaired and returned to service.

The earliest lighthouse tenders, like *Shubrick* and *Rush,* were named arbitrarily, but about 1860 the Lighthouse Service began a curious tradition that survives even today: Lighthouse tenders were christened with botanical names, larger vessels bearing the names of trees and shrubs native to the districts where they served, and the smaller tenders named for indigenous flowers.

A colorful bouquet of tenders serviced the various districts around the nation from 1869 to 1939: The Great Lakes had *Dahlia* and *Amaranth;* California was served by the *Columbine, Manzanita,* and *Madrono,* while the *Jonquil* and *Cypress* worked out of Charleston, South Carolina. New York City was minded by the *Tulip,* Boston by the *Lilac,* New Orleans by the *Pansy.* And surely it was no accident that the *Holly* and *Mistletoe* were assigned to look after the Chesapeake Bay and the Mississippi and Missouri rivers by the *Nettle* and *Bramble.* It seemed ironic that ships so rugged and homely wore such lovely names. Perhaps the tradition stuck, for the Coast Guard still has botanical buoy tenders such as *Red Birch, Sassafras, Bayberry,* and *Willow.*

When the Civil War began there were twenty-one tenders working in the Lighthouse Service and some, like *Shubrick,* did double duty supporting navigational aids and wartime commerce. Twenty years later that number had nearly doubled, as had the workload. The activities of the *Maple* along the mid-Atlantic Coast in 1894 give a sense of the busy schedule of the tenders:

"This steamer was in service during the whole year. She steamed some 18,520 miles and consumed about 1,425 tons of coal. Fires were hauled from under her boilers for 50 days; she worked 578 buoys; she visited 174 light-houses, delivered 229 tons of coal, 113 cords of wood, and left rations at 38 light-stations. The crew were employed in cleaning and painting buoys 70 days at buoy depots. She was on duty 17 days in the Sixth light-house district, and was eight days in towing barges from Baltimore to the new Cape Charles light-station, and 18 days in towing and attending to light-vessels."

By World War I forty-seven lighthouse tenders were at work along the nation's coastlines and larger inland waterways. Their duties increased as more buoys, lightships, and lighthouses were established, and sophisticated equipment was developed to run them. Automatic machinery for beacons and bells, and later, gas lighted buoys, placed the greatest demands on tender crews. Additionally, new construction burgeoned after the U.S. acquired territories in Alaska and Hawaii - thousands of miles of new coastline that needed to be surveyed and marked.

In response the Lighthouse Service ordered the construction of a new tender for service in the Hawaiian Islands. The 190 foot schooner-rigged steel steam tender *Kukui,* named for Hawaii's native candlenut tree, was launched in 1909 from the New York Shipbuilding Company in Camden, New Jersey. With a pricetag of $213,879 and steam turbines that moved it along at a swift 12.5 knots, *Kukui* was the toast of the tropics when it arrived in Hawaii and the fastest ship in the islands. During its first year of service it steamed nearly 9000 miles.

Because of its speed *Kukui* was often called upon for search and rescue operations in the Pacific. Chasing rogue buoys was part of its normal routine, but *Kukui* also searched for downed planes and derelicts. The tender's crew built or rebuilt nearly all of Hawaii's lighthouses, including the tiny beacons atop the lofty islets of Lehua and Ka'ula at the western end of the major island chain. Ka'ula was the less elevated of the islets but the most difficult to access because of its sheer cliffs, razor-sharp rocks, and pesky seabirds. In addition, trespassing on the islet worried some of the men. Ka'ula was believed by the Hawaiians to be the home of the legendary shark god, Kuhaimoana. When the chief engineer for the project caught two sharks, *Kukui's* superstitious crew, mostly native Hawaiians and Samoans, predicted bad luck. A week of storms and rough seas seemed to confirm the misdeed and cast a pall over the entire venture. Nevertheless, the little sentinel on Ka'ula Rock was completed and lit in August of 1932, without further interference from Kuhaimoana.

For all its good work, the *Kukui* was to leave a black mark on the reputation of lighthouse tenders. On March 1, 1911 in the darkness off Oahu, *Kukui* sideswiped the little fishing schooner *Moi Wahine* as it was returning to Honolulu. The schooner sank so quickly there wasn't time to lower the lifeboat, and the captain and seven crewmen were stranded in the water. The *Kukui* continued on course for some minutes following the collision, then stopped and scanned the tranquil sea with its searchlights. The crew saw nothing and proceeded on.

Sam Manu, the seventy-five year old skipper of the *Moi Wahine* and a survivor of two other shipwrecks, crawled on top of the wreckage. His shipmates were nowhere to be seen; alone, he floated to Lanai. When he finally reached Honolulu a few days later, he claimed *Kukui's* officers were to blame for the accident and afterwards had failed to make a thorough search. The ensuing investigation placed blame on the *Kukui,* but the Lighthouse Bureau refused to acknowledge any fault in the matter and made no reparations to Captain Manu. The event was the only blemish on *Kukui's* thirty-five year career.

For the rugged lighting of Alaska the tender *Armeria* steamed up the Inside Passage in 1902 to help build lighthouses at Sentinel Island and Five Finger. *Armeria* set buoys, charted Alaskan waters, and helped with the construction and maintenance of about a dozen Alaskan lighthouses before its career ended abruptly in May 1912. In an ironic turn of events, *Armeria* struck an uncharted rock near Cape Hinchinbrook Light in Prince William Sound. The lightkeepers aided in the rescue of the crew, but the tender was a total loss.

Armeria's replacement was the *Cedar,* built at Long Beach, California and assigned to Alaska's

The bow ornament of the old Lighthouse tenders was a handsome brass lighthouse 24 inches high. Crewmen, no doubt, were proud to keep it polished to a high luster. Note the date of approval: 6-26-17.

Courtesy of Shore Village Museum, Rockland, Maine
America's Lighthouse Museum!

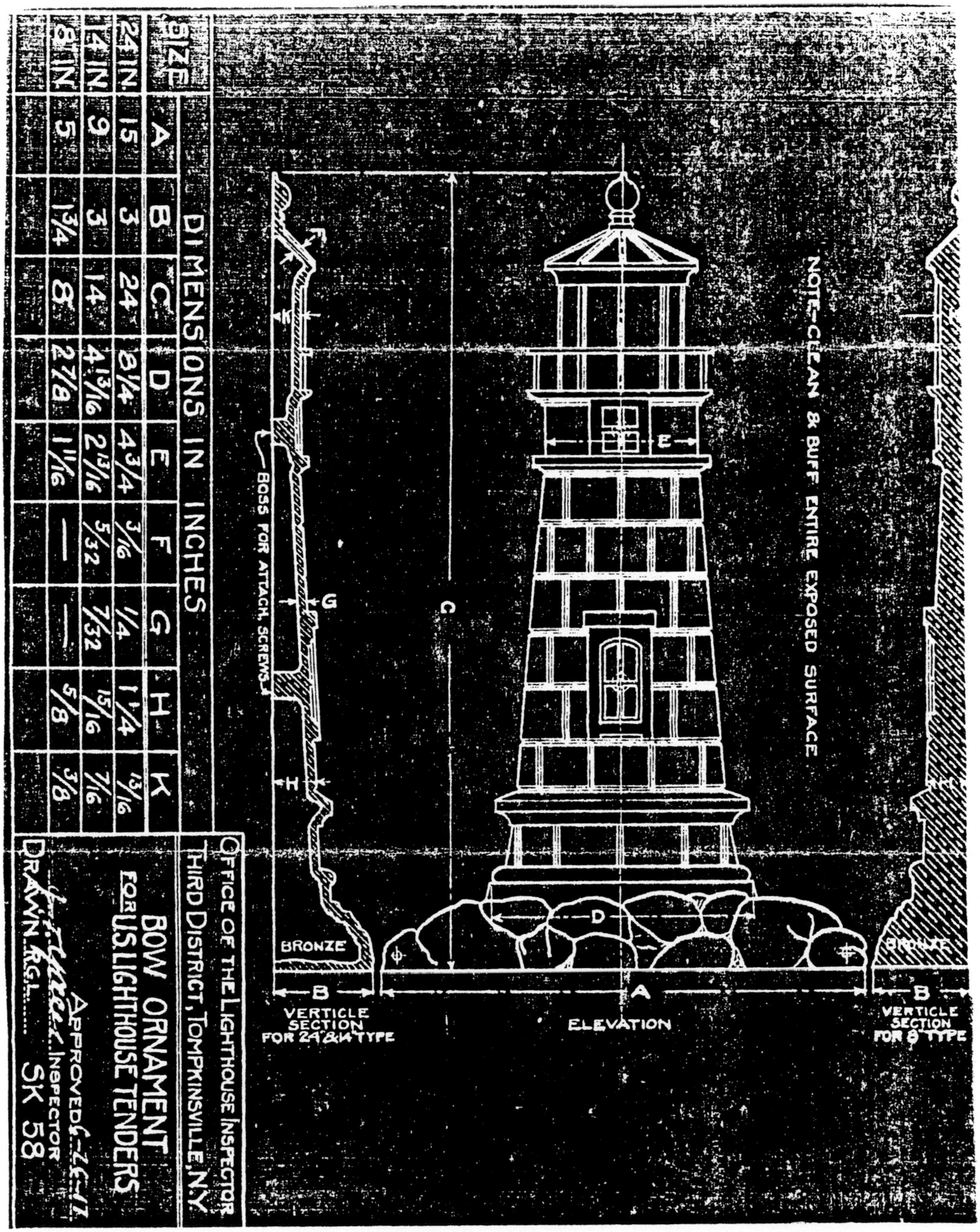
DIMENSIONS IN INCHES
SIZE A B C D E F G H K
24 IN. 15 3 24 8 1/4 4 3/4 3/16 1/4 1 1/4 13/16
14 IN. 9 3 14 4 13/16 2 13/16 5/32 7/32 15/16 7/16
8 IN. 5 1 3/4 8 2 7/8 1 1/16 — — 5/8 3/8
OFFICE OF THE LIGHTHOUSE INSPECTOR
THIRD DISTRICT, TOMPKINSVILLE, N.Y.
BOW ORNAMENT
FOR U.S. LIGHTHOUSE TENDERS
APPROVED 6-26-17
INSPECTOR
DRAWN R.G.L.
SK 58
BOSS FOR ATTACH. SCREWS
NOTE-CLEAN & BUFF ENTIRE EXPOSED SURFACE
BRONZE
VERTICLE SECTION FOR 24" & 14" TYPE
ELEVATION
VERTICLE SECTION FOR 8" TYPE

Lighthouse Depot at Ketchikan. A description of the tender appeared in the July 1915 *Lighthouse Service Bulletin:*

"*Cedar* is to be a double-bottom vessel, schooner rigged, 200 feet 8 inches over all, 36 feet molded beam, of approximately 1,750 tons displacement at 13 feet draft in salt water, and constructed of steel throughout. The propelling machinery will consist of a single screw, triple expansion engine of the vertical inverted type, with surface condenser, and the necessary auxiliaries which will be supplied with steam by two 3-furnace Scotch type boilers fitted for burning oil as fuel. Fuel oil will be carried in structural tank compartments located forward of the boilers."

The *Cedar* was big and tough, and the men who signed aboard knew they were headed for demanding duty in a desolate realm. The tender journeyed thousands of miles each year -- some 3000 miles alone, roundtrip, to the isolated sentinels on Unimak Island in the Aleutians. It was at Unimak's Scotch Cap Lighthouse in 1932 that the *Cedar's* crew solemnly attended to a final request for deceased lightkeeper Barney Lokken. His ashes were spread over the ground in front of the lighthouse.

Two years later *Cedar's* crew performed a more critical service, saving lives. The tender stopped at Five Finger Lighthouse in December 1934 to drop supplies and coal. The lightkeepers were ecstatic about the tender's arrival, since the entire lighthouse was frozen. One keeper was busy with a blow torch trying to thaw frozen pipes. Only moments after the *Cedar* came alongside, the lighthouse caught fire. With everything frozen, there was no water to fight the blaze. The station was completely destroyed except for a few outbuildings. Fortuitously, the *Cedar* was on hand to rescue the men, else they would have died from exposure. To the flustered lightkeepers *Cedar's* captain flippantly remarked: "I see you got the placed warmed up."

The early 1900s were the halcyon days for the tenders and their crews, with a high level of discipline and efficiency characterizing the service. Every tender flew the triangular Lighthouse Service ensign, a blue lighthouse on a white field bordered in red. Uniforms were authorized for tender officers and crewmen, both dress and fatigues. The masters of the tenders, stylish in dark blue wool jackets with gold braid and smart blue caps sporting the service insignia - a gold lighthouse and eagle - were tough-minded, durable men hand-picked by the Lighthouse Service.

Captain E. B. Johnson, master of the *Iris* and later the *Lilac,* was typically temperate:

"Captain Johnson was of the old school which sailed the seas before charts were issued. When cruising along the coast, Captain Johnson would make soundings, record them, and draw up his own charts. By doing this he was well equipped to sail in any waters he had heretofore navigated....Being a very religious man, he made a point of attending Sabbath services at whatever port he happened to be in on that day. If his ship was not in port, but was on a run down the coast, Captain Johnson would hold services in the after cabin. There was always some member of the crew who could play a melodeon, and the service would consist of hymns, a prayer, and a short talk on the Bible by the Captain."

The crews of tenders were hardy, sometimes raucous characters, willing to tackle long, grueling hours at sea doing jobs no one envied. Novice crewmen learned by doing, since there were no technical schools at the time to teach them the trade. Most started out as messmates, then went to deck jobs handling buoys and cargo or were assigned to the "black gang," an elite and bawdy fraternity comprised of oilers, firemen, and engineers who worked down in the greasy, torrid engine room. Some signed on quite young. A Ketchikan boy went to sea on the *Fern* in 1926 at age thirteen. He worked summers, seven days a week and earned $55 a month.

Many crewmen used tender work as a stepping stone to a better job. Swedish-American John Stenmark was serving aboard the *Madrono* in 1888 when a workboat, loaded with supplies for Point Conception Lighthouse, overturned. Stenmark courageously saved lighthouse inspector, Thomas Perry, who rewarded him with a transfer to a lightkeeper's post at Ano Nuevo. Similarly, Ted Pedersen was working as a deck hand on the *Cedar* in 1927 when a third assistant keeper's position came open at lonely Cape St. Elias Light in Alaska. (The third assistant had gone mad.) Pedersen, Alaskan born and half Aleut, convinced district officials that he was the right man for the job.

Tenders were lifelines to civilization for the keepers of remote lighthouses, and the call "tender comin'!" never failed to generate excitement. Most stations had a visit from the tender every three months; a few were lucky to have it visit once a year. As with most things in a lightkeeper's life, the tender's arrivals and departures depended on the weather.

When a North Pacific storm put out the light at Tillamook Rock off Oregon in October 1934, the keepers rigged a makeshift radio and called for help, as it was urgent that the light be restored before its absence caused a wreck. The desperate message made its way through the "wickwork," the lightkeepers' nickname for their communications network, and both the *Rose* and the *Manzanita* rushed to the station. Tillamook Rock was unapproachable, as rough seas continued to pound it. The keepers watched anxiously as the two tenders came in sight time and again, then moved off after deciding a landing couldn't be made. After three days the *Manzanita* risked sending a whaleboat to the battered rock. A hoist was improvised to haul up the whaleboat crew. The damage was so serious the *Manzanita* had to race back to the depot for repair materials. While it was gone two of the lightkeepers came down with influenza and were precariously taken off the station by crewmen from the *Rose*, then rushed to a mainland hospital. The "tender boys" were men of mettle.

From *All Among the Lighthouses*, By Mary Crowninshield
In the Collection of Barbara Gaspar

A more serious weather problem faced the tenders at lighthouses on the Great Lakes. At the end of the shipping season in December, they rushed to get the keepers off the lights before the winter freeze. All of the Great Lakes tenders had icebreaking bows, but if the freeze came too early in the season and thickened there was trouble. Just such an icy blast in late November 1929 sent the *Amaranth* steaming through the ice on Lake Superior to rescue the keepers at Stannard Rock Light, 30 miles off Marquette. It was dark when the *Amaranth* reached the lighthouse, whose keepers had switched on the low-intensity winter beacon in anticipation of their exit.

Amaranth slowed to a crawl and turned on its searchlight. An awesome spectacle of winter power greeted the tender crew. The tall tower was completely encased in ice and glistened like a castle from a fantasy tale. Long icicles hung from the gallery, and over the pier and the base of the tower the ice was several feet thick. The lantern, more than 100 feet above the lake, was wrapped in a shroud of ice, patiently deposited by minute droplets of spray. Were it not for the steady revolving of the winter beacon, Stannard Rock Light might easily have been mistaken for a frozen tomb. *Amaranth's* steam hose melted the iced entry door and freed the waiting keepers. In the spring when the tender returned to re-open the lighthouse, hours of chipping and steam thawing were needed before the keepers could go back to work.

Lightships that guarded the nation's far-flung navigational perils - Columbia River Bar, Nantucket New South Shoals, Blunts Reef, Diamond Shoals, Hen and Chickens, to name a few - were also cared for by the tenders. Many of the same tasks performed for lighthouses were also done for lightships. In order to service a light vessel, a tender had to moor off the ship's stern, then send pulling boats between the two vessels. With its go-nowhere mission, the lightship never traveled into port unless it needed repairs, and even then it did not move under its own power, but was towed by a tender.

Lightship crewmen saw the tender as their viable link to shore, for up until 1899, when the San Francisco Lightship was used to test Marconi's wireless communications, carrier pigeons and visits by the tenders were the only breaks in a lightship's monotonous routine. To the end, lightships were faithfully cared for by the tenders. As the lightships were, one-by-one, upstaged by modern technology in the 1970s and 1980s, Coast Guard buoy tenders towed them to shore and positioned the behemoth LNBs (Large Navigation Buoys) that replaced them.

Somewhat like floating warehouses, tenders brought everything lighthouse keepers and their families needed for life at sequestered islands, rocks, and seaposts. Food and household necessities came by tender, as did the 60-100 pound bags of coal for heating and to fuel the boilers in the fog signal house. These were unloaded directly onto a dock with a derrick or taken ashore by pulling boats if the dock area was too shallow for the tender to moor. Coal deliveries meant hours of backbreaking work, for the crews of both the tenders and the lighthouses, as the heavy bags were off-loaded and properly stowed.

In the 1920s coal for Boston Harbor's Lovell's Island Range Lights arrived in the early fall on the *Shrub* and was lightered to the beach and stacked in huge piles. The crewmen, mostly Cape Verdeans, carried the bags several hundred yards to the coal bin on their shoulders and sang as they worked. Light stations that were built atop steep cliffs had cable cars to haul the coal. Southeast Farallon Lighthouse off San Francisco had such a conveyance in the 1880s, pulled by a cantankerous mule who led the lightkeepers on a merry chase whenever she heard the tender's whistle, which signaled work.

Oil for lighthouse lamps (and later acetylene gas tanks) was also delivered by tender. The master or an inspector carefully measured the oil allotments and checked the keepers' account books to see that oil was not being wasted. There were serious consequences for discrepancies: Lighthouse Inspector A.M. Pennock, on his rounds in the Chesapeake Bay, reported, "The pay of the keeper of Turkey Point L.House has been suspended for the reason of her not rendering a proper account of the oil she should have on hand."

Frugality was the watchword of the Lighthouse Service, but it was, at times, carried to extreme. Inspector Harry Rhodes was said to have demanded that a California lighthouse keeper return an extra pencil to the stores of the *Sequoia* when it was discovered the keeper had accidentally been issued 13 pencils rather than the standard dozen.

Mail arrived at lighthouses by tender, as well as the keepers' pay, carried as gold coins in a special money belt worn by the tender's captain or the district inspector. Libraries of about 50 volumes in oak cases were circulated among the lighthouses as the tenders made their rounds, and an itinerant teacher was sometimes delivered to a station where there were school aged children, then picked up on the tender's next visit and transported to another lighthouse. Ministers were welcome aboard the tenders, and many a baptism or marriage ceremony took place with the tender crew looking on and the master as a witness.

If a new baby was expected at a lighthouse, a midwife might be taken aboard, and possibly a milk cow, whose seasick bawling could be heard long before the tender docked. Doctors traveled on tenders to care for the sick. In emergency cases, the tenders became waterborne ambulances. The *Goldenrod* found itself thus employed in the early years of this century when a keeper at Spectacle Reef Light on Lake Huron developed appendicitis. The tender pushed through December ice for 19 miles to reach the sick man, then rushed him to a mainland hospital.

Sometimes the sick weren't so fortunate. In the 1890s the *Madrono*, based in San Francisco, received a distress call from the keepers at isolated Southeast Farallon Lighthouse. It came by way of a sailing ship that had seen huge bonfires burning around the station. The desperate keepers, with no other means of communication, had been tending the fires for days, hoping some passing ship would see them and carry the news to San Francisco. With a doctor on board, the *Madrono* steamed to the island, but help came too late. Diphtheria had broken out; two of the children were returned to the mainland on *Madrono* in caskets.

The tender passenger who caused the most concern for everyone, including the crew, was the district inspector. His frequent travels aboard tenders assured their efficient operation and kept the lightstations and lightships on alert for surprise inspections. Lighthouse keepers were especially vulnerable, as they seldom knew in advance of an inspector's arrival. Most inspectors flew their personal flags as a courtesy, however. So the moment a tender was sighted on the horizon, a spyglass examined it carefully to ascertain if the inspector was on board.

Philmore Wass, who spent part of his childhood on Maine's Libby Islands Lighthouse, recalls the arrival of the inspector aboard the *Hibiscus* and his royal treatment:

"This was always a moment of high drama -- Father resplendent in his uniform, brass buttons shining, stepping forward to meet this godlike giant, Inspector Luther. Every eye of the audience was riveted upon them as they shook hands, turned, and marched through the boathouse and up the grassy path toward the houses. The urge to follow was too great to resist, so, keeping a safe distance, we all fell in behind, mothers with babes in arms, all the children, and, often, the horse, cow, and dogs. It was quite a parade."

The West Coast's legendary inspector was Captain Harry Rhodes, known for his trivial demands and parsimonious ways. He wore white gloves and checked every inch of a light station, examined the lightkeeper's books, eyeballed the brass for fingerprints, even perused the house in search of dust or bureau drawers out of order. He insisted a broom be used until it was stubble, a paintbrush not be discarded until the last hairs were worn down. While such extreme thrift caused many complaints, it earned Rhodes an enviable reputation as a tightfisted government manager.

Often, the most congenial characters found on the tenders were the crewmen themselves. These burly, hardworking men had big hearts, for those they served and for each other. Even the lowest hand was a trusted comrade and friend:

"Sport died of old age on July 19, 1926. He was sewed in canvas and buried at sea on the afternoon of the following day, 2 miles off Ludington, Mich. All hands were mustered on the spar deck where, with a few words for Sport to the effect that he had been taken from the waters and was now being returned to them, he was slid off the gangplank by a bunch of solemn-looking boys. He was given a salute and thus ended Sport, the best dog I have ever known."

The *Armeria,* from *Scribner's Magazine,* October 1896

Kirk Monroe, a 19th century reporter for *Scribner's Magazine*, described the arrival of the supply tender *Armeria* at Whitehead Lighthouse in the eloquent, though somewhat purple, Victorian style of his day:

....As the Armeria approaches Whitehead she is welcomed by a hoarse salute from its deep-toned, steam foghorn, and the inmates of the lighthouse gather on the rocks to witness this most interesting arrival of the year. She rounds the bold headland into a haven of glassy, forest-bordered waters, and her ponderous anchor rushes to the bottom, with a deafening roar of chain. Almost at the same moment the capricious freight-boat in which the supplies are to be carried ashore is lowered from the forward davits, and dropped back to an open port opposite the main hatch, from which the cases of oil are passed by a dozen members of the crew clad in working suits of brown canvas....

The grounds about the neat [keepers] dwelling-house are in perfect order; its exterior is bright with fresh paint and whitewash, and every inch of its interior is as scrupulously clean as soap, water, and persistent effort can make it. The assistant keepers appear in uniform; the women, if there be any, show to advantage in fresh calicoes, and the bashful faces of children, dressed in their Sunday best, shine above clean collars as though they too had been polished for the occasion. In the best room of the house, the walls of which are decorated with the keeper's marriage certificate, or honorable discharge from the army, in a neat frame, with photographs of light-houses or brilliant marine lithographs, the mate and clerk, pens in hand, seat themselves at a table and unfold portentous-looking papers. At the same time the yeoman opens his supply box on the floor, and displays its treasures as a peddler would those of his pack....

Author's Note

The Coast Guard recently introduced a new class of buoy tenders named, appropriately, for famous lighthouse keepers and lifesavers. The *Ida Lewis* was the first to roll off the ways. To follow will be such namesakes as the *Abbie Burgess* and the *Joshua James.* Flowers and shrubs and trees are being replaced by heroes! It's both a memorial effort and an educational effort - Tomorrow's students of maritime history will surely wonder what these people did to be so honored in the naming of important Coast Guard vessels.

Lightships

Lanterns of the Sea

No ship was ever pressed into service under greater need than the lightship, yet it remains one of maritime history's least celebrated vessels. It was ungainly in appearance, unpopular with seaman and cursed with a "go-nowhere" mission. An odd commingling of lighthouse, ship, light-keeper and sailor, the lightship struggled to claim its identity in an era when both lighthouse keeping and seamanship were admirable occupations. However, lightship service was afforded the glory of neither.

Its bulky hull and machine-cluttered deck lacked the sloping conical beauty of a headland lighthouse. No graceful stairs spiraled through its interior, nor iron-railed catwalk encircled its lantern. It did not anchor at distant ports as other ships did, and it returned home only for repairs and maintenance. Moored somewhere on the perilous border of land and sea - beacons lit, foghorn blaring and the doldrums of monotony bearing down upon its crew - the lightship gained attention only when it ceased to function.

England's Thames River is credited with the world's first lightship, the *Nore,* but in the days of Julius Caesar, Roman galleys were known to carry firebaskets on their masts as guideposts. No doubt other ships hung lanterns aloft and fired guns to signal other seaman, but the single-mastered sloop *Nore* was the first recorded ship whose sole purpose was to serve as a navigational aid. Its British designer received a patent in 1731 for the simple 12-foot crossbeam on the mast with lanterns suspended from either end.

The success of the *Nore* led to worldwide adoption of the lightship. In river estuaries, where mud and silt would not support a lighthouse foundation, and on harshly exposed rocks and reefs, where lighthouse construction was difficult, the lightship could anchor. It was also cheaper to build than a lighthouse and could be towed into port for repairs and maintenance.

In America in 1731, the lighthouse organization was still young and undergoing tremendous growing pains. It was slow to adopt many progressive ideas in pharology, a science dominated by the British and French whose navigational aids were the best in the world. Nearly 100 years after the *Nore* was lit, the United States recognized Britain's novel idea and placed lightships at Willoughby Spit, Virginia and Northeast Pass, Mississippi.

Virginia's lightvessel was moved to the less exposed location of Craney Island late in 1821. There it served successfully and prompted the government to put lightships at four more Chesapeake sites the following year. Most of these first lightships had no crew. A keeper, or lamplighter, was paid to row out to them at dusk and dawn to tend their lanterns.

Century Magazine, 1891

America's first "outside" lightship, or one that guards an exposed deepwater station, was anchored off Sandy Hook, New Jersey in 1823. It had a resident crew and guided sea traffic into busy New York Harbor. "Outside" lightships were also placed at Nantucket and Minots Ledge, Massachusetts, Diamond Shoals, North Carolina, Carysfort Reef, Florida, and Galveston, Texas. The bays, sounds and estuaries between Maine and Texas also received small lightships, but on the West Coast a lightvessel was not lit until 1892.

Initially, lightship design consisted simply of refitting an inactive ship of some type with lighting apparatus and crew. The *Nore* had been a cargo sloop, and many of America's first lightships were refitted revenue cutters. However, the lightship was soon designated a unique class of vessel with its own special problems, and architects began designing the lightship as a navigational aid afloat.

Among their considerations were the lightship's exposure to turbulent seas, its dual role as both ship and navigational aid, and its need to remain on position. The hull was flattened and bilge keels were added to reduce rolling in heavy seas. A huge mushroom anchor, weighing several tons, was installed to hold the ship in place, and living quarters were improved to ease the tensions of unhappy crewmen marooned at sea on a floating beacon.

Passing the Nore Lightship
From *Man on the Ocean*, 1883

Two sizes of lightships came into initial use. Small vessels displaced 100 tons or less, and larger lightships could go as high as 300 tons. The early lightboats had little or no motive power of their own. Experience with self-propelled lightships, able to keep their position in a storm or return to their position if mooring broke, soon proved the value of motive power.

The self-propelled lightships that appeared about the turn of the century were somewhat impotent, able to creep along at only about 8 knots. Their main concern was service as a navigational aid, hence most of the available space on board was devoted to the fog signal and lighting apparatus.

For many years, wood was the accepted hull material of lightships. Both captains and marine architects believed timber could withstand the seas pounding better than metal, but in warmer waters marine worms were a problem. A Charleston, South Carolina lightship rotted away in only 8 years, plagued by worms, and the *Carysfort Reef* off South Florida was eaten through in just 5 years. The careers of wooden lightships were more often thirty to fifty years, especially in colder seas, and only the apprehension of metal stress tolerance postponed the conversion to iron hulls.

The first American iron-hulled lightvessel was a refitted revenue cutter placed in service at Merrill Shell Bank, Mississippi in 1847. The problem of marine worms was absent, but limpets and barnacles encrusted its stationary hull. An instrument resembling a large hoe was used to scrape the pesky creatures away, and paint was added to inhibit rust. Most lightships were red, but a few yellow, beige and black were in service. They were identified at first by letters and later by numbers. This identification, along with the station name, was painted on the sides of the hull.

The first lighting apparatus consisted of lanterns encircling the masts. These were raised about 25 feet at dusk and lowered into a protective enclosure at dawn. The very oldest were simple oil lanterns with ten to twelve wicks. They rested on gimbals to keep them level as the ship rolled. Improved lamps and reflectors and fogbells, introduced at lighthouses in the 1820's, were also placed on lightships. Steam fog signals replaced bells about 1850, but most lightships retained a bell as backup in the event of boiler failure. At least one cannon was used as a lightship fog signal — the huge gun aboard the first *Diamond Shoals* lightship.

Being blown off station was a plight every lightship experienced, but *Columbia River #50*, the first West Coast lightvessel, embarked on the strangest lightship journey ever when it parted from its moorings in an 1899 storm. With no means of propulsion, the ship was at the mercy of wind and sea and drifted ashore at Cape Disappointment on November 29th. The Lighthouse Service had given it up for lost when a house moving company from Portland, Oregon submitted a bid of $17,000 claiming it could transport the lightship one mile overland to Baker's Bay and refloat it.

What followed was one of the most publicized salvage operations in maritime history. In only thirty-five working days, the #50 was moved through the forest and over a hill to the bay. Workers cleared a path through the trees, and a wooden cradle hauled by windlasses supported the lightship as it was pulled across land. It was successfully relaunched in the river and towed to Astoria for repairs. It then assumed the old station where it served until 1909.

Lightship #82, on Lake Erie near Buffalo was less fortunate. A November 1913 storm broke its anchor cables and swept its crew into oblivion. In May, the ship was discovered 63-feet underwater with its interior smashed. A titanic wave swamped the vessel and filled the interior before lifesaving efforts could be launched. A similar fate befell the *Cuttyhunk* off Cape Cod in a 1944 storm. It disappeared completely, and only the bodies of two crewmen and the anchor cable were ever recovered.

Ice was yet another hazard to lightship moorings. Seven Massachusetts lightvessels were torn off position in 1875 by floating ice. Worse however, was the total destruction of *Cross Rip Lightship* in 1918. Dislodged and crushed by a floe, it went down in pieces that were later discovered during dredging operations. Neither the bodies of the crew nor the moorings were ever found.

A second problem with lightship duty involved the crew itself. "Temperamental and impatient individuals are not for lightships," wrote James Gibbs in *Sentinels of the North Pacific*. Life on a lightship was both monotonous and terrifying, and crewmen had to be emotionally equipped to deal with the manic-depressive routine of daily lives.

A lightship crew averaged about seven men — no women ever served aboard lightships — whose actual workday was only about 4 hours. The men lived in cramped quarters, ate mundane meals, and did repetitious jobs without any change in scenery 8

New South Shoals Lightship, *Century Magazine*, 1891

months of the year. They took turns standing watch and doing mess duty, but there was usually only one cook. Meals often consisted of "scouse", a concoction of beef, potatoes, onions and whatever else the cook had on hand. Duff, sometimes flavorfully endowed with dried fruit, was the popular dessert.

Leisure activities were an important part of lightship duty, for there was plenty of time for relaxation. The usual nautical crafts of whittling, knotting and basket weaving were done, and a lighthouse tender brought libraries every few months. Occasionally, crews kept a pet. *Charleston #53* had "Tom", a hefty old, bristle-faced feline born on the lightship. His duties were simple — the eradication of rodents and the amusement of the crew — but the captain thought of him more as a typical sailor:

"When the boat comes to dock, he'll go ashore, get into a few scraps, and come aboard next morning with scratches and general evidence of having had a night of it. But you may be sure he'll never let the ship leave without him."

Disagreements aboard the lightvessel often came to a head at mealtimes, when men sat face to face partaking of one of the ship's few pleasures. On one vessel, the captain and chief engineer developed

74

such a distaste for each other, they hung a curtain across the table at mealtimes to separate themselves.

More often, seasickness kept shipmates separated at meals. Even the most seasoned sailors became queasy from the ship's ceaseless see-sawing. For the weak of stomach, lightship duty was a nightmare. A crewman assigned to the *Columbia River* light vessel became so violently ill he dropped 20 pounds in a week and had to be taken to a hospital by helicopter. In some instances, men plagued by seasickness had special amendments to their records excusing them from lightship duty.

The greatest danger for any lightship was not stormy seas or cantankerous crew, but the possibility of collision. Most reckoning vessels steered toward lightships, particularly in low visibility when fog signals were the only means of warning, and collisions were frequent. In fact, before the advent of radar, lightships could expect to suffer at least one collision a year. New York's *Ambrose* lightship was unlucky enough to be hit three times in one week, and *Cross Rip #5* was hit fifteen times in its 20-year career. Fortunately, most of these mishaps resulted in only moderate damage and lag time at a repair depot, but occasional serious losses occurred.

While off Cornfield, Connecticut in 1919, *Relief #51* was rammed by a barge and sunk in only 8 minutes. The crew narrowly escaped, having drilled faithfully in lifesaving procedures. Fifteen years later, *Nantucket #117* was severed in half in a dense fog by the 47,000 ton liner *Olympic*. All of the crew were picked up, but three later died from injuries.

The *Nantucket #117's* demise prompted architects to design lightships that were collision-proof. Watertight compartments and diesel-electric engines, that enabled a ship to get underway in five minutes should a collision impend, reduced the odds of fatalities. Heavier anchors were added — one weighed 14 tons — and better machinery was installed to reel them in. Finally, the silent signal of a radio beacon was given to lightships and a firm warning added about dependence on audible signals during fog.

Improvements aside, the spotlight on lightships was about to go dim. Lightvessel maintenance had become expensive, and manpower was needed elsewhere. The government had shown an established preference for lighthouses all along, and progress in lighthouse engineering had already upstaged a number of lightships. The *Minots Ledge* had given way to a huge, wave-swept, lighthouse. In mucky bays, sounds and estuaries, and on coral reefs, the revolutionary screw-pile and caisson lighthouses had sent dozens of lightships into mothballs.

Following World War II, the Coast Guard began a massive reduction in the number of operative lightships, replacing them first with super-buoys called LNBs, and later with huge, well-equipped Texas towers. One by one, American lightvessels went out of service until only the *Nantucket* remained. Many decommissioned lightships were converted to other uses, such as fishing boats. Some, like the lightship at Portsmouth, Virginia, were made into museums showcasing the history of the lightship era — a story that for the most part remains untold.

Lightships not only served where lighthouses could not, dropped anchor in waters other ships avoided, and remained on duty when other vessels ran for port, they also played significant roles in wars, participated in historical events, and taught marine scientists and architects much about the sea. During World War I, *Diamond Shoals #71* discovered a German submarine lurking off North Carolina. Knowing a number of nearby American warships were in danger, the lightship jeopardized its own safety by radioing a warning. The U-boat retaliated by torpedoing and sinking the lightship.

In 1988, scientists, reporters, and politicians boarded *San Francisco #70,* off the entrance to San Francisco Bay, to witness the first United States transmission of a wireless message. This unusual mission was a success. Despite an historic career of which 25% was spent under fog conditions, #70 was sold to private hands and later sunk off Alaska in 1941. In 1951, the *Barnegat* baffled scientists and seamen alike by surviving a May storm that neatly tied its anchor chain into a perfect overhand knot. The enormous anchor was found intact near position. The unexplainable mishap was rectified with the aid of the lighthouse tender *Sassafras* and a heavy boom.

When the career of the *Nantucket* ended, the last of America's active lightvessels disappeared — their gentle, rocking lanterns extinguished forever. In his book, *Keepers of the Lights,* H. C. Adamson paid humble tribute to the lanterns of the deep:

"Never in the entire history of the sea have smaller ships and fewer men been entrusted with bigger jobs or performed them with greater credit."

This article originally appeared in Mobil's *The Compass,* No. 3, 1984 and was reprinted in *Offshore,* June 1988, *Mariners Weather Log,* Winter 1988, and *Lighthouse Digest,* June 1994.

England's Great Storm

The Loss of the Eddystone Light

November 1703 was a month of turbulent weather throughout Britain, but especially in the south of England. A series of moderate gales began the second week of November and raged unremittingly for two weeks, keeping shipping impatiently in port, damaging the late autumn harvest, and dumping unseasonable amounts of rain on the English countryside.

Scoured by ceaseless winds, the English Channel churned like dirty water in a laundry tub. The lightkeepers on the Eddystone Rocks, 14-miles SSW of Plymouth, stood double watches in their 100-foot habitation — a wood and stone tower marking the channel's most disreputable navigational hazard. The tower's architect, Henry Winstanley, had planned to make repairs to the lofty sentinel before winter storms came. This was the second lighthouse Winstanley had built on the rocks, replacing a smaller one that had not withstood the powerful winter of 1698.

In the third week of November, the spell of foul weather finally broke, or so it seemed. Winds died down, and splotchy sunbeams peeked through the pall of clouds. Ships lifted anchor with overdue cargoes, fishermen headed out with their nets, and the keeper's of the Eddystone Lighthouse settled back into their normal routine, keeping watch both in the lantern and toward Plymouth's Barbican Steps where Winstanley and his repair crew would soon depart.

Hundreds of ships were already in the channel when Winstanley sailed for the Eddystone Light on Friday, November 26, 1703. Despite the widely-accepted superstition that setting sail on a Friday augurs misfortune, the sloop arrived safely at the lighthouse and began repairs. When darkness came late that afternoon, the beam of Eddystone Light, powered by an enormous candelabra holding sixty tapers, shone through the glass lantern. The lightkeepers had fastidiously polished the glass to produce the brightest possible beacon.

All was well for a time. The lightkeepers took turns in the watchroom and tended the candles, ever mindful to keep the tallow soot off the glass and to watch for birds that might collide with the huge beacon. Winstanley retired to his chamber to write in a journal and make plans for the morning's work, while his crew snored quietly from their cots.

A few hours after dark, bad weather returned, and by midnight a severe gale was blowing from the southwest. Heavy seas pounded the Eddystone Lighthouse, sending waves shooting up its walls and over the cupola. Each assault caused the great tower to shudder, and forced seawater through every fissure in its masonry and lantern. The powerful back-draught of water from each wave created a dangerous suction on the windows and doors.

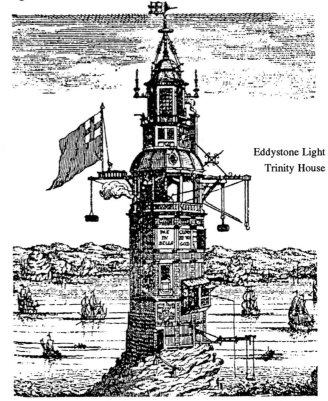

Eddystone Light
Trinity House

Winstanley reassured the vigilant lightkeepers and his terrified crew of workers. He believed the lighthouse, though in need of repair, was invincible. So firm was his conviction, some weeks earlier he had boasted to the press that he hoped to experience the worst storm in English history from inside his lighthouse. November 27 would grant his wish.

Residents ashore, occupied with their own survival, did not record exactly when the beacon on Eddystone Rocks disappeared. The tempest was at its peak between midnight and dawn on November 27, and at some point during those hours the lighthouse collapsed into the sea, leaving only a few metal bars protruding from the rocks as evidence that it ever existed. Winstanley, his crew, and the lightkeepers all perished.

The destruction of England's first offshore lighthouse was one loss of many in what has come to be called, simply, *The Great Storm*. Author Daniel DeFoe, well-known in later years for his classic tale, *Robinson Crusoe,* was intrigued with the disheveled landscape and shoreline he saw the day after the storm. DeFoe had written about two other calamitous events in England, the London Plague of 1665 and the Great London Fire of 1666, and he now resolved to chronicle this misfortune as well.

DeFoe traveled the countryside and circulated questionnaires to gather information about damage caused by the storm. Maritime investigations revealed that some 8,000 seamen had perished and nearly one hundred vessels, of all sizes, had gone down at sea, some without a trace. The quays in London, Yarmouth, Weymouth, Portsmouth, and Plymouth were virtually destroyed, and ships tied up at docks during the storm had been thrown high and dry. DeFoe was told that 700 sailing vessels moored along the Thames had been destroyed.

Daniel DeFoe, from the Library of Congress

"Several vessels had their sterns tossed up so high that the tide flowed through their forecastles," wrote maritime historian Edward Rowe Snow in *Astounding Tales of the Sea.* "The number of masts, bowsprits, and yards split and broken, the staving of heads and sterns and carved works, the tearing and destruction of rigging, and the squeezing of boats to pulp between other ships were beyond comprehension."

Huge tides raced up rivers, particularly the Thames and Severn. Livestock, including 15,000 sheep near Bristol, drowned. Riverbanks overflowed and inundated the land for 20 to 30-miles on either shore. Great loss was suffered by alehouses along the rivers, when cellars were flooded and kegs of beer were carried away.

Seawater and wind-borne salt intruded miles inland, spoiling ponds and coating pastures with a salt film so that cattle would not graze. Sheep who ate the grass on the downs near Lewes became sick and wandered about bawling for freshwater. At Cranbrook, 23-miles inland, all fresh water was spoiled. Hedges and vineyards at Tisehyrst, 20-miles from the sea, were coated in a fine white salt.

Hurricane-force winds and waves pounded dykes and banks, pulverizing the soil into minuscule particles that were carried inland on the wind and deposited on every object. Scientist Anton van Leeuwenhoek wrote: "The lower windows of my house, which are made of very fine glass and always kept well scoured...were yet so covered with the particles of the water which the whirlwind cast against them, that in less than half an hour thy were deprived of their transparency."

Leeuwenhoek also commented that at daylight on the morning of the storm, he took a reading of his barometer and "had never seen the quick-silver so low."

Only 123 people were killed inland, but damage to property and the land itself was inestimable. Daniel DeFoe was astounded to see the number of downed trees and attempted to make a count. He stopped when the tally in Kent alone reached 17,000! In areas such as Devonshire, Worcester, Gloucester, and Hereford, orchards were laid flat. In Oxford, a tornado leveled trees, barns, and homes and lifted a man into the air. Providently, he was deposited in a haystack and survived to relate his airborne adventure.

The harvest was nearly complete, and stacks of corn and hay lay in the fields. These were torn apart and scattered, as if some giant pitchfork had gone berserk. Barns were destroyed, often with livestock imprisoned inside. Windmills collapsed, but some caught fire before falling, due to the rapid turning of their blades that heated the wooden parts to kindling temperature.

In the cities, destruction was far worse. Brick chimneys and walls fell throughout London, killing many. Church turrets and steeples toppled. Lead roofs of London's churches, including Westminster Abby, tore loose and rolled up like paper scrolls. Streets and yards lay riddled with tiles and shingles, and many roofs were completely torn away. Demand for repairs after the storm inflated the price of roofing materials five times what it had been.

pass through unimpeded and relieved pressure on the upper part of the structure.

The wind was indescribably forceful at the height of the storm and left its mark on southern England from the Irish Sea to the North Sea. Its clamor caused people to mistake it for thunder, though there was actually very little rain during the storm. Church bells weighing several tons were tolled by the gusts, and buildings shook so hard their walls fell, leaving only the frameworks standing like skeletons. All over London, the din of wind and its destruction blared for hours.

Even the day after the storm, the wind still blew with ferocity. Milkmaids went out to find their

The Strand, 1907

Queen Anne and her royal family took refuge in the stone wine cellar of her palace at St. James until the storm passed. Nine of her royal guards were killed when the roof of their barracks collapsed on them. Nearby, the ornate weathervane at Whitehall was wrenched from its perch and flung into the street.

Despite violent winds on the rivers, the beautiful stone bridge over the Thames and the little houses atop its arches escaped injury. DeFoe believed the arches themselves were responsible for the bridge's durability, for they allowed the wind to

cows, but were bogged down in the swampy pastures. Some found their livestock drowned or hopelessly stranded in the muck. A few managed to fetch the animals, but found they could not carry pails of milk on their heads, as was the fashion, due to the strong wind. One young girl was blown into a pond and drowned after her head was injured by the wooden pail she carried.

Travel on land was nearly impossible for weeks after the storm, since roads were awash or made impassable by downed trees. On the water, it was even more difficult, due to the tangle of wreckage that blocked the harbors and the great damage to England's ports. Navigational charts required considerable reworking, since the erosive storm surge and tides had altered the topography of the sea and shore.

The Goodwin Sands off Dover were typical of the storm-wrought changes. Even in mild weather, these shoals shift constantly; but the storm of 1703 greatly reshaped them. At dawn on November 27, people ashore sighted castaways on the Goodwin Sands, seamen who had floated to the sandbanks at low tide on debris from their wrecked ships. A deep, tempest-torn channel separated them from the mainland; thus, their calls for help brought no response. As residents in the village of Deal watched in horror, the tide began to rise. Within hours, it would engulf the sands and drown every man.

Fortunately, there's a hero's tale to tell. Thomas Powell, a merchant in Deal and mayor of the town, offered a reward to anyone who would accompany him on a rescue mission. Several men volunteered, and Thomas was soon rowing to the Goodwin Sands in a sturdy boat. He was able to reach the sandbar before high tide and carried ashore half the survivors. The others were not so fortunate, as the tide broke over the sands before Thomas could return. Still, he was commended for his effort, but so grisly was the story of this tragedy that the government ordered a lightship anchored on the site to warn ships away from the treacherous bar.

The Great Storm, possibly the worst in England's recorded history, left scars on the landscape and in the hearts of those who experienced it. It has been likened to a New England nor'easter, an Asian typhoon, an Australian monsoon, a Texas cyclone, and a Florida hurricane all rolled into one. Without sophisticated weather instruments, scientists of the day had no accurate way to measure its severity. We will never know just how destructive it was, but descriptions from writers like DeFoe and Leeuwenhoek speak volumes.

An interesting footnote to the storm was the fate of the infamous Eddystone Lighthouse. It was said that on the night the lighthouse fell into the sea, a model of the tower in Winstanley's home in Essex crashed to the floor and shattered. Winstanley's widow saw to it that Parliament honored her husband as England's first offshore lighthouse builder and granted her a pension.

The dreadful Eddystone Rocks stood bare only a few years before a new lighthouse was erected by an architect who took his cues from Winstanley's

tragic finale. John Rudyerd built a simpler stone and oak tower on the rocks. It stood almost seventy years before being destroyed by a fire started by an overturned oil lamp.

Undaunted, England charged John Smeaton with the task of building a fortress on the rocks. He designed a stone lighthouse that appeared to grow out of the rock ledge and gave the tower a conical shape to throw waves back upon themselves. His lighthouse served a century before Trinity House decided to replace it with a taller, stronger edifice.

The builder of Eddystone's present lighthouse, James Douglass, was given knighthood for his accomplishment by Queen Victoria. The 133-foot monolith of stone remains one of the most exposed and dangerous outposts of the sea and a memorial to those who toiled to build all four Eddystone lighthouses.

Lightkeepers were removed from the tower years ago, due to the hazards and deprivations of serving there. It was converted to automatic operations that require maintenance only a few times a year. Storms still pummel it, but no human presence hears the crash of seas or feels the tower tremble in a gale. Only seabirds and spiders take notice when storm winds blow.

This article originally appeared in *Weatherwise,* October 1996.

The third and fourth towers at Eddystone in 1882

Bell Rock

Scotland's Proudest Sentinel

Robert Stevenson first saw treacherous Bell Rock at the age of 22, as he accompanied Scotland's first lighthouse engineer, Thomas Smith, on an annual inspection of seamarks in 1794. The rock lay 10-miles west of the Firth of Tay and was 16-feet submerged at high tide. It had devoured countless vessels with its elusive behavior. Young Stevenson was filled with dread as he watched its stealthy pinnacles disappear and resurface in a diabolical game of briny hide and seek. No peril in Britain more urgently needed to be marked. Little did Stevenson know he was destined to conquer Bell Rock in what would become known as one of the greatest achievements in maritime engineering.

Early Caledonians named the devious, reef Inchcape, but a persistent legend regarding the venerable Abbot of Aberbrothock, John Gedy, is responsible for its being called Bell Rock. He hung a bell on Inchcape in the 1300s to warn mariners of its rocky claws, but a villainous pirate named Ralph the Rover removed the bell to please an idle whim. Years later, his cruel joke forgotten, Sir Ralph came upon Inchcape in his own vessel and perished. The popular legend was later immortalized in a lengthy poem by Robert Southey who accurately captured the sly behavior of the Inchcape at low tide, when only the barest tips of its pinnacles showed —

No stir in the air, no stir in the sea.
The ship was still as she could be;
Her sails from heaven received no motion,
Her keel was steady in the ocean.

Without either sign or sound of their shock,
The waves flowed over the Inchcape Rock;
So little they rose, so little they fell,
They did not move the Inchcape Bell.

The pious Abbot of Aberbrothock
Had placed that bell on the Inchcape Rock;
On the waves of the storm it floated and swung,
And louder and louder its warning rung.

When the rock was hid by tempest swell,
The mariners heard the warning bell;

And then they knew the perilous rock,
And blessed the Abbot of Aberbrothock.

The sun in heaven was shining gay,
All things were joyful on that day;
The sea-birds screamed as they wheeled around,
And there was joyance in their sound.

The buoy of the Inchcape bell was seen,
A darker speck on the ocean green;
Sir Ralph the Rover walked his deck,
And he fixed his eye on the darker speck.

He felt the cheering power of spring,
It made him whistle, it made him sing;
His heart was mirthful to excess,
But the Rover's mirth was wickedness.

His eye was on the Inchcape float;
Quoth he, 'My men, put out the boat,
And row me to the Inchcape Rock,
And I'll plague the Abbot of Aberbrothock.'

The boat is lowered, the boatmen row,
And to the Inchcape Rock they go;
Sir Ralph bent over from the boat,
And he cut the bell from the Inchcape float.

Down sunk the bell with a gurgling sound,
The bubbles rose and burst around;
Quoth he, 'Who next comes to the rock
Won't bless the Abbot of Aberbrothock.'

Sir Ralph the Rover sailed away,
He scoured the seas for many a day;
And now grown rich with plundered store,
He steers his course for Scotland's shore.

So thick a haze o'erspreads the sky,
They cannot see the sun on high;
And the wind hath blown a gale all day,
At evening it hath died away.

On the deck the Rover takes his stand,
So dark it is they see no land:
Quoth Sir Ralph, 'It will be lighter soon,
For there is the dawn of the rising moon.'

'Canst hear,' said one, 'the breakers roar?
For yonder, methinks, should be the shore;
Now where we are I cannot tell,
I wish we heard the Inchcape bell!'

They hear no sound — the swell is strong;
Though the wind hath fallen they drift along,
Till the vessel strikes with a shivering shock
'O Heaven! it is the Inchcape Rock!'

Sir Ralph the Rover tore his hair,
He cursed himself in his despair.
The waves rush in on every side;
The ship sinks fast beneath the tide!

Down, down they sink in watery graves,
The masts are his beneath the waves!
Sir Ralph, while waters rush around,
Hears still an awful, dismal sound —

For even in his dying fear
That dreadful sound assaults his ear.
As if below, with the Inchcape Bell,
The devil rang his funeral knell.

When Robert Stevenson decided to attempt to construct a lighthouse at Bell Rock, he first investigated the legend of the bell, but could find nothing to substantiate it:

"Though a search has been made in the chartularies of the Abbey of Aberbrothock ...containing a variety of grants and other deeds from the middle of the thirteenth to the end of the fifteenth century, no trace is to be found of the Bell Rock or anything connected with it. The erection of the bell is not however," Stevenson concluded, "an improbable conjecture."

Stevenson had been appointed assistant lighthouse engineer to Thomas Smith in 1791 by the infant Scottish Northern Lighthouse Board. He had quickly absorbed all that his skilled master could teach him about the science of lighthouse construction and, had risen to a high level of respect among his peers. His work at the remote lighthouse sites of Little Cumbrae, Pentland Skerries and Cloch had so endeared him to the Commissioners of Northern Lights that they entrusted him with the development of the Bell Rock project, despite the fact that he held no University Degree and had never passed a Civil Engineering exam.

In 1800, only months after seventy vessels had piled up on vicious Bell Rock in one single storm, Stevenson landed on it for the first time to survey for possible sites for the proposed lighthouse. The need for a Bell Rock sentinel was more urgent than ever. Stevenson determined that a masonry tower approximately one hundred feet tall could be erected on the higher part of the rock for about 42,000 pounds sterling. He suggested a toll to raise part of the money, but it was 1806 before a satisfactory plan could be agreed upon in Parliament. The authorizing bill provided for a Treasury loan of 25,000 pounds sterling and a toll of 11 1/2d per British ton and 3d per foreign ton to be levied on all vessels passing the rock.

In the interim, Stevenson had married Thomas Smith's daughter, Jane. The couple had several children, one of whom would become the father of famous writer Robert Louis Stevenson. Robert Stevenson had thoroughly impressed the Northern Lighthouse Board with his supervision of the construction of lighthouses at Inchkeith and Start Point. With knowledge gleaned from a tour of English lights in 1802, Stevenson was able to design a tower and lighting apparatus for Bell Rock that combined the best ideas of the day.

Among his recommendations were the superior Argand lamp, which produced a cleaner, brighter and less fuel-consuming light; silvered copper reflectors to replace fragile mirror glass; copper or iron rooftops and galleries instead of flammable wood; and a tapered tower shape to reduce wave friction. Stevenson's vision into future marine construction was extraordinary, but as he began work on the bastion of Bell Rock, he had no idea he was building the model for many offshore masonry lighthouses.

Distinguished Scottish engineer John Rennie was appointed chief engineer of the Bell Rock project with Robert Stevenson as his assistant. Realizing the superior abilities of his younger colleague, Rennie voluntarily took a passive role in the design and construction of the lighthouse. Both Rennie and a now aging Thomas Smith were frequently consulted on matters concerning the tower, but in the end the Commissioners of the Northern Lighthouse Board agreed Stevenson was "...due the honour of conceiving and executing the great work of the Bell Rock Lighthouse."

In August 1807, actual work on the rock began. A workyard at Arbroath, twelve miles away, prepared the stone which was ferried out to the site by a sloop named the Smeaton in honor of the builder of England's famous Eddystone Lighthouse. A 67-foot Prussian fishing boat had been refitted as a lightship to house workmen on station. Aptly named the *Pharos,* its unique anchor was to forever alter the shape of vessel moorings. Stevenson and his crew had to contend with the North Sea's strong currents to keep the ship on station. A dead-weight anchor in the shape of a mushroom proved the most successful — so successful that it was adopted for lightship moorings worldwide. About fifty workmen lived aboard the *Pharos* in four-week intervals, chiseling away at the rock only at low tide. A forge was set up on the site to keep their pick axes sharp, but the sea allowed only fourteen workdays that first season. The men managed to erect a temporary beacon, build a 300-foot tramway for hauling the dressed stones, and begin excavation of the 42-foot diameter tower foundation. Highlighting the year for Robert Stevenson had been the birth of another son, Alan, who would achieve engineering fame on another rock of ill-repute — Skerryvore.

The first stone of Bell Rock Lighthouse was laid on July 9, 1808, after "much labour and peril, many an anxious hour," as Stevenson described it. The first course consisted of 123 stones weighing a total of 104 tons. It, and the 24-course above it, were solid through their interior to repel the heavy buffeting of the North Sea. Sandstone was deemed sufficiently strong for the center of these courses, but for the circumference Stevenson chose granite, making the Bell Rock monolith appear as if it grew out of the reef.

In order to expedite work and avoid danger rowing in from the *Pharos*, Stevenson decided to convert the temporary beacon to a barracks for the workmen. Seasick members of the work crew were happy to take up residence on the rock and, by the close of the 1808 season, they had completed three courses of the tower. It was not, however, until July 1809 that the lighthouse rose above the neap tide line and the crew was permitted full workdays. This milestone was justifiably celebrated with the firing of guns, hoisting of flags, and imbibing of rum by all hands.

The tower's solid cone of granite, through 25-courses, was completed by the end of 1809. Stevenson had prepared a special "Bell Rock mortar" for cementing the stone together in dovetail fashion. The final 66-courses were miraculously laid between May and July 1810. Ironically, it was always Stevenson who was last off the rock at the close of

each workday. Whether it was his devotion that inspired the workmen to toil so earnestly or their hatred of the rock, Stevenson was moved by their seemingly endless energies and later described them in his, *Account of the Bell Rock* as: "...somewhat like men stopping a breach in a wall to keep out an overwhelming flood."

The upper portion of the lighthouse consisted of five rooms and the lantern room, each 11-feet in diameter. To deal with the problem of confined space as the final courses were laid, one of Stevenson's men invented the balance crane to replace the derrick crane the tower had outgrown. This useful innovation saved much time and trouble. Stevenson, with characteristic regard for his men, was careful to give its inventor, Francis Watt, full credit for the idea.

The Strand, 1909

February 1, 1811 was a proud occasion for both Stevenson, now 39 years old, and the Northern Lighthouse Board. Bell Rock lighthouse was illuminated for the first time that night, closing a great void of darkness over Scotland's rock-riddled entrance to the Firth of Tay. A principal keeper and three assistant keepers, rotating leave ashore, were given care of the tower and its revolutionary beacon — the first colored light in service. Its red and white beams alternated by means of a revolving chandelier upon which seven reflectors and five red glass panels were attached. Scotland's first fogbells were also introduced on Bell Rock's christening night. Stevenson had ingeniously provided for their actuation by rigging them to the light's revolving mechanism.

There would be no confusing Bell Rock with its neighboring beacons of Scotland's East Coast. Its great red and white eye blinked with predictable regularity, and its bell tolled out in remembrance of the legendary Abbot of Aberbrothock.

Some 400 visitors came to the lighthouse during 1812, among them Sir Walter Scott who was a commissioner of the Northern Lighthouse Board and a friend of Robert Stevenson. Scott was very impressed with Stevenson's masterpiece of engineering, though his entry to it had been somewhat risky, up a 30-foot rope ladder.

When asked to sign the lighthouse record book the following morning, Scott composed a masterpiece all his own — *Pharos Loquitur.* Five years later, a shiny brass ladder replaced the rope Sir Walter had climbed to record his tribute to Bell Rock.

Robert Stevenson's achievement at Bell Rock was heralded worldwide as a milestone in pharology — the newly developed science of lighthouse construction and illumination — but his revolutionary ideas were to extend beyond the building of Bell Rock and into its keeper's realm. With the installation of the tower's unique reflector system, Stevenson realized that lightkeeping had reached a point of sophistication requiring its practitioners to be technically trained.

Hence, Bell Rock became the official training station for new Scottish lightkeepers. They were to be between the ages of 21 and 35, of sound mind and body, and willing to endure the dangers and monotony of life on a seawashed rock. Bell Rock's resident keepers received a higher salary than others due to the added responsibility of training incoming keepers and maintaining the newest and most treacherous beacon in the British Isles.

With the completion of Bell Rock Lighthouse, a great void of knowledge in marine engineering had been closed. It would not be the most awesome of Scotland's wave-washed sentinels nor the most tormented. Of Skerryvore Lighthouse, the most awesome, Sir Walter Scott said, "...the Bell Rock [is] a joke to it." But Bell Rock Lighthouse was the first and oldest of many successful rock lights in the British Isles.

Modernization, such as a hyperradial lens, electrification, RACON (radar-beacon) and a Tyfon fog signal have little changed Bell Rock's stalwart character through the years. Perhaps the best witness to its enduring importance can be found in the tower library — an inscribed, marble bust of Robert Stevenson and a copy of his *Account of the Bell Rock Lighthouse.*

Bell Rock, by Robert Stevenson's daughter, Jane.
Courtesy Northern Lighthouse Board

Neither bust nor book boasts a tale of personal triumph. They neglect to mention that Robert Stevenson never took out a patent on any of his marvelous inventions. They bear no testament to his establishment of pensions for widows of his workmen and lightkeepers or his discovery of the destructive marine worm, limnoria terebrans. They do not even allude to the fact that Bell Rock Lighthouse was and still is regarded as one of the ten great feats of marine engineering.

Stevenson's *Account of the Bell Rock Lighthouse* is merely what its title implies — an account of the planning and building of a monumental structure. In its day, it was required reading for every lighthouse builder and no doubt eased the apprehensions of American engineers who later faced such lighthouse projects as St. George Reef, Minots Ledge, and Sand Key. At the very least, it was Stevenson's tribute to the men who toiled on Bell Rock's ledges. His grandson, Robert Louis Stevenson, later called them:

> *...those, my kinsmen and my countrymen,*
> *Who early and late in the windy ocean toiled*
> *To plant a star for seamen, where was then*
> *The surfy haunt of seals and cormorants...*

This article originally appeared in Mobil's *The Compass*, No.3, 1985 and *The Highlander*, May 1988.

Recommended Reading

One of the most fascinating lighthouse-related biographies is Craig Mair's *A Star for Seaman: The Stevenson Family of Engineers*. It chronicles the dynasty of engineers who built Scotland's mighty sentinels.

Mair begins his story with Thomas Smith, the first "lighting engineer" in Scotland and mastermind of ten early lighthouses in that country. By 1719, Thomas was quite busy and needed an assistant. The man he chose was Robert Stevenson, then only 19 years old, but destined to build the infamous Bell Rock Lighthouse.

Ironically, the two men's lives would intertwine in more personal ways. Thomas Smith, widowed with a young daughter named Jane, became Robert Stevenson's stepfather in 1720, and in 1799 Robert married Jane. There began a blood-mixing of Smith and Stevenson skill and talent that would dominate Scottish marine science for almost two centuries.

The Stevensons built many lighthouses in Scotland, including Start Point, Dunnet Head, the massive Skerryvore, Muckle Flugga, Dubh Heartach, Flannan Isles, and Sule Skerry. But the most intriguing lighthouse legacy is the Bell Rock Light. As the foregoing article proves, it was an incredible undertaking, and it remains firmly fixed on its two-century-old foundation.

Mair capably tells the stories of all the Stevenson builders, combining technical information with human interest and gleaning previously unpublished information from family papers and interviews with descendents.

The book was published in 1978, but is still available at this writing.

Dramatic images of the lighthouse at Bell Rock, such as this one from the archives of the Northern Lighthouse Board, reveal a public fascination with this most dangerous yet compelling edifice!

Sir Walter Scott at the Bell Rock Lighthouse

"You must know that a committee of Commissioners for the Northern Lights are going to make a tour of Scotland and the isles..." excitedly wrote Sir Walter Scott to a friend in 1814.

Scott had been invited to accompany the Commissioners on a survey of the majestic masonry light towers that stood guard along Scottish shores. Leading the tour was Robert Stevenson, a renowned lighthouse builder, chief engineer for the Northern Lighthouse Board, and grandfather to the future poet and author, Robert Louis Stevenson.

Friends of Scott jokingly requested "that you do not break your neck or drown," and if he encountered any sea monsters, he should preserve them "in spirits." Lord Byron wrote a facetious letter to Thomas Moore suggesting Scott beware of wind on his adventure, and the Duke and Duchess of Buccleuch demanded Scott keep a journal detailing the voyage. Thanks to them, Scott left a first-hand account of the tour.

Many lighthouses were inspected, but the most memorable for Scott was the huge Bell Rock Lighthouse, fifteen miles off Arbroath, Scotland. The Commissioners' yacht anchored off the tower on the afternoon of July 29, 1814, and Scott stayed on deck until 11:00 that night watching the mesmerizing beam of the lighthouse.

The next morning, most of the group (but not Scott) were feeling seasick. Scott comically wrote that many "had a touch of a deep rolling pitching kind of heezie hozie, as the children call it, which forced the most reluctant and stout of the party to restore to Neptune our coffee and toast." Robert Stevenson wisely took the ill party to the lighthouse for a visit with the keepers.

Entry to the lighthouse was gained by a door thirty feet above sea. Visitors had a choice of being swung aloft in a chair, or clambering up a rope ladder with wooden rungs. Sir Walter Scott chose the rope ladder and noted that as he climbed, the pounding billows caused the tower to shudder and sent vibrations through the ladder. Once inside, the party ascended to the upper levels of the tower where the keepers had prepared a breakfast for them. Scott ate heartily, all the while amazed at the concussion of wind and wave on the huge tower.

Before the group departed, each was asked to write in the lighthouse logbook. Sheriff William Erskine of Orkney and Zetland, who was among the group, appealed to the poet in Scott: "You must give us something more than Walter Scott!"

Scott ascended to the lantern and peered out over the great expanse of gray sea, gathering inspiration. When he returned to the lower level, he took up the logbook and penned these lines:

Pharos Loquitur

*Far in the bosom of the deep
O'er these wild shelves my watch I keep;
A ruddy gleam of changeful light,
Bound on the brow of dusky night,
The seaman bids my lustre hail,
And scorns to strike his timorous sail.*

From a 19th Century Steel Engraving
Fords, Howard, & Hulbert

Writing from Abbotsford on July 24, 1814, Scott announced to Morrit his voyage in the lighthouse tender. 'I should have mentioned,' he adds, 'that we have the celebrated engineer, Stevenson, along with us. I delight in these professional men of talent; they always give some new light by the peculiarity of their habits and studies, so different from people who are rounded, and smoothed, and ground down for conversation, and who can say all that every other person says, and nothing more.' The anticipation expressed in this slipshod passage appears to have been partly realized. My grandfather was a man in whom Scott could hardly fail to have been interested and from whom he could scarce help but profit. Romantically minded, he had led a life of some romance. Two years before he had brought to an end the unique adventure of the Bell Rock Lighthouse; he had moved since boyhood as a pioneer among secluded and barbarous populations; his knowledge of the islands and their inhabitants was probably unrivaled; and his memory was rich in strange incidents and traits of manners, some of which have been preserved by Sir Walter in substance, while many others were doubtless boiled down into the general impression of 'The Pirate.'

Robert Louis Stevenson
"Scott's Voyage on the Lighthouse Yacht"
Scribner's Magazine, October 1893

Keeping Boston Light

America's First Official Lighthouse

Not only is it the oldest site of a lighthouse in America, Boston Light is also the only lighthouse that still has keepers on duty. Of the Coast Guard's 37,000 active duty billets, only three are for lighthouse keepers, and, at this writing, all three live at Boston Light.

The men - no Coast Guard women have served there - rotate duty two weeks on and one week off, with two men always at the station. They share many of the same tasks as the old wickies who cared for the beacon years ago. They clean, paint, groom the lawn, make weather observations, watch for boaters in distress, and keep the station machinery in order, including polishing of the second order lens.

What they don't have in common with their distant predecessors are the many comforts of modern lighthouse keeping. The station has a TV, VCR, and video games. There's a microwave oven in the kitchen, and of course, a telephone and radio.

"Lighting up" for the night has been greatly simplified too. Whereas the tower's first keeper had to kindle some fifty tapers on a huge candelabra and remain with them throughout the night, the current head keeper merely flicks a switch in the tower's base and heads off to bed. He's awakened by an alarm if the light fails during the night.

The station fog signal is even less demanding. In 1719 it was a booming cannon fired every half hour in fog. The current signal continually sends out a wire-thin beam of light to measure visibility and turns itself on when its probing beam fails to pierce the air. The keepers regularly fire up the old compressed air foghorns though, since they must serve if the high-tech signal fails.

No women have ever served at Boston Light, but many have left their thoughts in the station logbook. Until recently, families were permitted to live on the island, and a number of wives and daughters assisted the official keepers. Lucy Long lived at the lighthouse with her father from 1849 to 1851 and kept a colorful diary of life there. Her romance with harbor pilot Albert Small culminated in a proposal of marriage in the tower's lantern.

Georgia Norwood Emerson of Boothbay, Maine was born at Boston Light in 1932, the youngest of nine children, and claims to be the first child born at the historic light station. Her childhood was interrupted by a media blitz caused by author Ruth Carmen, whose 1937 novel *Storm Child* was loosely based on Georgia's early years. Travel and celebrity appearances related to the success of the book took Georgia away from her quiet island and family, and she was unhappy. Her family brought her home and suspended all contact with Ruth Carmen and her promoters.

In the 1970s the Coast Guard discontinued family assignments at Boston Light. The only female stationed on the island in 1992 when I visited was a slinky black cat named Ida Lewis. Her namesake was the intrepid 19th century lightkeeper of Lime Rock, Rhode Island. The feline Ida lived as comfortably as the three-man crew, but had to earn her keep. Without her expert ratting and mousing skills, the island would have been overrun with rodents.

Colonial Boston Light, courtesy of U.S. Coast Guard Archives

There was also a dog on the island, which the men had named Shadwell, in honor of the first keeper's black slave. The German shepherd was a useful watch dog and the first to alert the crew if visitors approached or a boat was in distress. He and the cat were companionship for the men, too. (See "Lighthouse Cats" and "Lighthouse Dogs" elsewhere in this book.)

Boston Light's premier keeper was George Worthylake, an honorable member of the Boston Bay Colony who lived on Little Brewster Island with his

wife and daughters and a black slave. The tower he tended was about 40 feet tall. Sadly, the keeper and his wife and one daughter died when the station boat capsized while returning to the island. With them was the slave, Shadwell.

The fiery Puritan preacher, Cotton Mather, delivered the funeral sermon for the Worthylakes, and Benjamin Franklin, a young apprentice in his brother's print shop at the time, wrote a poem about the family's loss called "Lighthouse Tragedy," and sold it on the streets of Boston. In later years Franklin recalled the piece as a wretched attempt at writing. No known copy of the poem exists. The Worthylake headstone still stands in Copps Hill Cemetery in Boston's North End.

Boston Light's history is replete with tales of storms, shipwrecks, and exciting events. Lightning hit the tower numerous times in its early years, because the Puritan ethics of the day forbid anything that might interfere with the powers of heaven. Lightning strikes in 1720 and 1751 resulted in fires that consumed all the wooden parts of the station and convinced the colony that Boston Light's great height tempted divine strokes a bit too much.

The lighthouse survived these early conflagrations, but not the American Revolution. It was occupied by the British during the war, then demolished with a keg of gunpowder as the defeated troops departed Boston. The current tower was completed in 1783. Historians believe some of its rugged stonework is from the original tower.

In the mid-nineteenth century, the lighthouse was increased to 102-feet and a spiral, cast-iron stairway was installed. The station was also increased in brilliancy with the addition of a new second-order French crystal lens that revolved on a series of small chariot wheels. The beehive of brass and 336 prisms still requires about four hours to clean. The oil lamps that illuminated the beacon a century ago have been replaced by a 1000-watt lightbulb.

Many keepers have chiseled their names and dates of service into the rocks around Boston Light, and there are several graves there. In November 1861 the square-rigger *Maritana* ran into heavy seas in Massachusetts Bay and approached the light in a blinding snowstorm. As the ship sighted Boston Light it ran aground on Shag Rocks. The lightkeepers were unable to render assistance. Bodies of the dead later washed ashore on Little Brewster Island and were buried by Keeper Moses Barrett.

One grave on the island is a recent one, nested amid plentiful dandelions behind the tower. The small gravestone marks the final resting place of Farah, "a mutt and keepers' companion for many years." She gave birth to eleven puppies while living at the lighthouse. Farah died in 1989. Many other dogs have lived at the station over the years.

The Blizzard of 1978 did considerable damage to the 4-acre island. Waves destroyed one of the concrete piers, boulders were tossed about like pebbles, and wind took a toll on the keeper's house and outbuildings. Though the city of Boston received 22 inches of snow, not an inch accumulated on Little Brewster Island due to the fierce wind. The old beacon remained lit throughout the storm, utilizing its emergency generator when power was knocked out from shore.

Surprisingly, only twice in its long career has Boston Light stood dark. It was put out by the British during the Revolution, but it was darkened deliberately from 1941 to 1945 to "avoid silhouetting ships for enemy submarines off the coastline."

Today, a host of caring preservationists look after Boston Light. The Friends of the Boston Harbor Islands conducts environmentally safe tours to the lighthouse. Visitors may climb the tower's 76 steps to see the beautiful optic. On the floor at the base of the tower is a rug with the image of the tower woven into its mesh. The Friends of the Boston Harbor Islands also have a home page on the web.

The local Coast Guard Auxiliary regularly relieves the keepers and helps maintain the station. And the Flying Santa Program sees that the men are remembered on Christmas Day for their steadfast duty to the light.

Hopefully, Boston Light will continue to be staffed with resident keepers, as a tribute to a long and venerable occupation and as a means for the public to learn about America's ligthkeeping past.

Versions of this article have appeared in *Mariners Weather Log*, Summer 1991 and *Navy Times*, March 9, 1992.

Boston Light Trivia

- In 1716 when the lighthouse was established, only about 70 lighthouses had been built in the entire world.

- Little Brewster Island has been called "Beacon Island" since the lighthouse was first built there.

- The beams from the tower's second-order lens cast ghostly images on nearby Great Brewster Island.

- The highest point of the island is a mere 23-feet above low water.

- The lens weighs 5-tons and turns on 12-inch chariot wheels.

- In the 1930s there were 19 children, belonging to three families, living on the island. They had their own school and an itinerant teacher!

- During World War II, when the government had concern about enemy submarines in the waters off Boston, the lightkeepers were issued two 30-calibre rifles for protection.

- The colonists of Massachusetts had to convince King George I of England to allow them to build the Boston Lighthouse. The king set the keepers' pay at 50-pounds per year, and a toll was levied on passing ships.

- In October 1994, Sally Snowman and Jay Thomson of Plymouth, Massachusetts were married at Boston Light. They are avid lighthouse enthusiasts and frequently stand in for the Coast Guard keepers of Boston Light so that the men can have "leave" ashore. I first met this special couple in 1995 and have since shared several lighthouse excursions with them. If Boston Light's strong beams have any influence over couples who tie the knot beneath them, Sally and Jay will have a long, happy life together! Every Christmas, they send me a lovely hand sketched card, like the one below, received in December 1996.

Old Boston Light, MA
Boston Harbor

89

Sentinel at Sandy Hook

Oldest Operating Lighthouse in the Nation

Sketch by Paul Bradley

Lighthouses are among New Jersey's most beautiful and cherished landmarks. More than a dozen of them once signaled to mariners at sea, extending both a welcome and a warning. Today, many have been discontinued and now serve as museums and the centerpieces of parks. Eldest of these sentinels is the Sandy Hook Lighthouse, guardian of the entrance to New York Harbor and one of the oldest structures in the state.

New Jersey's northernmost exposed beach is a 5-mile strip of natural sand that points like a finger toward busting New York City. In Colonial times this slender spit, called Sandy Hook, was likened to an extended arm holding a lamp that beckoned newcomers to the land of promise.

Perhaps the idea of the "lamp" came from the strand's first owner, an English Quaker named Richard Hartshorn, who probably kept a bonfire or fire-basket burning on the spit in the mid-1600s to warn ships. His beacon, though crude, would have been a truly welcome sight from sea, but also a dreaded one. Sandy Hook was, and remains, one of the most notorious navigational hazards on the Eastern Seaboard. It's estimated that if all the skeletons of shipwrecks off Sandy Hook were laid end to end, they would form a line that would stretch all the way to Barnegat, more than forty miles away!

In 1679 descendants of Richard Hartshorn suggested to Governor Carteret that a lighthouse be placed on the northern tip of Sandy Hook, but nothing was done until 1761 when a tract of four acres was purchased from the Hartshorn family for £750 and a lottery was established to raise funds to build a lighthouse.

In 1764 the lighthouse was completed, a 106-foot rubblestone tower of octagonal shape with a black iron lantern. Forty-eight oil lamps made a beacon visible almost 15 miles at sea. White-washed to make it stand out against the beige sands and cedar scrub, it was officially placed in service on the night of June 11, 1764. Taxes collected on passing ships, based on their tonnage, maintained the lighthouse and paid its builder, Isaac Conro, and the lightkeeper's salary.

The first keeper, though well-respected, had a difficult life. He was expected to remain at the lighthouse year-round, and if leave were necessary, to find and pay a replacement keeper. Firewood was at a premium, and winters on the spit were cold and windy. Two cows were kept, but they had little appetite for beach grass and stumbled about the dunes bawling from the bite of constant sand spray. The garden wasn't much of a success either, as few vegetables would grow in such a sandy, wind-scoured patch overlooking the sea.

During the Revolution, the Provincial Congress of New York decided to "render the lighthouse entirely useless" before the arrival of the British fleet, who might find the light to their own benefit. The illuminating apparatus was removed and hidden. Later, the British tried to destroy the tower with cannon fire but found its walls impenetrable. Impressed by its strength, they decided to use the tower as a base for raids on the Americans, and it remained under their control until the war ended.

Interestingly, during this time the peninsula of Sandy Hook was cut off from the mainland by a narrow inlet. General Howe, retreating from the

Battle of Monmouth in 1778, had to build a bridge to reach what he called "Sandy Hook Island." By 1800 the inlet had become choked with sand and was closed, but in 1810 and again in 1830 Sandy Hook was shown on maps as an island.

The strand has also altered its size and shape over the centuries, sometimes quite narrow in spots; sometimes acquiring peculiar bulges. A strong long-shoring effect, coupled with vulnerability to storm winds and waves, makes Sandy Hook a fickle strip of sand. When the lighthouse was built in 1764, it stood 500 feet from the northern tip of the peninsula. Today, it sits over a mile from the tip. Sand buildup continues to distance it from the channel.

Though the lighthouse stood on New Jersey soil prior to the Revolution, it belonged to New York and was called New York Light. After the Revolution, the two factions argued over ownership of the historic tower, while the new Federal Government, anxious to mollify each, assumed control of the sentry and changed its name to Sandy Hook Lighthouse. It was relighted, along with eleven other Colonial-period lighthouses. A long tenure of peaceful service followed, punctuated by occasional historic events and curious visitors.

Among the unusual guests were a continuous stream of treasure hunters lured to Sandy Hook by rumors that Captain Kidd had buried booty there. The area around old Horseshoe Cove was ardently combed, since near it stood a huge pine called "Captain Kidd's Tree." Supposedly, Kidd buried some of his treasure in the vicinity of the tree, but none has ever been found.

About 1850 a lightkeeper complained that there was no entry to the cellar under the house. No one knew why the cellar entrance had been closed off, but permission was granted to construct a door and stairway to the basement. When the keeper removed the floorboards to begin construction and climbed down into the dark recess with a lantern, he was greeted by an eerie scene.

Seated at a table was the skeleton of a man clothed in simple garments. Ashes lay in a makeshift fireplace along one wall. Later, a search revealed the skeletons of four other men and a woman buried beside the tower. Neither the skeleton in the basement nor those buried outside were ever identified. Some historians speculate these were American spies caught and executed by the British.

In the 1850s the Lighthouse Board inspected the lighthouse and found it quite sound. In fact, it was ranked third in the nation for efficiency and fitness. Eighteen Argand lamps and reflectors illuminated the lantern at this time. The Lighthouse Board suggested these be replaced by a Fresnel lens of third order — state-of-the-art in optics at the time. This was done in 1857, and a few years later the inside of the tower was lined with bricks for added stability and a new iron staircase replaced the old wooden one.

The only other changes to the lighthouse were the replacement of its iron lantern cap in 1880 and electrification around the turn of the century. Otherwise, it remains much the same as it was on the night it first shone a warning beam. Other than the short respite from its duties during British occupation, it has shone a light continuously since it was established in 1764.

In 1962 the lighthouse was modernized with automatic machinery to reduce operating costs. A timer switched the beacon on and off each day, and a bulb changer moved a new bulb into position when an old one burned out. With its lightkeepers gone, the ancient tower became vulnerable to the elements and vandalism. The public complained bitterly.

In 1964, the 200th anniversary of its service, Sandy Hook Lighthouse was declared a National Historic Landmark. Both the U.S. Coast Guard, which operates the beacon, and the Gateway National Recreational Area surrounding the lighthouse, vowed to help preserve this historic and vital relic.

The lighthouse was further honored in 1990 during bicentennial celebrations for the U.S. Coast Guard. Since it is the oldest lighthouse tower in the nation and still operating each night, it was featured on a commemorative series of five postage stamps.

Sandy Hook Lighthouse celebrated its 233nd birthday in June 1997 — an old soldier still on watch, with no plans to retire soon. It is the patriarch of American lighthouses and one of New Jersey's best-loved and most-visited landmarks. Who knows how much longer it will serve? A recent inspection of the tower showed it to be in good shape, and the Coast Guard has no immediate plans to remove it from their light list.

For more information on Sandy Hook Light and other New Jersey lighthouses, contact the New Jersey Lighthouse Society, P.O. Box 4228, Brick, NJ 08723.

This article is an updated version of "Sandy Hook Lighthouse," which appeared in *Mariners Weather Log,* Winter 1991.

MAIN LIGHT, SANDY HOOK, AND KEEPERS' HEN-COOP.

LIGHTING UP SERVICE STATION AT SANDY HOOK.

Upper Right: *From Wilderness to Sea*, 1866, A.B. Nims & Co.

All Others: "Sandy Hook in 1879," George Houghton, *Scribner's Magazine*, 1879.

Cape Florida Lighthouse

Oldest Structure in South Florida

Key Biscayne, with its graceful palms and tawny beaches, is one of Florida's most idyllic retreats, but it wasn't always so accessible. This barrier island's first inhabitants were probably the Tequestas, a tribe of the Calusa, who left behind shards of pottery, bones, and tools that fascinate archaeologists today. Ponce de Leon stopped here in 1513 and called the island Santa Marta. The origin of the name Key Biscayne is unsettled, but may have been given by a Spaniard shipwrecked there in the 1500s who pined away for his native Bay of Biscay.

Almost three centuries later, Florida became a territory of the United States. With miles of coastline and myriad perils, the government set about marking its shores. One of the strategic spots chosen for a lighthouse was Key Biscayne, at the northern fringe of the Florida Reef. The Gulf Stream hugs the shore closely here, and the strait is riddled with dragon's teeth coral capable of ripping open the strongest ship's hull.

The Davis family, who owned most of Key Biscayne but resided in St. Augustine, sold three acres of the key to the government for $225. On this plot on the south end of the key was built the Cape Florida Lighthouse and keeper's dwelling in 1825 at a cost of $16,000.

At the time, the only residents of the key were a few territorial squatters. John Dubose, the District Inspector of Customs and a former Navy officer, was appointed to keep the lighthouse. He brought to the key his wife, five children, and two free blacks - the first Americans to live on Key Biscayne. The family lit the tower for the first time on December 17, 1825.

Florida's Dade County was a virtual wilderness in those years. The tiny settlement of Miami would have fit inside a modern-day mall. There were no close neighbors for the Duboses, and the ships passing the lighthouse were only dots on the horizon. It was a challenging Florida frontier existence - insects, heat, isolation - but there were definite pleasures.

The golden sands, mangroves, and opaline seas teemed with wildlife. Manatees swam lazily offshore, turtles and conchs provided delicious stock for the soup tureen, long-legged birds strutted in the swaying grasses and tidepools. John James Audobon paid a visit to study and sketch the key's birds and was amazed to see first-hand a comely Great White Heron. Botanist and physician, Dr. Henry Perrine, sent plants and trees from Mexico for the Dubose family to cultivate.

In 1835 a hurricane swept the key and caused damage to the lighthouse and keeper's quarters. The storm surge also destroyed many of the imported plantings and left the key with much standing water. A more devastating invader arrived about this same time. Dr. Benjamin Strobel came from Key West by ship to collect sand, tons of it, to use in the construction of a hospital. While the beach appeared to have an endless supply, Strobel probably had no idea he was interfering with the ecological balance of the key.

The worst tribulation for the lighthouse came a year later when Seminoles, angered by government abuses and false promises, took revenge on the white settlers in the area. In January 1836 a family near what is today Ft. Lauderdale was massacred. John Dubose moved his family to Key West for safety and stayed on at the lighthouse with his assistant, John Thompson, and his helper, a free black named Aaron "Henry" Carter.

Courtesy Bill Baggs State Recreational Area

A dramatic 19th century engraving shows the burning of Cape Florida Light. Keeper Thompson is pictured on the lantern, as Seminoles fire at him from the ground and pillage the station.

Courtesy of the
U.S. Coast Guard Academy Library

Fortuitously, Dubose was in Key West celebrating his birthday on the afternoon of July 23, 1836 when Seminoles attacked the lighthouse. Thompson and Carter had taken refuge from the heat and were resting in the keeper's dwelling at around 4:00 p.m. when some fifty warriors came screaming into the compound. The two keepers ran into the brick tower and barred the door. Gunfire was exchanged, then the Seminoles shot a fiery arrow into the base of the lighthouse where barrels of whale oil for the lamps were stored.

Frantic, Thompson and Carter raced up the wooden stairs to the lantern. Within minutes, the tower became a blazing chimney. The lantern deck grew frying pan hot, and the men clambered to the edge to escape the heat, but they were met with a shower of bullets. Their dilemma was formidable - stay on the lantern deck and be fried alive or step to the gallery edge and be shot.

In agony, Carter attempted to jump but was shot and fell dead beside his comrade. Thinking to end his own misery, Thompson picked up a keg of gunpowder and hurled it into the inferno below him. The explosion shook the tower from top to bottom, but instead of killing Thompson, it caused the flaming timbers to drop to the floor of the lighthouse and smolder.

Nearly naked and badly burned, Thompson lapsed into a painful sleep. Thinking both keepers dead, the Indians departed, but not before they looted and burned the keeper's house and stole the station boat -- the only link to the mainland.

When morning came, the sun burned down on Thompson's tortured flesh. His hair was gone and several fingers and toes were shot off. Worst of all, there was no way to get down from the 65-foot tower. The scene below looked like a war zone.

Even the trees had been decapitated. Adding to Thompson's misery were the notorious Key Biscayne mosquitoes feasting on his flesh.

Carter's body had begun to reek in the heat. As noon approached, and the scorching July sun blazed down on him, Thompson passed out. A short time later, voices jarred him to consciousness, and he was able to raise himself enough to see a schooner at anchor just offshore.

It was the USS *Motto*, a Navy ship that had seen the glow of flames at Cape Florida the night before and came to investigate. Imagine the crew's surprise when they discovered Thompson on top of the 55-foot lighthouse, clinging to life. There began the ordeal of rescuing Thompson. Numerous contraptions, including a kite, were tried to get a line up to Thompson. After several hours, a line fired from a musket snagged on the lantern, and a crewman was able to scramble up the lighthouse to rescue the agonized keeper. Carter's body was brought down and buried beside the lighthouse.

Thompson's burns and musketball wounds healed, but he was too crippled physically and emotionally to return to duty at Cape Florida Light, and the tower was in such terrible condition many months would pass before it returned to duty. It was repaired with new brickwork and relit in 1846 after troubles with the Seminoles died down. By this time Key Biscayne was a more peaceful place, and it was beginning to attract more settlers and speculators.

The cost for the refurbished tower was $7995. Winslow Lewis let out the contract for construction and installed his patented illuminating apparatus. (Joan Gill, author of *Key Biscayne*, relates that Lewis overcharged the government and reportedly pocketed an 800% profit on the deal!) Reason Duke was given the job of keeper at a salary of $600. per year. Duke relit the tower for the first time on the night of April 30, 1847 -- a much-needed sentinel after the loss of lighthouses on Sand Key and at Key West in the terrible hurricane of October 1846.

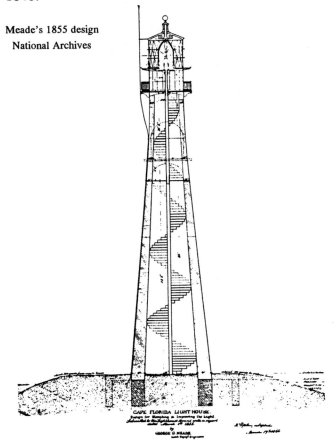

Meade's 1855 design
National Archives

In the 1850s, the tower's height was increased to 90-feet and it was given a sparkling new second-order fixed Fresnel lens. It was also whitewashed to make it easily visible against the golden sands of Key Biscayne. These improvements came after an inspection of lighthouses and a reorganization of the government body that oversaw them. More than 500 wrecks occurred off Florida's Atlantic Coast between 1840 and 1850, and many were blamed on the inefficiency of navigational aids. George Gordon Meade, then a lieutenant and a civil engineer working for the newly-formed Lighthouse Board, was given the task of making the improvements. His decision to add height to the tower and increase its brilliancy made it visible at least 20-miles at sea -- a necessity to assure that vessels did not run aground on the reef looking for the beacon. (Later, Meade would gain fame as the general who defeated Robert E. Lee at Gettysburg.)

The handsome new optic at the taller Cape Florida Light was barely baptized before it was destroyed during the Civil War when rebels put out the beacon to prevent it from aiding Union forces. Keeper Simeon Frow was helpless to halt the angry men who barged into his home in August 1861 and held him a gunpoint while others climbed the tower and shattered the great lens. The beacon was not returned to service until 1868. Frow's son, John, became the new keeper.

With the construction of Fowey Rocks Lighthouse in 1878, only a few miles offshore on the perilous reef where the HMS *Fowey* wrecked in 1748, the Cape Florida Light was discontinued. The tower stood dark and neglected for many years. In the 1880s its empty keeper's house burned, leaving only a shell of brick. In a letter to the Dubose family in 1890, John H. Duke wrote: "The old brick Tower stands there Solitary and alone like it was a monument for some departed one."

In 1903, Waters S. Davis, heir of the Davis family that had served at Key Biscayne before its demise, bought the abandoned lighthouse property from the government for $400. Waters had moved back to Key Biscayne a few years before and had made money farming such crops as pineapple, bananas, bamboo, coconuts, coffee, oranges, and lemons. He had rebuilt the old keeper's cottage and returned the compound to its former beauty. About this same time, tourists to Florida began to enjoy trips to Cape Florida to see the old lighthouse.

Some ten years later the lighthouse was passed into the care of James Deering, a wealthy and retired entrepreneur who had come to Key Biscayne to found his own private paradise. The transfer of the lighthouse into his hands came with the promise that it would be restored; hence, Deering sent to Washington for blueprints. His letter stirred up enormous controversy about the legality of anyone, save the government, owning the lighthouse and its surrounding property. Deering won a temporary deed and spent considerable money and manpower in 1918 and 1919 restoring the aging lighthouse.

In the 1920s, development of Key Biscayne for housing began. A causeway was built to nearby Virginia Key in 1941 then extended to Key Biscayne in 1947, opening the area to further development. Resorts and beach clubs followed. A wealthy Cuban couple bought the lighthouse property and other acreage from the Deering estate in 1948 for a hefty $1.5 million, despite the tower being dangerously close to the water's edge and boarded up and the keeper's cottage in a shambles. The couple offered the lighthouse to the National Park Service, which refused it at first but later helped the State of Florida buy it for a pricetag of $8.3 million.

By 1960 more than 3000 people had taken up residence on the key, and not surprisingly, the first high-rise came in 1967. This same year the Bill Baggs Cape Florida State Park opened, named for a Miami Herald editor who had been instrumental in its creation. The lighthouse was again restored and a replica of the old keeper's cottage was built beside it.

In 1978, a century after its decommissioning, the tower was ceremoniously relit by the Florida Department of Parks and returned to the Coast Guard *Light List* as a navigational aid. In 1996 more renovations to the tower and keeper's house were completed. The most striking change was the addition of a coat of bright white paint to the tower, returning it to its former 19th century glory. As the oldest standing and operating structure in South Florida, it has been given a new lease on life and long overdue honors for its unique contributions to the settlement of the Sunshine State. Preservation of this lighthouse and others in Florida has become the cause of the newly-formed Florida Lighthouse Association, which met for the first time in July 1996 at Cape Florida Lighthouse.

This is an updated version of an article that originally appeared in *Mariners Weather Log*, Summer 1988.

Recommended Reading

It was unfortunate that during the four years I resided in Florida (1979-1983) there was no definitive book on Florida's lighthouses. The Sunshine State has the second longest coastline in the U.S. and a colorful maritime history, complete with the tales of more than 30 lighthouses. Love Dean's *Reef Lights* was handed to me in 1982 by a librarian at Sanford Public Library, a lady who knew I was searching desperately for information on Florida's lighthouses. Dean's stories of the screwpile lights only whetted my appetite for more information, but there was little to be found without the resources of time and money to dig. I managed to do a modicum of research, much of it on-site, and recorded material remotely related - stories people told me, descriptions of the towers, and comments other authors had written about them. Eventually I had enough material to write my own book, albeit a small tome with its share of errors and gaps. Thankfully, readers welcomed it, pleased to have something in hand about the Sunshine Sentinels. Since the publication of my *Guide to*

Florida Lighthouses, several books have followed on the subject. Four authors deserve mention here for their excellent work:

Thomas Taylor's *Territorial Lighthouses of Florida 1821-1845* is thoroughly researched and readable. Tom's love for lighthouses began in childhood on Monhegan Island, Maine, and he now has a book underway on the lighthouse there. Tom also wrote a fine short history of the Ponce de Leon Inlet Lighthouse. Both books can be obtained by writing P.O. Box 238014, Allandale, FL 32123.

Kevin McCarthy's *Florida Lighthouses* is a handy paperback with interesting history and lovely paintings by William Trotter. Especially helpful are detailed directions for reaching the accessible lighthouses. The book was published by University of Florida (where McCarthy teaches) at Gainesville.

Coast Guard Officer Neil Hurley has self-published three fine books on Florida's sentinels and has a great site on the World Wide Web that is one of my favorite stopping places when I'm "surfing" for lighthouse information. His *Lighthouses of the Dry Tortugas* is my favorite, but also he has produced *Keepers of Florida Lighthouses 1826 - 1839* and *An Illustrated History of Cape Florida Lighthouse*, which is certainly apropos here. Hurley's three books are reasonably priced and can be ordered from Historic Lighthouse Publishers, 4511 Lark Lane, Alexandria, VA 22310.

For readability and broadness, Joan Gill's *Key Biscayne* is the best book yet to chronicle the Cape Florida Lighthouse. Though it treats only the lighthouses at Cape Florida and Fowey Rocks, their stories are detailed and deliciously intertwined with the larger picture of the settlement and growth of South Florida. All lighthouse history is set against the backdrop of larger stories of our nation and its development from fledgling colonies to a premier national power. Florida's role in that story is particularly fascinating, since it was among the first areas explored by westerners and always a sought-after peninsula.

Joan Gill has a wonderfully deft pen, which combined with a multitude of archival material and tedious research, presents a compelling story. I owe Joan many thanks for providing important information for the update of the previous article on Cape Florida Lighthouse, which appeared in print eight years before Joan's *Key Biscayne*. For anyone who's ever been to Key Biscayne or likes lighthouses, Joan's work is a "must read." Write Pineapple Press at P.O. Box 3899, Sarasota, FL 34230.

Tybee Island Lighthouse

Old Sentinel of the South

To give some hint of their state's size, Georgians recite the phrase, "From Tybee Light to Rabun Gap." This near 300 mile stretch traces the twists and meanders of Georgia's most important river - the Savannah - and defines the state's northeastern border. Where the Savannah River opens to the sea is one of the South's most elegant and active ports, marked for more than two centuries by the tall lighthouse at Tybee Island.

Historians can't agree as to when a beacon was first placed at Tybee Island, but an official one was certainly in use by the American Revolution, for among Georgia's gifts to the fledgling Federal Government in 1791 was the brick lighthouse at the mouth of the Savannah River. General James Oglethorpe, founder of the Georgia Colony, had ordered a watch tower built on this site in 1736 to aid the growing commerce in the south's second-largest port, but the tower was quickly destroyed by a storm. A second wooden tower was built in 1742 but it too was smashed by a gale, as was its 1748 replacement.

Determined to outwit the ravages of wind and sea, Georgians built their first true lighthouse in 1773, abandoning wooden walls for brick and a lantern in which a candelabra burned each night. Tybee's feeble beacon joined a mere half dozen other lights in the colonies at this time, but it had the distinction of being the southernmost lighthouse and one of only two sentinels in the South. The other was at Charleston, South Carolina.

When Tybee Lighthouse came under Federal control in 1791, it stood about 90 feet tall, topped by a wooden lantern and illuminated with spermaceti candles. Official records lack further details, indicating only that it was tended by a keeper named Higgins. A better account of the happenings at Tybee Light came a year later when the tower caught fire, due to a candle dropped on the tallow-soaked wooden floor. The Savannah customs collector attempted to fight the blaze and later colorfully remarked: "...it was so very hot I was not able to tarry half a moment and I saw it was in vain to attempt to save it."

Presumably, some of the brickwork survived the fire and was used in the construction of the new lighthouse. Wood was prudently rejected altogether, in favor of an iron lantern and stairs and iron window casings. Within a few years the beacon was fitted with 15 oil lamps and reflectors, as was the custom with most major estuary lights during the early 19th century. These were clean, hollow-wicked Argand lamps intensified by Lewis's parabolic reflectors.

By the 1820s, commerce in and out of Savannah was burgeoning. Larger vessels found the river entrance difficult to navigate, necessitating the construction of a smaller sentinel, called the Tybee Beacon, not far from the main lighthouse. When its dimmer light was lined up underneath the Tybee Light, piggyback fashion, the two served as a range for ships entering the river channel.

In the 1850s, reorganization of the Lighthouse Service brought Tybee Light under serious scrutiny. A series of inspections revealed the United States to be far behind Europe in its lighthouse technology and listed many towers in desperate need of repairs and improvements. Inspectors weren't in agreement as to Tybee Light's fitness, but all felt it needed renovations.

Lieutenant David Porter arrived at Tybee Light in July 1851 aboard the Navy mail steamer *Georgia*. Overall, he gave the light station a good review but suggested it be given a fixed light rather

than a revolving light so as not to confuse it with the beacon at Charleston, South Carolina. He also felt a fog signal was needed:

"Tybee Light, though a very good one, cannot be distinguished in foggy weather. Tybee shows at a distance of 12 miles, which is quite sufficient, as the water is bold right up to the bay and the light and beacon show plainly before you reach the outer buoy. Tybee Light should also be provided with a steam whistle, or there should be a bell buoy on the bar, which is about four miles from the lighthouse."

The newly-formed Lighthouse Board, in its report to the government in 1852, did not concur with Porter's findings. The board suggested Tybee Light be raised to a height not less than 150 feet and given a first order Fresnel lens. It was described as "inferior," and placed on the board's list of lighthouses needing immediate attention. Only about 20 feet of additional height was added, however, and the board settled for a second order lens.

A decade of quiet followed, then in 1862 Confederate forces occupied the lighthouse in order to attack nearby Fort Pulaski. All of Savannah's beacons were extinguished, and in the struggle that ensued Tybee Lighthouse was burned and damaged by a gunpowder explosion. It stood dark until the end of the war.

lies immediately in the rear of the keeper's dwelling." Engineers discovered that a drain that had been dug years before had become obstructed during wartime operations, causing the swamp to fill and spawned an army of mosquitoes from the foul, stagnant water. A quick unclogging of the drainage system solved the difficulty.

A year later new troubles began. Cracks appeared in the tower walls after a severe hurricane. The inspector for that year warned that Tybee Light could "fall at any time" and recommended it be torn down and rebuilt. Five of the tower's eight faces had cracks, and they continued to widen over the next fifteen years. Though inspectors repeatedly stated the need for demolition and rebuilding in subsequent years, nothing was done. Another vicious storm in 1878 added to the damage, and in 1886 an unusual earthquake widened the cracks and broke the huge prism lens.

For some inexplicable reason, the government ignored all pleas to replace the tower, though concerns seemed well-founded, and the $50,000 proposal for a new structure would have put little strain on the Lighthouse Service's purse. Perhaps some perspicacious bureaucrat knew Tybee Lighthouse was as stubborn as its builders and firmly anchored to the Georgia shore. Despite its frightening scars, it hasn't fallen yet.

Tybee Light being destroyed by Confederates

A hasty attempt to relight it was foiled by an outbreak of cholera. It was not repaired and relit until 1867. Workers used what remained of the old tower to build the handsome 144 foot structure that still stands today. Its current daymark clearly delineates where the old tower ended and the new one began.

It wasn't long before new problems beset Tybee Light. An 1870 inspection reported: "This light station is very unhealthy, which is mainly attributable, it is believed, to a small swamp which

An interesting postscript to this august old sentinel's career is the story of Florence Martus, whose name has become synonymous with keeping a watch for the sailor returning home to Georgia. In 1883 her brother was appointed lightkeeper at the Elba Island Range Lights, about six miles inside the Savannah River. Along with the Tybee Island lights, these beacons assured large ships could make safe passage in and out of the bustling port at Savannah.

A gregarious teenager, Florence often visited nearby Tybee Island Light and was the belle of Fort

Pulaski, where her avid appetite for meeting people was satisfied by the history tours she gave to visitors. It was on one of these excursions that Florence met and became smitten with a handsome sailor from a ship that had stopped in Savannah for a few weeks. On the eve of his departure, the sailor asked Florence to be his wife and promised to return for her as soon as he could. He had no ring to offer, but instead left her with his handkerchief, which she promised to wave from the shores of Tybee Island when he returned.

Weeks passed, then months; yet Florence heard nothing from her beau. She asked about him on the docks at Savannah, but no one seemed to know him or the whereabouts of his ship. Grief stricken, Florence began to wave the handkerchief at every ship that passed on the river. At first she waved in hopes someone would get word to her sailor that she desperately awaited his return, but as time passed and there was no news of him, her greeting to ships became a salve for her wounded heart.

Soon, sailors everywhere knew of the "Waving Girl of Elba Island," who beckoned them with a white handkerchief by day and swung a lantern to and fro at night. When her brother retired from lighthouse keeping in the 1930s, she had been waving to ships for more than 40 years. Though Florence died in 1944, she hasn't been forgotten, nor have sailors lost their waving girl. A statue of her stands on the Savannah waterfront, frozen in eternal greeting.

This article first appeared in *Mariners Weather Log*, Summer 1993.

Interesting Trivia

While doing research at the Mariner's Museum in Newport News, Virginia in June 1996, I discovered an undated news clipping concerning a 70th birthday party held in Savannah for Florence Martus. The day was August 7th. (I estimate it was about 1935. Dates for her birth conflict, depending on the source.) The celebration was held at Fort Pulaski, where she had been born shortly after the Civil War and spent so much of her time. Some 3000 people attended, including a Georgia Congressman who gave a speech in which he called Florence Martus "the sweetheart of mankind." Florence was asked to speak, but she was overwhelmed by the events of the day. She scribbled a note and asked a friend to read it. It said: "This is

the grandest day of my life." After her brother's death, Florence spent her last years in a Savannah hospital, grief-stricken and dazed. She died in 1944.

My husband and son visited the "Waving Girl" statue with me in April 1995. We couldn't find out when it was erected, but it was certainly after Florence Martus' death. A collie dog stands next to the slim, alert figure of Florence as she lifts a handkerchief into the air. The flowerbeds and stone patio around the statues are lovely, and the view over the Savannah River is peaceful. Florence would be speechless, once again, to know how appreciated she is. She'd be pleased to know someone, albeit a statue, still waves to the ships.

When I told Scott, my son, about Florence's dedication to waving at passing ships, he nodded his head in appreciation of a good tale, then suggested that someone dedicate a statue to me upon my decease, which he hastened to add should not be too soon, in honor of my flag-waving campaign in print. Such an effigy would reflect what he calls "Lighthouse Mode" - a state of mind that overtakes me when I am proximate to a lighthouse. The mission to find it and photograph it and study it eclipses all else, including obedience to traffic signals and no trespassing signs. Scott has experienced this transformation on many occasions, and I suppose he worries it may someday result in my demise.

Yes, officer, I did run that red light back there, and I admit I was driving the wrong way on a one-way street and a bit too fast; but you see...there's a lighthouse up ahead I need to photograph before the sun gets too low in the sky.

TYBEE ISLAND
HISTORICAL SOCIETY

West Quoddy Head Lighthouse

Candy-Cane Sentinel of Maine

The easternmost soil on the mainland of the U.S. lies near the quiet town of Lubec, Maine on a slender peninsula called West Quoddy Head. It points like a long accusing finger at Sail Rocks, a jagged pile of offshore granite that resembles a ship's sail. The Passamaquoddy believed these rocks to be the stepping stones of a giant that lived on Canada's Grand Manan Island.

Champlain navigated his way around these rocks almost four centuries ago on his way to nearby Dochet Island in the St. Croix River. The French colony he helped establish there was called Acadia and was the site of the first Christmas celebration in North America. Snow-frocked and framed by majestic spruces, it lies almost halfway to the North Pole.

Vessels still give the Sail Rocks a wide berth, but since 1808 navigators have used the warning beam of West Quoddy Head Lighthouse to help them avoid this dangerous ledge. Built by direction of President Thomas Jefferson, it is one of the prettiest sentinels in New England.

When the last Coast Guard keeper was removed from West Quoddy Head Light in 1988, the town of Lubec petitioned for a caretaker. There was concern about the safety and upkeep of the tower. In addition, many residents felt West Quoddy Head Light's long tradition as a sentinel should be preserved as a museum with a resident curator. Although Lubec has yet to find funding for this project, the State of Maine has assumed responsibility for the lighthouse grounds.

Part of the lure of West Quoddy Head is its rugged coastline, cut by glaciers and delicately carved by the massive tides of Passamaquoddy Bay. The sea sometimes rises as much as 30-feet at high tide. When it recedes, a curious art show of rock sculpture is exhibited — marvelous caves and arches, lonely stacks, and cobble-strewn beaches. Sail Rocks and its many toothy, offshore neighbors seem to have been tossed into the sea mindlessly by King Neptune himself. Throughout the day they play a hide and seek game as the enormous tides alternately submerge and expose them.

The Acadia Coast is also known for fog — the pea soup kind that smothers even the brightest navigational beacon and plays nasty tricks with sound. West Quoddy Head Lighthouse was the site of numerous experiments with fog signals in the 19th century. Its first fog warning device was a 5-foot long cannon fired in response to the whistle of a nearby ship. Although the lightkeeper could sometimes hear a ship 6-miles away, the cannon's report was too brief to be of great benefit. The gun was also dangerous, and keepers complained about having to fire it.

In 1820 the nation's first fogbell was tried at West Quoddy Head. It weighed 500-pounds and was struck by hand. To assuage the discontent of keepers, who sometimes stood hammering the bell for days, the government added a $70 bonus to the annual salary of $250. (An additional $50 had been given earlier, after complaints that the soil around the lighthouse was too poor for a garden.)

Pen and Ink Sketch by Jessica De Wire, 1990

Although the bell was an improvement over the cannon, its sound did not carry well in dense fog. A smaller, higher-toned bell weighing 241-pounds was tried, but it too failed to be heard through West Quoddy's murk.

It was upstaged by a titanic 1565-pound bell with an irreverent bong that vibrated through the entire station and kept everyone awake. It hung in its own bellhouse above the surf with a weight that descended down to the beach to actuate the striker, somewhat like the clockworks of a cuckoo clock. But even the low, mournful song of this monstrous bell could not penetrate the thick air.

the unhappy beasts when it was time to be hooked to the wagon for a trek over the potholed, rut-riddled road to Lubec.

A better choice was to take the station boat. Still, this meant a perilous climb down a ladder to the beach and tide-propelled trips going and coming. In winter the sea was usually too rough for small boats, and ice was a danger. Large chunks sometimes rode the tides in and out of the bay. Not until motorboats and cars came along was the semi-isolation at West Quoddy Head broken. Even today the nearest neighbor is over a mile away.

Sketch from All Among the Lighthouses, Collection of Barbara Gaspar

Stamp courtesy of Ed Nickerson's "Lighthouse Post," sent to me on the first day of issue, 4-26-1990

In desperation, the Lighthouse Service installed an experimental steel bar in the shape of a triangle. Its base was 14-feet across and it was struck much like a dinner bell. Either the bell worked satisfactorily, or fog signal funds ran out because the bar remained in service until a modern diaphone horn replaced it near the turn of the century.

Life was not easy for families at West Quoddy Head Lighthouse prior to electricity and automobile travel. Though situated on the mainland, access to mainland comforts was limited. The road connecting the station to civilization was little more than a widened deer path. Early keepers had poor pasture for their horses and a lot of trouble catching

A serious difficulty for early lightkeepers was the constant sweating of the interior masonry walls and the iron lantern cap. This was especially bad in winter when the moisture froze and glazed up the lantern windows, obscuring the light. A stove had to be kept going inside the lantern for most of the year to keep it dry, and it required much more coal and wood than keepers would normally have used.

In 1842 Alfred Godfrey revealed another expensive practice at West Quoddy Head Light, however, this time a simple solution was offered. Godfrey noted that the lantern had lamps facing all different directions, including the forested area behind the lighthouse. He proposed removing the lamps that faced landward, thus reducing the lighted arc to 240°. His suggestion resulted in considerable savings on oil each year.

The current masonry tower at West Quoddy Head was built in 1858 to replace the original rubblestone sentinel. Sometime after its commissioning, it was given its famous red and white stripe daymark. The Canadians popularized the practice of painting red stripes on lighthouses. Though handsome, the stripes are not cosmetic; rather, they show up well in regions where snow blankets the coast. Only one other U.S. lighthouse sports red and white horizontal stripes from lantern to base — Assateague Light in Virginia.

The visual appeal of West Quoddy Head Lighthouse has earned it many honors over the years, but none so lofty as its inclusion in the U.S. Postal Service's 1989 commemorative series of lighthouse stamps. Only five were chosen to represent the 650-plus sentinels that still stand in our nation. West Quoddy Head's bold stripes clearly dominated the series.

Unfortunately, there is a small error on the stamp, a mistake that matters little considering the benevolent intent of the series. Lighthouse fanciers will spot the flaw immediately. Count the number of strips on the stamp, then count the number of stripes on the real tower. A few stripes are missing.

This article originally appeared in *Mariners Weather Log,* Fall 1990.

Author's Highlight

About those pretty stripes -

I have several slide shows I give to groups interested in lighthouses and lighthouse lore. The favorite is, hands down, *I Brake for Lighthouses.* It's light and fun and gives folks from eight to eighty a broad look at the diverse locations and architectural styles of our nation's lighthouses.

The show begins with West Quoddy Head Lighthouse. The moment its image flashes on the screen, a crescendo of *ooooohhhs* and *aaaaahhhhhs* begins, which sets the tone for the entire program. I call it the "Pete's Dragon Response," because I feel it's somehow connected to those old, nostalgic and romantic images people have about lighthouses. Yes, lighthouses are beautiful, and West Quoddy is, without a doubt, one of the prettiest. No matter the time of year, it's candy-cane stripes stand out starkly against the evergreens and rocks and blue sky.

During winter snowstorms, those red bands show up very well in the swirl of white flakes and spume.

I visited West Quoddy Head Lighthouse in June 1990 with my son, Scott, who was then fourteen. We were returning from a visit to St. John, New Brunswick where my husband's duty station, the USS *Fulton,* had pulled into port. The St. Croix River was muddy and fast-moving as we drove southeast from Calais (which Mainers pronounce like that tough skin we get on hands and feet from overwork). We glimpsed Lubec Channel Lighthouse on the way.

A parking area near the lighthouse worried me. I had left my pickup truck in a similar parking area at Owls Head, Maine a few years before and returned to find the window broken and much of my stuff stolen. Scott and I locked everything in the trunk of the car and hiked down to the lighthouse. Luckily, our car was safe.

The stripes were bright, even under overcast skies. The old fogbell sat on a platform, reminiscent of the first bell that served here in 1808. I gonged it gently with my knuckles and drew into my ears its sweet, melodic tone before the persistent wind snatched away the doleful sound. Dandelions sprinkled the green lawn, and wet, brindled rocks shimmered in the sea.

Scott galloped about, with gangly legs and arms whirling like a windmill, free to be a kid. His assessment of the place was a simple, "Cool, Mom!" He counted the stripes on the tower and agreed with me that the recent U.S. Postal Service stamp was in error. But what's a stripe or two when it comes to lighthouses? Artistic license is much like literary license, and I'm all too familiar with that!

Afterwards, we drove across the water to Campobello Island and visited Head Harbor Lighthouse - a typical Canadian beauty. We scampered down the metal ladder, in spite of a sign warning of the danger below. Such signs may as well say, "We dare you!"

Head Harbour Lighthouse, *Harpers Magazine,* 1874

Biloxi Lighthouse

Mississippi's Highway 90 has an unusual traffic light at which no motorist is required to stop; yet many do. It's the old Biloxi Lighthouse, which stands in the grassy median strip where the highway skirts by Mississippi Bay. This parcel of historic ground was part of the Old Spanish trail that linked Florida to California in the years before American colonization. Later, it became the capital of the French Province of Louisiana, better-known to historians as the Louisiana Purchase.

Biloxi Lighthouse was built in 1848 to serve the Gulf of Mexico's lucrative shrimp and oyster fleets, as well as schooners bringing timber down the Tchouticabouffa River estuary. The lighthouse, prefabricated in Baltimore then shipped in sections to Biloxi, is thought to be the first cast-iron sentinel built in the south. The 61-foot tower was lined with brick and bolted to a stone foundation. Nine brass lamps with reflectors served as a beacon, which showed a distinctive three-second flash.

Six years after its completion, it was necessary to build a seawall around Biloxi Light. Storms and high tides had eroded the beach and threatened to undermine the tower. Also in 1854, the first of three women to keep the lighthouse arrived — Mary Reynolds, a Baltimore native and mother to a small band of orphan children. Her appointment was arranged with the help of her good friend and Mississippi senator, Albert Gallatin Brown, whose family had intimate ties to the Lighthouse Service.

Reynolds' income was a paltry $400 a year, considerably less than men were paid for the job, but among the better salaries for women of the day. By all reports, Reynolds was an excellent lightkeeper and, with the help of her children, kept the station in good repair. Their life was idyllic. Days were spent fishing, swimming, and boating. Balmy breezes blew in off the gulf, and the heady scent of camellias wafted through the air.

But there was a down side to life too. Biloxi Light stood watch in Hurricane Alley, where severe storms slammed the Mississippi coast about once a decade. After the destructive 1860 storm, Reynolds told Mississippi's governor, "I ascended the tower at and after the storm, when men stood appalled at the danger I encountered."

During the Civil War, Biloxi Light was extinguished to prevent it from aiding Union forces. Mary Reynolds remained at the lighthouse, though there was no work to do. Ironically, she devoted her time to sewing clothing for Confederate soldiers while watching over the federal supply of oil and equipment in the lighthouse.

In 1866 Reynolds was replaced by Perry Younghans, who probably had the right political connections. (Lightkeepers positions were politically controlled until Grover Cleveland's presidency.) Younghans died only a year after his appointment and was succeeded by his wife, Maria. She cared for the tower's new beacon, a fifth-order Fresnel lens illuminated by lard oil lamps.

About this same time, the lighthouse was painted black. Rumors quickly circulated that the daymark was a drape of mourning for President Lincoln and a woeful reminder of the death of the Confederacy, for Beauvoir, the home of Confederate president Jefferson Davis, sat just behind Biloxi Light. It's more likely the color was intended to make the lighthouse show up against the tawny beach in bright daylight. Regardless, the paint scheme lasted only a few years before the government restored the tower's white daymark.

Maria Younghans and her daughter, Miranda, proved themselves capable lightkeepers, despite repeated tests of their fortitude and skill. In 1867, when erosion caused the lighthouse to lean, the two women managed to keep the beacon lit while workers dug away at the foundation to right the tower. They also kept the light going during the hurricanes of 1870, 1888, and 1893.

A 1916 storm hurled a pelican through one of the lantern windows and tore up the breakwater, causing severe flooding in the Younghans' house. The women installed a temporary window and restarted the revolving lens. Though the tower groaned and trembled mightily during the worst hours of the storm, they did not abandon it. The danger was real, for only a decade before, the 1906 hurricane had killed the keepers of nearby Sand Island Light and completely destroyed the tower.

After Maria Younghans retired in 1919, Miranda Younghans took over the light and served another ten years, during which time the lighthouse was electrified and tourism began to increase. By

1948, when the lighthouse celebrated its 100th birthday, it had been automated and the keeper's house was home to the Biloxi Chamber of Commerce. The citizens of Biloxi honored the lighthouse with a brief ceremony and a fresh coat of white paint.

In 1969, Hurricane Camille destroyed the lightkeeper's house, but Biloxi Light stood firm. Minimal repairs put it back in service as a navigational aid. Today it is operated as a private light by the city of Biloxi.

This article originally appeared in *Mariners Weather Log,* Summer 1994.

Recommended Reading

Lighthouses of the Gulf of Mexico have been largely ignored by maritime historians and travel writers. Many of the Gulf towers are difficult to reach unless by boat, and admittedly, most lack the romantic, masonry beauty of the sentinels along other shores. Still, they possess those all-important lighthouse traits of solicitude, strength, and beauty.

David L. Cipra, former photojournalist with the Eighth Coast Guard District in New Orleans, pulled together archival material and, I'm certain, personal experience in his *Lighthouses & Lightships of the Northern Gulf of Mexico*, published by the Department of Transportation in 1976. Though the writing is plain and straight-forward (as we would expect from a government publication), Cipra exumed much interesting material from Coast Guard files and gave us a broad look at the kind of sentinels that stood guard in the stormy waters of the southeast.

Old photos, maps, blueprints, and handsome charcoal sketches by Gyuri Hollosy, then a Coast Guard Yeoman, complement Cipra's 62-page text. A brief glossary appears at the end, opposite a startling rendering by Hollosy of the destruction of Horn Island Lighthouse off Mississippi, where the keeper, his wife, and daughter died in a 1906 hurricane.

The text covers lighthouses from the Florida Panhandle west to the lower Texas Coast, with more than sixty towers included. Among the Mississippi sentinels profiled are Cat Island, Pass Christian, Round Island, Chandeleur Island, Biloxi, Proctersville, Ship Island, Pascagoula River, St. Joseph's Island, Merrill Shell Bank, Horn Island, and Lake Borgne.

A picture of Biloxi Lighthouse as it appeared in 1892, when Maria Younghans and her daughter kept the beacon, is included. Cipra noted that "beach surrounded the station on three sides and the keeper crossed only a small shell road to reach the tower." Today, a four-lane highway skirts the old lighthouse.

Though out of print for years, *Lighthouses & Lightships of the Northern Gulf of Mexico* was recently reprinted by Cypress Communications, P.O. Box 791, Williamsburg, VA 23187.

Tillamook Light

Oregon's Sentinel on the Rock

About a mile off Oregon's Tillamook Head is a chunk of basaltic rock that protrudes above water like the humped, barnacle-covered back of an ugly sea serpent. This forbidding piece of briny real estate lies some 20-miles south of the treacherous Columbia River Bar. Here, the rushing waters of the river estuary meet the ocean flood tide in a maelstrom of churning, surging sea. Maritime historian James Gibbs estimates more than 2000 shipwrecks have occurred in this area in the past few centuries.

Years ago, the only witnesses to this destruction were the thousands of sea lions that lounge on Tillamook Rock and frolic in the deep, cold waters around it. After 1881 though, a single watchful eye took over the vigil - the eye of Terrible Tillie.

This is the nickname given to Tillamook Rock Lighthouse by its earliest keepers. The unflattering moniker was well-deserved, for Tillamook Light was not only a terror to build, but many of its lonely lightkeepers likened a tour of duty in it to a prison sentence. Tillamook Rock is among the most desolate and dangerous light stations in the United States and reflects the ever-present struggle between sea and shore along the rugged Pacific Northwest Coast.

The need for a lighthouse at Tillamook was recognized soon after the acquisition of the Oregon Territory, but it wasn't until 1878 that decisive action was taken. In that year, Congress appropriated $50,000 to build a sentinel on lofty Tillamook Head, located on the mainland south of present-day Seaside, Oregon. Engineers cautioned against this, however, since Tillamook's extreme elevation often left it shrouded in clouds and fog. A better site appeared to be a mile offshore nearer the north-south shipping lanes at Tillamook Rock.

From the outset, getting on and off the rock proved the most difficult aspect of building and later tending the lighthouse. When the district superintendent was sent to survey the rock, he was forced to leap onto it from a pitching surfboat. Unable to get his instruments landed safely, he proceeded to survey the rock with only a tape measure.

From the moment the first pick and chisel hacked into the rock, the public became mesmerized with the awesome danger involved in the undertaking. The sheer cliffs of Tillamook Rock drop straight down into the sea, and depths around the site range between 96-feet and 240-feet. The water is seldom calm here and never warm - a place fit for birds and sea lions, but not for people.

In September 1879, not long after blasting of the foundation began, master mason John Trewares drowned trying to leap onto the rock from a launch. Public outcry arose, and people demanded the project be abandoned. But construction boss Charles Ballantyne cleverly rounded up a new crew and sequestered them away at Cape Disappointment where gossip and inflammatory talk would not reach their ears.

While working on the site itself, crewmen lived in canvas tents lashed to iron rings that had been driven into the rock. Seawater often soaked their tents and ruined provisions. In addition, the men had to stand on a scaffolding of sorts to work on the rock face. When the wind kicked up or seas ran high, the scaffolding pitched and reeled, sometimes awash.

A barracks was eventually built for the workmen, with a storehouse nearby for supplies. While the derrick was under construction, men got on and off the rock by means of a lifeline and breeches buoy, similar to the apparatus then in use to rescue shipwreck victims. The breeches buoy was far safer than the dauntless leaps the men had been making from the surfboats, but it was a less than comfortable ride. The supply vessel rolled miserably in Tillamook's unsettled waters, making the lifeline alternately slack and taut. The breeches buoy usually rode like a bucking horse. Rare was the occupant who was put ashore dry and unbruised.

Two and a half years after the initial survey of Tillamook Rock, the lighthouse was completed. Its beam flashed out for the first time on January 21, 1881 to the cheers of crowds ashore, despite the cold weather. The beacon, elevated 131-feet above water and with a 75,000-candlepower beam, could be picked up 22-miles at sea. The lighthouse had cost $123,000 and was among the nation's most expensive to build.

Life on the station was tolerable at best. Five keepers were assigned to duty there with one always on leave. At first the men served three months, followed by two weeks leave, but discontent and a number of unusual ills, both physical and emotional, convinced the Lighthouse Service to institute a 42-day duty followed by 21-days leave. Since the government had stipulated Tillamook be a stag station, "far too confined for both sexes," no women ever served or lived on Tillamook Rock.

In 1890, to answer keepers' pleas for better communication with shore, a submarine telegraph cable was laid between Tillamook Light and the mainland. Only a year later, it was severed by stormy seas and had to be reconnected. This scenario was to be repeated many times in the lighthouse's career.

Numerous storms have battered the lighthouse, and the cost to repair it afterwards has far exceeded the original pricetag. In 1882, only a year after the beacon was commissioned, a storm threw seawater over the lantern dome, causing considerable damage. An 1894 storm tossed large boulders against the tower and smashed the lantern. The light was out almost 24-hours while the keepers cleaned sand, seaweed, and dead fish from the priceless prism lens.

The worst storm, though, came in 1934 when winds of 110-mph lashed the rock, and stones as heavy as 150-pounds were hurled against the tower and onto the base platform. Henry Jenkins, the youngest of four keepers on duty at the time was washed out of his brass bed after the sea broke off an estimated 25-ton piece of the western overhang of the rock. The severed chunk plunged into the sea and created a huge wave that swamped the lighthouse.

Tillamook's keepers have told many incredible stories about life on the rock; many of the keepers were unbelievable characters themselves. Bob Gerloff, the "Grand Old Man of Tillamook Rock," became so enamored of the solitude and danger of the place he once did a 5-year stretch of duty with no leave. After retirement, he asked to rent a room in the lighthouse but was denied. The government also disallowed his request to be buried at the station.

Keeper Roy Dibb played golf at the lighthouse by teeing off on a hard cotton ball attached with a cord to a railing stanchion. He also got exercise by jogging around the tower platform.

In 1957 the Coast Guard decided to close Tillamook Lighthouse. Its functions could, by then, be performed by a large buoy, and it had proven a very difficult station to man and maintain. It was ceremoniously closed up by the last keeper, Oswald Alik, on September 10, 1957 with a poetic log entry: "Farewell, Tillamook Rock Light Station. I return thee to the elements...May your sunset years be good...your purpose is now only symbol."

Following retirement as an active beacon, the lighthouse held down a variety of occupations. A preservation group had not been able to raise funds to use the lighthouse for historical purposes, so it was put on the auction block. The high bidder was Academic Coordinators of Las Vegas, who bought the structure for a mere $5600 in 1959.

Their use of it as an educational site never materialized, and it was resold in 1973 to a New York executive who wanted it for a vacation retreat. He used it just twice before selling it in 1978 to a wealthy Portland, Oregon bachelor.

The pricetag had inflated to $27,000., and by now the lighthouse was covered with guano and inhabited by hundreds of seabirds. A lawsuit against the estate of the bachelor put the lighthouse in the hands of an elderly Eugene, Oregon woman. She doubled the price and immediately resold it to a group of speculators in Portland.

What started out as a joke for this group - the conversion of the lighthouse into an offshore mortuary - turned into a serious financial operation. Eternity By the Sea Columbarium fetched up to $25,000 per niche for those desiring to have their ashes interred on the rock. More than 40,000 niches were made available, from the basement all the way to the top of the lantern.

With so many spirits inhabiting it, Tillamook Lighthouse truly has found life after death. Prospective lighthouse keepers can be found in every nook and cranny of the station, though they needn't worry about the storms that still pound the rock or sharing their cramped, secluded quarters with seabirds. Tillamook has become a sanctuary for departed souls who cannot leave the sea, even in death. Had devoted lightkeeper Bob Gerloff lived a few more years, his wish for an eternity at Tillamook could have been granted.

This article originally appeared in *Mariners Weather Log*, Winter 1990.

Recommended Reading

James Gibbs, who lives in his own lighthouse called Cleft of the Rock in Yachats, Oregon, has been a favorite author of mine for years. His many lighthouse books are part of my treasured collection, and I've read a number of other things he's written on Pacific maritime history. His *Sentinels of Solitude*, written to compliment photographer Chad Ehlers spectacular pictures of West Coast lighthouses, is a handsome, readable piece, recently re-issued by EZ Nature Books of San Luis Obispo, California.

In my opinion, Mr. Gibbs is the premier West Coast lighthouse author, a man whose love for the sentinels was gained firsthand and has endured over the years. During World War II he served in the Coast Guard and, among other duties, was assigned as a keeper at Tillamook Rock Lighthouse. His experience there was harrowing at times, but undoubtedly helped launch his successful career as a journalist, for shortly after he arrived at the lighthouse he discovered a room full of musty books. He read and read, and he grew fond of both the site and its odd but lovable attendants.

Years later, in 1979, Gibbs published *Tillamook Light*, a wonderful little paperback that tells the history of the station and Gibbs' experiences serving there. It's well-written in comfortable, conversational style, but not without all the pertinent information. My favorite chapter is called "A Night of Horror." In it, Gibbs crafts a delightful true tale about a mysterious and, at first, frightening intruder in his bedroom not long after his arrival. It turned out to be a large goose that had collided with the

tower, broken its wing, and wandered down into the lower part of the lighthouse. Gibbs dutifully took the beleaguered bird outside and turned it loose. The loose goose must have found a way to fly on one wing, for it was not seen again!

Gibbs has also written *West Coast Lighthouses, Lighthouses of the Pacific, Oregon's Seacoast Lighthouses,* and most recently, *Twilight on the Lighthouses*. Each one is uniquely informative and entertaining, as Gibbs always delivers a balanced menu of material.

I've not had the pleasure of meeting him, so I will thank him here, publicly, for his contributions. His books have helped me on many occasions with research for articles, lectures, and my own books.

A brief quote from his Introduction in *Oregon's Seacoast Lighthouses* gives the flavor of Jim Gibbs' wonderful work and helps us think about the many ways lighthouses reach out to us:

What does the reader think when the word "lighthouse" is mentioned? Sentinels of solitude are endowed with multiple personalities and have different meanings to different people. The navigator looks upon them as the protector of the sealanes; the photographer and artist as a premier subject for a camera or canvas; the clergy likens them to a spiritual monument; travelers see them as a roadside attraction. Writers and poets view lighthouses as subjects to appear in print. Nothing is quite so thought-provoking as the sight of a tapering lighthouse tower reaching skyward with a shining jewel in its crown.

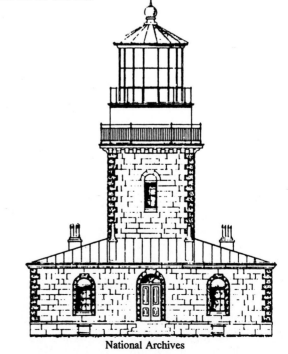

National Archives

Beacon on the Nubble

Cape Neddick Light Station

Unnumbered rays sweep the sky,
a thousand lighthouses shining high;
beacons white, gold, and red —
stars for the seaman, 'Robert Louis' said...

Elinor De Wire
The Celestial Lights

Billions of miles from earth, far beyond the frigid perimeter of our solar system, the *Voyager II* probe drifts aimlessly, its antennae pointed inquisitively into the vast black abyss that lies between us and other star systems in the Milky Way. Its mission to explore the outer planets is complete. Dazzling, animate images of the giant gas planets now splash the pages of science books and spin across computer screens, dressed in gaudy stripes and ringed by icy debris and herds of moons.

But one small part of *Voyager II's* mission remains. Having exited the solar system and traveled beyond the range of communication with home, it is perhaps the most far-flung human-made object in the cosmos. It has no destination, no itinerary, no crew, not even an auto-pilot. It's a derelict interstellar ship floating in vast unexplored seas of emptiness. Only the stars beckon it, like celestial lighthouses.

As such, *Voyager II* has become the first ambassador from our planet to other worlds. Inside its small main compartment, resting quietly beside obsolete cameras and radio equipment, is a canister containing a disk filled with images of earth. Should extraterrestrials exist and encounter *Voyager II*, its time capsule will tell them who we are and where to find us.

What's inside the capsule? Astronomers selected a variety of sights and sounds that exemplify our world, digitized them on disk, and sealed the disk inside the capsule, along with a plaque showing a sketch of a man, a woman, and our location in the known universe. Among the digitized images is a picture of Maine's Cape Neddick Lighthouse. It is hoped that this quaint little sentinel will convey an important message about the nature of earth and earthlings.

What would it say? Perhaps -

We are the keepers of ourselves and others, no matter from what destination they travel. Follow the beacons of space to our beacons of Earth and find a world of which 75% of the surface is covered by water, where people go about in boats and need guidance. Welcome.

* * * * *

In May 1602, when English explorer Bartholomew Gosnold sailed down along the Maine coast near present day Cape Neddick, he could hardly have imagined that ships would someday fly into the heavens, or that the tiny islet he saw would be the site of a lighthouse that might eventually beckon distant travelers to our earth. His journal tells of a friendly encounter with the Abenaki on the pleasant offshore islet they called Savage Rock. The islet was small — only a few acres — and capped by a lush carpet of green grass, wildflowers, and gray boulders strewn haphazardly. In Abenaki legend, the giant Glooskap had made the rock-riddled coastline here and used the little islet for a pillow when he slept in the ocean on hot summer nights.

The Abenaki drew a map of the coast for Gosnold and included Savage Rock on it. The name seemed ill-fitting, though the tide-rushed channel separating the islet from shore was dangerous, and a number of submerged rocks made approach to the islet tricky. If Gosnold was puzzled by the islet's name, those who followed him years later would not be. A century after Gosnold's peaceful meeting with the Indians, Savage Rock lived up to its name when the Abenaki, disgruntled with the English, slaughtered the first settlers at Cape Neddick.

Today the pretty little islet wears a more pleasant title and a better reputation. Local residents affectionately call it The Nubble. In summer, when Cape Neddick is teeming with vacationers, shutterbugs congregate on the point across from The Nubble to picnic and photograph its picturesque little lighthouse. Officially called Cape Neddick Light Station, the Nubble Lighthouse has appeared on countless postcards, calendars, and jigsaw puzzles, and in TV and magazine ads. According to the

Maine Publicity Bureau, it's one of the most photographed lighthouses in the nation.

Surprisingly, Nubble Light is one of Maine's youngest sentinels, established in 1878. Requests for a navigational aid on this spot began much earlier though, spurred mainly by the lucrative Down East fishing industry of the early 19th century.

had more pressing projects than the design and construction of a lighthouse at Cape Neddick. Critical landfall lighthouses near main ports needed to be repaired and upgraded with new lenticular optics that vastly improved range and clarity. When attention could be turned again to the Nubble, war intervened.

Sketch by
Paul Bradley

In 1837, a government lighthouse inspector pointed out the need for a lighthouse at Cape Neddick, but his suggestion was ignored until 1842 when the bark *Isadore*, out of Kennebunkport and on its first voyage, tragically piled up on Bald Head Cliffs north of the Nubble. One survivor insisted the bark's demise had been revealed to him in a dream the night before, and his graphic recollection of the horrid shipwreck caught the interest of newspapers. Bombastic accounts were written, vividly describing the pain and suffering of the victims and suggesting that a navigational beacon in the vicinity of the wreck would have averted the tragedy.

Public outcry was enormous. A hasty appropriation of money was made for a lighthouse on The Nubble, but the amount was too small, and internal problems within the Lighthouse Service prevented its immediate increase. A brief period of upheaval ensued, after which the Lighthouse Board was established in 1852. But the newly-created board

Cape Neddick Light Station finally was completed in 1879, a conical iron tower standing 41 feet tall and exhibiting a fixed red beacon from 88 feet above water. The original illuminating apparatus was an incandescent oil vapor lamp that diligently served until electrification in 1938.

The tower was painted in various experimental colors during its early career but has shown a spanking white daymark since about the turn of the century. A narrow catwalk encircles the lantern, with each of its iron railing posts capped by a charming, miniature lighthouse. The outbuildings are bright red against the Nubble's green crinoline lawn and gray rock trim. The Coast Guard decided to paint the buildings white a few years back, but local residents objected so strongly the red color was restored.

Between the mainland and The Nubble is a little channel nicknamed the Hellespont. Lightkeepers traveled across it in a station boat when supplies and mail needed to be fetched or a visitor had to be transported to the station. At low tide, it's sometimes possible to wade across to the islet, but not recommended due to the tidal rip. A lightkeeper's wife once called a repairman to fix her sewing machine. She planned to row to shore and transport him, but to her surprise, he knocked at her door with pantlegs rolled up above his knees and his shoes in his toolbox.

From the outset, rats were the bane of lightkeepers at The Nubble. After Cape Neddick became a popular tourist spot, the rats took up summer residence on the mainland rocks across from the lighthouse, where they could forage in the garbage left by picnickers. In winter, when the tourists were gone, the rats swam out to The Nubble to raid the lighthouse stores.

Traps and poison were a partial remedy, but a more effective and pleasant solution was discovered — cats. Some of lighthouse history's most famous felines have lived at The Nubble, one so popular he appeared in newspapers and was briefly profiled in the annual *Lighthouse Service Bulletin*.

The hefty, 19-pound tomcat was a gift to 1930s lightkeeper, Eugene Coleman, from the keeper he relieved. Called Sambo Tonkus, the cat amused tourists and townspeople alike with his love of the water and insatiable appetite for rodents. Sambo was content to remain on The Nubble most of the time, but when the rat population on the islet dwindled, or he wanted to carouse in town, Sambo went ashore. He was captured by many a camera as he ambled down to the Hellespont, dove in and swam to shore, his big paws cutting the surf like paddles. Often, he'd return with a fat mouse or rat clenched in his big jaws, and swim back home as ably as a water spaniel.

A problem all Nubble lightkeepers faced was getting their children to the mainland for school. Most youngsters were rowed across the Hellespont in the station boat, or they lived ashore with relatives during the school year. In 1967, keeper David Winchester came up with an alternative that made front-page news. He rigged a cable from the boathouse to the mainland and attached a small wooden box to it. Each morning, he placed his son, Rickie, in the box and hauled him across to the schoolbus waiting on the mainland. Rickie's method of conveyance caught the attention of the media, and reporters flocked to Cape Neddick to see the devoted schoolboy.

When a picture of Rickie, suspended over the Hellespont, was released by the Associated Press, along with a caption extolling his determination to get to school each day, the Coast Guard halted the practice, deeming it too dangerous. But Keeper Winchester and his son were already celebrities. Letters arrived from near and far, offering to help Rickie get to school. Trips in the station boat resumed, however. Rickie's predicament had brought to light one of the many tribulations of growing up on an island.

Since 1989 Cape Neddick Light Station has operated automatically, without a keeper; but public fascination with the little sentinel continues. Tourists line the shore in the warmer months to photograph, paint, and admire it, and during the Christmas season, the town of York decorates the station with lights and holds a festive celebration in the mainland parking area overlooking the islet. The success of this event has spawned a summertime clone called "Christmas in July," where mittens and hot cocoa give way to swimsuits and cold sodas.

Despite its popularity, the holiday lighting of the Nubble has its detractors — those who say the gaudy lights cause confusion for mariners who still need the beacon and those who feel the practice commercializes a much-respected symbol of safety at sea. Still others insist the brightly lit Christmas Lighthouse is symbolic of the peace and goodwill of the season and a reminder that every day signals a need to be "thy brother's keeper."

Either way, the stigma of Savage Rock has long-since vanished. The Nubble's peaceful image has welcomed, warned, inspired, and soothed earthbound travelers for over a century now and will likely continue to do so for years to come. Someday it may issue the ultimate greeting — a shining welcome to extraterrestrials as they journey into our small corner of the cosmos.

This is a updated article that originally appeared in *Mariners Weather Log*, Summer 1990.

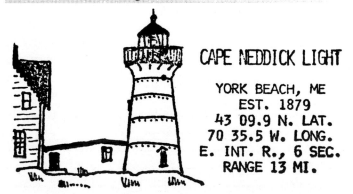

CAPE NEDDICK LIGHT

YORK BEACH, ME
EST. 1879
43 09.9 N. LAT.
70 35.5 W. LONG.
E. INT. R., 6 SEC.
RANGE 13 MI.

Rubber stamp image used by Nubble Coast Guard keepers in the 1980s.

Minots Ledge Lighthouse

...sea monster floating on the waves...
Henry David Thoreau

A mile off Cohasset, Massachusetts is a forbidding ledge of granite that bares its teeth at low tide. The Quonahassits believed the evil demon Hobomock lived beneath this ledge. When he grew irritable, Hobomock roared to the surface and churned up a nasty storm. To appease him, the Quonahassits paddled out to the ledge at low tide and left offerings, which Hobomock greedily devoured when the tide rose.

A 97-foot stone lighthouse stands over Hobomock's home today. Although it hasn't altered his mercurial temperament, its bright flash has kept ships away from his treacherous lair for over a century. Officially listed as Minots Ledge Lighthouse by the Coast Guard, the beacon is affectionately called "Lovers Light" by smitten couples ashore. Its famous 1-4-3 flash in the dark seems to be a pledge of *I love you*.

The dark granite tower at Minots Ledge has been awash for most of its career. Built in 1860, it is considered a marvel of marine engineering. Its illustrious designer, Joseph G. Totten, was the first American to successfully build a masonry lighthouse on a wave-swept, offshore ledge. He borrowed his design from the British, who had built huge, offshore towers at such formidable spots as Eddystone, Inchcape, Skerryvore, and the Lizard.

But Totten learned more from his predecessor, William Swift, than from British engineers. Swift had designed and built the first Minots Ledge Lighthouse in 1850. This peculiar tower stood less time than it took to build it and gave its name to one of the worst storms in New England history - the Minots Light Storm of 1851.

About a century before this costly storm, a colonial merchant named George Minot lost a valuable, cargo-laden ship on the ledge. Thereafter, the rocks were known as Minots Ledge. Though the settlers of Cohasset did not believe in the demon Hobomock, they were respectful of Minots Ledge.

Between 1832 and 1841 alone, it destroyed more than 40 vessels. Merchants and seamen alike pressured the government for a beacon on this spot, since it lay very close to the shipping lanes of Boston.

Up until this time, the United States had confined its lighthouse building to onshore sites or rocks and islands in protected areas. The British, as mentioned, had developed several revolutionary designs for lighthouses on exposed unstable sites. Captain William Swift, of the U.S. Army Topographical Corps, was sent to study Britain's offshore towers, then to examine Minots Ledge and design a tower suitable for it.

The first tower on Minots Ledge. National Archives

Swift was impressed with the screwpile lighthouse design, used in estuaries and bays in England. It was already being studied for use in the Florida Keys, as well as the Chesapeake and Delaware bays. Swift felt the screwpile's open framework design would offer less resistance to wind and waves than would a solid masonry tower. He also liked the idea of anchoring piles into the ledge itself.

111

Swift's plans were approved early in 1847, and construction began that summer. A schooner was tied up at the ledge to house workers. They could work only at low tide, and with the ledge dry a mere 3 or 4 hours a day, the foundation proceeded slowly.

Eight holes were drilled in a circular pattern over the 25-foot ledge, with a ninth hole in the center. Each hole was 12-inches in diameter and 5-feet deep. The drilling machinery washed off the ledge several times before all nine legs of the tower were secured in their foundations with cement.

Atop the legs was hoisted a keeper's house with a 16-face lantern room. The result was perhaps the most peculiar lighthouse ever to stand in New England. When Henry David Thoreau passed it on his travels up the Massachusetts Coast, he likened it to "...the ovum of a sea monster floating on the waves."

On New Year's Day 1850, Keeper Isaac Dunham illuminated the strange tower for the first time. Its light was a long-awaited blessing to shipping, but within a month Dunham was convinced the tower was unsafe. He requested it be strengthened with crossbraces, but the government declined. As a result, Dunham resigned only nine months after assuming his duties.

From *Frank Leslie's Illustrated Newspaper*, 1884

He was replaced by John Bennet, who after only a week at the lighthouse also warned of its instability. Bennet noted that during gales dishes danced off the table in the kitchen, and the entire structure rocked and reeled "like a drunken man."

In April 1851, Bennet went ashore on business and left the lighthouse in the care of his two assistants. The following day, a storm blew up and prevented Bennet's return. He watched anxiously from shore as the tower was pummeled by high winds and heavy waves, some so powerful they washed over the top of the 70-foot structure.

The storm intensified as night approached, and Bennet feared for the safety of his assistants. Around midnight, the men began hammering on the fogbell in distress, but no one could help them. Shortly after 1:00 a.m. the iron legs of the lighthouse snapped like matchsticks. The huge tower sank below the waves, taking its keepers to their deaths.

Following the disaster, the steam towboat *R.B. Forbes*, and later the lightship *Brandywine Shoal*, were moored off the ledge to serve as temporary beacons until a new tower could be built. Joseph Totten, Chief of Engineering for the United States, began to look at new designs. He was impressed with Britain's offshore masonry towers and determined that this was the most suitable design for Minots Ledge.

Combining practical principles of offshore marine engineering, such as a foundation sunk directly into the ledge, the center of gravity as low as possible, and a tower that was smooth and sloping to throw waves back upon themselves, Totten came up with a solid design that closely resembled the famed Eddystone Lighthouse of the English Channel.

The 114-foot tower took five years to complete. It was ceremoniously illuminated for the first time on the night November 15, 1860. But the celebration was quickly marred by reports of strange happenings at the new lighthouse.

Its two new keepers heard tapping sounds in the tower and believed them to be the ghosts of the former keepers, as it was known that these men often signaled to each other by tapping on the stovepipe in the old tower. The lens and lantern were mysteriously polished on several occasions, and passing ships began to report a spectral figure seen clinging to the ladder at the base of the lighthouse.

Haunted or not, a tour of duty on Minots Ledge was like a prison sentence. Keepers nicknamed it "The Rock," and many resigned or were removed under odd circumstances. One man

Getting off Minots Ledge Light
Harpers Magazine, 1874

much-loved part of Cohasset's coastal scenery. Each year, thousands of visitors peer across the waves at its hulking, gray form. Perhaps they view it with a mix of admiration and dread, as Henry David Thoreau did in 1871 when he saw the replacement for that first "sea monster":

"The lighthouse rises out of the sea like a beautiful stone cannon, mouth upward, belching only friendly fires."

This article originally appeared in *Mariners Weather Log,* Summer 1989.

Author's Highlight

Minots Light was the first lighthouse to capture my interest and fire my imagination. I was 19 years old when I first read the account of the Minots Light Storm of 1851, of how the tower swayed and groaned in the hurricane, terrifying its human occupants before it hurled them to their deaths beneath the cold, dark waves. My husband had brought me Edward Rowe Snow's *The Lighthouses of New England* from the library at Brunswick Naval Air Station, Maine, and it was my page-turner for the winter of 1972-73. It was closely followed by Ross Holland's *America's Lighthouses*, still hot off the press, and John J. Floherty's *Sentries of the Sea*. Twenty-five years later, I own a personal collection of some 150 lighthouse books - five of them my own - and am still dazzled by every lighthouse I see.

Many years after my initial encounter with Minots Ledge Light, I finally got to see it up close! In June 1996 George Morgan, the Flying Santa of the Lighthouses, invited me on a boat cruise out of Hingham, Massachusetts. The skipper brought the boat close to Minots Ledge, quieted the engines, and let us float aimlessly on the sea for several minutes. It was a sobering experience, to say the least.

The bottom of the tower was submerged, and algae clung to its base. Waves washed about its lower course, occasionally revealing the teeth of the ledge. High up on its side was an access door reached by a tiny ladder.

"A round prison cell at sea," I said to Doug Bingham of New England Lighthouse Foundation, who stood along the rail with me. He nodded. The shore seemed a million miles away, yet we both knew only about a mile separated us from land.

"I'd like to get inside it one day," I added.

Doug chuckled. "Yeah, but you wouldn't want to stay long. Creepy place, you know."

complained that the tower had "no corners," while another was killed when he fell from the top of the tower in the station lifeboat; a third man was driven to suicide after ice sealed shut the tower door and temporarily trapped him inside.

The misery of serving at this desolate and wretched site ended in 1947 when the Coast Guard installed automatic machinery. Since then, the light has been visited only for periodic maintenance. Its damp, musty interior is occupied by spiders, and birds find the lantern a comfortable perch.

In 1977, Minots Ledge Lighthouse was made a national historic landmark by the American Society of Civil Engineers. Its uniqueness, and the extraordinary achievements of its designer and builder were finally recognized, nearly a century after its construction.

The Coast Guard made extensive repairs to the tower in 1987. It continues to operate and is a

Old Barney

Beacon at Barnegat Inlet

When Quakers settled on New Jersey's Long Beach Island in the late 1600s, the only beacon to guide their benevolent mission to lend assistance to those at sea was the light of kindness shining in their hearts. The Society of Friends prayed for "those in peril on the sea," but earned a large part of their livelihood salvaging life and property from the many shipwrecks that occurred along their shores.

Barnegat is one of the half-dozen places along the Eastern Seaboard that lays claim to the grisly title, Graveyard of the Atlantic. As in colonial times and its early years of statehood, it remains one of the U.S.'s most dangerous coasts, keeping the Coast Guard busy year-round. Shoals and bars extending out from its barrier beaches, odd currents and weather conditions spawned from the nearby Gulf Stream, and the prevalence of gales and hurricanes are among the perils here. Additionally, it was and remains a the major thoroughfare of shipping between important ports in New England and the mid-Atlantic.

With such a gruesome reputation, one might imagine Barnegat was one of the first places in colonial America marked by a lighthouse. Unfortunately, some two centuries passed after settlement before a lighthouse came to Barnegat. The solicitous Quakers did what they could. A privately owned beacon — probably a fire bucket mounted on a tripod — was exhibited on the beach from time to time prior to the American Revolution, but it was not until 1835 that a lighthouse was built there.

Losses from shipwrecks were numerous prior to the establishment of the lighthouse. An early colonial newspaper, the *Boston Newsletter,* gave an account of a spring storm off Barnegat:

New York, April 30. -- Yesterday came hither the masters of three sloops which were cast away near Barnegat by the late easterly storms, viz: Archibald Morris, who was bound from Pennsylvania for New York and Boston,; one Jones who was bound from Horekill to Boston; and one Saunders, bound from Roanoke to Boston. Saunders had one man drowned and saved nothing at all, and the others saved very little besides lives.

Among the most horrid wrecks was that of the *Rose-in-Bloom.* (The late maritime writer, Edward Rowe Snow, gave a stirring account of the event in his *Famous Lighthouses of America,* from which the following information is taken.)

The ship left Charleston, South Carolina August 16, 1806 and was overtaken by a hurricane off Cape Hatteras a few days later. Storm winds pushed the ship northward, where it battered to pieces off Barnegat. More than half the 41 on board drowned as the hull was broken apart. Survivors floated on the remains of the hull, spars, and cargo until they were rescued by the crew of the Canadian brig *Swift,* which had encountered the tempest just south of Barnegat.

During the worst part of the storm, the *Swift's* captain, Richard Phelan, claimed a sulfurous smell pervaded the air. Lightning and thunder were intense, and rain came down in sheets. Phelan swore the devil himself was aboard ship. When the wind finally died down and skies cleared, Phelan's crew sighted the remains of the *Rose-in-Bloom* and launched the jolly boat again and again to rescue the survivors.

Wrecks occurred in calm weather as well, attesting to the dangers of Barnegat. In April 1815, the Danish schooner *Surprise* was headed to New York with veterans of the Lake Ontario campaign when it struck the shoals off Barnegat. Thirty drowned. Five years later, three vessels wrecked on these same shoals, all within a year's time and in mild weather conditions. Public demand for a lighthouse at Barnegat was loud and insistent, yet another fourteen years would pass before a government beacon was established.

In 1834, several acres of beach near Barnegat Inlet, situated about 100-yards from the water's edge, were purchased from Bornt Slaught. Nathan S. Crane was contracted to build the 40-foot brick tower for $6000. It was whitewashed to show up against the beige sands of Barnegat and showed a fixed white light produced by eleven oil lamps placed in front of reflectors.

Its first keeper, Henry V. Low, had been on duty only two years when the brig *Morgania* went aground in a storm. Barnegat's handsome lighthouse had made passage along mid-coast New Jersey safer, but it could not prevent every wreck. Low brought the *Morgania's* survivors ashore, including the skipper, who had smallpox. The lightkeeper kept the captain quarantined at the lighthouse until he recovered. Fortunately, no outbreak of smallpox in or around Barnegat occurred, and even Keeper Low escaped contracting the disease. He died the following year, however, and was succeeded by his son and daughter-in-law.

The strangest wreck that occurred off Barnegat Light was that of the *Adelaide*. The sloop struck the bar in September 1846 while trying to pass through Barnegat Inlet to take refuge from a sudden gale. The vessel capsized and all were presumed lost. When the battered hull washed ashore a short distance from the lighthouse, local residents went to see what could be salvaged. Imagine their surprise when tapping sounds came from inside the up-side-down hull.

After much anguish and hard work, a hole was cut in the hull, and a lone, drenched, terrorized survivor was pulled out. She turned out to be the captain's teenage daughter. The girl eventually recovered from her ordeal and married a local fisherman.

From the beginning, navigators complained that Barnegat Light was too weak and was easily confused with other lighthouses or mistaken for a ship at anchor. "I generally steer for Barnegat, frequently passing without seeing it, owing no doubt to the low position of the light. I came very near losing my ship in consequence," said E.R. Smith, captain of the *Tropic* in the 1840s. Navy lieutenant, David Porter, noted that Barnegat Light could easily be confused with a ship's light, so feeble it was. He, and others, suggested it be made a flashing beacon.

An investigation about this same time noted that the tower was poorly constructed with inferior materials. At 54-feet above sea, and still operating an archaic lamp and reflector system, it was neither tall enough nor brilliant enough to do its job. But the Lighthouse Service was embroiled in controversy in the late 1840s, and nothing was done to improve Barnegat Light until 1855 when plans were made to build a new tower and install a stronger beacon.

Lt. George Gordon Meade, who would later distinguish himself as leader of the Union forces at Gettysburg, was at this time a respected and proven engineer with the Fourth Lighthouse District. Meade suggested Barnegat be given a first-order sentinel, due to its importance for ships from Europe making landfall at this spot before proceeding up the coast to New York. Meade's recommendation was favorably received, and he proceeded with design and construction of the new lighthouse.

But as the new tower went up, the old one collapsed, and Meade hastily erected a temporary beacon to serve until the new structure was completed. On the night of January 1, 1859 the elegant new Barnegat Light was lit for the first time. The 150-foot tower held a first-order Fresnel lens that weighed five tons and had been manufactured in France in 1847 by Henry LaPaute. Its 1000-plus prisms and 24 flash panels gathered and magnified the light of kerosene lamps to produce a powerful beam that flashed over the sea once every ten seconds.

Meade's noteworthy engineering achievements are aptly described by Jerome Walnut in *Barnegat Lighthouse*, a small booklet produced by the Barnegat Light Historical Society Museum:

"Its twin walls of brick...were designed with an air space between to produce ventilation and a certain amount of 'give' in high winds....the cast iron stairway was installed as the walls were built, so that the inner wall fits the stairway like a jacket, and the two reinforce and support each other."

Lovely Victorian keepers' cottages were built a few years later for the station's three lightkeepers. They survived until shortly after the turn of the century, when erosion destroyed them. Erosion continued to re-shape the shoreline at Barnegat until the tower itself was threatened in the 1920s. Despite the construction of jetties and several attempts to shore up the area around the lighthouse, in 1927 the government decided to remove the lens and abandon the tower. It's beacon was replaced by a lightship, stationed a few miles offshore.

Local residents pulled together to save the aging tower by creating a breakwater of old cars. These were dumped into the inlet just off Barnegat Light in hopes they would deter the onslaught of erosion. The effort seemed to work, since the tower remained out of harm's way until the 1940s when the Army Corps of Engineers built two new, strong jetties and a dike.

Barnegat Light found itself at work again during World War II, but this time as a lookout tower for the Coast Guard, keeping watch for enemy submarines. At the end of the war, the lighthouse was handed over to the State of New Jersey and made the centerpiece of a park. The ecology around the tower is being preserved with special plantings and fences that slow erosion and hold the dunes in place.

This is an unpublished article in the author's files.

Author's Highlight

In the summer of 1991, as a graduation gift to my daughter, Jessica, I gave her a 3-day trip of her choice anywhere within driving distance from our home in Connecticut. She picked Atlantic City. No doubt my stories of fun in New Jersey during my high school years in the 1960s fueled her interest. Friends of hers had recently visited the Jersey Shore and raved about it. She enthusiastically added, "You can stop at all the lighthouses you want, Mom!" I did, of course.

As it turned out, Jessica enjoyed Barnegat far more than Atlantic City. We were both disappointed with New Jersey's most famous city and noticed a definite duality to the place. There were rich casinos and hotels and clubs, or there were old, run-down, has-been places. There seemed to be nothing in-between. The boardwalk wasn't nearly as quaint and fun as I remembered, and the bathhouses were filthy. Trash lay everywhere, and a coke was far over-priced and watered down. Even the long, flat, sandy beach seemed less beautiful.

Absecon Light stood in a run-down, dirty part of town, surrounded by litter and weeds growing up in its pavement. Its red band was faded to a pale pink, and nowhere was there evidence of its former Victorian beauty. (I'm pleased to report it's doing better these days.) We didn't get out of the car to see it, choosing instead to snap a few quick pictures

with the windows down and high-tail it for safer streets.

A short time later we arrived in Barnegat. It didn't disappoint either of us. We parked and played for several hours. I snooped around the lighthouse, which was open for climbing, explored the area along the jetty, and spoke with some of the people I encountered - all friendly and smiling. Jessica soaked up the sun and made sand sculptures and played in the waves.

As I watched her, all grown up and ready to go off to college, I thought of all the beaches she had played on in her life, such a lucky kid to have a dad in the Navy and a mom who can't stay away from lighthouses. We drank many sodas that afternoon, ate many bags of chips, walked many miles of beach together, wrote silly messages in the wet sand, fed the seagulls, and let a generation fall away between us.

As the sun dropped low, we headed back to our car, beach bag bulging with shells, beach glass, and assorted treasures. Motoring into town, we aimed to visit the museum, but it had closed at 5:00. I left a note on the door saying I regretted having played so long at the beach and missed seeing Barnegat's beautiful lens. Dinner was wonderfully "beachy greasy" seafood, as Jessica calls it, from a roadside stand, topped off with hot fudge sundaes.

At dark we headed to King of Prussia, Pennsylvania to visit Jessica's favorite aunt, MaryJo Feldman. I fear we carried pounds of sand into her apartment, as well as left tell-tale signs of our day's fun in the shower, the beds, and on the bathroom floor. It was Barnegat sand though - wonderful, variegated bits of quartz and feldspar that represent the child in us all.

Jessica's sketch of Barnegat Light, 1991.

Fire Island Lighthouse

Beacon on a Barrier Beach

Viewed from the deck of a ship, lofty Fire Island Lighthouse dominates the beach on the south shore of Long Island, sporting a cheerful black and white daymark and extending a bright welcome to the traveler headed into New York Harbor. It has greeted millions of sojourners during its many years of service, from pioneers to cruise ship passengers, fishermen to ferrymen, sailors to soldiers. Whether departing, returning home, or working the local waters, their trip was made safer by this well-known seamark.

For my father, coming home on a troop ship after World War II, the first glimpse of Fire Island Light was an emotional experience. As its lantern inched over the horizon and flashed a grateful salute to the returning veterans, a cheer went up, and some cried. Not only was the lighthouse a long-awaited signpost on the searoad home, it was also an inspiring reminder of the values Americans had fought to preserve. Many an uncertain immigrant also has seen Fire Island Lighthouse as a reassuring light in the dark night, and one of hope for a bright future in America.

Prior to the appearance of the Statue of Liberty in New York Harbor in 1886, Fire Island Light was the first glimpse of the "American Dream" for most newcomers. Ironically, the story of the lighthouse itself is much like that of the immigrants — a tale of opportunity, determination, and adjustment to change in a strange but wonderful land.

Tall, masonry towers are not ideal structures for an unstable and windy beach such as Fire Island has. A massive pillar of bricks — 800,000 in all — towering 170-feet above the golden dunes, Fire Island Lighthouse has had to contend with the vagaries of sand and sea for more than a century. The original 85-foot tower, built in 1825 at a cost of $10,000 was an octagonal stone sentinel much like the old tower at Eaton's Neck, on the sheltered north shore of Long Island. Fire Island Light was built to mark hazardous shoals along the open approach to New York Harbor, but it also gave guidance to ships entering Great South Bay.

The name "Fire Island" was apparently derived from "Five Island," the name used in colonial times when there were five inlets cutting across the island. Try-pots for whale blubber boiled over open fires on the beach in those days, and it's probable "Five" was misquoted as "Fire."

In 1858 the old tower, nearly undermined by erosion, had to be demolished, both for safety reasons and because mariners felt its beacon was too low to be seen a safe distance at sea. A taller, more impressive lighthouse was built 200-yards northeast of the original site. It was given a heavy coat of yellow paint to protect the brickwork from the constant sandblast. Almost immediately, sailors began calling it "the Winking Woman" because from a distance its bright daymark and flared base presented an image of a statuesque lady in a long, yellow dress.

There was also a state-of-the-art prism lens in the new lighthouse, recently purchased from France and of much greater brilliancy than the old reflector system used in the first tower. Keepers had to install white draperies in the light room to shield the lens during the daylight hours; otherwise it could start a fire by directing magnified sunlight into the brush and pine groves surrounding the compound.

Harper's Magazine, 1874

In 1871 the second tower began to show signs of deterioration, so the government had the entire exterior of the masonry column sealed in a thick layer of Portland cement. A few years later it was painted in the distinctive black and white bands it still wears today. This daymark is more easily seen against the beige sand and distinguishes Fire Island Light from other towers in the area. Also about this time an electrical generator was installed, making this one of the first American lighthouses powered by electricity. For reasons not known, the system was removed after only a few months and replaced by an incandescent oil vapor apparatus. Electricity was not reinstated until 1939 when a submarine cable was laid from the mainland.

Duty at Fire Island was "preferred" by lightkeepers and their families. Except for the intermittent pummelings by storm waves, and the poor soil for gardening and grazing livestock, the island was an idyllic place to live. New York City's bustle and excitement was only a boat ride away from the serenity and beauty of Fire Island's lonely miles of beach. The lightkeepers were highly respected for their solicitous work, since the sea occasionally cast ashore gruesome evidence of the need for lighthouses and lifesavers. Shipwreck losses were made more bearable by the presence of the huge tower, working alongside the rugged surfmen and beach horses of the island's neighboring lifesaving stations.

Coast Guard lightkeeper Gottfried Mahler was stationed at Fire Island Lighthouse with his wife, Marilyn, and three sons when hurricanes Carol and Edna hit Long Island in 1954. The storm surge of Carol came to within six inches of the base of the lighthouse and powerful winds caused the tower to vibrate. The children were young, ages 8, 4, and a newborn. It was a terrifying experience for all, but the lighthouse and keeper's quarters survived both storms.

Fire Island Lighthouse served faithfully until 1973, when its duties were taken over by a flash tube array of lights on the Fire Island National Seashore water tower. The lighthouse was abandoned and began to deteriorate from lack of care and vandalism. In 1981 the National Park Service obtained custody of the tower, and funds were raised for its restoration through the incorporation of the Fire Island Lighthouse Preservation Society.

By 1986 enough work had been accomplished to open a small museum in the keeper's quarters and relight the beacon. An emotional ceremony, attended by some 800 boats and a number of dignitaries and celebrities, marked the joyous rekindling of this old and much-loved landmark.

I was fortunate to be among the honored guests aboard the flagship *Evening Star* that night and spoke with several descendants of the lighthouse's civilian keepers. Peter Nappi, then 14 years old, told me how proud he felt to be present as a representative for his great-great-great-great-great grandfather — the station's first keeper!

Grace Humes of Long Island remembered living at Fire Island Lighthouse as a child shortly after the turn of the century. Lightkeeping blood ran true in the family: Her father, grandfather, and great grandfather had kept this light, and she recalled climbing the tower's 192 stairs to tend the beacon herself or to help her mother, who stood in when her father had to be away or when the assistant keeper got drunk.

According to Grace, "Not all of them [Keepers] were saints." But of her father she said, "He was a good, hardworking man and well-liked by everyone."

Grace also remembered the tower being struck by lightning, which hit the ball on the cupola, burned through the roof, and made the 170-foot trip down the stairway to the house. Fortunately, no one was injured, but the powerful stroke knocked out the new telephone system. With the typical good humor of a lighthouse keeper's daughter, Grace remarked that this event reminded everyone "how much a tall lighthouse tempts the powers above."

Fire Island Lighthouse Preservation Society Logo

One of the goals expressed by preservationists at the historic relighting ceremony was to restore the exterior of the tower. The concrete covering was peeling off, and the banded daymark had faded. "The Winking Woman needs a new dress!" one society member enthusiastically told everyone.

That goal was achieved, and today the lighthouse proudly wears a fashionable gown of black and white, and its beacon remains shining as a sentry for vessels, large and small. The society hopes to keep the museum open and to continue giving tours of the tower, which affords a seagull's view of the counterpane of sand and sea around Long Island. Their efforts have paid off handsomely in many ways, but especially in the living heritage that has been returned to the region.

The public can visit Fire Island Lighthouse as part of the Fire Island National Seashore.

This article originally appeared in *Mariners Weather Log*, Summer 1992.

Paul Bradley's Fire Island Light

Paul Bradley
Lighthouse Artist

Fort Lauderdale, Florida's Paul Bradley, Jr. is a retired architect and artist who truly appreciates lighthouses. Paul has drawn more than 100 of America's beautiful sentinels, including Fire Island Light at left. Each tower is painstakingly researched to produce a rendering that is not only pleasing but accurate as well.

Paul usually travels to a lighthouse before beginning his drawing. He takes numerous photos, studies the textures, tones, and perspectives of the site, and makes preliminary sketches. Back in his studio in Fort Lauderdale, the final drawing emerges -- an amalgamation of the sensory experiences and feelings of being at a lighthouse.

My friendship with Paul began in the mid-1980s when he wrote to comment on one of my articles. He enclosed a sketch, and I have since collected many of his beautiful drawings. His sketches have illustrated a number of my lighthouse profiles for *Mariners Weather Log* and were important in the production of my *Lighthouse Activity Book* for kids. Several illustrate this book, too.

Paul's work has appeared in many other publications. It regularly appears in *The Keeper's Log,* the journal of the U.S. Lighthouse Society, based in San Francisco, and his renderings are available as notecards from the society's Keeper's Locker.

Among my favorites of Paul's lighthouse sketches are his wonderful Christmas cards, always drawn with a special holiday touch -- a wreath on the tower door or the Bethlehem star in the night sky -- and handsomely colored. Large mylar reproductions of his Colchester Reef Lighthouse and Tibbetts Point Lighthouse hang in my office, ever the inspiration I need when writing about my favorite subject!

As one who preserves and appreciates lighthouses with words, I owe Paul an enormous "thank-you" for helping my readers see the lights. Many artists have illustrated my work over the years, but Paul Bradley has been the most supportive and encouraging. May he enjoy his retirement and sketch hundreds more lighthouses for all of us to enjoy.

Thank you,
Paul!

Point Reyes Light

Sentry on a Perilous Cliff

As Sir Francis Drake sailed down the West Coast on the *Golden Hinde* in the summer of 1579, he searched for a calm spot in which to anchor and repair his damaged ship. In mid-June the ship passed a great outcropping of rock some 40 miles north of present-day San Francisco. His crew stared up at the forbidding cliff in awe. Just south of it lay a calm harbor where Drake anchored for over a month and befriended the native Miwok, who provided food and took the Englishmen exploring.

Drake named the area Nova Albion, or New England, because its sheer cliffs reminded him of the shores of his own English Channel. Two decades later, Spanish explorer Don Sebastian Vizcaino gave the rocky point the name by which we know it today. His ship sailed beneath *La Punta de Los Reyes* on the 12th day of Christmas, or the Feast of the Three Kings. The name was shortened to Point Reyes when American pioneers arrived in the 19th century.

Perched 300 feet above the Pacific Ocean on the bold headland is squat little Point Reyes Lighthouse. First illuminated in 1870, it guards the treacherous point where the San Andreas Fault trails out to sea. The West Coast's first known shipwreck occurred here in 1595 — the *San Agustin* — and so frequent were wrecks after the Gold Rush, San Francisco newspapers kept heading slugs that read "Shipwreck at Point Reyes."

The station holds the distinction of being both the windiest and foggiest lighthouse on the West Coast. Winds, averaging 23 mph, continuously scour the promontory. One clear-weather gust in 1895 was clocked at 93 mph! Fog shrouds the area about one-third of the year as well, rolling and churning over the jagged headland in thick, cold clouds almost daily during the summer months.

Point Reyes Lighthouse has been unattended for several years now and operates on an automatic beacon. One of the highlights of Point Reyes National Seashore, its history is among the most fascinating of the sentinels of the old Lighthouse Service — a grueling saga of hardship and adversity set against the sprawling wilderness of the Northern California coast.

Lightkeeping is often regarded as a romantic, relaxing occupation, but a visit to this lighthouse will put such notions to rest. Some 308 steps lead down to the beacon tower from the keeper's residences, and it's another 338 steps to the fog signal house. During the last century, one keeper suffered a heart attack climbing the blustery stairs; another was nearly killed when a cable car hauling coal to the foghouse snapped its line, went careening down the staircase, and smashed into the lighthouse.

Wind has always been a hazard on the point. Keepers were sometimes marooned in the lighthouse for hours, knowing they might be blown off the cliff were they to venture out. When cleaning the exterior glazing, they tethered themselves to the gallery railing with a stout rope, lest they be blown off the tower.

Harpers Magazine, 1874

120

Sand grains spun upwards from the beach like tiny meteors stung their faces and frosted windows; wind kidnapped laundry from the clothesline and shredded the station flag. One gusty night a keeper left his bed to assume the watch and was nearly impaled when a splintered timber was hurled through his window, snared the bed sheet, and pinned it to the opposite wall!

Battling the elements was a constant burden for lighthouse keepers during Point Reyes Light's early years, but there were worse headaches to endure than those caused by nature. No roads connected the point with civilization until the 1930s, and the only visitors were the crew of the district tender, which brought supplies and fuel to the keepers.

Firewood and extra water, in case the cistern went dry, were hauled over an Indian trail from a distant ranch. As if there weren't enough difficulties, this task also tested the men's fortitude, for the station mule was afraid of water and had to be led across the point blindfolded.

Not long after its addition to the West Coast's string of navigational aids, Point Reyes Lighthouse was deemed "the most undesirable [station] in the district" by the Superintendent of the San Francisco Lighthouse District. Finding keepers for the remote station was hard enough; keeping them on duty was almost impossible.

A January 1889 logbook entry for the station read: "The Second Assistant Keeper went crazy today and was handed over to the constable at Olema."

Keepers lost patience with the cantankerous machinery that ran the light and fog signal, with each other, and with their families. There was constant bickering, aggravated by the eternal din of the foghorns and the ever-present fog or wind. A meteorological curiosity and a calamity for the lightkeepers were days of both fog and wind!

One disconcerted lighthouse keeper was prompted to pen a verse he knew:

O Solitude where are thy charms that
Sages have seen in thy face?
Better o dwell in the midst of alarms
Than reign in this terrible place.

But not everything was dreadful at Point Reyes. California poppies set the headland ablaze with color during the warmer months, and gray whales surge by the point on their way to warmer breeding grounds to the south. The persistent fogs,

botanists remind us, have always brought vital moisture to California's majestic redwoods. The wives of Point Reyes' lightkeepers noticed it made their complexions softer too.

Historian Ralph Shanks pointed out that even if adults did not particularly enjoy duty at Point Reyes, their children did. A favorite amusement was riding down the precipitous coal chute in a box slathered with axle grease. Another was trying to slide down the steep stair railing to the lighthouse without touching feet on the steps.

With all the steep rocks to play on, Point Reyes children became as sure-footed as mountain goats, and they swam like merfolk in the point's surf, which is thought to be the roughest on the California coast. Youngsters learned to take naps and concentrate on school books to the accompaniment of the loud bellow of foghorns. One lighthouse mother noted that her baby's first words were not the expected "mama" or "dada," but the resounding "beeee-oooohhhh!" of the Point Reyes fog signal.

Harper's Magazine, 1874

121

Many changes have occurred at Point Reyes Light since it went into service in 1870. The fog signal has been moved a few times to compensate for the cliff's dead spots and odd acoustics, and it now operates electrically rather than gobbling 80 tons of coal a year as it did a century ago.

Although the original French prism lens is still in place, illuminants have kept pace with progress. Lard oil was used initially, followed by an oil vapor lamp in 1877, and finally electricity in the 1930s. The sentinel was also a weather station from 1900 to 1927 and had a radiobeacon installed in 1949. The titanic lens, with its 1000-plus glistening prisms, was retired in 1975 and replaced by a more modern beacon on the roof of the tower.

Today the lighthouse and its remaining buildings are a highlight on a visit to the Point Reyes National Seashore. Visitors sense the isolation of the station's early keepers as they travel out a narrow, winding road to the point, high above the sea. Cattle and Tule elk pause in their grazing to stare; terns wheel overhead, and wildflowers wave in the wind.

On the point itself, a sign warns of the dangers - wind, fog, the blast of the foghorn, the strenuous climb down to the lighthouse and back. The Pacific laps against the cliff far below and stretches to the west like an immense blue carpet upon which rocks have been carelessly thrown. To the north stretches a long, beige beach where the Point Reyes Lifeboat Station once stood, to help the shipwrecked.

Without too much imagination, one can conjure an image of the old days, when lightkeepers kindled the oil lamps in the lofty lighthouse and surfmen pounded the misty beach on patrol, lanterns swinging in the dark.

This article is an updated version of one that appeared in *Mariners Weather Log*, Spring 1988.

Author's Note

Some years ago, my good friend Ken Black, director of the Shore Village Museum in Rockland, Maine, gave me a poem called "Lighthouse Keepers." No one knows who wrote it, but I've always thought the author of these quaint verses must have known about Point Reyes Light. Perhaps he was a lightkeeper there and anxious to hand over his duties to someone else, or she was a keeper's wife at the station, eager to be off to a better assignment.

Point Reyes is a piece of fickle real estate, to be sure.

Lighthouse Keepers

Lighthouse keepers have it easy;
All year long their homes are breezy.
Noises don't disturb their labors,
For they haven't any neighbors!

They don't need nine holes or twenty;
They get exercise aplenty:
Each trip up the stairway
Equals three around the fairway!

They don't need big waste baskets
For old papers, orange peels, or gaskets;
Just one carefree motion,
And their trash dumps in the ocean!

Window shades? They're never needed;
Lighthouse keepers dress unheeded.
Their wakeful babes don't have conniptions
To make the neighbors give long descriptions.

When I'm old and don't need pity,
I shall leave the sullied city,
Climb a lighthouse, bar the door,
And trim those wicks forever more!

The Cape Henry Lights

Old & New Beacons of the Bay

Looking out over the sand and sea from Cape Henry, Virginia is like looking at the past and present all in the same moment. Big supertankers glide silently through the yawning mouth of the Chesapeake Bay, over barnacle-riddled ribs of sunken sailing ships and the huge concrete tubes of the Chesapeake Bay Bridge Tunnel. Sunbathers sprawl on the beach, and Army LARCs (Lighter Amphibious Resupply Cargo vehicles) prowl the dunes.

Beneath it all, some of Blackbeard's pirate booty could be buried, or possibly the body of some unfortunate castaway from one of the hundreds of ships lost off this cape.

The most obvious and handsome landmarks at Cape Henry are its two lighthouses — one an old masonry tower with cracks running up its walls; the other a tall, iron sentinel with a checkerboard daymark and a blinding beam in its crown. Embracing both old and new, they are bold reminders of the cape's importance and its ever-changing topography.

When the first Virginia colonists landed here in April 1607, they raised a wooden cross to mark the spot where they had first set foot on American soil and honored the eldest son of King James I by giving the tawny, sweeping cape his name — Henry. The cape they spied some ten miles to the north was named for the king's younger son, Charles.

There were no buoys or beacons to guide these first colonists through the mouth of the Chesapeake and on to the James River where they would eventually settle. Though their colony was nearly wiped out by disease and starvation, others bravely followed, and the need for navigational aids was quickly recognized.

The earliest residents of Cape Henry probably kept bonfires burning or post beacons lighted to aid vessels approaching the bay. During periods of fog, they may have pounded drums or rang bells. But it would be many years before ships found safe passage into the Chesapeake guided by the beam of a lighthouse.

In 1721 Virginia governor Alexander Spotswood urged Maryland to join him in petitioning the British Board of Trade for a lighthouse at Cape Henry, but nothing was done until 1774. In that year, tons of stone was quarried along the Rappahannock River and transported to the cape. A foundation for the lighthouse was laid, but money ran short, and the project was abandoned. A year later the Revolution broke out, further delaying the construction of the lighthouse at this important location. The stones and foundation soon drifted over with sand, never to be retrieved.

Courtesy of Association for the Preservation of Virginia Antiquities

Following the war, the care and administration of about a dozen colonial lighthouses was transferred to the new Federal Government.

Virginia gave two acres of ground at Cape Henry to the government in hopes a lighthouse would be quickly built. One of Congress's first actions in 1789 had been the passage of a bill providing for the "Establishment and Support of Lighthouses, Beacons, Buoys, and Public Piers." Cape Henry was considered one of the most critical spots in need of a beacon, since it marked the way to a number of burgeoning mid-Atlantic settlements and ports.

The Treasury Department, under Alexander Hamilton, allotted money for the lighthouse almost immediately. President Washington himself made suggestions as to the materials, dimensions, and type of illuminant to be used in the tower. New York bricklayer, John McComb, was contracted to build the lighthouse. He began work in August of 1791. A year later, on October 1, the beacon was lighted for the first time by keeper Laban Gossigan. The tower was 90 feet tall, octagonal in shape, and constructed mostly of sandstone.

Fish oil was burned in the crude lamps until the early 1800s when it was replaced by whale oil in new lamps with parabolic reflectors. About 1855 a fogbell was installed to answer ships during periods of poor visibility, and two years later the lantern was equipped with a sparkling new Fresnel lens imported from France. It increased the beacon's range considerably, but at the same time made it more difficult to discern from nearby Cape Charles Light which had been built in 1828.

The tower's expensive new optic served only a short time before the outbreak of the Civil War. Confederate soldiers stormed the lighthouse, put out its beacon, and damaged the lens and tower — a scene repeated at many southern lighthouses during the war. The Union moored a lightship off Cape Henry to serve as a beacon until the lighthouse could be repaired. The tower returned to operation in 1863.

A decade later, inspection revealed several dangerous cracks in the tower walls. The structure was lined with bricks, but since it had been built on a 30 foot high sand dune, engineers decided that the unstable foundation would eventually open the fissure wider, and the lighthouse would topple. Plans were made for a new lighthouse to be built 340 feet southeast of the old tower.

The new Cape Henry Lighthouse was illuminated for the first time in December 1881. Made of cast iron plates painted in alternating faces of black and white, it was the tallest cast iron lighthouse in the nation, rising 165 feet. Its first-order lens also made it one of the most powerful beacons on the Eastern Seaboard. The distinctive checkerboard daymark distinguished it from the white tower to the north at Cape Charles and its red brick tall sister to the south at Currituck Beach, North Carolina.

Despite claims that the old tower would collapse, it survived beyond the turn of the century and remains standing today, a stubborn and battered sentry that refuses to succumb to the ravages of time. In 1930 it was placed in the care of the Association for the Preservation of Virginia Antiquities, which opened it to the public. By that time the Fort Story Army Training Base had grown up around it, along with a Navy explosives handling operation. Cape Henry had a very different seascape than when colonists first stood on its beach n 1607.

In 1939, the Coast Guard joined the military operations at the cape when it assumed operation of the new Cape Henry Lighthouse. That same year also marked the 150th anniversary of the U.S. Lighthouse Service, and old Cape Henry Light was chosen as the centerpiece of the celebration. Former Lighthouse Commissioner George Putnam gave a stirring speech from the steps of the old beacon that was heard on national radio. He praised the men and women who had stood vigil at American lighthouses since colonial days and paid tribute to all the beautiful towers guarding our shores. Old Cape Henry Light seemed to epitomize the hope, solicitude, and restless spirit of those early pioneers who struggled to make America their home.

It still inspires visitors today with rugged endurance and simple beauty, despite having given over its duties to a younger, more modern sentinel. Both the old and new Cape Henry lights are viewed by thousands each year. During the warmer months the interior of the old tower is open for climbing, and a small gift stand operates at its base. The climb up the spiral stairway is steep and tiring, but the reward is a seagull's view of the bay and the sea beyond. To the north the Chesapeake Bay Bridge Tunnel stretches out like a gigantic serpent sunning itself on the surface. To the south lie the famous beige sands of Virginia Beach, with its glamorous hotels and condos. But looking east is the most sobering view, a vast emptiness as far as the eye can see that's equally inviting and forbidding. It reminds us why lighthouses stand watch.

This article originally appeared in *Mariners Weather Log,* Fall 1988.

Author's Highlight

Dear Mrs. D.,

My family went to the black and white lighthouse at Cape Henry. It was so cool, just like you said! If you come down to Virginia Beach sometime with Mr. D., write to me, and maybe we could meet at the lighthouse.

Love, Nancy

In addition to my work as an author, I'm also a teacher. My two careers mesh well - each one helps the other. I've always felt I'm a better teacher because I'm a writer and a better writer because I'm a teacher.

Part of being a teacher is seeing students move on, both to new grades and to new schools. While teaching in a predominantly military-dependent elementary school, I was able to see the "moving" take place literally and frequently, as students came and went with their families on military assignments. This was not unfamiliar to me, since my husband has had a long career as a Navy Officer, and we have moved many times.

Certainly, the good-byes and repeated adjustments are hard for both the kids and me, but something wonderful came from many of those relocations. Some students stayed in touch with me through their love of lighthouses. I have many delightful letters, postcards, and drawings from students who have "moved on" and found a memory of me in a lighthouse they've visited. I consider it an honor to be symbolized by a lighthouse. What more could a writer and teacher ask?

I first saw the two Cape Henry lighthouses in 1975 when my husband drew orders to the USS *Shenandoah*, a destroyer tender, in Norfolk, Virginia. Looking out over the mouth of the Chesapeake - the beautiful Mother of Waters revered by the Potomacs and Rappahannocks and Choptanks - I felt a special connection to my past.

My maternal ancestors had come to this area long before, sailed up the Chesapeake, and eventually settled around Frederick, Maryland. In my blood is brackish water, oyster-shuckin', crabcakes, guitar-pickin', and duck huntin'. I still chuckle at the way my Uncle Brantley said *Baldmer* when speaking of the Chesapeake's primary port. We called it *baywooter* instead of baywater and always enjoyed a good time when somebody came home from the bay with a mess of crabs. You had to work hard to get that sweet crab meat. Aunt Grace taught us how to suck the meat out like "them crab legs is soder straws."

The family farm in Frederick County, where I was born, the youngest of many children, was far from the place where the Chesapeake cries tears of reunion with the sea, but my roots go back to it as surely as old Cape Henry Lighthouse still stands firm at its mouth. Perhaps this is why I love lighthouses so much. There's a little bit of brine in my blood. And, I like to pass it on to my students.

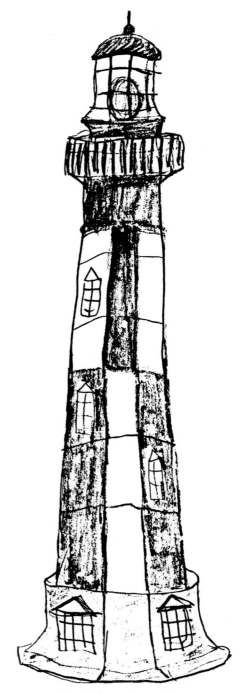

This is Nancy's pencil sketch of new Cape Henry Light. Maybe Mr.D. and I will meet her there someday.

Split Rock Lighthouse

Sentinel on Lake Superior

As the Great Lakes shipping season neared its close in 1905, carriers began tallying up their purses with excitement. More freight had been moved in and out of the lakes that year than ever before and, with several hundred vessels yet to complete their runs before the December 1 deadline, it promised to be a record season.

And record it was, but in a way no one expected. On November 23, just three days before shipping ended for the winter, a violent gale blew up, sending blinding snows and 60-mph winds ripping across the lakes. On Lake Superior alone, 29 ships were damaged or sunk. Three of these were stricken in a remote area of northern Minnesota known as Split Rock.

The powerful Lakes Carriers Association pressured Washington to build a lighthouse and a signal station at Split Rock. Among their arguments was the fact that magnetic characteristics in the rocks around Split Rock caused a compass deviation that put ships on a collision course with shore. Compounding the situation was the extreme depth of water so close to shore — too close and too deep to allow soundings to verify position.

Congress assented. In March 1907, $75,000 was appropriated for the building of a lighthouse and fog signal at Stony Point some 50 miles northeast of Duluth and only a few miles north of the tiny settlement of Two Harbors. The site was a sheer precipice rising 178 feet above Lake Superior. Like many of the rock formations in this region, it was dappled gray and topped by graceful, wind-driven evergreens. But it was the deep vertical fissure running down its face that made it so striking when viewed from the water.

The brilliant kernel of the night,
The flaming lightroom circles me:
>   *I sit within a blaze of light*
>   *Held high above the dusky sea.*
>   *Far off the surf doth break and roar*
>   *Along bleak miles of moonlit shore...*

> Robert Louis Stevenson
> **The Light-Keeper**

Sketch by Leo Kuschel

Ironically, a surveyor mapping the coast in the 1850s had noted that Split Rock was "good for a lighthouse." No doubt he was anticipating the onslaught of capitalist interests that the 1855 opening of the Sault Ste. Marie Canal would bring. But he couldn't have envisioned anything quite so picturesque as the Victorian-style sentinel that first illuminated this spot in 1910.

Once funds had been approved for the building of Split Rock Lighthouse, the government began an earnest search for an engineer to do the job. The winning candidate was a young civil engineer named Ralph Russell Tinkham. His experience on the remote vertical cliff at Split Rock would groom him for later projects on distant and dangerous islets in Alaska and Hawaii.

No roads connected Split Rock to civilization when construction of the lighthouse began in May 1909, and conquest of the cliff from water was complicated by foul weather and the sheer rise of the cliff face. Tinkham first ordered a zigzag path blazed out to the site from a nearby cove. A derrick and engine were then carried to the summit so building materials could be hoisted up the precipice from the scow-pulling tug *Red Wing*, out of Detroit. The entire station was completed in the summer of 1910 and put into operation without fanfare, for it was too isolated to attract many celebrants.

In the early years of its career, Split Rock Lighthouse was virtually inaccessible, except by water. Its three caretakers, a head keeper and two assistants, lived double lives. They and their families were brought to the lighthouse every April just before the opening of the shipping season. They kept the light burning and the foghorns blaring until mid-December when the station was shut down for the winter and the families returned to their permanent homes in the nearest towns. This practice of closing up the light for the winter continued until 1930 when families began living at the station year-round.

In summer, Split Rock was a pleasant, pastoral spot, set atop its speckled cliff and backed by miles of untouched forest. Ileana Covell Meyers, who spent her girlhood years at Split Rock, remembers feeding the chipmunks she and the other children had tamed and "summer nights so idyllically quiet fish could be heard jumping far below on the dark water..."

But tranquil evenings were matched one-for-one with nightmares. Waves sometimes pounded the rock face so furiously it seemed as if all 170 miles of open lake had hurled itself at Split Rock. Wind could shred shirts on the clothesline or send pedestrians sprawling. Snow squalls came so thick that keepers were forced to tether themselves with ropes for fear of losing their way. And as winter's deep freeze overtook the lighthouse, ice ground against the cliff with such force it seemed as if the ancient glaciers that carved the lakes had returned.

Isolation made life difficult too. The lighthouse tender *Amaranth* stopped by about every three months, bringing supplies, amenities, and guests — if they were prepared to stay awhile. Keepers willingly made the 12 mile trip by rowboat to Beaver Bay once a week to get mail and extra supplies, or to fetch a doctor when needed, but always at the mercy of the weather. Split Rock families accepted the possibility that they might be marooned in the wilderness for weeks, unable to get in or out.

Contact with the outside world burgeoned in 1924 when the North Shore Highway was built and a dirt road was cut from the highway to the light station. Isolation ended and visitors poured in by the thousands, drawn to Split Rock's majestic, lakeshore setting and the curiosity of the lighthouse and its keepers.

Pen & Ink by Lee Radzak

Orren Young and his assistant, Frank Covell, began wearing two hats — lightkeeper and tour guide. At first, tourists came only on Sundays, but soon they were arriving by the bus loads every day of the week during warmer months. In 1937, for example, Covell estimated that as many as 60,000 visitors came to the lighthouse.

These large numbers necessitated the establishment of visiting hours and rules of conduct while on the lighthouse grounds. Guests were permitted in the lantern room until scratches began to appear on the valuable Fresnel lens. They were allowed to climb out on the lofty lantern deck until several people were knocked down by the wind. Split Rock became known as "the showplace of the district."

Fences and signs were put up to steer tourists away from trouble and ensure privacy for the families. In 1938, at the strong recommendation of Keeper Covell, a safety fence was placed at the base of the tower where the cliff dropped 178 feet down to the lake.

Split Rock Lighthouse became obsolete as a navigational aid in 1969, but its popularity as a tourist spot encouraged the state of Minnesota to open it to the public in 1971. Its current resident caretaker, Lee Radzak, and his family feel a kinship with the old keepers who long ago tended Split Rock's magnificent beacon. Though they operate a gift shop, show a movie about the light's history, and oversee the site's many trails and campground, there are still days when the reality of living at a Great Lakes lighthouse becomes clear.

Radzak admits he and his family have been "captivated by the same sunrises and moonrises over Lake Superior that the keepers saw during their long nights on duty." He's also had to endure power outages, waves throwing spray over the cliff, and blizzards that bring everything to a halt. In Radzak's words, the place never shows "the same face two days in a row."

Every year on November 10, the Radzaks light the beacon as a tribute to the ore carrier *Edmund Fitzgerald*, which went down with all hands in a November 10, 1975 storm. In doing so, they retrace the steps of Split Rock's early keepers and remain mindful of Lake Superior's split personality — an inland ocean that is both serene and terrible, even for modern mariners and lightkeepers. On this commemorative night, the original 4.5 ton lens turns on a mercury float, powered by clockworks and 250 pound weights which must be wound up by hand, just as they were in 1910.

To find out more about Split Rock Lighthouse, write 2010 Highway 61 East, Two Harbors, MN 55616.

This article originally appeared in *Mariners Weather Log*, Spring 1991.

Author's Note

I am indebted to several artists whose work has complimented my writing over the years. Leo Kuschel, of Taylor, Michigan, remains a constant friend, though we have never met in person. Every Christmas I receive a hand-sketched card from him of a Great Lakes beacon; to date, my collection of these is quite large. He has generously given me artwork to use on several occasions. His lovely renderings of the lights at Split Rock and Fairport appear in this book and in *The Beacon*, the quarterly publication of the Great Lakes Lighthouse Keepers Association.

Lee Radzak also has kindly provided artwork for this endeavor. Those of us who love lighthouses consider him the luckiest man on earth. He lives the romantic life we can only dream of, caring for the beautiful lighthouse at Split Rock, Minnesota. His surroundings, coupled with considerable indoor time in the winter months, provide a plethora of fascinating subject matter for his ink pen.

Over the years, Lee has been a great letter-writer and has helped me with research and pictures. He supplied photographs when this article originally debuted in *Mariners Weather Log,* and his photograph of Split Rock Light in autumn appears on the back cover of my *Guardians of the Lights*. His intense devotion and hardworking hands keep Split Rock Lighthouse alive, though its usefulness as a navigational aid is long past. Lee often wears an old lightkeeper's uniform, and rightfully so, for he is a lighthouse keeper in the spiritual sense. His wife and children bring laughter and togetherness to the remote point, even when winter winds howl at their back door. The Radzaks truly are a lighthouse family.

Several of Lee's sketches appear in this piece. I can see the sensitivity and sincerity of his work, and I am grateful he has chosen to capture the natural world at Split Rock, for much of the color and texture of its history derives from the seasonal changes there.

Thank you Leo and Lee!

The deft pen of Lee Radzak captures the natural beauty of Split Rock.

129

Lighthouses
of
Block Island

Sentinels of a Faraway Isle

Out on the broad Atlantic rises an Island fair,
Her beacons gleaming brightly,
guarding the waters there.

Ethel Colt Ritchie

Midway between Narragansett Bay and Montauk Point is a small, tear-drop shaped island that seems to drift on the sea like a nautical mirage. When conditions are right, light fog rises from the surrounding ocean, causing a soft lavender haze to float over the island. The Pequots say it's smoke from the pipe of Hobomock, their mythical hero.

Block Island is the official name, but this eleven-square-mile piece of briny terra firma has had numerous titles during its long tenure of human occupancy. The current enticing moniker, "Bermuda of the North," derives from the island's clement weather — a gift from the warm northern edge of the Gulf Stream — and lures thousands of visitors to its shores between April and October.

The island's permanent population is less impressive — a scant 300. Most year-round residents descend from sturdy founding families who fished and farmed, salvaged shipwrecks, gathered tug for their fires, and built the miles of stonewalls that riddle the island's face. Today their incomes are earned in restaurants, bed & breakfast inns, bars, and gift shops. Perhaps the most lucrative business is bicycle rentals.

Biking south along the Mohegan Cliffs yields breathtaking vistas of the sea and Block Island's majestic Southeast Lighthouse. Rolled back from the

cliff's edge in 1992 in a much-publicized feat of ingenious engineering, the handsome Gothic-style sentinel has become Block Island's biggest celebrity, outshining even the fabled death ship, *Palatine*. Hardly a tourist departs for the mainland without some souvenir of the famous sentinel. Southeast Light appears on everything from beach towels and T-shirts to mugs and magnets. "Seen the light?" asks a popular bumper sticker.

Verrazano found no such mementos when he passed here on his early 17th century voyage along the Atlantic Seaboard. He jotted notes in his journal describing the island's hills and the precipitous cliffs on its southern tip. Dutifully, he drew its shape on his charts and called it Claudia in honor of his Italian queen. Had he dropped anchor in one of the protected coves, he would have met the natives, who called their home Isle of the Little God in honor of their great sachem, Chief Sassacus. There was no lighthouse in those days, but the Pequots occasionally lit a bonfire on the island's highest hill to guide their canoes home.

In 1614, Dutch trader and explorer, Adriaen Block, chanced upon the island and, in a moment of self-obsession, gave it his own name. Twenty years later, a Massachusetts colonist named John Oldham sailed to *Block Eyeland* to trade with the Pequots, but his Puritan principles were marred by duplicity. He gave them onion seeds that he promised would grow gunpowder. When his absurd trick was realized, the Pequots killed him.

The Massachusetts Bay Colony retaliated by driving the Pequots from Block Island and taking control. For some time no one dared venture there, for fear the Pequots would return. Finally, in 1661, a group of freemen purchased Block Island and began settlement with sixteen families. It was a winning proposition, for there were more than 300 ponds, many spring-fed, and plenty of hardwoods for building homes and boats. Weather was milder than on the mainland of New England, and the location was central to the burgeoning shipping routes that were rapidly growing between Boston, New York, and Philadelphia.

The tiny community began to prosper, and it wasn't long before Block Islanders discovered a most profitable enterprise — wrecking. While fishing and farming were mainstays of income, salvage and rescue of wrecked ships and their crews often filled a bigger purse, so lucrative at times, Block Islanders were accused of mooncussing, the unscrupulous practice of exhibiting false lights to lure ships to their doom. Bonfires to guide the island fishermen blazed sporadically on the island's northern tip at Sandy Point, atop the southern Mohegan Cliffs, and on Beacon Hill, the island's highest point; but it was easy for a vessel unfamiliar with the surrounding shoals and rocks to become disoriented. Wrecks were accidental, but disaster could be assured with a little imaginative misguidance. A lantern slung about a horse's neck and paraded along the shore bore amazing resemblance to a ship making safe passage. The uncertain sailor steered for such a ruse and ran aground, only to have his ship pillaged and a brick in a sock slammed against his skull.

Was Block Island a stronghold of ruthless mooncussers? Popular literature of the day perpetuated the rumor, and governments, both Colonial and Federal, made no serious attempt to mark the perils around the island, despite the numerous wrecks. Navigators, unsure of the tricky course in and out of Long Island Sound sailed, not by dependable beacons, but by the seat of their pants. The grisly reputation of the island might more reasonably be attributed to resentment: Fortunes in lost cargo did not readily spill onto mainland shores.

Despite its sullied character, Block Island attracted celebrities of the day. Benjamin Franklin was among the dignitaries who regularly visited Block Island to rest and socialize in its briny taprooms. Though there were no lighthouses in his time to guide vessels into the main port at Old Harbor, Franklin no doubt entertained thoughts of them, for he was much concerned with the safe passage of mail packets into Long Island Sound.

Shipping losses in the vicinity of Block Island were costly in those years. Some estimates put the total number of wrecks as high as 1000, with most occurring off the island's north point, which is part of a long shoal that geologists say once connected Block Island with the mainland. Not until 1829 was any government effort made to light this treacherous spit of sand, which marked the approach to important ports like Newport and Providence.

To prevent confusion with the single white beacon at Montauk Point, it was decided that Block Island should have twin lights. These were built at Sandy Point — two short towers attached to either end of a 25-foot house. They served mariners for about a decade before erosion and complaints about their inefficiency forced the government to replace them. The second set of double towers fared no better and were abandoned in the 1850s in favor of a single tower. It lasted until the Civil War; then sand and water destroyed it.

The fourth and final lighthouse at Sandy Point was built in 1866, a sturdy granite house with a small tower rising from its roof. It was confidently dubbed "Old Granitesides" in hopes the erosion problem had ended, but the elements began a renewed assault and sand was soon stripped from its base. A solution came in 1873 when the immediate area around the lighthouse was paved with blocks to stabilize the lighthouse plot. Erosion continued but at a snail's pace. The old North Light still stands today, though its duties as a navigational aid have ended. It now houses a museum.

"Old Granitesides" by Paul Bradley

Shortly after a lighthouse was established at Sandy Point, a second sentinel was built atop the Mohegan Bluffs on Block Island's southern shores. Southeast Light, perched 204 feet above sea level, is the highest lighthouse in New England. Its Gothic Revival architecture and the spectacular Mohegan bluffs below it make this sentinel one of the nation's most scenic.

The lighthouse overlooks the sea where the fabled Palatine Lights are sometimes seen. According to legend, the ship *Palatine* caught fire off Block Island. All aboard were rescued except for a frightened woman who had hidden below deck. As flames consumed the ship, her screams echoed across the water to the watchers on shore. A boat was launched, but the blistering heat and falling rigging prevented any rescue effort. Since that time, islanders claim to have seen eerie, unexplained lights over the sea on calm, clear nights; and occasionally those lights are accompanied by the distant wail of wind, so like a woman crying in distress.

A number of Block Island lightkeepers and their children have shared memories of life on the island in the days before automation of the lighthouses. Barbara Beebe Gaspar, now a resident of Providence, Rhode Island, has fond recollections of growing up at both of the Block Island lights where her father served some 29 years beginning in the 1920s. Barbara walked across the long spit at Sandy Point to catch the bus to Old Harbor School. Blowing sand stung her face, and during one windstorm her raincoat was shredded. In winter, the block pavement around the lighthouse iced over, and Barbara's father had to pull her up to the door on a rope, which she considered great fun.

Marie Carr, wife of lightkeeper Earl Carr, lived at Southeast Light during the 1938 hurricane. The storm tossed stones up the cliff and hurled them through her living room window. Electricity failed in the afternoon, causing the emergency generator that powered the beacon to kick on, but the keepers still had to turn the lens by hand, since the rotating mechanism was not emergency powered. While the tower suffered little damage, 25 feet of the cliff behind the lighthouse washed into the sea.

Southeast Light, by Paul Bradley

Subsequent storms brought the edge of the cliff dangerously close to the lighthouse. Block Islanders realized it would not be long before their beautiful and historic lighthouse tumbled over the cliff and into the sea. The Coast Guard also recognized the threat and relocated the beacon to a skeleton tower local residents derisively nicknamed "The Erector Set Lighthouse."

To save their beloved sentinel, Block Islanders formed the Southeast Lighthouse Foundation and raised $1.8 million to move the tower 200 feet back from the cliff. The relocation was completed in the summer of 1992. International Chimney Corporation, which specializes in large-scale projects, used hydraulic jacks and a custom-made railway to lift the lighthouse off its foundation and slide it slowly away from the bluff. On its new site, safe from the sea, the beacon was relighted in the summer of 1995.

This article originally appeared in *Mariners Weather Log, Spring, 1992.*

Interesting Trivia

Relocating lighthouses seems suddenly to be in vogue! At this writing, three in New England have been moved back from the sea to save them for future generations to enjoy. Over the next decade, I suspect more sentinels will be uprooted from their old foundations and rolled to safe spots farther inland.

There is considerable debate over whether to apply this technology to the beloved Cape Hatteras Light. I visited the site in the summer of 1996 and was shocked to see how close to the tideline the great spiral-striped tower stands. Huge sandbags are piled around its base to hold back the sea, but they will not keep time and tide from having their way.

Some believe a lighthouse, once doomed to collapse, should be allowed to die - no matter how historic or revered it is. In the case of Cape Hatteras Light, I can't agree. This tower is one of the best-known in our nation and a talisman of sand and sea for thousands who visit it every year. It's massive height and brickwork astound even the most astute engineers. Once you've climbed to its top, you cannot imagine our nation ever being without this handsome symbol of safety and guidance. How will it be saved? I think it's destined for a trip west.

Large lighthouse relocation projects like these are fascinating, but not new. The old Lighthouse Service moved a number of its lighthouses when erosion threatened them or changes to the profile of the shoreline rendered them useless. The tall, cast iron towers at Cape Canaveral, Florida and Hunting Island, South Carolina are well-known examples.

Nauset Light, which took a ride to the west in December 1996, had a much longer journey in the 1920s when it was moved up the cape from Chatham to Nauset Beach. The difference between that move and the recent one is technology. Moving lighthouses may seem new and exciting, but it's really an extension, albeit more technologically sophisticated, of an old practice.

Fairport Harbor Light

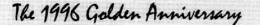

The 1996 Golden Anniversary

Fairport Marine Museum

Lighthouses are responsible for saving lives, but this is the story of a lighthouse that was *itself* saved. Fifty years ago, the old Fairport Lighthouse was a dark and disheveled sight. Local youngsters found it the target of the perfect late night dare. Weeds had grown up around it, paint was peeling on the door and ironwork, and cobwebs festooned the windows like lace curtains.

Though it had served Lake Erie shipping for a century and beckoned thousands of immigrants westward, a new, more efficient beacon had taken its place at the end of the harbor breakwater. Like many of its sister sentries, Fairport Lighthouse was no longer needed. Even the government viewed it as useless and appropriated $10,000 to demolish it.

The citizens of Fairport had other plans, however. Bound together by affection for the historic sentinel and an emerging sense of obligation to preserve the maritime heritage of the lakes, they convinced the government to grant the town a probationary lease on the lighthouse for five years. If in that time a suitable use was not found for the aging structure, it would be torn down.

No wrecking ball was necessary. The Fairport Historical Society formed to rescue the cherished old sentinel, and funds were raised to "establish a marine museum in the lightkeeper's dwelling...and preserve the lighthouse as an historic monument for posterity."

When the Fairport Marine Museum officially opened its doors in 1946, it held the distinction of being the first marine museum in Ohio and the first lighthouse museum in the Great Lakes. In addition, Fairport Lighthouse was acknowledged as one of the oldest standing structures in northern Ohio.

"We started the trend of converting old lighthouses into museums. For years, ours was the only one on the lakes and one of only three in the nation," recalls the museum's former curator, Pamela Brent, who until recently made her home in the upstairs of the old keeper's quarters.

"It's a romantic idea — living at a lighthouse — but it's not at all like it was in the old days," says Brent. "Lightkeepers had to stay on watch; they trimmed the wicks several times a night. It was especially demanding work if the weather was bad. Curators are really just caretakers. Besides, there hasn't been a light to tend here [Fairport] for years."

Thousands of visitors tour the lighthouse and museum each summer, and in the off-season school children and special interest groups arrange for special tours. Discovering a lighthouse in Ohio surprises many travelers, as does the size and power of Lake Erie:

"Visitors from other parts of the country stop at the museum and think they'll be able to see the other side of the lake," continues Brent, laughing. "They're very surprised that Lake Erie is so big, an inland sea really. The size of our lighthouse and the maritime relics on display say a lot about the lake's importance and the dangers here. I used to tell people to stop by in January if they didn't believe the weather could get serious on the lake."

Though not the tallest lighthouse in the Great Lakes, Fairport Harbor Light tops out at about 70-feet. In its active years, it was a crucial link in a string of beacons that guided shipping in and out of the upper lakes. Originally called Grand River Light, the beacon owes its existence to a sheltered lake-harbor that feeds into the Grand River. It was here that the gateway to the famed Western Reserve was established. A fertile tract of Lake Erie shorefront some 120-miles long and owned by the Connecticut Land Company, the Western Reserve attracted droves of homesteaders and speculators from the East.

No decent wagon roads had been cut across the wilderness of western New York and Pennsylvania in the early years of the 1800s, so most settlers traveled to the Western Reserve by water. A few of the more intrepid pioneers came in the winter months on heavy, ox-drawn sleighs, with the wind howling up their sleeves and the surface of Lake Erie like frosted glass.

They were attracted to the Western Reserve for the same reasons the great Iroquois tribes had migrated there centuries before: The land was rich and arable, and there was bountiful fish and game. O-he-yo, the place of the beautiful river, was a wide-open frontier waiting to be mastered. By the time settlers began putting down roots, most of the Iroquois had moved further north and west, but their liquid language still echoed in the names of many twisting rivers feeding and siphoning Lake Erie — Cuyahoga, Chippewa, Mohican, Huron, Tuscarawas, and even the "beautiful river" itself, the Ohio.

It was the French, however, who named the river and the harbor over which Fairport Lighthouse would shine. Trappers had found profitable trade here with the Indians and called the handsome estuary "La Grande Riviere." The Connecticut Land Company must have thought it a suitable name, for they translated it into the English "Grand River" and dubbed the tiny settlement "Grandon."

About 1818 a traveler named William Darby passed through Grandon and left a simple description of the river in his journal:

Pen & Ink by Leo Kuschel

134

"Grand River is a stream of some consequence....about 70-yards wide at the mouth, with a 7-foot water on the bar near the entrance to the lake. The east bank rises to a height of 30 or 40 feet according a very handsome site a village. The harbor is excellent for such vessels whose whole draft of water will admit entrance. Preparations are making to form wharves...to afford a harbor to vessels of any draft."

Steamboat traffic into the Grand River increased considerably in the early years after settlement. By 1825, when the population of Grandon had grown to about 300 and steamboat navigation was in full swing on Lake Erie, the harbor's future looked bright indeed. Citizens abandoned the name Grandon and proudly announced their town's new name would be "Fairport" — a moniker sure to attract hardworking folks from back east.

Soon there was so much activity in the harbor, it seemed sensible to build a lighthouse on Fairport's bluff. The March 26, 1825 issue of the *Painesville Telegraph* carried a notice asking for bids on the proposed lighthouse and keeper's quarters. Specifications for the sentinel included a stone or brick tower 30 feet tall. A two-story dwelling house with cellar and well was also described.

Separate bids were taken for fitting up the lantern with patent lamps and reflectors. These were most likely fueled with whale oil, as whaling was at its peak in New England and whale oil was inexpensive and accessible. The light of the beacon was intensified with silvered, parabolic reflectors placed behind each lamp. Among the lightkeeper's duties was the daily polishing of the reflectors to keep a clear, brilliant light.

Jonathan Goldsmith, a Connecticut native who had moved to Painesville, Ohio in 1811, won the construction bid for $2900. He completed the tower and keeper's house in the fall of 1825, but became embroiled in a dispute over the cellar beneath the keeper's house, which he claimed was not included in the plans he had been given. He submitted an exorbitant bid for the addition of the cellar, and since the expense of hiring another contractor was inhibitive, the Collector of Customs at Cleveland had no alternative other than to accept Goldsmith's high price. This brought the total bill for the project to $5032 — almost twice Goldsmith's original bid.

Though a respected Western Reserve architect, Goldsmith's work came into question within a decade of completion of the lighthouse and quarters. The foundation of the tower settled so much it became necessary to replace it in a costly and time-consuming project. An ironic turn of events occurred six years later when Goldsmith applied for the position of lightkeeper. He was denied when his application fell into the hands of the same Collector of Customs who had handled both the unfair bidding and the repairs to the faulty foundation. The position was given to Samuel Butler, the first of seventeen keepers to serve at Fairport Lighthouse.

The town of Fairport burgeoned over the next few decades. It served as fueling station and supply harbor for vessels headed to other ports on the lakes. These ships carried pioneers and all their earthly belongings west to new lands beyond the reserve. Everything from oil of peppermint to upright pianos sailed into the harbor and passed under the scrutiny of the lighthouse keepers, whose job included keeping records of incoming and outgoing marine traffic and collecting wharf fees.

In 1847 alone, during the tenure of keeper Isaac Spear, 2,987 vessels entered Fairport Harbor with cargoes valued at almost a million dollars. Records also indicate that other cargoes passed through the harbor at this time, buoyed by the beams of hope and freedom streaming from Fairport Light. Historians believe these priceless "goods" were hidden in the cellar beneath the keeper's house — fugitive slaves passing through Fairport Harbor on the Underground Railroad.

By the time the Civil War began, the lighthouse was in terrible condition and its archaic lamp apparatus lagged far behind the technology of the day. An 1868 inspection revealed that one of the iron bands supporting the tower had snapped, and the keeper's dwelling was dilapidated. The tower was braced to stand through the winter of 1868-69 while plans were made for a new lighthouse. A temporary beacon was erected and lit in the winter of 1869 so that the old tower could be dismantled.

With an appropriation of $30,000 work began on the new Fairport Lighthouse on April 4, 1870. Rather than repeat the same mistake Goldsmith had made with the old foundation, contractors for the new structure prepared an elaborate foundation some 12-feet deep with piles encased in concrete and a grillage of 12-inch timbers. The gray Berea sandstone tower was built on top of this sturdy base and completed up to its twenty-ninth course when work was halted due to suspension of funds.

An unpainted board cover protected the tower during the interim period, but the exposed skeleton of the keeper's house began to deteriorate almost immediately under the constant pummeling of Lake Erie wind and rain. In the spring of 1871 when work resumed, an additional $10,000 was required to rebuild the house.

On August 11, 1871 a light shone in the new tower for the first time, produced by oil lamps positioned inside a glistening third-order fixed Fresnel lens. The new illuminating apparatus with its hundreds of prisms and huge convex belt of magnifying glass was encased in a handsome brass framework and pedestal. The entire mechanism weighed several tons. Keeping the magnificent jewel polished was the bane of the lightkeeper, assuaged only by the benevolent beam cast 18-miles over the troubled waters of Lake Erie.

It wasn't until November that the keeper's quarters were complete, so Captain Joseph Babcock, whose family would tend the lighthouse for the remainder of its career, rented a house in town until his home was ready. Cost for the new tower and Babcock's dwelling was almost six times that of the original lighthouse built by Goldsmith in 1825.

The new tower was 70-feet high and had a spiral iron staircase with 69 steps leading to the light room. The tower was whitewashed in its early years of service, but later wore its natural gray garb. It was easy for approaching vessels to see, day or night, since it was situated on a slender finger of land elevated 102-feet above the lake on the east side of the river entrance.

The Babcock family tended the lighthouse for more than fifty years (1871-1925) and are its most remembered keepers. Captain Joseph Babcock escaped death in an Indian massacre at Sandusky at the age of eight, because his mother was Indian. Babcock fought in the Civil War before accepting the position of lightkeeper. His son Daniel served as assistant keeper from 1901-1919, then as head keeper until the lighthouse was decommissioned in 1925.

Two of Joseph Babcock's children, Hattie and Robbie, were born in the lighthouse. Robbie died there of smallpox at about age five. The boy's ghost is believed to haunt the downstairs of the museum. Staff describe him as "a presence of dread" sometimes accompanied by cold air and a foul smell of decay.

Pamela Brent also remembers a shadowy catlike form that was seen from time to time in her upstairs apartment. She believed it to be the apparition of one of the many beloved felines belonging to Mary Babcock, wife of Captain Joseph

Babcock. Mrs. Babcock was bedridden on the second floor for a long period during her stay at the lighthouse and was entertained by a kindle of kittens. Brent said the harmless little wraith she encountered looked like a small puff of gray smoke "skittering around on the floor as if playing, but without feet."

In 1910 the management of navigational aids was handed over to the newly-created Bureau of Lighthouses, headed by a practical and thrifty chief named George Putnam. Within months Putnam began tightening up the purse strings and making more efficient use of funds. A long overdue appropriation of $42,000 was made to improve Fairport Harbor. It provided for a new lighthouse and foghorn on the west breakwater pierhead and the deactivation of old Fairport Lighthouse.

But the nation went to war before the funds could be spent. Construction of the new lighthouse was delayed until 1921. It was completed and placed in service in 1925, the centennial of the original lighthouse. The new, 38-foot Fairport Breakwater Light had been prefabricated at Buffalo Lighthouse Depot in 1921 and shipped 147-miles across the lake to its destination, where it was quickly assembled. About $10,000 had been saved by this method of construction. The sensible Putnam earmarked the savings for the demolition of the elder sentinel.

Public outcry at the loss of Fairport Lighthouse was overwhelming. Putnam had not expected such opposition and chalked it up to local sentimentality. Feeling certain the protests would die down, he temporarily shelved demolition plans, then forgot about them. When the Coast Guard assumed control of the abandoned lighthouse in 1939, the idea of razing it revived. Again, it met with opposition, but this time the citizens of Fairport were prepared to offer an alternative — community care.

"Being a landmark in a small, close-knit community was the key," remembers Pamela Brent. "Many lighthouses are too remote to really belong to a community, and except for their keepers there's probably no one intimately tied to them. The people of Fairport banded together to save their lighthouse because it had become something more than an old abandoned building. The government was surprised that people felt so strongly about the lighthouse. It wouldn't surprise anyone today, but back then it was something new."

Much has changed at Fairport Lighthouse since it was saved fifty years ago. The Fairport Marine Museum, located in the downstairs of the old lightkeeper's house is run by about fifty volunteers. Displays showcase Lake Erie's maritime past and lore, as well as the crucial role of the lighthouse at Grand River. Among the treasured relics are the old third-order fixed Fresnel lens and the pilothouse of the Great Lakes carrier *Frontenac*. The tower is open for climbing and affords excellent views of the lake.

Fairport Marine Museum is open Saturdays, Sundays, and holidays 1:00-6:00p.m. from Memorial Day through Labor Day. Group tours are given year-round by special arrangement. Fairport Historical Society — founder and custodian of the old lighthouse and museum — celebrated its Golden Anniversary in 1996. Historian Helen Kasari says the lifeblood of the museum is its volunteers and membership, which donate hours of work and much-needed funding to maintain the museum.

This is an unpublished article in the author's files.

Recommended Reading

About ten years ago, when I first became interested in the Fairport Harbor Lighthouse, I wrote to the Fairport Historical Society for information. Their generosity was immeasurable. Among their suggestions was a book called *A History of Fairport Harbor, Ohio, 1976.*

The book was produced by the sixteen-member Fairport Harbor Bicentennial Committee. Though it sounded a bit dry, I ordered it on the recommendation of Helen Kasari, historian at the lighthouse. She said the book contained considerable information about the lighthouse and its keepers and was good reading. She was right. While Chapter 6 concentrates on "Fairport's Lighthouses," the entire book gives a well-rounded perspective on this community's history and diverse ethnic groups. Of course, no lighthouse's history exists in isolation, rather is colored by the community of which it is a part.

Of particular value to me was a clipping from the *Painesville Telegraph,* March 26, 1825, describing the proposal for construction of the lighthouse. We tend to think our government today mires itself in paperwork; this clipping proves it's been an American tradition for most of our nation's history!

There are photos as well. One special photo shows the Babcock family of lightkeepers having Thanksgiving dinner in 1912. The book is available from the Fairport Historical Society, 129 Second St., Fairport Harbor, OH 44077.

Author's Trivia

There are numerous stories like this one languishing in my files, stories written on speculation for a particular magazine or assigned by an editor only to be refused when completed. Writers, as you've probably guessed, are the world's most devoted masochists. We like to work hard on projects, knowing full well they may be rejected by editors and end up in desk drawers where they fade to various hues of yellow. Editors have all sorts of reasons for rejecting writers' work. They normally present these in list form on a rejection slip and check those reasons that apply. (Some are kind enough to pay a "kill fee" - isn't that an inspiring phrase? - when they reject work they've assigned.)

Rejection is the story of this piece. I queried an Ohio-based history magazine a few years back and got the "go-ahead" to write this article. I delivered it, as promised, only to get it back with a brief note explaining that "our editorial needs have changed since your query was approved." Where did that leave me? Perhaps I spent 10-12 hours researching and another 6-8 writing. It cost me postage two ways, plus paper, envelope, etc. It was my loss. But it was theirs too, I think.

Such attitudes about the craft of writing have always amazed me. What would our plumber say if, after he fixed the sink, we informed him: "Our needs have changed since we called for your services, so we don't intend to pay you, even though you've done the job we asked you to do."

I suppose the answer to this dilemma is, you have to love the writing more than the tangible reward. I guess I do, because this isn't the only unpublished piece in my files!

Colchester Reef Light

Little Sentinel on Lake Champlain

At the turn of the century, Electra Havemeyer Webb inherited a fortune from the sugar cane industry and began collecting assorted antiques, beginning with a cigar store Indian in 1906. As her passion for Americana swelled, so did her collection. By World War II she had decided to put it on display and chose Shelburne, Vermont as the site for her museum.

The collection soon outgrew its single-building, eight-acre home, because Mrs. Webb became enamored of American architecture and began collecting historic buildings and structures. One of the earliest of her large-scale collectibles was the Colchester Reef Lighthouse, retired to the Shelburne Museum in 1952 after a long and eventful career as a navigational aid on Lake Champlain.

Colchester Reef Light was one of about ten sentinels to serve the steamers of the lake, many of them hauling lumber down from Canada to Burlington and Albany. It sat on a stone foundation surrounded by water and warned of a group of dangerous reefs off the tip of Grand Isle, which jutted southward into the middle of Lake Champlain.

According to author Gorden P. Manning, the design for the Colchester Reef Lighthouse was obtained through a contest held by the Lighthouse Service in 1869, meant to interest notable architects and engineers in the business of lighthouse building. The present exhibits in the Colchester Reef Lighthouse include the presumed winning entry, a handsome design by Burlington engineer Albert R. Dow that looks remarkably like the actual lighthouse.

However, no mention is made of such a competition in the reports of the Lighthouse Board during those years, nor was the parsimonious and business-like government organization apt to have conducted such an activity. It's likely the "contest" was more fable than fact, and Dow probably negotiated a contract for the design.

The annual report for 1871 does detail the placement and blueprints for the lighthouse at Colchester Reef, as well as its cost:

"After a careful examination and survey of the locality, it was found that the rock called 'Middle Bunch' was the proper place for the new Light-house. This rock is in the middle of the channel, with seven feet of water over it at low water, and deep water on either side. With a Light thereon a vessel can pass on either side close to the rock...."

The crib for the light's foundation was made in Burlington, towed to the site, sunk, and filled with concrete and stones. Two courses of the foundation stonework were laid before the work season ended in 1870, just high enough to bring the structure above water. The following spring's ice jams tore away some of the stonework, as if to give a hint of the challenges that lay ahead.

Drawing by Paul Bradley

The lighthouse was completed and lit in December 1871, exhibiting a fixed white beacon visible for 11 miles. Kerosene oil lamps were used with a Fresnel lens, probably fourth order. There was also a fogbell, operated by an automatic bell striker, that sounded once every 20 seconds in periods of poor visibility. The crank for winding up the striker's weights was conveniently located inside the house.

Herman Malaney was the first keeper, with Walter M. Button as his assistant. When Malaney retired in 1882, Button became the head keeper, and the government decided that an assistant was no longer needed, especially since Button had a wife to live on the light with him and to help with the work. Harriet Button turned out to be a steadfast assistant, but she soon realized that the lake ruled her life.

That fact became miserably apparent in 1888 when the couple's fifth child was born. They had arranged to signal a friend ashore when the doctor was needed. It was hoped the lake would be clear enough of ice to allow the doctor to ferry across to the lighthouse, or frozen enough for the doctor to walk the mile from shore to the sentinel on the reef. January 29, 1888 turned out to be neither.

A thin sheet of ice covered the lake that evening when the Buttons' friend and the doctor reached shore opposite the light. But knowing Harriet Button needed help they risked a crossing on foot. When they were about halfway to the lighthouse, a wind came up and the ice began to crack. Terrified, the two watched as a fissure opened between them and the lighthouse, and the floe they were occupying began to move northward, away from their destination.

Standing at a window in the lighthouse, Walter Button watched in horror as the men hopped from one cake to another then disappeared in the darkness to the north. A short time later he welcomed his new daughter, who arrived hale and hearty and screeching a typical newborn's protest. The Buttons' friend and the doctor drifted in the darkness for several hours, then were able to wade ashore and hail a ride home.

The six Button children found ways to entertain themselves on the cloistered reef. The lighthouse had a four foot wide walkway around it, and the reef was above water on two sides of the stonework foundation. So the youngsters did have a small playground of sorts. They were permitted to take the boat to a nearby island where the family kept a garden. And there was always an assortment of pets at the lighthouse, including two squirrels that mysteriously appeared one winter day, were caught and eventually persuaded to stay as house pets.

Walter Button retired in 1901 and handed the lighthouse keys to his son, Chester, who served eight years. Though shipwrecks were not common on Lake Champlain, one is recorded in the younger Button's logbook. On a June evening in 1905 the 27-ton steamer *Mariquita* was returning to Burlington from Plattsburg when it hit Colchester Reef, in spite of the fact that the night was clear and the lighthouse was brightly lit. A great celebration might have been underway on board the steamer, since its passenger list included the Burlington baseball team and their fans. Perhaps the skipper was caught up in the revelry and forgot to watch out for Colchester Reef.

The sentinel's most devoted lightkeeper was a hulking German immigrant named August Lorenz. He spent 22 years alone on the light, unmarried and as penurious as the service that employed him. Lorenz' guests often groused that he boasted about his bankroll while serving them beans and bread. Lighthouse keepers were poorly paid, but Lorenz managed to save $28,000 during his career, cleverly deposited in three different banks so that no one would know his total worth.

Many of Colchester Reef's lightkeepers went ashore in the winter when navigation shut down on the frozen lake, but not Lorenz. The lighthouse was the center of his life, and he refused to leave it even when chunks of ice ground against it and Old Boreas came howling down the lake. Most winters the lake froze over entirely so that ice fishermen could set up camp near the lighthouse and adventurous shore residents could visit the keeper in horse-drawn sleighs.

Having watched many unfortunate souls fall through the ice, and pulled them out both alive and drowned, Lorenz determined that such a fate would never befall him. Whenever he ventured out on the frozen lake he carried a long, spiked pole that he could use to snag the ice and pull himself out in the event he crashed through the lake. Fortunately, he never needed it for this purpose, but it did come in handy on another occasion --

It was spring, and the lake had begun to break up and clog in places with huge cakes of ice. On this particular day a brisk southwest wind pushed the floe around the lighthouse. During the day Lorenz kept watch over the ice floe to see that it moved along without too much interference, but throughout the dark evening hours he could only listen to the grinding and rending of ice along the sides of the lighthouse's stone base. He was worried that the ice would pile up against the stones on a windy night and push the lighthouse off its foundation.

That evening, it almost happened. Lorenz was in the lantern working when a terrible crash and screech of wood splintering sent him rushing down the stairs. As he entered the lighthouse kitchen, oil lamp in hand, the southwest corner of the room split open, and huge pieces of ice pushed through. Lorenz danced about the kitchen in fright, avoiding the small frozen chunks that scuttered across the floor. After a minute or two the wind reversed, and the monstrous intrusion of ice slid back out, leaving a gaping hole in the kitchen wall.

Residents ashore grew uneasy at the sounds coming from the lake that night -- the ice gnawing at the lighthouse foundation; they worried for August

Lorenz's safety. Imagine their relief the next morning when the familiar profile of the keeper was seen at the railing of the lighthouse deck.

Later in the day he was seen gingerly leaping about on the ice surrounding the lighthouse. His dory, ripped from its davits and carried away during the night, was sitting up-side-down on a floating ice cake not far from the lighthouse. He was determined to rescue it, since he had saved his own money to buy the dory, and he wasn't about to let the lake have it. The wind was slowly moving the little ice cake toward him, and at the right moment he reached out with the long pole -- the one he always carried while on the ice -- and snagged the vagabond vessel.

Lorenz retired in 1931, not by choice but because the Lighthouse Service decided he was too old to remain on duty. The lighthouse was briefly tended by Joseph Aubin, then decommissioned in 1933 after an automatic flashing beacon replaced it. Shuttered and locked, it sat dark for twenty years before the Coast Guard put it up for sale. The buyer was Electra Havemeyer Webb, who thought a lighthouse would be the perfect companion for the sidewheeler *Ticonderoga,* which she had just purchased and given a new home in the grass at Shelburne Museum.

Colchester Reef Lighthouse was carefully dismantled and removed from its stone foundation, then transported to the museum piece by piece. There it was lovingly reassembled on a replica of the stone base. Huge rocks were piled around it, as if it were still vulnerable to those punishing chunks of ice. The interior was refurbished and opened as a gallery of marine art. Later, some lighthouse artifacts were acquired and put on display, among them a melodious old fogbell like the one that long ago bonged across Lake Champlain when the air was thick.

Visit the Colchester Reef Lighthouse at the Shelburne Museum in Vermont. From its landlocked perch on the grassy grounds of the museum, it's now a sentinel shedding light on history.

This article appeared in *Mariners Weather Log,* Winter 1994.

Author's Note

At right is a list of the lightkeepers who served the Colchester Reef Lighthouse during its 62-year career. The names and dates provide interesting grist for thought. Walter M. Button had three stints as keeper and handed the lighthouse keys to his son, Chester, upon retirement. The Buttons

and August Lorenz aside, most Colchester keepers served short terms. Perhaps they were not so well suited to "water, water everywhere." Oddly, James Wakefield, Jr. served before James Wakefield, Sr., and the elder Wakefield served a mere 23 days. The folks at Shelburne Museum could shed no light on that situation. My guess? Could James, Jr. have died while in service at the light, and his father kept the beacon going until Walter Button arrived?

Colchester Reef Lighthouse Keepers

- Herman Malaney, 1871-1882
- Walter M. Button, 1882-1888
- August Pare, 1888-1889
- James Wakefield, Jr., 1889-1890
- Walter M. Button, 1890-1892
- James Wakefield, Oct.- Nov. 1892
- Walter M. Button, 1892-1901
- Chester F. Button, 1901-1908
- William H. Howard, 1908-1909
- August Lorenz, 1909-1931
- Joseph Aubin, 1931-1933

Recommended Reading

Manning, Gordon P. *Life in the Colchester Reef Lighthouse,* Shelburne, VT: The Shelburne Museum, 1958.

National Archives

Tibbetts Point Lighthouse

Sentinel on the St. Lawrence Seaway

There was a time when only lightkeepers and their families knew what it was like to live at a lighthouse. The rest of us had to be content with romanticized stories of dangerous storms and shipwrecks, pea-soup fogs, ghosts, pirates, and daring rescues. But today, with many lighthouses open to the public as museums and centerpieces of parks, all that has changed. A new kind of lighthouse keeper has emerged — with a title such as curator, caretaker, host, or site manager — who will help us recapture the bygone days of wooden ships and the lights they steered by.

Of the more than 100 lighthouses in the U.S. now open to the public, almost all are accessible only during daylight hours. Lighthouses, however, are much more impressive after dark. Probing the night with their silent, piercing beams and sounding a doleful warning through the fog, they reveal the true picture of lightkeeping as a largely nocturnal vocation.

At Tibbetts Point Lighthouse on the Lake Ontario end of the St. Lawrence Seaway, visitors may stop by the station during the day, but it's more fun to spend a night at the light! Tibbetts Point is a lighthouse hostel operated by the Syracuse Council of American Youth Hostels, Inc. It opened for hostel guests in 1985 in the two keeper's houses next to the lighthouse, which is still an active navigational aid.

Facilities are sparse and homey, but very affordable considering the unique setting. Tibbetts Point Lighthouse Hostel is one of only a few lighthouses in the nation offering overnight accommodations and the momentary experience of living at a lighthouse. In these days of automation, it's as close as we can get to authentic lightkeeping.

In 1990, when I visited the lighthouse, Tom Kenny was manager of the hostel. He resided at the station from May to October with his dog, Caesar, keeping the buildings shipshape and entertaining guests with his stories about the lighthouse and the history of the region. Caesar tagged along everywhere Tom went and never missed a chance to ham it up for a visitor's camera. When my visit ended, Caesar escorted me to my car and tried to jump in!

Tibbetts Point Lighthouse sits on scenic Cape Vincent, New York, looking across the mouth of the St. Lawrence to the shores of Ontario, past the islands of Wolfe, Grenadier, and Carleton. The point was named for Captain John Tibbett of Troy, New York who owned 600 acres here in the 18th century. In 1827 the U.S. government obtained three acres of the Tibbett land and built a stone lighthouse to mark the entrance to the St. Lawrence River. It was illuminated with whale oil lamps and reflectors and cast a beam visible about 10-miles. The tower was part of a string of beacons needed by vessels entering and leaving the Great Lakes.

These rich, deep blue waters — home to bass, muskie, trout, and pike — had become important shipping routes following the American Revolution. Grain, lumber, coal, and ore were transported eastward to the hub of American society, while manufactured goods traveled west to the flourishing heartland..

Tibbetts Point Light, like others on the lakes, showed a beacon April to December, then closed for the winter. Great chunks of ice piled up around it in January and February, creating a glistening spectacle that attracted stouthearted winter sightseers who arrived by sleigh or walked over the ice. After a storm, the lighthouse sometimes became encased in ice from top to bottom, with long icicles hanging from its lantern like magnificent spires on a cathedral. In the spring, when the jam began to break up, the clamor of grinding and gnawing ice could be heard miles inland.

In 1854 the old lighthouse was demolished and the present 69-foot masonry and stucco tower was built. A beautiful Fresnel lens was purchased for it from Paris to be used with oil lamps. It exhibited a fixed white light of the fourth order. After electrification in the 1930s, Tibbetts Point Light was changed to a flashing signal, on for 6 seconds and eclipsed for 4 seconds.

A steam fog signal was installed in 1896 operated by a coal-fired compressed air boiler. Thirty years later the fog signal was converted to two diaphone horns run by a Diesel engine. Their mournful groan could be heard about 5 miles, and though they were discontinued in 1972 in favor of a radiobeacon, the old horns can still be seen protruding from the fog house in back of the tower.

Tibbetts Point Light has had many keepers in its long career. The Montonna family is the most remembered, having tended the station more than 50 years beginning in the 1880s and ending just prior to Coast Guard takeover of the station. "Semper Paratus" resided at the lighthouse from 1939 to 1981 when automation arrived, and the Coast Guard began operating the beacon and foghorns remotely from Oswego. About two years after its last lightkeeper was transferred, the station was leased to American Youth Hostels. Tibbetts Point was again occupied, this time by happy vacationers and travelers.

The community of Cape Vincent launched the Tibbetts Point Historical Society in 1988 to help restore and preserve their lighthouse and its ancillary buildings for educational purposes. A group of seventh graders at a local school pitched in to clean up the grounds, mow grass, and paint. The small square lighthouse that once stood at the end of the town breakwall and had been moved to the southern approach to Cape Vincent was spruced up and made a welcome landmark.

Society member Shirley Hamblen rallied tremendous support for the lighthouse restoration project. It included plans to install an exhibit hall featuring the history of the region and the light's important role as a Great Lakes sentinel. She enthusiastically steered visitors from her gift shop in Cape Vincent to the spot where Tibbetts Point Lighthouse stands its windy, lakeshore watch. If visitors couldn't stay the night at the hostel, she advised them to take in the sunset over Lake Ontario. It's the next best thing to having the beacon sweep over your bedroom window at night.

Sadly, Shirley Hamblen passed away in 1996, but her love and devotion for Tibbetts Point Lighthouse lives on in the hearts of many Cape Vincent residents who hope to realize her dream of restoring the lighthouse and preserving its history. For information on the project or the hostel, write Tibbetts Point Lighthouse Hostel, RR1, Box 330, Cape Vincent, NY 13618..

This article is an updated version of the original which appeared in *Mariners Weather Log*, Fall 1991.

Sketch by Paul Bradley

142

Saugerties Lighthouse

Visit to a Sentinel on the Hudson

The wind was blowing briskly out of the southeast on a clear day in October 1993 as I followed the wet, sandy trail to the old sentinel at Saugerties, New York. Sea oats waved their blonde heads, gulls cried, and water bubbled up around the soles of my sneakers, reminding me that the Hudson River is still a tidal estuary here, some 100 miles north of the sea.

There's seldom a day when the wind doesn't buffet the narrow point where the lighthouse sits perched on its round stone pier. Curator Steve Thomas grew accustomed to the eerie, high-pitched squeals coming through the cracks in the walls, the muffled thump of the bell rope against the house, and the rattle of window panes.

He would go up to the lantern gallery at least once a day to untangle "Old Glory," and occasionally to replace the flag if its edges had become too tattered. Rarely did he hang his wash outside, for the wind would spirit it away, the same way it stole his cap when he escorted me up to the gallery high above the river.

"I'm not a lighthouse keeper in the traditional sense," Thomas admitted. Yet his life wasn't really much different from the keepers who lived here in the 1940s. Though the modern beacon in the lantern operated automatically, and the extra bedrooms upstairs held displays and B&B accommodations, Thomas still kept the place in good order. I suspected he was more "keeper" than he thought.

There was no TV, but I heard a radio quietly playing as we entered the kitchen. It was chilly in the house. Thomas said heat was a luxury. Sometimes he looked forward to crawling in bed under his electric blanket. Electricity was meager too -- supplied by a small generator.

"I can't keep ice cream in this frig," he laughed. "Not enough power. Of course I could store it outside in winter, but it's always summer when I want it!"

He was alert for trouble on the river, though it came less often during his tenure as caretaker than in the past when Lighthouse Service keepers kept watch, and Steve's concerns usually involved recreational boaters rather than commercial vessels. In summer when the lighthouse is open to the public, he patiently greeted visitors, showed them around the restored station, and enthusiastically recalled the days when sloops, barge tows, ferries, steamboats, and little periaugers passed the lighthouse.

Thomas reminded me that in those days there was no electricity and plumbing. Telephone service didn't arrive until World War II. The earliest Saugerties lightkeepers were, like their forebears, hardworking river valley folk who loved the water and earned their livelihood from it. Some fished or cut ice; others ran ferries or lightered cargo. They knew every twist and turn, shoal and sandbar of this deep and vital waterway; some even boasted the ability to pilot it blindfolded.

As commerce increased on the Hudson River in the early 19th century, lights were needed to guide those less familiar with the vagaries of its 140 mile navigable northward reach into Appalachia. The opening of the Erie Canal in 1825 and the Delaware and Hudson Canal in 1828 made the river a critical link between the rich importers and manufacturers of New York and the burgeoning agricultural communities of the Midwest.

Sketch by Paul Bradley

143

"Very historic place," Thomas mused from a stool in the small exhibit room after he had shown me the interior of the lighthouse.

Indeed, Saugerties Lighthouse was the first sentinel established on the Hudson River. In the early 1830s Congress appropriated $5000 for its construction and selected the north bank of the mouth of Esopus Creek as the best site. By 1835 the station was operating. A stone crib served as the foundation for a square house with a lantern on its roof, 42-feet above water. Five whale oil lamps, fitted with parabolic reflectors, produced enough light to guide vessels into or past Ulster, as the town of Saugerties was then called.

Abraham Persons, the light's first keeper, served only two years before being dismissed. The government discovered that he was living several miles from the lighthouse and had hired someone to tend the light for him. This sort of "subcontract" activity was strictly forbidden by the Lighthouse Service. Persons' replacement, George Keys, was reminded to reside on site and to tend the beacon himself.

With the decline of whaling in the 1850s, the lamps were switched to mineral oil. A short time later the station got its first prism lens, a sixth-order Fresnel made in France and fitted with hollow-wicked Argand lamps. Thomas told me Saugerties' lightkeepers spent much of their workday cleaning and polishing the prisms and brass of the lens. (Nowadays, a modern, plastic beacon does the job. It requires practically no maintenance. Thomas had to wipe down the windows when cobwebs formed and give the beacon a dusting when the spirit moved him. It's a self-sufficient system.)

Saugerties Light was rebuilt in 1867 on a larger stone pier next to the original beacon. The Fresnel lens was moved to the new lighthouse, and for a few years, the two sentinels sat side-by-side -- one dark, the other lighted. The elder sentinel was sold and dismantled in 1872.

The second and present Saugerties Light saw 85 years of continuous service before it was automated in 1954 and its keepers were removed. Twenty-two keepers, two of them women, had served at the station since its inception in 1835. But with no one to maintain it, the lighthouse rapidly deteriorated and was deemed a fire hazard. The Coast Guard removed the light, set up a post beacon to replace it, and announced plans to demolish the historic lighthouse.

Local residents, moved by the entreaties of retired Saugerties keeper Chester Glunt and his wife Ruth Reynolds Glunt, a local historian and author of *Lighthouses and Legends of the Hudson,* mounted a campaign to save their cherished sentinel. For twenty years, the lighthouse languished while the Coast Guard and the public debated the options.

In 1976 the Saugerties Arts Council pushed forward and managed to transfer the property into state hands. The Saugerties Lighthouse Conservancy then formed and acquired the lighthouse from the state in 1987.

The group labored to restore Saugerties Light, preserve its history, and make it accessible to the public. Steve Thomas did much of the carpentry work on the interior, but he was quick to give credit to a long list of other talented contributors. "It was practically a shell. We've truly rebuilt the place," he told me with a satisfied nod.

The beacon was returned to the lantern in 1990, though it is a modern solar powered aero-marine that doesn't quite match the old-time ambiance of the station. But the 1909 fogbell does. As I stood on the gallery looking downriver, hair flying in the crisp Hudson breeze, Steve Thomas indulged my desire to hear the fogbell's lilting bong. I could see the worn spot on the bell lip where the striker had pounded it year after year. The bong was low and mellifluous and quickly snatched up by the wind. Some hikers on a trail far below turned and stared, as if wondering what the mournful sound meant.

"Wanna hear it again?" Thomas asked me, grinning like a ten-year-old.

This article originally appeared in *Mariners Weather Log,* Spring 1994.

For information on visiting Saugerties Lighthouse and B&B accommodations contact the Saugerties Lighthouse Conservancy, P.O. Box 654, Saugerties, NY 12477, (914)246-9170.)

On your way to the lighthouse, stop by the Hudson River Maritime Museum at Kingston, New York. Exhibits in the museum detail the history of Hudson River lighthouses, and a 40-foot liberty boat runs out to Roundout Lighthouse several times a day. Special events are held at the lighthouse, and visitors may make arrangements to spend the night in the historic sentinel. Call (914)338-0071 for more information.

Cape Cod's Sister Sentries

The Triple Beacons at Nauset Beach

Cape Cod's steep cliffs at Nauset and Highlands overlook the sea from the center of the cape's infamous backside beach, an eroded strand of bluffs and hollows and salt marshes that receives the brunt of Atlantic wind and has witnessed numberless maritime tragedies.

Near this beach the Nauset Indians came to the aid of the survivors of the *Sparrow Hawk,* an English ship bound for the Virginia Colony in 1624 but forced ashore along the cape by scurvy and near-mutiny. Henry David Thoreau beachcombed here and spent a night with the lighthouse keeper at Truro. Years later, Henry Beston lived a hermit's life in a spartan beach house near Nauset and penned a tribute to the beauty of the sweeping seascape:

I see the lantern now as a star of light which waxes and wanes three mathematical times, now as a lovely pale flare of light behind the rounded summits of the dunes. The changes in the atmosphere change the colour of the beam . . .

Beston's "three mathematical times" describes well the first beacon at Nauset Beach. In 1838 the nation's only set of triple lighthouses was built here — three diminutive white towers capped with black lanterns. The little sentinels were intended to assist coastwise navigators hugging the backside of the cape, and they were quickly dubbed the "Three Sisters of Nauset," due to their striking resemblance to three dainty ladies in white dresses and black hats.

The government opted for triple lights at Nauset to distinguish these beacons from other lighthouses in the area. At Monomoy a single beacon guided shipping around the cape's southern extremis; at Chatham, near the elbow, there were twin lights; on the Highlands north of Nauset a landfall beacon stood, the brightest on the cape. The European system of flashing lenticular optics was not yet in use in the U.S. in the 1830s, so multiple lights provided the answer to the problem of identifying lighthouses in close proximity.

The three small Nauset lighthouses were constructed in only 38 days, each one of brick, 15 feet tall, with iron lanterns and granite stairways. They were situated 150 feet apart atop the 70 foot high bluffs at Nauset Beach. Their builder, Winslow Lewis, also constructed a keeper's house and dug a well, in addition to outfitting the towers with old-fashioned oil lamps and reflectors — all for a prudent pricetag of $6,549. His work was severely criticized, for he had not built the towers in the exact positions surveyors had chosen, and they were built directly on the sand with inferior materials.

National Park Service

In 1858 the archaic oil lamps and reflectors of the Three Sisters were upstaged by sixth-order Fresnel lenses imported from France, which greatly improved the range and clarity of the lights. Ten years later, blowing sand had so badly frosted the lantern windows they had to be replaced. By this time, it was apparent that erosion was claiming the bluff at a measurable rate and would eventually topple the little lighthouses.

Recognizing the threat, the Lighthouse Board in 1892 replaced the old brick sentinels with three 22 foot wooden towers situated farther inland. The original lantern caps and prism lenses were moved onto the new towers. Within a few years, the decapitated brick towers tumbled over the cliff and disappeared into the sea. Beachcombers still occasionally find pieces of their brickwork, smoothed by decades of tumbling in the surf, and an occasional low tide uncovers the old foundations.

In 1911, the penurious chief of the newly-formed Bureau of Lighthouses, George Putnam, decided the beach at Nauset was a prime example of "overlighting." An inspection revealed that erosion was again threatening the station and that the yearly consumption of 300 gallons of oil could be reduced to 100 gallons if two of the lighthouses were discontinued. In addition, sailors claimed the triple lights merged into a single or double light from certain positions at sea, causing confusion.

Putnam extinguished two of the Nauset triplets and ordered the third triplet moved next to the keeper's house where it was attached by a covered walkway. Its brilliance was increased with a fourth-order flashing lens, but the keeper complained that the little tower vibrated in the wind, causing the light to pulse. Guywires were installed to stabilize it and no further vibrations were reported. The two abandoned towers were decapitated and sold for $3.50 each to a local resident, who converted them into a summer cottage.

In 1923, one of the twin lights at Chatham was also discontinued. Since it was tall and a sturdier, cast iron tower," Putnam decided to move it to Nauset Beach and decommission the remaining "Sister." The new Nauset Light was painted lower half white and upper half red to distinguish it from Highland Light and its Chatham twin. Though Putnam was noted for his solemnity, he gave the new Nauset Light a triple flash, in honor of the lost little trio that had served mariners for 85 years.

The last, headless little "Sister" was hauled away and underwent a facelift similar to its siblings'.

It served first as a cottage, then a hamburger stand for the tourists who flocked to Nauset Beach in the summer. No one protested the irreverent fate of the Three Sisters. Hardly anyone was aware of their historic importance as the only triple light station ever built in the U.S. and one of few worldwide.

The Casquets off Cherbourg, France once had triple lighthouses, as did the dangerous Lizard in the Scilly Isles at the entrance to the English Channel, but neither set of triple towers stands intact today. Time and tide have reduced the Casquets to stumps and obliterated the Lizard's trio.

In the 1960s, when the National Park Service established Cape Cod National Seashore, interest in preserving cape heritage burgeoned, and the uniqueness of the Three Sisters was realized. Fortunately, it was not too late to save them. One by one the hapless, little towers were purchased by the park service and placed in storage until funding became available to refurbish them.

In the late 1980s the towers were repaired. Only one, "The Beacon," had its lantern intact, and not enough money was appropriated to fabricate new lanterns for the other two. Rather than wait for additional funding, the National Park Service went ahead with restorations, for the Sisters were badly deteriorated.

The Three Sisters now sit in a wooded park a safe distance from the erosive beach. Though they no longer function as active navigational aids, they shed great light on the seafaring history of the 19th century and stand as small monuments to Yankee ingenuity.

Occasionally, when severe storms pound the backside of the cape, the old brick foundations of the previous Three Sisters are uncovered by the waves. Tourists question each other in fascination, but the cape's old-timers understand the significance of this hide and seek game of the tide. Such occurrences are grim reminders that the sea still holds claim to Cape Cod and is pushing it ever westward, inch by inch. The tenure of the Three Sisters has been a mere wink of the cape's geologic eye.

This is an updated version of an article that appeared in *Sea Frontiers,* March 1986.

Recommended Reading

Life on the Edge, a small, privately published booklet about the lighthouses of Nauset by J. Brian West, is an excellent, concise history of the Three Sisters. Contact Cape Cod National Seashore.

Nauset Light

Guardian of the Backside Beach Cape Cod

High on the steep bluffs of Cape Cod's Nauset Beach stands a weatherworn cast iron lighthouse. Its revolving signal of alternate red and white flashes duplicates the conspicuous daymark, a bright, candy-stripe color scheme seen 19-miles at sea. It overlooks a panorama of sea, sky, scrub pines, and dunes and is the guardian of centuries of cape history.

Here, the Nauset Indians traded corn and beans with the Pilgrims long ago, and countless castaways washed ashore from shipwrecks after running amok of the cape's notorious backside perils. Their misfortunes would result in Houses of Refuge — tiny, weatherbeaten shacks with basic supplies for survival — and launch the U.S. Lifesaving Service, a precursor to the Coast Guard whose intrepid members were dedicated to search and rescue.

Somewhere beneath the drifted dunes of Nauset, under the vigilant beam of the red and white tower, also can be found the footprints of American literary "beacon" Henry David Thoreau, who walked the entire length of the cape twice to experience its raw power and beauty. Henry Beston was drawn here too, and lived a solitary existence in his famed "Outermost House."

When Thoreau passed by in the 1840s, three tiny lighthouses stood side-by-side on Nauset Beach. They were still there when Beston lived in his tiny cottage at the turn-of-the-century. These triple beacons — designed to differentiate themselves from the numerous white, fixed lights of the cape — were barely 30-feet tall and stood 300-feet apart. Sailors affectionately called them the Three Sisters, because of their resemblance, from a distance, to three ladies in white dresses and black bonnets.

Over the decades, erosion toppled several sets of triplet towers, and their foundations now lie submerged under the sea, as do the sands where Thoreau and Beston walked. The most recent set of triple towers, built in 1892, served only three decades before being deemed frivolous and an obvious case of "overlighting." At the beginning of the 20th century the triple lights were discontinued, upstaged by beacons with flash sophisticated characteristics. Nauset Beach still needed a lighthouse, however, and the Bureau of Lighthouses didn't have to look far to find one.

Chatham, some 15 miles south, had cast iron twin lights that had been built in the 1870s. About 1920, the 48-foot tall north twin was deemed unnecessary and was darkened. Three years later, it was dismantled and moved by barge up the cape to Nauset Beach. There it was bolted to an exposed concrete perch on the high bluffs some 115-feet above the sea. A fourth-order prism lens was installed, fueled by kerosene and powered by clockworks with huge weights suspended in the tower. The lightkeeper, George Herbolt, had to wind up the weights every eight hours.

Nauset Light, 1923, Nauset Light Preservation Soc.

The old, handsome keeper's house from the Three Sisters' site was moved back from the sea's edge and next to the tower. There were few trees on the beach in those days and the lighthouse was the most conspicuous structure. It was also a safe distance from the cliff's crumbling edge. In 1940 the tower was painted with a bright red stripe to set it apart from its neighboring beacons at Chatham and Truro. As if to preserve the nostalgia of the defunct Three Sisters lighthouses, the beacon flashed three times every ten seconds.

Over the years, Nauset Light served quietly in its picturesque setting. Summer tourists enjoyed being photographed with the pretty sentinel in the background, and weddings were sometimes held on the grounds of the station. The keeper's cottage was occupied by numerous Lighthouse Service and Coast Guard personnel.

Among the station's most colorful families were the Haskins, who served the lighthouse from 1932 to 1938. Allison Haskins was a much-respected man with many talents who won the coveted First District Pennant while stationed at Nauset Light in 1934. His three daughters attended a one-room schoolhouse in Eastham and enjoyed memorable childhoods at Nauset Beach. Leona Haskins, wife of the keeper, could always find her husband by attaching a note to the family dog's collar. The loyal canine was seldom away from his master.

The last resident keeper of the light was Eugene Coleman, who left his post in 1952. At this time, the lighthouse was made automatic with the installation of a modern aerobeacon. The unneeded keeper's house was sold and has been since occupied by private individuals.

In winter, storms and wind pound the cape, weathering away the steep cliff at Nauset — sometimes consuming as much as three feet of ground per year. The entire backside of the cape — from elbow to fingertips — is moving westward, and no amount of shoring up the beach will halt its march. This has been a concern at many light stations on the cape and the primary reason Nauset Light is built of cast iron plates. If erosion threatens, it can be moved back from the sea.

In the early 1990s, the Coast Guard, realizing the Nauset Lighthouse would soon fall over the cliff, announced plans to decommission it. Residents of the cape could not imagine Nauset Beach without its beautiful lighthouse. It had been admitted to the National Register of Historic Places some years earlier, and there was no argument as to its historic significance. The Nauset Light Preservation Society quickly formed, and efforts began to raise funds for the relocation of the lighthouse. The little garage built for the first keeper in 1926 was turned into a gift shop and donation station.

The tower's new site, a safe distance from the cliff, was donated by the National Park Service. Funding was provided also by the Federal Intermodal Surface Transportation Enhancement Act and the Massachusetts Department of Environmental Management. The relocation process was begun in the fall of 1996 by International Chimney Corporation of Buffalo, New York, a firm which had successfully moved two other lighthouses.

A special cross steel and dolly system was designed to move the tower after it was hoisted out of its old foundation. The dolly had a unique three-point suspension to keep the tower level on its downhill journey to the new site about 300-feet southwest of the original location. The historic oilhouse also was moved to the new site. Eventually, it is hoped the historic keeper's cottage will join the tower in the new location.

This article is scheduled to appear in *Mariners Weather Log*, Fall 1997.

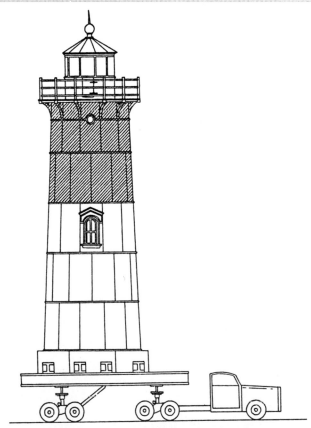

Courtesy of International Chimney Corporation

Mount Desert Rock

Lonely Luminary on the Sea

"What mad misanthrope chose to build a lighthouse on this hostile, forsaken rock?" asked a 19th century writer. Storm waves often breach Mount Desert Rock, the wind scours it mercilessly, and on many occasions huge rocks — some weighing as much as 75 tons — have been tossed onto its craggy plateau. Sequestered and exposed to the full fury of the Atlantic, it is among the nation's loneliest outposts.

On this barren, half-acre shelf of granite 24 miles out in the Gulf of Maine stands Mount Desert Rock Lighthouse. The 58-foot, rough-hewn tower appears to grow out of the jagged ledge, as if carved by the waves. But human hands built this sentinel at great risk, for the sea here seems never still and safe anchorage for a boat is nearly impossible.

A lighthouse was first placed here in 1829, a ramshackle affair consisting of a small wooden house with a beacon on its roof. The lightkeeper and his family led a wretched and isolated existence, plagued by the weather, hunger, and separation from civilization. To assuage their misery, fishermen brought them barrels of soil and flower seeds, which they crammed into the crevices of ledge to make rock gardens.

In 1893, the current stone tower was built. Its rotund, sloping form, gray and sturdy, was designed to direct waves back upon themselves and to discourage the wind from lingering. Despite its age, the tower remains strong and still serves the fishermen and boaters of Blue Hill Bay and Frenchman's Bay.

Mount Desert was among the most challenging assignments for lightkeepers, even after the Coast Guard took over in the 1940s and such amenities as a television and video games broke the monotony and solitude. Under Coast Guard management, Mount Desert was a "stag station," with only men serving, but early in its career, families lived at the secluded beacon. A year's supply of provisions was kept in the storerooms, in the event the supply tender could not make regular visits. Children were tethered to prevent falls from the 20-foot cliffs surrounding the rock, and wives seldom got off the rock. One woman who lived at the lighthouse at the turn-of-the-century did not visit the mainland for seven years.

Winters were especially difficult. Wild Atlantic storms raged over the rock, imprisoning the lightkeepers for days at a time. When they had to clean the exterior of the lighthouse lantern, leather harnesses were used to prevent falls. The rock was bitterly cold and ice build-up in the lantern and house was a problem. No wood was available on the rock, so the families had to ration coal and kerosene carefully for the stoves.

Numerous wrecks have occurred near the lighthouse, including the ocean tug *Astral,* which crashed into the submerged north end of the ledge at Mount Desert in a December 1902 gale. The lightkeepers heard the *Astral's* whistle screaming through the flying vapor and went to the tug's assistance. Despite frigid temperatures and a hampering high tide, they were able to rescue all but one of the crew of 18 using ropes and life preservers.

Mount Desert Rock Lighthouse withstands some of New England's heaviest weather. The gale of 1842 dislodged a 57 ton boulder from the tideline of the ledge and tossed it on the rock's plateau. Another storm moved a 75-ton rock a distance of 60-feet. The station's earliest fog signal was a large bell rung by hand. The bell keepers were relieved when a steam foghorn was installed in the 1890s. Its harsh wail was more audible than the lilting tones of the old fogbell, and its coal-fired bellows operated the signal automatically.

Mount Desert Light was completely automated in 1977 and its last two Coast Guard keepers were removed. Both were happy to leave the lonely station, but they were quickly replaced by other attendants. Today the College of the Atlantic in Bar Harbor, Maine utilizes the station for marine studies.

Students live on the rock for varying periods and keep watch from the lighthouse lantern for whales and other marine life. They also conduct bird banding of the tiny pelagic Leach's storm petrel which seeks refuge on the rock but does not nest there because there is no soil to burrow.

Information is collected on the types of whales sighted and their behavior patterns. Large baleen whales and small-toothed whales frequent these waters and vary in population according to the availability of herring and plankton. Because of Mount Desert Rock's remote offshore location amid colliding currents, its waters are rich in marine life and whale behavior is undisturbed by boat traffic.

The lightkeepers of yesterday considered Mount Desert Rock a dreadful assignment, but for the 40-some volunteer researchers who come to the rock each year, it's one the world's finest living laboratories and a beacon of light for marine science.

This article appeared in *Mariners Weather Log*, Spring 1996.

Author's Note

Over the years I've written a number of short stories where the setting was a familiar friend - a lighthouse. I don't consider myself a strong writer of fiction (although one of my stories won a literary prize in 1992), but I do feel one of my best in the lighthouse genre is "Mainland Soil." Not surprisingly, it is set at Mount Desert Rock, and the plot concerns a young woman awaiting her husband's return from the mainland. He brings her a gift, something you or I would consider a strange offering to one's beloved. But for her, it is sweet and treasured, and a symbol of her strong bond to the land, despite her sequestered existence on a barren and distant rock.

I dare not tell more, else I risk spoiling the ending. Suffice it to say, this tale is a bittersweet mixture of hardship and happiness. I have presented it in various ways in *The Keeper's Log, Guardians of the Lights*, and *Lighthouse Victuals & Verse*. Often, I tell it to school children. Even they grasp the message that we all need things to remind us of home and family when our loved ones are far from us.

People wonder what is lost when lightkeepers are removed from a lighthouse, when it no longer requires human hands to tend its beacon. What remains is a soulless, silent tower - home to no one but spiders and seabirds. No laundry waves on the clothesline, no children scamper about in play, no footsteps are heard on the stairs, no sweet smells of bread and pies waft from the kitchen, and no rough, over-worked hands cram dirt and seeds into rocky crevices to bring color into a life of dismal gray.

We should be thankful people no longer endure a miserable existence at Mount Desert Rock. Yet, something precious and pious and pure is gone from its gray pinnacles and can never be replaced.

Point Cabrillo Lighthouse

An Old Time California Light Station

In the purple twilight of June 10, 1909 a placid, pastoral scene greeted mariners along the northern California shore near Mendocino. At first glance it appeared to be a quaint country church with a lamp flickering sleepily in its steeple--a beacon of salvation for the coastwise sailor. But the structure had a more earthly mission. It was to guide the doghole schooners of the Pacific Northwest lumber trade and serve as a navigational beacon to any other shipping that passed by.

In its halcyon days, the Point Cabrillo Lighthouse could easily have passed for a seaside chapel and its caretaker a minister of deliverance, for such metaphors are easily attributed to lighthouses. Throughout its 65 year career numerous offshore calamities occurred, and the nearby Coast Guard patrol and rescue units were kept busy answering distress calls, some placed by the Point Cabrillo lightkeepers themselves.

Fittingly, a light that served the lumbermen was made almost entirely of wood, except for its iron lantern. The beacon itself was a flashing third order lens on top of a 47 foot octagonal tower attached to one end of the fog signal house, where twin sirens faced seaward ready for the murk that frequently plagued the area. Three keepers homes, for the principal keeper and two assistants, were surrounded by bent, gnarled cypress trees and several small outbuildings. The whole complex was situated on a dramatic, spray-dashed cliff that reminded well-traveled seamen of the Cornwall Coast of England.

Wilhelm Baumgartner appears to have been the station's first keeper, and he was, no doubt, pleased with such a pleasant assignment. Point Cabrillo Lighthouse was not as cloistered as many of its companion sentinels on the West Coast, nor as

dangerous. The access road was clear and smooth, and the comforts of civilization were close by--a school, stores, a church, a doctor, friendly neighbors.

Like all lighthouses, this one had its drawbacks, though they were small by comparison. Fog was persistent, demanding that the sirens be put to work on the station's first night of duty. Eventually, the lighthouse would be assigned three lightkeepers, owing to the prevalence of fog and the work required to keep the fog signal going. Wind blew incessantly, causing the hunched-over stance of the trees, shredding the station flag, and challenging the clothespins to hold fast to their wash-day charges.

An occasional severe storm threw waves over the point too, bringing heavy rains that made the cliffs so sodden they crumbled underfoot. One of the cows living at Point Cabrillo fell victim to the unpredictable terrain when the ground gave way beneath her and sent her tumbling down the cliffs into the sea. The keepers rescued her with a makeshift hoist powered by the head keeper's car.

A more serious consequence of the point's precarious topography was the near death of keeper Harry Miller in the 1940s. Miller, as other keepers before him, was plagued by flooding in the basement of his house when rains were heavy. During a particularly troublesome storm, he and his assistant, Thomas Atkinson, decided to dig a trench behind their homes to carry the rainwater into the sea.

When digging reached a depth of about 8 feet Miller suddenly felt the bottom of the pit fall away beneath him. Sinking in the saturated sand, he was quickly mired up to his knees. Atkinson realized his friend was being sucked into a subterranean cavern; he grabbed Miller's arms and pulled. Miller's feet came out of his boots with a loud *whoosh,* and he clambered up the walls of the pit in his socks, thankful to be alive.

In 1952, veteran lightkeeper Bill Owens came to the station with his wife, Isabel. The parents of four lively daughters, they had served at several other California lighthouses and would be the last civilian family assigned to Point Cabrillo. Owens' tenure was relatively uneventful until February 8, 1960 when a savage storm arrived from the west and pounded the point.

Owens and his assistants had turned on the beacon a few hours before the storm hit, and one man had gone on watch in the small building adjacent to the lighthouse. As steady westerly winds pushed against the shore, the seas heightened and began breaking over the point. Spume so obscured the light that the keeper on watch knew the fog signal had to be turned on. The ground was awash, and he was unable to go to the building that housed the horns.

The storm raged throughout the night and much of the following day. The light continued to operate, despite the heavy weather pummeling the walls around it. When the fury abated, the landscape was strewn with debris and rocks, some of them weighing as much as two tons. The seaward side of the lighthouse had been stripped of its siding, and the doors to the fog signal room had been smashed. A generator and air compressor were pushed to one side of the room, and nearly a foot of pebbles and sand covered the floor. Fortunately, the beacon had weathered the storm and was still operating.

Resident lightkeepers continued to tend the 35-acre Point Cabrillo Light Station until it was automated in the 1970s. Like many self-sufficient lighthouses, it was then locked and the property around it posted with warnings against trespassing. Soon after it closed, concerns over the future of the point were raised, especially about issues of subdivision and residential development.

In 1978 the California Coastal Conservancy was enlisted to help establish a workable plan for the preservation of Point Cabrillo. The Conservancy was able to acquire the property around the lighthouse from the Coast Guard and then purchase privately owned land bordering the station. In all, 300 acres were acquired, including considerable waterfront where wind-blown cypress trees stand hunched over and the shore is carved into deep recesses and caves.

Public use guidelines for the point were established and a plan was developed to carry them out. As of 1993, the final chapter in the Point Cabrillo story was yet to be written and will likely depend on the amount of funds raised to preserve the old station.

The Conservancy envisions the development of an educational park where whale-watching, beach activities, natural history tours, and a small museum are enjoyed by visitors to the lighthouse. The station's original Fresnel lens is still intact although it has been upstaged by a strobe beacon, and the buildings are in good shape. West Coast lighthouse historian Ralph Shanks describes Point Cabrillo as "the best example of a complete, old-time light station in northern California."

For more information on Point Cabrillo Lighthouse and its scenic seaside surroundings, contact the California Coastal Conservancy at 1330 Broadway, Suite 1100, Oakland, CA 94612-2530.

This article originally appeared in *Mariners Weather Log*, Spring 1993.

Recommended Reading

When it comes to West Coast lighthouses, Ralph Shanks is an acknowledged expert. His books include *Lighthouses and Lifeboats of the Redwood Coast* and *Guardians of the Golden Gate*. Both are excellent reading — chocked full of history and interesting lore written in an easy anecdotal style that does not detract from their accuracy. Shanks keen sense of the inter-relationships of the old Lighthouse Service, Lifesaving Service, and the emerging Coast Guard define his work. To discover more about the history of Point Cabrillo Light and other sentinels of the California shore, refer to Shanks' *Lighthouses and Lifeboats of the Redwood Coast*.

James Gibbs, as previously mentioned, is also an excellent West Coast lighthouse historian and one of my favorite lighthouse authors. While Shanks has concentrated mainly on the sentinels and lifesavers of California, Gibbs' work takes in the entire Pacific Coast, from Southern California to Alaska and even far-flung Hawaii. Point Cabrillo Lighthouse appears in his *West Coast Lighthouses* and *Lighthouses of the Pacific*.

Author's rough sketch of Point Cabrillo Light
(Perhaps I should stick to writing and leave the art to true artists.)

The Lone Star Lights

Sentinels of Texas

Southern sentinels, particularly those in the Gulf of Mexico, have never enjoyed the same public acclaim given New England's rustic old lighthouses. Yet many of the Gulf lights bear striking resemblance to traditional Yankee towers, with long careers in perilous places, ably tended by stouthearted men and women of inimitable spirit.

Texas alone, with 400 miles of hurricane-battered, shoal-riddled shore, could rival any of our nation's coastal states for the grim title, "Graveyard of Ships." But the Lone Star State isn't celebrated for its maritime past the way New England is. Tall ships, smoky port taverns and crowded wharves, and those majestic masonry lighthouses spewing their bright beams seaward seldom conjure images of Texas; yet these things were part of the past in our second largest state, long before its bronze sands were turned black with oil and the profiles of derricks stood like skeletons along its shores.

No roads led into Texas in the early 1800s, only cow paths and Indian trails; hence pioneers and land speculators came by ship, dodging stealthy shoals and searching for the few known landmarks among the look-alike barrier islands that form a protective ribbon along the Texas shore. Despite inadequate charts, vicious storms, and a host of coastal hazards, ports gradually grew up along Texas, and the cry went out for lighthouses.

Sam Houston lobbied for navigational aids in 1845, and although two lighthouses were planned in 1847 at Galveston and Matagorda bays, impending statehood and government reorganization of the Lighthouse Service held up construction. There was also an unexplainable air of indifference to the Gulf of Mexico, expressed by the overseer of the nation's navigational aids--Stephen Pleasanton. He seemed much more concerned with the lighthouses of New England and the Great Lakes, and though the Southeast was burgeoning during these years, only the Mississippi River received serious consideration from Pleasanton.

An investigation in 1851 brought the plight of the Gulf Coast and Texas in particular to the attention of the newly formed Lighthouse Board. A year later a cast iron lighthouse was built at Texas's Bolivar Point and painted red--a distinctive daymark against the low, flat beaches and beige sands of the Gulf Coast. Other Texas lighthouses soon followed, and by 1859 the shores of the Lone Star State were arrayed in a bright, beneficent necklace of lights extending from its Sabine River border with Louisiana to its southern limit at Brownsville.

About a dozen of these lighthouses remain standing. Each is, in the words of lighthouse historian F. Ross Holland, "a window on the past." Among them, Bolivar Lighthouse seems to best exemplify the legend and fact surrounding Texas lighthouses. Its physical history and human story intertwine in a career that was both ordinary and extraordinary, in a landscape centered along the sultry, flat Texas coast where hurricanes plow across the barrier islands yearly, where cranes and herons take measured steps among the marshes, and sea oats rock peacefully to and fro in the Gulf breeze.

Point Isabelle Light

Bolivar Lighthouse was fabricated in Baltimore by the iron company of Murray and Hazlehurst, then shipped in pieces to the Texas coast and assembled on its foundation in 1852, the first light shipping would see on the approach to Galveston. At the same time the company also built Matagorda Lighthouse, with the pricetag for the two sentinels tallying up at $23,400. Both lights were fitted with Boston-made 21 inch silvered reflectors and lamps--archaic for the time considering Europe had been using the revolutionary Fresnel lenses for two decades. A wooden keeper's dwelling completed the Bolivar station, and it was lit shortly after the New Year in 1853.

As with many engineering projects of importance in a growing territory, Bolivar Light was almost immediately made inadequate by the influx of settlers and businesses on the Texas frontier. The old lighting system was feeble, and the tower was too short to meet the needs of increased shipping. The same company that had fabricated and built the light returned in 1857 to heighten it an additional 24 feet and to install a third-order Fresnel lens.

Ironically, three years later the light was extinguished by Confederate soldiers who did not want to see it aid the Union in any way. As a further assurance of Southern protection, the entire lighthouse was taken apart, plate by plate, and hidden. Historian T. Lindsey Baker believes the plates were eventually melted down to manufacture war materials for the Confederacy.

A temporary wooden beacon went into service after the war and served until 1872 when a new cast iron tower was built. It was modeled after the handsome Pass a l'Outre Lighthouse in Louisiana and sported a black and white banded daymark and a brilliant third-order, fixed Fresnel lens. The lens was upgraded to a second-order flashing beacon after shipping increased and mariners began to complain that the lighthouse could not be seen at a great enough distance.

Life at Bolivar Light was anything but idyllic. Nothing would grow in the sand around the tower, so keepers spent much of their time rowing to a nearby settlement for food, which had to be nonperishable because of the Texas heat. Mosquitoes were thick and soiled the lens and the brasswork. Birds crashed into the tower frequently and sometimes took refuge in the lantern if a cold snap, locally known as a Blue Norther, set in. And the heat and humidity could be oppressive on summer days when the Gulf breeze died down. It exacerbated

many a disagreement into a full-fledged fight that had to be settled through either a reprimand or a transfer of personnel, and sometimes even a dismissal.

But the curse of Bolivar Light was its vulnerability to storms. Though it always stood firm when tropical corkscrews of wind and rain slammed the coast, keepers were usually terrified when its metal joints began to creak and groan and it swayed like a giant reed under the stress of hurricane winds.

Henry Claiborne served at Bolivar Light through two of the most destructive storms in Texas. The 1900 hurricane struck on September 7th and 8th, inundating Galveston and its surrounding shores with a monster storm surge and estimated 120 mph winds. The lighthouse proved to be one of the most stable structures in the area, in spite of its height. The homeless took refuge inside it, welcomed by Henry Claiborne and his wife, who dutifully fed her frightened guests a meal of boiled beans. Before the storm ended, 124 people clambered onto its spiral stairs, two on a step, while in the bottom of the tower the water had risen to the chest of the lowest person. Keeper Claiborne stood watch in the lantern throughout the storm and at times was forced to cling to handholds to keep from falling as the 117 foot tower reeled in the gale.

Fifteen years later another powerful hurricane hit the Texas coast in August. Keeper Claiborne stated in his logbook that the 1900 storm paled in comparison; this 1915 cyclone tore the keeper's house from its foundation and tossed it into a pit that the sea had gouged out farther down the point. The assistant keeper's house, along with all other outbuildings and objects at the station, disappeared in the surge. Only the lighthouse remained, a sanctuary from the tempest for dozens of local residents who had lost their homes and still lighted when the winds died down and the waters receded--a tribute to its two courageous keepers.

From *The Strand*, 1909.

An interesting sidenote concerning the storm was the bravery of Assistant Keeper J.P. Brooks who stood watch in the lantern as the hurricane made landfall on the night of August 16. Brooks reported that the revolving mechanism of the light failed about 9:15 that evening, and he was forced to turn it by hand. He remained in the lantern until the storm threatened to shatter the windows, then trimmed the wicks and left the light shining on its own.

As he descended the stairs, stepping over one after another whimpering soul, he felt wind howling up the shaft of the lighthouse. The iron door at the base of the tower had come open and water had risen some six feet high. Fearing the erosive force of the water would undermine the lighthouse foundation and topple it, Brooks tethered himself with a rope and jumped into the seething maelstrom in the bottom of the lighthouse and attempted to close the door. After much exertion he managed to secure the door and returned, bruised and spent.

Two new keeper's homes were built following the hurricane, this time perched on stilts to allow floodwaters less opportunity to demolish them. Life resumed as usual until a year later when something entirely unexpected happened: Bolivar Lighthouse was accidentally attacked. Keeper Claiborne was astounded that November afternoon in 1917 when shells began bombarding the compound and continued for about two hours. "One 3" shell struck the front of the Tower making a 3" hole through the steel plate a little above & to the eastward of the entrance door," Claiborne reported. The Coast Guard rushed to investigate and discovered that soldiers from nearby Fort San Jacinto had been conducting gunnery practice with what they thought were weak powder charges. The ammunition tested well, however, and within range of the lighthouse.

In 1907 Bolivar Lighthouse was downgraded to a third-order harbor beacon, since the new Galveston Jetty Light better served the needs of shipping nearer the channel entrance to Galveston Bay. When the younger and more proximate sentinel was increased in brilliance in 1930, the Bureau of Lighthouses announced that Bolivar Light would be abandoned. Barraged with protests and tearful entreaties from local residents, including a prominent Congressman, the government backed down; Bolivar Light was allowed to burn, but only temporarily.

Budgetary concerns in the Depression years forced the government to reconsider the necessity of keeping a beacon lit for the sake of sentimentality. In 1933 the Bureau of Lighthouses issued a firm directive that Bolivar Light be discontinued; the mandate went virtually unchallenged this time, and on May 29, 1933 the sentinel was extinguished for the final time.

For a time the lighthouse was used by the Army at Fort San Jacinto as an observation tower during maneuvers. But after World War II the lighthouse was of little use to the military, so it was auctioned off as surplus real estate. The buyer was E.V. Boyd; he purchased the station for $5,500 and converted it into a summer vacation retreat. It still remains in the Boyd family today.

The tower's magnificent third-order lens was given to the Smithsonian Institution's National Museum of American History and is currently on display in the maritime industry hall.

This article originally appeared in *Mariners Weather Log*, Winter 1993.

Recommended Reading

When we think of lighthouses, Texas doesn't usually come to mind. Texas is where there are oil rigs and cowboys, longhorns mooing from cattle pens, and business men dressed in suits and sharp-toed boots and Stetson hats. Texas has all these things, true; but it also has a rich and colorful maritime past.

Texas settlers came mostly by water. They faced a treacherous coastline of low, flat barrier beaches that constantly changed shape. Surreptitious sandbars hid just beneath the tide. The territory desperately needed guideposts into its harbors and bays. Yet, Texas was the last state bordering the Gulf of Mexico to receive aids to navigation.

Its maritime story, including its lighthouses, has been overshadowed by more romantic locales. Thankfully, this oversight has been rectified to some degree. T. Lindsey Baker, who researched lighthouses as part of a project to document the Lone Star State's historic sites, "caught the lighthouse bug." The result was *Lighthouses of Texas*, published in 1991 by Texas A & M Press.

It's a well-researched and skillfully-written over-sized book, perfect for the coffee table. Paintings by Harold Phenix, on the cover and in a lavish centerspread, add to its appeal, as does a forward by Ross Holland. Also included are many archival photos of Texas sentinels and numerous useful endnotes. This is a scholarly work, but with strong readability and charm.

Beacons of the Delaware Gateway

Replica of old Cape Henlopen Light
from a postcard in author's collection.

From Cape May to Cape Henlopen

In 1623, Cornelius Jacobus Mey of Holland's West India Company sailed into the Delaware Bay, passing between a pristine point of sand and sea oats on the southernmost tip of New Jersey, which he called Cape Mey, and a pine forested beach on the Delaware side, which Mey dubbed Cape Cornelius. He named the tawny sands farther south along the Delaware shore for a compatriot in Amsterdam — Thymen Jacobsen Hindlopen.

Over the centuries, Mey's conceited christenings and the capes themselves have been altered: An early mapmaker dropped the name Cornelius in favor of Hindlopen, which, along with Mey, became Henlopen and May. Erosion has redrawn the shoreline, particularly on the Delaware side where a mile-long finger of sand called Point of Capes has been deposited. The character of the capes has changed too, from sleepy strands of spindrifted dunes to bustling resort towns with hotels, shops, restaurants, and the busy Cape May-Lewes Ferry terminals.

Mey had neither the benefit of a local pilot's keen navigational skills or a beacon to guide his way. Were he to venture into the Delaware Bay today, he would encounter tugs pulling barges, mammoth tankers, 100-car ferries, and a regatta of pleasure boats gliding across the estuary mouth. Lighthouses would blink a greeting from both the northern and southern hinges of the gateway, and more lights would beckon inside this vital artery to the ports of Wilmington and Philadelphia. In the last two centuries, some thirty lighthouses have been built and rebuilt on the Delaware Bay.

The first sentinel to stand watch over the entrance to the bay was the Cape Henlopen Light, built in 1767 on the Delaware side. Wrecking had been a profitable business along this shore prior to the building of Cape Henlopen Light. No doubt the lightkeeper was welcomed with ambivalence, for his work was a boon for mariners but a bane for wreckers. Legend contends mooncussing was practiced here on inky black nights, using Judas Lanterns — oil lamps suspended on poles and rocked gently to and fro in imitation of a ship safely at anchor. The idea was to lure vessels onto the shoals, then board them and claim rights of salvage.

The original Cape Henlopen Light burned during the Revolution and was rebuilt in 1784, octagonal in shape and resembling its sister-sentinel 150-miles to the north at Sandy Hook, New Jersey. Throughout its career, the lighthouse was plagued by erosion, but it remained in service until 1925. When the foundation became undermined, the lens was removed and the lightkeeper sent to a new assignment. By then, another sentinel had been built on a breakwater off Lewes.

The new beacon was thoughtfully named the Harbor of Refuge Light when it flashed on in 1901, but only seven years later it was leveled by a storm. Its successor was also toppled in 1921. The current Harbor of Refuge Light, a cast-iron tower on a concrete caisson, has stood firm since 1926. But in that same year the abandoned Cape Henlopen Lighthouse collapsed in an April storm. The site is now under the ocean, but beachcombers occasionally find small chunks of brick at the tideline, smoothed by the sea and hurled ashore — battered mementos of Delaware's first lighthouse.

On the north side of the bay entrance is Cape May Point Lighthouse, tall and distinctive with its red lantern and beige walls. The first tower here was built in 1823, but local residents may have operated some sort of beacon prior to this time, as Cape May was home to pilots, shipbuilders, and whalers in the 1600s and was an important colonial port for Philadelphia commerce. The original light was brick, 68-feet high, and lit by 15 lamps with reflectors. It had to be abandoned in 1847 due to the encroaching shoreline. The site of this tower is now about 300-feet offshore, and like old Cape Henlopen Light, shards of its masonry occasionally wash ashore.

Cape May Light, by Paul Bradley

A second brick tower, 78-feet tall, was built. Four years later it was inspected by the newly-formed Lighthouse Board and found to be in poor condition, with an outdated illuminating apparatus and a less than model keeper. The current 157-foot Cape May Point Light was built in 1859 and has operated continuously since that date, except for a brief period of darkness during World War II because of the presence of enemy submarines off the New Jersey Coast.

During the years when families lived in the two keepers' houses, the station was an idyllic, shoreside assignment. Children passed the days swimming, building sandcastles, and beachcombing for shells and the water-smoothed shards of glass tourists called "Cape May Diamonds." Summers at the lighthouse are quaintly recalled in *Mary Elizabeth and the Cape May Point Lighthouse* — the memoirs of Mary Elizabeth Bennett Rott, niece of an assistant keeper in 1912. Her uncle Ed Hughes was paid $480

a year and supplemented his income by "making bait boxes and selling them to tourists."

The last Cape May lightkeeper was Harry Palmer, a fastidious and well-liked man who raised prize-winning hydrangeas and in the 1920s won the Lighthouse Service's award for "best kept lawn." Palmer was forced to hand over the lighthouse duties to his wife in 1933 after suffering a heart attack. Ada Palmer kept the beacon until it was automated in 1936.

Thereafter, trips up the 199-step spiral stairway were made only during periodic maintenance checks. The Coast Guard assumed care of the lighthouse in 1939, and seven years later the tower's antique, revolving, first-order lens was removed and a modern rotating beacon was installed. The classical Fresnel was given to the Cape May County Museum for display. The tower lantern still sports a mesh birdscreen, however, as it stands watch along the Great Atlantic Flyway and is sometimes hit by birds.

In 1983 the Mid-Atlantic Center for the Arts expressed interest in the tower for educational purposes. A few years later, a grant from the New Jersey Historic Trust allowed MAC to restore the lighthouse and invite in the public. The tower now belongs to the State of New Jersey and is a popular landmark with Cape May's summer vacationers and traveler's on their way to the ferry terminal.

This article appeared in *Mariners Weather Log*, Fall 1994.

Recommended Reading

Cape Henlopen Lighthouse and Delaware Breakwater, written in 1970 by John W. Beach and privately published, is an excellent overview of the history of the light at Cape Henlopen. I bought my copy at the gift shop at Cape May Lighthouse.

After a ferry ride to Lewes, I found the small replica of the lighthouse that stands in town, oddly facing a street of traffic and a gas station. The site of the old lighthouse is now under the tide.

Beach's work is a reminder of Cape Henlopen Light's prominence in Colonial navigation and its tragic ending. The book has excellent archival pictures that detail the career of the lighthouse and its gradual decline, as erosion gnawed away its foundation and finally toppled it.

There are also interesting photographs of the breakwater lights that replaced it, including the vanished Strickland Light on the west end, and the East End Light and Harbor of Refuge Light.

The Paradise Lights

Sentinels of Hawaii

An old Hawaiian legend tells how a canoe bearing Kamehameha I was once caught in a cruel wind off the Big Island's Kona Coast. As the king's oarsmen struggled to find their way in the stormy blackness, a glimmer of light appeared on the shore. It flickered, spread itself broadly, then danced in a huge, orange fan. A second light appeared, then a third. Their flames merged and sparks hissed skyward until the darkness was consumed. Knowing their king was in peril, the people of Nawawa had torched their village to give him a beacon.

The king's predicament on that blustery night was somewhat irregular, for early Hawaiian seafarers were keen navigators seldom plagued by the sea's natural hazards. They had little need for manmade navigational aids. Every current, reef, rock, and anchorage in their remote Pacific domain was well-known to them. Fogs and mists were virtually nonexistent in the Islands, enabling Hawaiians to employ their sophisticated knowledge of celestial navigation, guided by the sun, moon, and stars.

Sequestered in the center of the vast Pacific like tiny green sequins on blue silk, Hawaii was one of maritime history's best-kept secrets, and it remained so well beyond Polynesian discovery.

Perhaps the Spanish encountered Hawaii as they sailed between Mexico and the Philippines from 1550 to 1750. Subtle evidence substantiates this possibility. The most convincing clue is a map taken from a Spanish galleon in 1742 clearly charting islands in nearly the same latitude and longitude as Hawaii. Cook's visit in 1778 removed the mystery concerning the Islands. Even with Hawaii's new-found link to the West and a continuous parade of ships into its harbors, nearly a century passed before the first lighthouse was built in the Islands.

Natives had been content with shoreline bonfires such as the crude beacon at Kukui-o-Lono heiau on Kauai that guided night fishermen and war canoes. "The Light of God Lono," however, proved inadequate for New England whaling captains who were accustomed to such magnificent sentinels as Boston Lighthouse, Nantucket's handsome Great Point Lighthouse, and the unique twin lighthouses at Chatham, Cape Cod.

From the time of their arrival in Hawaii in the 1820s, whalers protested the Islands' lack of navigational aids, but their licentious behavior appalled resident missionaries and impeded efforts to light commercial ports.

Henry T. Cheever, a minister traveling in Hawaii in the 1840s, described the "ribald oaths...language of lewdness...and ready wages of sin" earned by Lahaina's whalers. He dubbed the town "one of the breathing holes of hell," but merchants and monarchs were less critical of Lahaina's absence of propriety. They eagerly supplied materials for a small lighthouse at Keawaiki in 1840 to aid the raucous but profitable whaling industry.

Hawaii's premier lighthouse was neither grand nor lofty. It stood only nine feet high and was shaped like a box with a small, four-window compartment on top. Dual, piggyback lanterns inside its tiny lightroom cast a feeble beam less than five miles, and the first keeper of the Whaler's Lighthouse was paid twenty dollars a year to keep it burning.

The lighthouse soon became a pawn between warring factions of whalers and missionaries. Lahaina's more pious residents sometimes extinguished the light to spite the vulgar whaling fleet. In turn, vengeful seamen sent cannon fire screaming over Lahaina's churches on Sunday mornings. The scuffles continued until about 1860, when the whaling industry went into a deep recession.

A crude channel beacon, lit about 1853, marked the entrance to Honolulu Harbor until treacherous Kaholaloa Reef was officially given a lighthouse in 1869. Honolulu Harbor Light, as it was listed on pilots' charts, stood on a long pier 26 feet above water and sported a fourth-order Fresnel lens manufactured in France.

Such lenses were state of the art in 1869, refracting the weak light of oil lamps through prisms and magnifying it into concentrated beams. The little harbor beacon cast its light more than ten miles, but local residents were unimpressed with its prismatic optic. They degradingly referred to it as "The Wink" and described it as "an infantile structure which more closely resembles a birdcage than a lighthouse." The small beacon survived until 1925 when it was upstaged by the light atop the Aloha Tower.

During the reign of King Kalakaua, more navigational lights were established, but most were poorly constructed and barely visible beyond the perils they marked. A flimsy wooden lighthouse went up on Molokai's Laau Point, along with post lanterns at Lauphoehoe and Mahukona on the Big Island. Kitchen lamps served as markers at Maui's lava-strewn Kanahene Point and Maalaea Bay, while a lookout station on Diamond Head displayed a weak oil lamp.

lantern of the kind with crimson cloth tied around it to give it a red glow." Several of the lights had been built by shipping companies desperate to provide assistance to their lucrative vessels.

Congress released funds to upgrade existing lights, install modern optics, and build new lighthouses. By 1906, the searoad to Hawaii was satisfactorily marked by 19 lighthouses, 20 buoys, and 20 daymarks, but three costly shipping disasters in September of that year proved that more were needed.

The monarchy's grandest lighthouses were the 42 foot coral tower at Laeloa, now known as Barbers Point, and a steel-framed stone tower on the slopes of Diamond Head. Both lighthouses were sturdy masonry structures utilizing modern optics. Along with the Honolulu Harbor Light, they assured safe passage around Oahu's southern shore.

The United States Lighthouse Service assumed control of Hawaii's lighthouses in 1904, and the Islands officially became a sub-district of the Twelfth Lighthouse District in San Francisco. Headquartered in Honolulu, Hawaiian district personnel began the arduous task of assessing the Islands' navigational aids and making recommendations to Congress. Inspections revealed that most lights were inferior, including "the one on top of the Customs House in Honolulu, being a

Worst of these was the wreck of the Pacific mail liner *Manchuria* off windward Oahu. Caught in a freak night mist, the ship ran aground near Waimanalo. The skipper blamed the unfortunate accident on "the lack of lighthouse facilities on Makapu'u Point," but lost his license in spite of an impeccable record and corroborative opinion of the district inspector.

In a report to Congress, the inspector stated: "All deep-sea commerce between Honolulu and Puget Sound, the Pacific Coast of the United States, Mexico and Central America, including Panama, passes Makapu'u Head."

The government responded by allotting $60,000 to build a lighthouse on the lofty 647 foot headland. When completed in 1909, the squat, 46 foot tower was the most elevated in the Pacific. Its advanced illuminating apparatus was a gigantic, five-ton lens known as a hyper-radiant type. It measured 13 feet in height, 8 1/2 feet in diameter, and was composed of 1140 highly polished glass prisms. True to its name, which in Hawaiian means "the bulging eye," the monstrous beacon was sometimes seen as far away as 40 miles at sea.

Makapu'u lightkeepers and their families lived in three handsome stone houses behind the lighthouse. Life was often difficult at the remote station. Keepers traversed a 300 yard, serpentine trail along the cliff face to tend the beacon. Rockslides were frequent, and diverging tradewinds continually scoured the headland, at times so strong, laundry on the clothesline was shredded. It was nearly impossible to get a doctor or a babysitter to brave the steep, winding road to the station, but the ocean view atop Makapu'u Head is unparalleled, and keepers' wives admitted they were never bothered by door-to-door sales people.

Also completed in 1909 was the tall sentinel at Makanalua Peninsula on north Molokai. Old Lighthouse Service records reveal apprehension on the part of Congress to appropriate funds for a navigational aid so close to the Kalaupapa leper colony, but the importance of providing a landfall light for shipping bound from the West Coast eventually outweighed the fear of Hanson's Disease. The lighthouse tender *Columbine* and its hearty island crew were sent to Molokai to build the tower, but great care was taken to avoid contact with the residents of Kalaupapa.

The peninsula's sequestered northern tip was walled in by 2000 foot cliffs. Materials for the tower were brought in from the tender, then loaded onto donkeys for the overland trek to the construction site. Freshwater was brought in via a wooden pipeline from distant Waikolu Valley to ensure that it was free of disease contamination. Upon completion, the 138 foot octagonal concrete lighthouse became the tallest structure in the Islands and was illuminated by a first-order Fresnel lens with a focal plane 213 feet above the sea.

Molokai lightkeepers were given precise instructions regarding the handling of packages dropped by the tender. Everything was double-wrapped to prevent contamination. The outer wrap was removed and burned, then the keeper washed his hands before removing the inner wrap. These regulations continued until after World War II when sulfone drugs and increased understanding of Hansen's Disease reduced public fear.

Ninini Point, Kauai and Ka Lae, Kawaihae, and Keahole, Hawaii also received lighthouses in 1906. Ka Lae, also called South Point, is the southernmost point in the United States and the presumed landing place of the first Polynesians to arrive in Hawaii. Eruptions of Kilauea have often obscured its beacon. Wrote one keeper: "For the past ten days this station has been enveloped with smoke, at times so dense that nothing could be seen for a mile..." This same keeper requested a windmill which he cleverly connected to the light's power source to produce one of the first wind-powered lighthouses.

Ka Lae's cliffs are riddled with spikes, rings, and holes where vessels have moored over the centuries. Nearby is the ancient Kalalea Heiau where some Hawaiians still make offerings before going to sea to fish. A functional, battery-powered post lantern, or monopole light, replaced the old lighthouse some years back.

Kauiki Head Lighthouse was established in 1908 on a small islet off the rustic village of Hana, Maui. Legend holds that a god once stood on this spot and threw his spear beyond the sky. Fittingly, Kauiki means "the glimmer."

Vessels have anchored at Hana throughout Hawaiian history. More than 1000 war canoes filled its bay during an early 18th century invasion from the Big Island. Captain Cook dropped anchor in Hana in 1778, and precious Maui cane sugar was once carried away from here in cargo ships. The present miniature beacon was built in 1914 and still casts its beam eastward.

Kauai's most elegant sentinel, perched 216 feet above the sea near Kauapea Beach, is Kilauea Lighthouse, now obsolete as a navigational aid, but preserved as a historical maritime monument. It was built in 1913 to provide landfall for shipping from the Orient. The engineers who built it were unfamiliar with Hawaii's clear sea air and included a fog signal in the original plans. The droning foghorn fortunately was never installed.

Kilauea Light's $12,000 clamshell lens weighed 4 1/2 tons and turned in a low-friction, high-density mercury float. The Garden Island newspaper likened it to "the famous Cyclops of old" when it was lighted May 6, 1913, adding that "it winks at old Neptune every ten seconds." Huge weights, working on a principle similar to a cuckoo clock, were suspended in the tower to rotate the lens. The keeper had to wind them up every three hours.

In June 1927, aviators attempted the first trans-Pacific flight from Oakland, California to Honolulu. They overshot their destination, but recognized the brilliant beam of Kilauea Lighthouse as they passed north of Kauai, recalculated their position, and landed safely at Hickam Field, Oahu. Installation of a radiobeacon at Kilauea Lighthouse in 1933 simplified flights from the Mainland. Among the first to benefit from the marvelous "silent signal" were six Navy pilots from California. A young Kilauea lightkeeper named Fred Robbins manually worked the radiobeacon to steer them in. Thirty years later, he retired from the lighthouse service as the last of Hawaii's old lamplighters.

persistent seasickness — to build lighthouses, lay buoys, and render assistance to vessels in distress.

Among the *Kukui's* most praiseworthy achievements was the illumination of the small sentinels at elevated Kaula and Lehua islets. Crescent-shaped Kaula Rock is a hazard that forced Japan-bound ships to pass Kauai on the north rather than along the south shore near Niihau. A beacon atop Kaula Rock meant considerable savings in miles and money, but conquest of the 562 foot islet proved a forbidding task.

Guardian of Kaula was Kuhaimoana, the shark god. No one had ever reached the pinnacle of the rock prior to the arrival of *Kukui's* crew. The

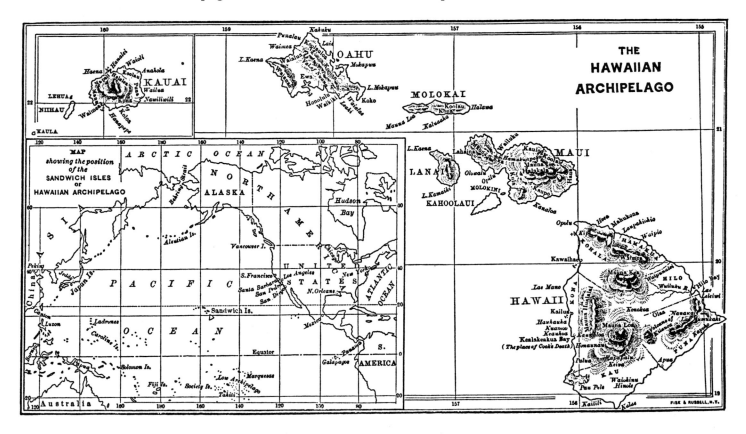

The task of building and maintaining Hawaii's lighthouses fell upon the crewmen of the lighthouse tenders, particularly the *Kukui* which served in the Islands from 1909 to 1939. These hearty men hauled construction materials to Hawaii's untouched corners, cleared roads, erected derricks, and toiled in the tropical sun to raise the towers that would safeguard Island shipping.

Duty aboard the tenders was strenuous and risky. Anchored where other vessels would not venture, crewmen clamored over wave-washed rocks to chisel away at precipitous, volcanic cliffs, and intrepidly faced myriad dangers — including

men chose to scale Kaula's sheer walls on its leeward side, driving metal handholds into the rock as they inched upward. Seabirds pecked at their hands, and the stench of guano was unbearable, but they managed to reach the summit in only three days.

An automatic acetylene gas beacon was firmly anchored on the peak, facing the full force of northeast tradewinds. Its feeder tanks were attached to the leeward pali (cliff) 80 feet above the waterline. The lonely little sentinel was left to operate on its own, and crewmen gratefully bid farewell to Kaula Rock until a maintenance crew would check the beacon six months later.

Nearby Lehua Rock was one of the last shipping hazards in the Islands to be marked. A half-moon of dry, barren earth, it rises abruptly to 704 feet. Since Hawaii is rarely cursed with the fog and low cloud cover that plagues New England and the West Coast, Lehua Rock is the ideal site for a lighthouse — a true sentinel whose watch stretches far out to sea. When illuminated in 1931, it became the highest elevated lighthouse in the United States. Though Kaula Rock's beacon has been upstaged by modern technology, Lehua's white flash continues its warning on Hawaii's western fringe.

On the easternmost point of the Big Island, a 124 foot skeleton tower guards the low lava stretches of the harsh Puna Coast. Cape Kumukahi Lighthouse has been in service since 1929 and provides landfall for shipping from Central and South America. The Coast Guard calls it "The Lucky Lighthouse" because it barely escaped destruction during a 1960 eruption from Kilauea volcano. Fingers of lava passed within inches of its base and spared only the light tower and an ancient burial ground before pouring into the sea.

In 1939, Hawaiian navigational aids, along with the rest of the nation's aids, were placed under the care of the U.S. Coast Guard. Hawaii was established as the Fourteenth District, and its civilian lamplighters were given a choice between joining the Coast Guard or finishing their careers as civilians. Most opted for the former and were given rank and pay equivalent to their time in service as lightkeepers.

The Coast Guard gradually moved toward a more efficient lighthouse system by replacing high-maintenance equipment with automatic mechanisms. Electric lights phased out the old oil and gas lamps powered by weights. Light-sensitive timers turned the lights on and off. Automatic bulb changers moved new bulbs into position when old one burned out. Old-fashioned, prismatic jewels were upstaged by modern, low maintenance optics.

The era of the lightkeeper was rapidly coming to a close. Men like Samuel Amalu, whose career as a Hawaiian lamplighter spanned 33 years, and Fred Robbins, a lifelong servant of Hawaii's lighthouses, became faint silhouettes against the brilliant advances in maritime technology. The heroism of Barbers Point lightkeeper, Manuel Ferreira — running three miles in a hurricane to telephone for help for a stranded ship — was quickly forgotten.

In April 1974, the last Hawaiian lighthouse keeper, Coast Guardsman Ron Cianfarani, took a final walk along the windy path to Makapu'u Lighthouse and activated its newly-installed automatic beacon. For more than a century, human hands had tended Hawaii's lighthouses. As Cianfarani stood on Makapu'u's iron-railed catwalk and surveyed the great expanse of blue stretching out before him, he felt a small pang of regret.

The Fourteenth Coast Guard District currently maintains some 700 navigational aids within its 12-million square mile domain — the largest geographic command in the United States Coast Guard. About forty of those aids are lighthouses, and all economically operate with modern, automatic equipment requiring only periodic maintenance.

Considering that Hawaii's only link to the rest of the world is by ocean and air, and an estimated 85% of its population lives within sight of the sea, the old sentinels serve a vital purpose while reminding us of Hawaii's past — of boisterous whalers, the creaking timbers of square-riggers, and shiploads of anxious immigrants.

Few structures transcend time and civilization or so accurately mirror the complexion of a nation the way lighthouses do. Like old soldiers still standing watch, they proudly refuse to give up their posts.

This article first appeared in *Aloha: The Magazine of Hawaii and the Pacific,* October 1986 and was reprinted in *Hawaii Magazine,* June 1987 under the title "Island Sentinels Signal Aloha." A special piece on Kilauea Lighthouse appeared in *Mariners Weather Log,* Spring 1989.

Lahaina, Maui, pictured here in the 1880s, had settled down considerably from its raucous days as a prime whaling port. No doubt a beacon of sorts was in use when this drawing was made, but it would have been small. The probable location is just to the left of the church. Note the mountain peaks behind the village — 19th century navigators memorized the outlines of mountains on various Pacific islands, including the Sandwich Islands, as Hawaii was called, and used these for daytime navigation. Sailing directions gave detailed descriptions of mountain profiles, their colors, and distinctive features. The plumes of smoke from Hawaii's Big Island volcanoes also guided ships.

On that same subject - Hawaii's volcanoes have been called "Nature's Lighthouses." By day they send banners of smoke, and by night their fiery streams of lava are seen for miles. Perhaps the Polynesians used these natural beacons on their way to the islands nearly a thousand years ago.

Interesting Trivia

In the 1870s, Charles Nordoff, the roving reporter of his day, sailed to Hawaii to learn about the natural history of the islands and their people. There were no lighthouses to greet his ship, save the crude beacons that supposedly shone from Diamond Head and "The Wink" in Honolulu Harbor, but Nordoff's description of the voyage is noteworthy, for it gives the flavor and tenor of a time when Hawaii was an exotic destination dreamed about by many Americans. We still dream of going there and escaping to paradise, if only for a few days or weeks.

The voyage from San Francisco to Honolulu lasts from eight to ten days, and is, even to persons subject to seasickness, very enjoyable, because after the second day the weather is charmingly warm, the breezes unusually mild, and the skies sunny and clear. In forty-eight hours after you leave the Golden Gate, shawls, overcoats, and wraps are discarded. You put on thinner clothing. After breakfast you will like to spread rugs on deck and lie in the sun, fanned by deliciously soft winds, and before you see Honolulu you will even like to have an awning spread over you to keep off the sun. When they seek a tropical climate, our brethren on the Pacific coast have no such rough voyage as that across the Atlantic to endure. On the bay you see flying-fish, and if you are lucky, an occasional whale or a school of porpoises. And you sail over the lovely blue of the Pacific Ocean, which has not only softer gales but even a different shade of color than the Atlantic.

We made the land at daylight on the tenth day of the voyage, and by breakfast-time were steaming through the Molokai Channel, with the high, rugged, and bare volcanic cliffs of Oahu close aboard, the surf beating against the shore vehemently. An hour later we rounded Diamond Head, and sailing past Waikiki, which is the Long Branch of Honolulu, charmingly placed amidst groves of cocoa-nut trees, turned sharp about, and steamed through a narrow channel into the landlocked little harbor of Honolulu, smooth as mill-pond....Your first view of Honolulu, that from the ship's deck, is one of the pleasantest you can get...

All engravings are from "Hawaii Nei," *Harper's Magazine*, 1873.

The generosity of the U.S. Coast Guard is largely responsible for much of the first-hand information I've collected about lighthouses. The 14th District was especially kind. This trip provided vital research for all my Hawaiian lighthouse articles, but particularly "Makapu'u: The Bulging Eye," *The Keeper's Log,* Summer 1986.

U.S. Department of Transportation

United States Coast Guard

(flp)

Commander
Fourteenth Coast Guard District

Prince Kalanianaole
Federal Building
300 Ala Moana Blvd.
Honolulu, Hawaii 96850
Phone (808) 546-5523

4000
Serial 23028
25 January 1985

Mrs. Elinor De Wire
USLHS Hawaii Rep
6368B Ibis Avenue
Ewa Beach, HI 96706

    Subj: PERMISSION TO VISIT MAKAPUU LIGHT STATION FOR
             RECREATIONAL PURPOSES

Dear Mrs. De Wire:

Your request to visit the Coast Guard Makapuu Light Station property, as outlined in your letter dated 23 January 1985, is approved. This letter grants you and approximately four (4) persons permission to visit the Coast Guard property on 6 February 1985 from 12:00 noon to approximately 4:00 PM.

So that you may fully enjoy your visit, we ask you and members of your group to be aware of the potential hazards which exist at Makapuu, including:

    a. a very narrow access road to and from the summit of the property. This road has potholes, broken pieces of asphalt, sunken areas and no guard rails;

    b. steep cliffs, jagged/slippery rocks and soft, loose soil;

    c. rusted and deteriorated metal railings on the concrete pad near the summit;

    d. buildings on the property which may contain broken glass, protruding nails and other possible hazards to visitors.

No fires are permitted, and your litter is to be removed from the premises. We recommend using vehicles no larger than a station wagon and ask that vehicles not go beyond the parking area located near the summit. Overnight visits are prohibited.

Please brief all members of your group on normal safety precautions, with particular attention to the above conditions prior to entering the area.

The key to the Makapuu property gate is available from the Chief, Aids to Navigation Branch, room 9139, 14th Coast Guard District, Prince Kalanianaole Federal Building, 300 Ala Moana Boulevard, Honolulu; telephone 546-7130. Office hours are 7:00 AM to 3:00 PM, Monday through Friday. District offices are closed on all Federal holidays. Please lock the gate behind you as you enter and lock it upon departure. Return the key to the Chief, Aids to Navigation Branch (room 9139).

To fulfill our requirements, please complete the bottom blocks of this letter and return the second copy to reach this office prior to your visiting date.

                      Sincerely,

                      E. NEIL ERICKSON
            Chief, Logistics & Property Branch
           By direction of the District Commander

Diamond Head Lighthouse

Light Over the Reef

Tourists arriving in Hawaii by air are treated to an unusual view of the fiftieth state's most famous landmark. Diamond Head's aerial vista is less familiar, but infinitely more interesting than its hackneyed postcard profile as a backdrop for the Honolulu skyline. From the air, its eroded crater and sharp sloping sides bear a remarkable resemblance, according to H.C. Adamson, to "a great decayed tooth in want of a filling."

Also visible from the air is lovely Diamond Head Lighthouse, which appears as a tiny white spike dwarfed by the huge mountain behind it. Since 1899 this beacon has warned shipping away from the coral reefs that extend several miles off Oahu's southeastern tip. It also has blinked a welcome to ships approaching Honolulu.

Centuries ago, Diamond Head was its own natural lighthouse, shooting flames, turrets of smoke, and rivers of orange lava that could be seen miles at sea. Native Hawaiians called it Lae Ahi, or "wreath of fire," and they kept a navigational bonfire lit near its summit to guide fishermen and war canoes. Their homecoming was announced to the tiny village of Honolulu by a chain of conch shell blowers.

When British sailors scaled the volcano's 760-foot slopes in 1825, they found hard, clear calcite crystals among the black lava rocks. These were quickly mistaken for diamonds, and the name Diamond Head was coined, though some mapmakers continued to use the Hawaiian name.

With the increase in commerce to Hawaii in the 19th century, island merchants established a lookout station on the south slope of Diamond Head. The idea was more profit-motivated than benevolent, but the keeper of the station, whose job was to announce the arrival of ships by means of signal flags, also relayed distress calls to Honolulu.

"Diamond Head Charley," as John Charles Peterson was nicknamed, was a retired Swedish sailor who had dropped anchor in Oahu in the 1870s and married a native woman. She died in childbirth, but the baby, Melika, survived. The small community of Honolulu was saddened by Charley's misfortune, and as small propitiation, offered him the job of lookout on Diamond Head. The pay was $50 a month.

Charley and his bronze-skinned little daughter lived a happy life in a tiny cottage on the southern slope of the mountain. Melika walked along Waikiki Beach — then a quiet and sparsely populated strand — to get to school each day. She spent her leisure hours fishing and swimming and helping her father. Charley devoted much of his time to the big telescope Honolulu businessmen had given him as a gift.

But even his telescope could not see the changes on the horizon. The Hawaiian monarchy fell in 1893 with the deposition of Queen Lilioukalani, and in 1898 Hawaii became a U.S. territory. Within a decade, its relaxed Polynesian charm gave way to modernization and a fast-paced economy. Among the first improvements sought by Congress were navigational aids, mostly buoys and lighthouses.

Because of its status as a landfall for Honolulu, Diamond Head was one of the first sites selected for a lighthouse. Several wrecks off the point had convinced shipping interests that the beacon was crucial to safety. The SS *Miowera* was among these. It grounded on the reef on a black, moonless night after steaming too close to shore looking for the familiar profile of Diamond Head crater. The great steamship *China* had also foundered here, trying to make landfall from the south.

In 1899, the quaint little lookout tower was upstaged by the long-awaited Diamond Head Lighthouse. Honolulu Ironworks fabricated the iron framework and lantern. The tower stood 145-feet above sea and mounted a third-order prism lens which was illuminated by oil lamps and had a red panel inserted in it to shine a warning over the reefs.

Within a few months, the first lightkeeper, John Kaukaliu, reported that the tower was unstable in high winds and asked to have it strengthened. The open framework was enclosed with brick. Kaukaliu was paid $75 a month and traveled to the lighthouse every day from his home in Kaimuki. Diamond Head Charley continued to live in his little cottage by the lighthouse until his death in 1907.

In 1910 the beacon was upgraded to an incandescent oil vapor system. Not long afterwards, and for reasons unknown, the superintendent of Hawaii's navigational aids decided to switch the keepers at Diamond Head and Barbers Point lighthouses. It's likely neither man was disappointed with the change in scenery, for both stations were idyllic assignments.

By World War I, cracks had appeared in the brick walls of the lighthouse, and money was appropriated for a new tower. It was completed in 1918 at a cost of $6109. The construction process is noteworthy: A scaffold was built around the old tower and the lantern was lifted and braced. The old tower was demolished, and the new 55-foot tower of reinforced concrete was poured. When it had cured, the lantern was gently lowered onto the new tower and a bright electric beacon was installed.

In 1921 a keeper's house was finally built next to the tower, but only four years later the lighthouse was automated. Hawaiian lighthouses were among the first to be automated by the thrifty Bureau of Lighthouses, which was looking to recoup savings in salaries for keepers and upkeep on their homes. According to historian Love Dean, "Automation was made possible because of the development of highly efficient incandescent lamps and reliable electric-generating equipment that could be used in case commercial power failed."

The empty keeper's house at Diamond Head became the home of the superintendent of Hawaii's lighthouse district, who soon admitted he had one of the best backyards in the world. In 1939, after the Coast Guard assumed control of lighthouses in the U.S. and its territories, and the 14th Coast District was headquartered in Honolulu, the district's Commandant expressed interest in the pretty house with its elegant arched doorways and polished wood floors. Commandants of the 14th district have resided in the house ever since that time.

Today, Diamond Head Lighthouse continues to signal "aloha" over the opaline reefs off Oahu. It was placed on the National Register of Historic Places in 1980 and is a popular subject with tourists and photographers. The beacon is especially beautiful at night when its amber beam sweeps over the water like the eye of some great bird of paradise.

This article originally appeared as the cover story in *Mariners Weather Log*, Spring 1995.

Interesting Trivia and Reading

When I lived in Hawaii from 1983-85, there was no single book on the subject of our 50th state's lighthouses. James Gibbs had written a little, and a small amount of material was in the files of the Coast Guard Public Affairs Office in Honolulu. I searched local libraries and the Bishop Museum, then decided the only way I could truly find out about the lighthouses was to travel to them myself. It wasn't always easy.

The Coast Guard kindly lent me the keys to the gate at Makapu'u Point. It was memorable day for my entire family. We picnicked, saw humpback whales frolicking in the deep several hundred feet below us, and admired the breath-taking beauty of the cliff where lightkeepers had once lived. We were sad to discover that the hyper-radiant lens inside Makapu'u Light had been pierced by a bullet.

On separate occasions we journeyed to lighthouses at Barbers Point, Kilauea, Cape Kumukahi, Nawiliwili, Pawela Point, Lahaina, MacGregor Point, and Pyramid Rock. The treks to each tower were wonderful experiences, but local people seemed to know little, and research was frustrated by time and money constraints. I did manage to write a few articles about the lights, for *Aloha* magazine, *Hawaii,* and *The Keepers Log.*

One of the most memorable trips was to Kaena Point Light on the northwestern tip of Oahu. A road traveled around Kaena Point - remnants of the old railway that once took tourists to see the gigantic winter waves that form between Oahu and Kauai. But it could hardly be described as a road when I trekked over it! It was barely passable in an all-terrain vehicle. In fact, my efforts to rent one from local car rental agencies were futile the moment I revealed my destination - Kaena Point.

"Too risky," was the excuse from the rental companies. Some told me they had lost 4-wheel Jeeps out at Kaena because the road was so bad. "Walk," they said. We did - 7 miles out and 7 miles back.

My family accompanied me on this jaunt. Jessica was a sixth grader at the time. (She's now 23.) Scott was in first grade. (He's now 19.) Jon, my husband and president of my fan club, served as pack mule. He carried our lunches and drinks and, occasionally, a tired kid. I had the camera.

A guidebook about the natural history of the point made the long, dry walk more interesting. It advised us to carry plenty of water and sunscreen, which we did, but everyone still came back sunburned. Goddess Hiiaka's chant about Kaena being "salty and barren" was true. The leeward sides of islands are always drier and hotter than the windward coasts. As we walked, the kids ducked off the rough trail to play in tidepools and explore little spouts and caves. They drank a lot and frequently asked, "How much farther is it?"

The point itself was a sad sight. Trash lay about the beach area, and the little lighthouse was covered in graffiti. Disappointed, I took pictures anyway, not realizing they would become some of the most important photos in my collection. I've published them many times and shown them in slide talks as examples of what happens when a lighthouse has no resident keeper. They never fail to bring a response, and I feel it would not be an exaggeration to say they've inspired a few people to join the effort to save lighthouses.

The high point of the visit to Kaena was seeing "Soul's Leap," a large rock that Hawaiians call Leina-a-ka'uhane - *the leaping place of ghosts.* Hawaiian legend says the souls of the dead leap off for heaven or hell here, depending on which way the gods intend to send them. If they are heaven-bound, they walk up the first rainbow to appear. At Kaena, rainbows are infrequent, due to the arid climate, so a soul would need to pay close attention to the skies to catch a ride. My children were enchanted with this legend and stood on "Soul's Leap" imagining what it might be like to walk up a rainbow, using each color as a step to heaven.

We arrived back at the parking area at Yokohama Beach tired and dusty, but happy. My husband commented that it was an experience few tourists to Hawaii ever know. Kaena is not high on the list of travel destinations, but it is a glimpse of the "real" Hawaii. Later, I wrote several articles about the point for science and travel magazines, and I included little Kaena Point Lighthouse in my articles for *Aloha* and *Hawaii* magazines.

To get back to my original thought:

There were few sources of information about the lighthouses of Hawaii during my years in the islands, but thanks to Love Dean, there's now a definitive book on the subject. *The Lighthouses of Hawai'i* appeared in 1991 and is an excellent history, painstakingly researched and illustrated. My favorite Hawaiian lighthouse appears on the cover — Makapu'u Point. Dean's research notes are priceless. Oh, how I could have used them in 1983!

Jessica's memory of Hawaii, sketched at age 13.

The
Eskimo Lights

Lighthouses in Alaska

The first lighthouse on North America's Pacific Coast was established in 1805 at the quaint port of Sitka, Alaska. Flanked on the east by towering, ice-capped mountains and to the west by the mercurial Gulf of Alaska, Sitka was then a Russian trading post under the shrewd management of entrepreneur and governor, Aleksandr Baranov.

The governor's home, known as Baranov Castle, was a bold citadel facing the sea. It served not only as a welcome landmark for vessels headed into Sitka Bay, but also as a fortress against the native Tlingits who had destroyed a previous outpost at Sitka after mistreatment by Russian traders. Atop the castle was a cupola where a light was shown. In addition, Baranov ordered a small lighthouse built on an island at the entrance to the bay.

The island light vanished sometime in the 1830s, but the beacon in the castle was still shining when the U.S. annexed the Alaska Territory in 1867. An army post was quickly set up, with an ordinary officer given responsibility for the beacon. He was paid an extra 40-cents a day to keep its seal oil lamps burning and the windows clean. The beacon was maintained for ten years, then abandoned when the army withdrew from Sitka. From 1877 to 1902, the Alaska shores — with half again as much coastline as the continental U.S. — were dark.

Gold was the spark that finally lit the Alaskan coast. Klondike prospectors arrived by the thousands in 1897-98 via Lynn Canal and Skagway. While gold fever raged, shipping attempted to keep up with the need for transportation of people and goods. By this time, a number of buoys had been placed along the perilous Inside Passage, but fog, swift currents, and hidden rocks still exacted a heavy toll. The Alaska that had once been dubbed "Seward's Folly" and the "Ice Box of America" beckoned with boundless opportunity. Lighthouses were needed to show the way.

Baranov Castle, Sitka, as pictured in 1867.
U.S. Coast Guard Academy Library

168

Perhaps the government was slow to act because of the enormous expense and hardship of lighting the nation's largest piece of real estate. Urgent sites for Alaskan lighthouses were isolated and treacherous, some more than 3000 miles from the Lighthouse Depot at San Francisco. Eventually, a separate district was established for Alaska, headquartered in Ketchikan and later moved to Juneau. The early lights were built by the crews of steam-powered tenders out of Seattle — tough little vessels with dainty floral names like *Rose, Fern, Armeria,* and *Columbine.*

In 1902, the first major Alaskan light stations were established at Southeast Five Finger Island in Frederick Sound and Sentinel Island in Lynn Canal. Despite the wet, chilly climate, and the ever-present threat of fire in the lantern, the towers were built of wood to save money. They were handsome Victorian structures though, with comfortable living quarters and state-of-the-art fog signals to blast through Alaska's relentless murk.

To guide shipping into the Bering Sea, lights were also built at Scotch Cap and Cape Sarichef as guardians of Unimak Pass in the Aleutians. These were made stag stations - only men could serve there - since they were deemed too remote for families. The keepers who served at these stations often were chosen from the stalwart native population, for enormous fortitude was required to handle the deprivations of life on a barren island.

Ted Pedersen was such a man — born in 1905 on remote Samalga Island to an Alaskan fur trader and his Russian-Aleut wife. Pedersen served aboard the tender *Cedar,* which supplied the outer Alaskan lights in the 1920s, then received an appointment to Kayak Island's Cape St. Elias Light after one of its keepers went mad.

Pedersen disliked duty on Kayak Island, calling it "the worst in Alaska." Storms were terrifying and living conditions so dangerous the service tender came just once a year. Often, supplies ran low and meals were lean.

"If we saw seagulls flying around eating something — halibut or rock cod washed up — we'd go down and look, and maybe we'd take it away from the gulls," Pedersen recalled.

Within a year, another position opened at isolated Cape Sarichef Light. One of the assistant keepers had suffered a breakdown after two years at the lonely station. Pedersen replaced him and, having spent part of his childhood in the Aleutians, found life at Cape Sarichef more to his liking. He

hunted, explored the island, and read hundreds of books. A magazine article described him as "The Lighthouse Keeper at the End of the World" and noted that he wore a reindeer parka with as much finesse as a three-piece suit.

Cooking was one of Pedersen's favorite pursuits, and he was known for his Mulligan Stew made from fresh caribou meat. In deep winter, when the station was shut down for three months, Pedersen sometimes made hikes around Unimak Island. One of these was a 263-mile trek to see a schoolteacher. Pedersen was 29 at the time, and women were a rare sight on Unimak Island.

Other less hardy keepers did not adapt as well as Pedersen. In 1981, one of the Cape Sarichef crew became ill, and a tender was summoned to take him to a hospital. When the tender arrived, the sea was too rough to dock. A launch was sent to the lighthouse, but waves swamped it, drowning everyone aboard. While the tender waited at anchor for calmer seas, the sick lightkeeper died. He was buried behind the station on "Graveyard Hill."

A bureau bulletin mailed to lighthouse keepers nationwide in February 1921 carried a firm warning about the dangers of the Alaskan wilderness. The notice was occasioned by the loss of two men near Mary Island Lighthouse. Keeper Herbert Scott and two friends from nearby Ketchikan had gone to the aid of a stricken boat. As they returned to the lighthouse, they lost the trail in fresh snow and wandered off into the dense woods. Two of the men, including Scott, froze to death. The Bureau of Lighthouses called it "a needless accident."

At times, even the greatest fortitude, outdoor skill, and common sense weren't enough on the rugged Alaskan landscape. Five keepers lost their lives at Scotch Cap Lighthouse in 1946 after a seismic disturbance in the Aleutian Trench spawned a monster tsunami that destroyed the station. The lighthouse was battered to pieces and washed into the sea.

During Prohibition, the keepers at Guard Island Lighthouse discovered a boat adrift and rowed out to investigate. They found the mangled bodies of two men stuffed inside a locker in the boat cabin. The shocking crime was blamed on bootleggers. Guard Island's lightkeepers began carrying guns at all times. This station was one of only three in Alaska where families were permitted to live, and the men were concerned for the safety of their wives and children.

Most of the old wooden lighthouses in Alaska were replaced with more durable concrete structures by the time the Coast Guard took over navigational aids in 1939. Because of the emotional and physical hardships of keeping Alaska's outer lights, some new rules were instituted. Keepers were required to serve only a year at remote stations and were visited by tenders more often. In addition, plans were made to automate these lonely outposts as soon as possible.

By the close of the 1960s most of the Eskimo lights were self-sufficient and their keepers transferred back to civilization. The Northern Lights began to dance a new song — the hum and click of automatic machinery. No one remained to hear the Taku winds whispering through cracks in the walls or feel the shudder of the sea throwing itself against the shore. Bears no longer had garbage cans to raid; the caribou had no risk of becoming steaks in a lighthouse freezer.

A cute family of martens took up residence at Cape St. Elias Light, and the Coast Guard's periodic maintenance team sometimes left food for them. Seals and seabirds made themselves at home around Eldred Rock, Cape Hinchinbrook, Cape Spenser, and other sentinels in the far north, but they shun human contact, preferring to watch from a distance when tender crews arrive to check the lights.

Such changes seem to suggest sequestered spots like these are better suited to beasts than people.

This article originally appeared in *Mariners Weather Log*, Winter 1992.

Recommended Reading

Because of their remoteness, the lighthouses of Alaska have received little study from historians, not even during the years they were attended by on-site keepers. Perhaps they were too far-flung and unromantic to capture public interest. Indeed, some were and remain so, for it's always a surprise to audiences at my slide programs when pictures of Alaskan lighthouses appear on the screen. They forget our 49th state has a long and fascinating maritime history.

The story, according to Shannon Lowry, of the "lighting of the liquid highway" to Alaska is important and riveting. She captures it well in her *Northern Lights: Tales of Alaska's Lighthouses and Their Keepers*, published in 1992 by Stackpole Books. It exceeds anything else written about Alaska's sentinels and is handsomely illustrated with both archival and modern-day photos.

The text is strong on information but also emotion, portraying the heyday of Alaska's lighthouses, the character of those who tended them, and the ultimate decay following automation. Jeff Schultz' pictures of rusty locks, peeling paint, and cobwebbed windows stir the heart. So far from civilization are most of these sentinels, we wonder who, if anyone, will care for them the way lighthouses in the lower forty-eight are being preserved.

Silhouette of Cape St. Elias Light

Index

Race Rock Light, by Paul Bradley